Alastair

PHARMAGEDDON

Pray it's only fiction!

P O Box 335
Stellenbosch 7599
South Africa

grantalastair@yahoo.co.uk

ISBN: 1453635122
EAN-13: 9781453635124

Pharmageddon is a work of fiction.
The characters populating the story are all imaginary, and
some of the 'facts' have been massaged a little for dramatic effect.

Readers are encouraged to search the internet for the truth.
It is a lot closer to fiction than you may think.

I'm very grateful to the friends and family
who helped in a hundred ways to get this
book out of my head and onto paper.

I dedicate the end result to my wife,
who has always believed in me -
even when I've had my doubts.

PHARMAGEDDON

PART I

Chandigarh, India
06:00 Sunday 2 January

Anil Sirkandar knew he shouldn't be drinking bhang at work, but it was just over an hour to the end of his shift and the cannabis drink made the time pass quickly and painlessly. These were special circumstances, he told himself. For one thing it was freezing in the unheated building, and for another this was a holiday, when bhang was traditionally drunk. But most of all, this was his way of getting back at the production manager for springing this shift on Anil and his team at the last minute, when they were supposed to be off duty.

He took another sip and let his thoughts drift back for the millionth time to the car he was due to collect in a couple of days. Instead of queuing for a bus or flagging down a surly auto-rickshaw driver at the end of each shift, from next week he would walk casually to the staff car-park, step into the shiny blue Nano, turn on the radio and drive through the factory gate just as the company executives did. When he sat in the car at the Tata showroom last week he was shivering so hard with excitement he'd barely been able to say 'I'll take it.'

For a Dalit – an untouchable – whose family had been sweepers since the beginning of time, the idea of owning a car was as far-fetched as... being called into Dr Chaturvedi's office, asked to sit down, and offered the job of shift supervisor. But that is exactly what happened, barely six months ago. Anil still felt light-headed when he thought of it. The manager of the plant, a Brahmin, shaking the hand of a Chura, inviting him to sit – on a chair – and offering him a supervisory position! Truly, this was a new and wonderful world.

Anil kept imagining his mother's expression when he parked the new Nano outside her shack and offered to whisk her and his two sisters off to the market to do their shopping, just like the higher castes did. His father had never dared to dream of owning a scooter and here Anil was, not quite 24 years old, able to borrow enough on the strength of his salary and prospects at Maurya Pharmaceuticals to buy a car. He could barely bring himself to think about what this might mean for his marriage prospects. Surely a Chura in his position could be introduced to girls from a higher caste? Someone who could be presented to Dr Chaturvedi at the next staff party, a year from now. The girls he'd met would faint at the very thought of looking a Brahmin in the eye, smiling, and saying 'pleased to meet you.'

In truth Anil was more than happy to work this shift, supervising his team while they readied the laboratory for the return of the production staff in a couple of days. Working on a Saturday night meant double-pay, as did working during the holidays. A Saturday during the holidays meant three times his regular wage which, on a supervisor's pay-scale, was a huge sum

– thousands of rupees! Anil could almost picture the money gushing into his bank account. Come to think of it, he was actually grateful to the production manager for canceling his day off, even though the man always spoke to him in the contemptuous manner of a higher caste addressing a Dalit, ignoring Maurya's policy of equality at work. But Anil's skin was thickened by centuries of abuse, and money had no caste.

The work tonight was particularly hard for his team because the engineers who installed and serviced equipment during the holidays had left a mess in the normally spotless laboratory. But Anil was careful and methodical, qualities which Dr Chaturvedi had noticed and mentioned when he promoted the young cleaner, even though he had worked at the plant for only three years. Now, as a supervisor, he did not clean anything himself but he made sure his team embodied the same qualities, frequently telling them that if he could become a boss – and buy a new car – so could they.

Anil swallowed the last of the bhang just as his new Casio watch chimed stridently. He pressed the button to turn on the backlight, even though he didn't need to, and read the time although he already knew from the wall-clock in the tiny supervisor's cubicle that it was 6am. Time for a last inspection. He straightened the black surgical scrubs which he wore over his regular clothing because of the cold, pulled on his surgical mask and cap, and a fresh pair of white cotton gloves, and headed into the laboratory hall.

He knew the plant manufactured a range of ingredients used to make drugs – 'active pharmaceutical ingredients or API' he told his friends, with the air of one who knows much more than he is permitted to disclose. The laboratory was a huge space filled with work-benches, each fitted with basins and faucets, gas and electrical connections, and stacked with computers and other apparatus which did things that he could not even guess at. Along the two longer walls, 20 glass doors opened into smaller rooms, each containing a mystifying collection of glass, steel and plastic tubes, bulbs, cylinders and machines. All Anil knew was that his cleaners were only allowed into those spaces when they were empty, or if they were told to clean specific surfaces under the supervision of a chemist.

At the far end of the hall an airlock led to an area where raw materials were stored. Chemists or their assistants collected materials from the store before measuring, testing and preparing them, after which the materials were taken to one of the 20 small rooms – called reaction chambers – where the mysterious equipment somehow transformed them into tiny quantities of powder or liquid which were vastly more valuable than gold. These precious essences were then packaged and sent off to hundreds of pharmaceutical plants around the world, where they were made into medicines to save or improve the quality of countless lives.

Usually Maurya's Chandigarh plant was open around the clock, working a three-shift system, and the main laboratory was a hive of quiet, ordered activity. Staff wore different colored surgical scrubs – green for chemists, blue for assistants, and orange for cleaners. Supervisory staff wore a darker shade of the same color while executives wore black and visitors, on the rare occasions they came into the laboratory, wore white.

However the dress code was sometimes bent during the night shift, from 23:00 to 07:00, when chemists deliberately wore the wrong colors. It was all done in good spirit, and nobody would dream of committing a serious breach of the rules by, for example, working without a mask, gloves or hat. Tonight, in a moment of recklessness when he entered the deserted laboratory, Anil put on a set of the black executive scrubs and invited his team to wear any color they wished, although they all put on the familiar orange. And, because the heating was turned off, they all wore their own clothes underneath their scrubs. Even though Chandigarh is only 300 meters above sea level it lies in the foothills of the Himalayas and winter nights can be chilly, sometimes falling below freezing.

Production at the plant stopped only four times a year, each time for a week or ten days. The breaks were timed to coincide with each of the major religions – the Christian Easter in March, the Muslim Eid al-Fitr in September, Diwali, the Festival of Lights celebrated by Hindus, Sikhs and Jains in November, and of course the current break for Christmas and New Year.

These were the times when professional staff took their vacations but they were also the busiest times for the plant's engineering staff and cleaners. Anil's team had worked every night during the past week, cleaning and sterilizing empty reaction chambers before the engineers filled them with new equipment.

But Saturday night was supposed to be his team's night off.

Anil walked along the north wall, stopping at several benches to check they were free of dust by running his gloved fingers over various surfaces. His crew were well-trained to know what to clean, and what to leave alone. They had been shown videos of the invisible animals called bacteria which live on surfaces that look clean but are not. The age-old trade of the sweeper had been updated and they were now equipped to sweep away all of these tiny animals – using special machinery and chemicals – so they would not interfere with the work the chemists were doing. And they took pride in their work, which was essential to making the drugs which saved many lives.

Right now Anil could see only Parvati working in the main hall, but he wasn't concerned. He knew she was finishing off the last of the benches and floors, while two of her colleagues had gone to help the remaining two cleaners finish sterilizing reaction chambers seven and 13. Outside chamber seven Anil saw the steam-cleaner standing alongside cases of equipment which would be unpacked and installed by the engineers later today. Through the glass door he could see Amit and Kavita drying the walls and floor with disposable swabs. He knew the chemists would find no invisible animals in chamber seven.

Anil continued around the perimeter of the hall, pausing to check the airlock area. Cleaning the storage section beyond the airlock would be the responsibility of the cleaners on the next shift. Outside reaction chamber 13 he saw another cluster of packing cases, but no steam cleaner. Inside, as he feared, he found Suresh and Arpita were running late, so he briefly reminded them how privileged they were to be on his team and to be earning triple time for this shift, and how happy every other cleaner at the plant would be to do this work if they found it too tiring. He left them working frantically to catch up.

The plant had fifteen cleaning teams in all, one team for each shift in each of five zones, which included the laboratory itself; the workshop, boiler-room, generator and water-purification plant; the administrative offices and executive suites; the canteen, changing rooms and toilets; and the exterior of the building and grounds. Anil had worked every shift in each zone before being promoted to one of the three elite laboratory teams and then, quite unexpectedly, to the post of shift supervisor! Truly he felt good in these black scrubs!

On several occasions he had seen the owner of Maurya Pharmaceuticals, Dr Shan Gupta, inside the laboratory, accompanied by Dr Chaturvedi. Both men would be wearing the same black scrubs with hats and masks, but the older and heavier plant manager was instantly distinguishable from the slim, youthful figure of his employer. Dr Gupta was world famous, one of the richest men in India. He usually arrived at the plant in his black helicopter from his headquarters just outside Shimla which, thanks to the mountainous terrain, was a couple of hours away by car or train but only a few minutes by helicopter.

Dr Chaturvedi himself was reputed to be one of the best research chemists in the world, although you'd never guess it to meet him. He usually arrived early at the plant in his modest Honda Accord, and he made a habit of stopping to chat to any staff he encountered – even cleaners – asking after their families and checking whether there was anything he could do for them.

And these weren't empty words. Dr Chaturvedi had encouraged Anil to improve his education so he could progress beyond cleaning, suggesting he enroll for an engineering diploma at the Chandigarh Technical College. Naturally Maurya would provide letters of recommendation to the college. Both men knew a Dalit would never be admitted without this letter, but that with the company's endorsement his acceptance was assured. Anil was waiting for the offer to be repeated, as protocol demanded, before accepting it. But in the meanwhile he saw no reason not to use his vastly improved income to buy the little Tata car, and to tell his family he was ready to marry.

Moving back towards the supervisors' cubicle Anil imagined he was already a company executive, wearing these black scrubs not as a prank but as an entitlement. He surveyed the vast laboratory with a proprietary air, clicking his tongue with displeasure at the stacks of rough crates and grubby tool-boxes cluttering this normally pristine space. Still lost in his fantasy Anil imagined reprimanding the engineers, telling them to take their dirty tools back to their workshop while the laboratory was being cleaned.

Then he spotted a tool box on top of a work bench and yanked himself back to reality. He hadn't noticed it earlier because it was hidden between two large pieces of laboratory equipment. Engineers were strictly forbidden from putting anything on the near-sterile workbenches. As a junior cleaner he would never consider moving an engineer's tools, but as a supervisor he was expected to show initiative. Hopefully the engineer who put it there would realize his mistake when he found the toolbox had been moved to the floor, and would be suitably grateful that he had been spared a tongue-lashing by the production manager.

Anil called to Parvati, telling her to bring her cleaning trolley. He explained that she was right to have left the toolbox when she cleaned this area, but she should have told him about it. She stepped forward to move the toolbox but he tapped her arm smartly.

'No, it is not your place to move something belonging to the engineers.'

Parvati lowered her eyes respectfully and stepped back – something she would never have done before Anil was promoted to supervisor, since she was of the same caste as he, but older and married. As he stepped forward to take hold of the toolbox himself, Anil's Casio chimed the half hour. In the same instant he had a fleeting impression of light, heat and sound, then nothing.

The explosive in the toolbox was so powerful that it reduced both Anil and Parvati to a spray of tiny fragments, which were evenly distributed over the western end of the laboratory. The laminated glass doors to the reaction chambers lining the north and south walls were designed to resist fires, but were no match for the enormous pressure of 30 kilograms of military-grade explosive, which transformed the thick glass into millions of sharp-edged projectiles, shredding everything inside the chambers.

In chamber seven Amit was killed instantly when a cube of glass entered his brain through his right eye. The pressure of the blast knocked Kavita unconscious, while one of the several hundred shards of glass which sliced into her body nicked an artery in her neck. She awoke in the semi-darkness to find Amit was taking a nap. It didn't make sense, but she was so tired herself that she decided to close her eyes, just for a moment.

Across the hall in chamber 13, Suresh recovered consciousness and picked himself up, then lost his footing on the slick blood pouring from countless lacerations all over his body and fell heavily, striking his head hard on the corner of the steam cleaning unit.

When she regained consciousness, Arpita was deaf and confused, and her clothes and flesh were hanging in ribbons. However she was able to walk, and she stumbled from chamber 13 into the darkened laboratory hall, picking her way between overturned benches and scattered equipment, heading toward the light from the gaping hole where the front airlock had been.

When she was almost there, one of the plant's security guards appeared in front of her, silhouetted against the light but recognizable by his black turban and uniform, his shotgun held ready across his chest.

In the same instant, clouds of invisible and odorless LP gas and oxygen, streaming from a dozen broken gas lines, reached a smoldering fragment of black cloth from Anil Sirkandar's illicit scrubs, stuck like a funereal Post-It to the west wall of the laboratory.

Guard Nirmal Singh was standing motionless in the broken airlock, transfixed by the sight of some kind of prehistoric creature shuffling out of the darkness toward him. Beyond this viscid figure, the laboratory looked more like the charred maw of a dragon than the bright sterile workplace he knew. Before he could make sense of these images, or decide what he and his shotgun should do about them, the dragon breathed blue-white fire on them both.

Istanbul, Turkey
04:00 Sunday 2 January

In my dream Emily and I were hosting a party at the villa. It was great fun, even though nobody spoke English. Emily had no trouble speaking to them in Turkish and Hindi and Croatian, but it was all Greek to me. But it made no difference – when we raised our glasses and toasted the new year we were all good mates, and life was good.

The bash was in full swing when my phone rang. I struggled to hear the caller over the din but finally made out that it was Jim. I was so relieved that he was speaking American that I didn't ask myself why he wasn't at the party, or why he wanted me to get my ass into the office. He said something about one of Shan's factories being blown up, which made no sense, but I didn't argue because it was, after all, just a dream. The next thing I was in the Aston, rumbling across the Bosphorus Bridge and into the jeweled arms of European Istanbul.

Only… it wasn't a dream. At least, not all of it. It felt like I really was driving across the floodlit bridge, which was practically deserted at this hour. Em and I really did host a New Year's party in Fenerbahçe, but it ended 24 hours ago. And, even though our guests came from many countries, they all spoke perfect English. Except for Emily, of course, who could no longer wrap her tongue around any of the seventeen or so languages she understood.

Jim's call must've been real, too, but I couldn't be sure. The champagne from the party had worn off, but Em had insisted we stay awake for the first day of our first full year in Istanbul, so we'd only got to bed a couple of hours ago, and I was more unconscious than asleep when Jim called. If he called. Maybe I was dreaming that I was driving? What if our party was just part of the dream? Shit, what if Istanbul, the Aston Martin and my job were all just figments of Bollinger-induced unconsciousness? In fact, if I woke up right now, where would I be – how far would my story rewind?

I pushed on the Aston's horn, which was piercingly real. And if this was just a dream, how would I know that this bridge is usually crammed full of crawling traffic? Or how to drive toward the thousand-year-old Galata trading district, and my place of employ in Karaköy?

We could have chosen to live on the European side of this ancient city, say in Baltalimani or Etiler-Levent, but we both liked the idea of living on one continent and while I worked on another, so I bought the south-facing villa in Fenerbahçe with its great views over the Sea of Marmara and the Princes' Islands. Not that I was at home much to enjoy the place, but Emily loved it.

Like the other senior editors I spend most of my time on the road. Or rather, in the air and in hotel rooms. Usually I could count on being with Emily over Christmas and New Year, because it's a flat period for the news industry. The silly season. But, unless I'd imagined Jim's call, the silly season had ended early… and with a bang.

Jim's call must have woken Em as well. She never grumbled about being disturbed in the middle of the night, or about me having to leave her at a moment's notice. Sometimes I wished she would, but I suppose she felt it was the one thing she could do for me. Give me space. She must have watched this morning while I dressed and grabbed my carry-on – a familiar sight for her and something which, evidently, I could do in my sleep.

In Karaköy I aimed the Aston into the underground parking at the TWO headquarters. Even at this hour there wasn't any space at the kerb. Street parking is rarer than a pork pie in Istanbul. Then I took the lift – or should I say 'elevator', since we've standardized on lingua Hollywood. I normally take the stairs for the exercise but this was my dream, so I took the elevator.

I wasn't surprised to find the fourth floor hopping at 04:30 on a holiday Sunday – there's always something happening somewhere, somebody writing about it, and somebody wanting to read about it, even in the silly season. So we're always here, serving up fresh-baked news to the global village.

It looked like every workstation in the ECO – the editorial coordination office – was filled, and I knew it would be the same one floor down, in the content section where they pull it all together. Or at least where they oversee the process – all the heavy lifting is done by contractors scattered around the world. Karaköy is simply where the puppet-masters sit, jerking the threads, 24–7–365.

As I walked through the ECO I laid a hand on Nerisha's shoulder. She was the editorial coordinator on duty for the health section that night, talking into her headset as usual. She gave me a big smile and I gestured not to interrupt her call. Then past the row of editors' offices, including my own, and into the executive editor's suite. His assistant's desk was empty but Jim saw me through the open door and came out to give me a hug.

'Gip. Glad you're here. Sorry about the time. Come on in.'

His office looked like a boardroom. No desk, just a table running down the middle and a huge plasma screen taking up the whole wall next to the door. At that moment the screen was showing half a dozen cable news channels and a bunch of online news services, including our own. The end wall and the one to my left were made of glass, giving his office one of the most impressive – and expensive – views in the world.

Without asking, Jim poured Turkish coffee into a tiny cup and handed it to me and then slid a plate of pastries within grasping distance. Since the usual rules don't apply in the virtual reality of dream-world, I grasped.

Jim's face suddenly filled with concern. 'So, how are you feeling?'

I cocked an eyebrow at him. 'Probably a damn site better than you, Jimboy. If I remember correctly you had at least two ambers for every glass of champers that I put away.'

He dropped the fake concern and laughed. 'Naah, I think that's two beers for every BOTTLE of champagne you had, Gip. Sheesh, but you ozzies can put it away! Your party invitations should come with a government health warning!'

We chuckled, sipped and nibbled, thinking back to the rowdy do. It was good to have a bunch of colleagues over, and I knew Em had made quite a few new friends. Certainly she was the center of attraction, despite her mangled speech, even if I was the life and soul. I was happy to chew over the gory details, even at this time of night, but I wasn't surprised when Jim got serious.

'Gip, like I told you on the phone, Shan's factory in Chandigarh blew up... was blown up... about an hour ago. Of course they thought it was an industrial accident, but then they heard two other pharmaceutical plants in Hyderabad were sabotaged at exactly the same time. Three different companies, a thousand miles apart.'

'Jesus! And we thought competition in the news business was tough!'

He gave a thin smile, but didn't play. 'Thankfully all three factories were closed for the holidays or we'd be talking hundreds of deaths, but they did lose half a dozen cleaning staff and a couple of guards.'

'Did Shan call you himself?'

'Yeah. Then I called you.'

'Does he know why they were targeted?'

'He said there are a few possibilities. Actually he didn't say very much, except that he thought it would be a good idea if you were there.'

'Where? In India?'

Jim nodded and smiled as he watched me struggling with my biorhythmically challenged brain.

'Hey, I like India and all, but... isn't this a crime story? More than health? Unless you are one of the dead people, of course.' I also wanted to remind him that TWO editors don't generally run after breaking news – that's why we've got stringers – but, shit, that would be like reminding the Pope that he's Catholic.

'He's sending his jet for you.'

'He's... you're kidding! Are you kidding?'

'I never joke about executive jets. He said his plane was already en route from Frankfurt to Delhi, so he diverted it. Should be landing at Ataturk about now.'

'Jesus! That's... fucking amazing! Aah... d'you think he'd mind if we stopped off in Paris while I pick up a few clothes – I could use some new threads.'

This time he played. 'Sure, wherever. Rome, Milan, New York.' We sat smiling at each other as we lived out this little fantasy. A dream within a dream. My turn to get serious.

'So... are we getting coverage on this from our stringers? And the competition? I didn't have a chance to check it myself.'

He reached for the remote lying on the table in front of him. 'Yeah, I got Nerisha to wake up some guys in Chandigarh and Hyderabad. In the past few minutes they've posted stuff from the cops, fire brigades, eye witnesses.'

As he jabbed at the remote a couple of the windows on the massive monitor expanded. One showed our page on the breaking story, featuring video clips of the bombed factories with firemen rushing about, and stills of Shan and the other CEOs.

'We've got some comment from pharma in the US. Shock, horror, the usual. The opposition are a bit slow off the mark...' he pushed another button and his monitor returned to the default collection of opposition electronic newspapers and TV networks. 'They started reporting it just a few minutes ago, but so far they're having to credit us.'

This was good. The name of the game is to get the opposition to admit to the world that they are relying on TWO for their news. Do our advertising for us. And we have a talent for putting other media in that position. They hate us for it.

'Then again, Jim, it's not their owner who's been bombed. D'you think they're holding back their own reporters? Professional courtesy?'

He gave a scornful laugh. 'Yeah, right!'

I slapped my jeans. 'So... that's it? I'd better get going.'

'I guess so. I'll see you back here tomorrow, I suppose. Unless it gets interesting. You want me to do anything... for Emily?'

'No worries Jim, I'm sure she'll be fine. I'll call her, and she's got the barbarian and the others to look after her. But of course she loves it when you drop in. If you want to spend the night in the guest room, she'd be very happy.'

'Sure Gip. You know I'm here for you both.' He stood to give me another hug, and walked me out.

After a brief stop with Nerisha I was back in the Aston and on my way to Ataturk International, also an easy drive at this time of day. Now that I was fully awake I felt a little regretful. It would've been nice to spend a bit more time with Em before disappearing on yet another crusade. I knew she wouldn't be sleeping, so I called her to tell her what was going on. I also told her that it felt like a dream, and I kept expecting to wake up alongside her.

'Happy somnambulations, lover. Bring me something from Shimla.'

'Sure babe. Go back to sleep.'

Then I focused on the next thrilling installment. It didn't disappoint – a uniformed steward waving a placard with my name on it, valet parking, VIP passport facilities. At 5am! I could get used to this!

If anything, it felt even more like a dream as I settled into one of the sculpted seats on Shan's black Gulfstream, with the gleaming golden logo of Maurya Pharmaceuticals on its tail. A beautiful girl in a black silk sari with the same emblem embroidered on it offered me spiced tea and asked me to fasten my seat belt.

After we were airborne the pilot (black suit, gold logo on pocket) came back to tell me it would be a five-hour flight to Delhi's Indira Gandhi Airport. Unfortunately we couldn't fly direct to Shimla – something about runway length and immigration facilities – but there would be a helicopter standing by in Delhi to take me to the Maurya headquarters.

Oh sure. Of course. Warm up the chopper, Jeeves. And while you're at it, top up my tea, wouldya? Just kidding. Send the babe.

Washington DC
21:00 Saturday 1 January

Yvonne Delgado felt a fluttering in her chest and goose-bumps on her arms as the cellos poured their rich cream into the auditorium, sprinkled with the sweetness of the violins. The sound flowed thickly and then vanished, as if imagined. Before the audience fully registered the silence they were pummeled by the bass drums. Another in-breath of silence, and a lone soprano began her bitter-sweet story.

Delgado looked over at her husband and daughter. Vernon and Halley were completely engrossed in the familiar story, waiting for the appearance of the lover. That's what's important, she thought. Not how far I've come, or where I'm going. You. The fact that we have each other. Suddenly the opera seemed contrived and false by comparison. She looked back at the stage and raised her opera glasses to hide her bright tears.

After a moment she felt a touch on her elbow and heard the whisper. 'Madam secretary?'

Outside in the hall, when the door to the private box had closed behind her, her personal assistant told her the UN secretary general has asked that she receive the head of the World Health Organization as a matter of extreme urgency.

'What's it about, Harry? Did she say?'

'Only that it relates to the sabotage of some pharmaceutical factories in India a couple of hours ago.'

Delgado knew better than to ask if it could wait. Harry was a fierce watchdog. He would never allow anyone to waste her time, especially these precious moments with her family.

'Secretary general Kapur said she would have come herself but she's currently en route from Karachi to New York. And she says it can't wait.'

'Well, I'd better see him then. Is he here?'

'Any minute, ma'am. The theatre manager has made his office available.'

'Thank you Harry. I'll just tell Vernon and Halley that I'm deserting them.'

Whispered apologies made, and received stoically, secretary Delgado was escorted downstairs and offered refreshments. Five minutes later the director general of the World Health Organization, Dr Jean Folbert, was shown in. Introductions and courtesies were kept short and Folbert came to the point.

'Madame, we are facing a major crisis and we need your government's support.'

'Go ahead, Doctor.'

'Are you aware of the sabotage of three pharmaceutical plants in India?'

'Yes, I saw something on the news this evening, just before we left for the theater.'

'Bon. I regret to inform you there was another act of sabotage at the same time. It was at a UN warehouse on the outskirts of Stockholm, where we store drugs and emergency supplies for global disasters and epidemics.'

'That's... very bad news. I assume there is a connection?'

'Oui, madame. The Indian factories were the biggest producers of the active ingredients for antiretroviral medications, and our warehouse contained the world's largest stockpile of those drugs.'

Delgado stared at the Frenchman for a moment, wondering if she had misheard. 'Antiretrovirals? For AIDS?'

'Precisely. Those three factories together manufacture the molecules which are used in the manufacture of more than ninety percent of generic first-line antiretrovirals.'

'My God! I had no idea... when I heard about the blasts...'

'No, that information has not yet reached the public domain. And we have prevailed on the Swedish authorities to say nothing of the fire at our warehouse, or what we lost.'

'Why?'

'The factories in India produce many ingredients, not only those for antiretrovirals. It is unlikely anyone will make the connection, for a while at least. But the incendiary device in Stockholm... well, it is obvious the target was ARVs.'

'And you don't want the public to know this fact?'

Folbert stared at the secretary of state for a moment as if gathering his thoughts. 'Madame, as of today about nine million people depend on antiretrovirals to stay alive. Most of them are using generic first-line medications.'

Delgado had heard the numbers before. The State Department controls the US foreign aid program, which in turn donates huge quantities of ARVs to developing nations.

'I understand this, Dr Folbert. Are you suggesting this sabotage poses an immediate risk to those people?' She was expecting a reassurance from the UN executive, and was shocked when he did not immediately reply. She took a deep breath. 'Okay. How bad is it?'

'Madame, for several years the producers of antiretrovirals have had difficulty keeping up with demand. The rapid rollout of treatment in many low-income countries has given them no opportunity to build any... safety margin. I would be surprised if global reserves are sufficient for more than a few weeks. In some countries it could be a matter of days.'

'How long will it take to restore production?'

Again Delgado's heart lurched as Folbert hesitated. 'We can only guess at this stage, madame. As I said before, this is a major crisis...'

'What are you asking for, Dr Folbert?'

'Madame, our immediate concern is that the existing reserves of these drugs will... disappear... when word of this gets out.'

Delgado's hand flew up to her mouth, and she stared at Folbert for a moment. 'Of course! They will be worth a fortune on the black market if they are no longer freely available.'

Folbert nodded. 'Yes, and they could be used for political leverage. To control those who depend on those drugs. We are also concerned about people selling fake medications to people who cannot get the real thing.'

'But Dr Folbert, surely it's just a matter of time before word gets out?'

'Oui madame. But we are hoping to secure a significant quantity of the drugs in the high-prevalence countries within the next day or two. With your help.'

Suddenly the penny dropped for Delgado. She sat back in the theatre manager's chair, and looked at Folbert. 'You're asking us to store these drugs in our embassies. To... withhold them from host governments.'

Folbert returned her gaze. 'Embassies are effectively foreign territory, madame. Since the attacks in Kenya and Tanzania in 1998, your embassies have been the best fortified of all foreign missions. And your government has paid for most of those drugs through your foreign aid program. In my view, this is no more than safeguarding your investment.'

Delgado put her elbows on the theater manager's desk and massaged her temples while the WHO chief continued.

'We wouldn't ask this of you, or any country, if it were not a matter of life or death for... many.'

She looked up. 'Many? How many, Dr Folbert? What's the worst-case scenario?'

'Our concern is not only for patients dying from AIDS. We are concerned that these events could destabilize some countries. In some African states there are more soldiers and policemen living with HIV than without it. The problem extends across many categories of workers in industry and public service. And there are the unemployed, who are the most vulnerable and unstable group in society. An interruption of the supply of antiretrovirals could be a catalyst for... catastrophe, madame.'

Delgado had not been long in office, and so far she'd managed to tip-toe along the knife edge of history. But she saw immediately that the new administration's mantra of 'incremental progress in all areas' simply didn't fit this situation. This was all or nothing – back away, or take a giant and dangerous leap into the unknown. Either decision could change the world, and America's place in it.

She sighed. 'How do you suggest we proceed, Dr Folbert?'

Over Turkey
06:00 Sunday 2 January

For a while I followed the bombings using the internet setup on the Gulfstream – a smaller version of Jim's monitor. All the major networks had contacted an assortment of cops and commentators but their stories were the same – horror, outrage, sympathy, incomprehension.

Our own worker-ants were doing a good job of picking up crumbs and delivering them to the TWO inbox, but that's all they were – crumbs. Shocked families, bewildered managers, stoic firemen and EMTs, opportunistic politicians... the usual suspects. Our forums were already overflowing with theories and emotions, but no hard evidence. It wasn't long before I lost concentration and started scanning other news, even though I was being paid to follow this story. And paid very well!

Two years earlier I had been holding down a great job as health correspondent for The Economist. Emily and I were nesting in the Cotswolds. Apart from Em's health, life was good. Then came The Call from Jim Wallace.

'How would you like to work for Shan Gupta?' It sounded like the opening line of a joke. Knock knock. Shan Gupta was a medical doctor, chemist, and the creator of a huge pharmaceutical empire in India. A self-made billionaire. As a medical journalist I'd met him, of course, and emailed him once or twice, but I didn't expect he'd remember me.

'What's the punch-line, Jimboy?' He knew how crazy it sounded. I could hear him smiling.

'Here's the thing, Gip. He's planning to launch an online newspaper. Do for the internet what Ted Turner did for cable news.'

'CNN is doing it already. Everybody is.'

'Yeah, but Shan's been doing some research. Well, actually, he hired me to do the research. I reckon there are two big gaps. One is for a publication which is online first, not the bastard child of some newspaper or TV network. And the other is for a global medium which isn't associated with a particular country or religion.'

'Oh... kay,' I said slowly. 'But why his interest in the media?'

'Same as all those other billionaires, I guess. Turner, O'Reilly, Murdoch ... something to play with.'

'And your interest? Other than the research, I mean?'

'He wants me to run it. Choose my own team, complete editorial freedom, blank check. The usual Maurya working conditions.' Shan's company, Maurya Pharmaceuticals, was famous for spoiling their staff rotten.

'But... you're at the top of your game, Jim. You've only been at Newsweek for what... a year?'

'Yeah. But so are you, Gip. At the top of your game. Did you hear when I said blank check?'

'So, it's true!'

'What?'

'That everybody has their price!' Fortunately I've known Jim for years, and he knows when to take me seriously. I hope.

He chuckled. 'So what's your price, Gip?'

I pumped up the accent. 'A lobster dinner and an bonzer bottle of Chablis, Bruce. What's he offering?'

'Think of a number and treble it.' He paused just long enough to show he wasn't bullshitting. 'But... the money is only part of it. Shan is planning to base his new outfit in Istanbul, because he says it's the middle of the world. In several senses. But only a core team will actually work there, all the grunt work will be contracted out, and you could live wherever you like. You'd get your own full-time research and support team – I'm thinking 10 people for each beat. And we'll have stringers all over the world. Thousands of them. Tens of thousands.'

'Jesus! Are you serious?' You have to admit it sounded pretty far fetched.

'You have no idea. Most of our material will come from citizen journalists – stringers, blogs and forums. I know it's not new, but we'll go the whole nine yards – a news wiki, in real time.'

'But… you'll need a magic ingredient, Jim. There are lots of chat forums out there. The net is chocka bloggers…'

'You're right, Gip, and the magic ingredient is money. We're going to pay these citizen journalists, and we're going to moderate, sub-edit and translate their stuff into all the major languages in a couple of minutes.'

'Fucking hell, Jim. How to make a small fortune on the internet…'

'Yeah, I've heard that one already – start with a big fortune. But that was my brief from Shan. To tell him what could be done if money wasn't a limiting factor. Once I started thinking about the possibilities, it's like there was no end to them.'

'But… shit, Jim, how do you know that he's… serious?'

'He's already put up the money! It's in a trust fund in the Channel Islands. I've already had it checked out. It's… enough money to buy a country. He's not messing around.'

'So… you're really thinking about doing this?'

'Sure. Do you think I'd be wasting your time otherwise? It's the real deal. Fair dinkum, Sheila. Whaddaya think?'

Jim did a lot of things well, but an Australian accent wasn't one of them.

'I don't know Jim. I'm completely fucking gobsmacked to tell you the truth. Listen, Em and I are in the groove, you know, but… shit, when opportunity knocks. So, whose doors are you knocking on?'

'For the health beat, just yours Gip.'

'I'm flattered. And the other beats?'

'Georghe Dorin for politics, Russ Kleinschmidt for economics, Mikaela on the environment, Ume Noburu on science, José Guevara on sport…'

'Holy crap, Jim, that's like an international who's who. Whatever you're smoking, I want some!'

'Well, to be fair, none of them has committed yet. Shan has asked if we can all fly to Istanbul next weekend. Meet him and get the feel of the proposal before we make any decisions.'

'We?'

'Yeah – the whole crew. I haven't committed either. If I can't get my dream team I'll just go back to my life.'

It sounded suspiciously like he was saying if we didn't take the job, he wouldn't either. But for once I didn't say the first thing that came into my mind.

'A freebie to Istanbul? No strings attached? Why didn't you say so in the first place?'

He laughed again. 'So you were right after all, Gip. Everybody has their price!'

The gorgeous life-jacket demonstrator broke into my reverie to ask what I'd like for breakfast. 'I'm sorry, we don't have any bacon on board, miss. We weren't expecting a passenger. But we have eggs, and I can make Indian breakfasts...' She was so beautiful, and so anxious to please.

'What does the crew normally have?'

'We are having idli sambar...'

'I'm sorry, my knowledge of Indian food is limited to dishes that begin with tandoori.'

She laughed, showing perfect white teeth.

'Oh, no problem, miss. It is like a pancake made with fermented rice and dhal – lentils – and served with a vegetable curry. I could make scrambled eggs to go with it.'

'I'd love to try that. Thank you!'

As she glided away to the galley I thought of asking how she got into that sari. Maybe she'd demonstrate... Then I remembered we both worked for the same man, and decided I'd ask instead if she could make an espresso to go with the pikelets and cackle-berries. See if she could figure that out.

I used the keyboard and trackpad built into my seat, and the oversize monitor on the wall in front of me to scan for the latest on the bombings but there was nothing new so I let my mind drift back to that first meeting in Istanbul.

We were sitting on packing cases in the unfurnished building in Karaköy, with those incredible views across the waters of the Golden Horn to the iconic mosques of Constantinople.

I knew everyone in the room, some more by reputation than in the flesh. Jim, of course, is right up there – the guy who really did write the book on the way the world produces and consumes news.

Amanda Jones is a legend in the arts world, not only for her profound understanding of every form of creativity and culture, but also for her ability to put it across to cretins like me.

Linus de Boer is that most unusual animal – an expert in everything to do with the military, who is also a paid-up pacifist. I call him Oxy, short for oxymoron, like 'military intelligence'. He sometimes calls me Darwin, when he's out of reach, for reasons best ignored.

Enoch Mabuza is an inspiration, not only for his commentaries on life in the third world, but because his own life is an example of what can happen when you connect the dots of opportunity, talent and hard work.

If I sound star-struck it's because I was. These were the gods of my world.

Shan Gupta was there too – a god from another world. He didn't make a grand entrance, or arrive with a flock of acolytes, just a flask of coffee and a cooler of sodas. He shook hands with everyone and knew who we were without needing introductions. This is a guy who does his homework.

He was forty something, slim with dark hair and eyes, clean shaven, café au lait skin, features which would not be out of place anywhere in the middle east or northern India, but put together really well. About my height, five nine or ten, and slim – no evidence of affluence around the circumference, as Em would say.

He spoke with the accent of his public schooling in England and medical degree from Cambridge. Like me he never actually practiced medicine, but he went into R&D for a pharmaceutical company in Germany, then left to set up his own lab in India, and suddenly was producing patents of a quality and quantity which made the industry sit up and notice.

He began working with a small manufacturing firm to produce his formulations, for sale in India and neighboring countries. His drugs proved to be far more profitable than the company was expecting which, paradoxically, left them with a major headache. Their agreement allowed them to use Shan's patents with no upfront payment, but a large royalty on sales. This formula, together with sales volume, meant their chemist was now making more money than they were. Before long he bought the company and renamed it after an ancient Indian empire.

Shan proved to be even more adept in the boardroom than in the laboratory, and soon Maurya became a major player in the Indian pharmaceutical industry. After a string of corporate acquisitions in Europe and the far east, Shan was heading a mid-sized global corporation churning out products from micronutrients and cosmetics to over-the-counter, generic and proprietary drugs. Then there was the ARV thing in the nineties, which he used very effectively to promote his other lines, and suddenly Maurya was in the big league and a household name. Literally. Take a look in your own bathroom cabinet.

Russ and Georghe were the last to join our little gathering – their connection in Budapest had been delayed. Russ Kleinschmidt was Europe's answer to Jim Wallace, a professor of journalism and an economist of note, while Georghe Dorin was the consummate global political analyst.

After a few pleasantries, Shan got down to business with a refreshing lack of false modesty. 'I've been fortunate enough to become quite wealthy, and in India we believe it is important to share good fortune with others. Of course I could simply continue to give away a lot of money to the underprivileged, but I want to give them something even more valuable. The truth.' He looked at us steadily, to make sure we understood this wasn't bullshit.

'We live in the information age, but information isn't the same as truth. There's a premium on information which isn't... manipulated... by someone for their own benefit. If you don't believe me, try asking your friends whether your breath smells! You'll probably end up paying a dentist to tell you – and even then you'll probably keep breathing into your hand!' He waited for the inevitable joshing to die down.

'When I began to make money, one of the first things I discovered was that I could afford much better information, and this meant I could make better decisions. Of course it helped me to become even richer, but it also made me realize that a lack of good information is one of the key reasons why poor people stay poor. And that restricting access to information is a key strategy used by the wealthy and powerful to... close the door behind them.'

Once again he looked around to see if we were with him. I could see Enoch nodding. If anyone knew the link between ignorance and poverty, Enoch did. But most of our small group looked neutral, or skeptical. Every hack has heard the old gag: 'Never let the truth get in the way of a good story,' but I knew of very few who bought into it. We all did our best to bring 'the truth' to the people.

As for sharing the truth with the world's poor – a couple of years earlier someone would have pointed out that the masses didn't have access to the internet. But the explosive growth of cellular networks in the developing world, together with huge increases in bandwidth and decreases in user-fees, had changed all that. Today pretty much everyone could connect to the internet. Automatic translation and voice synthesis meant language and literacy were no longer barriers, either. In short, online news was no longer the preserve of the rich and educated. For the poor and illiterate it was the only way to go.

'Dr Gupta, may I ask a question?' Ume Noburu's name was synonymous with science and technology. Fortunes had been made by companies whose gadgets, software or sites she endorsed, and lost by those she didn't. I wondered if she would raise the issue of internet access in the developing world after all.

'Only if you call me Shan.'

'Sure, thanks Shan. What you said about the truth being more expensive than spin – it's very true. I see it all the time. Free is the magic word, but somebody has to pay, eventually, and there's only so much advertising to go around. There are a few paid-subscription sites, but they target very specific markets and they're generally small operators. Murdoch's News Corporation tried to sell quality journalism online, but he was hoping that a generation raised on bootleg music would pay for their news...'

Shan nodded, but waited for Ume to finish.

'So... what I don't get is the math of your plan. Who's going to pay? I know you can afford to get it off the ground, but sooner or later even you will run out of money. This is a seriously expensive project you're talking about.'

The Indian must have read the small nods and shifting of bums in seats, and known that Ume had raised a concern we all shared. He didn't look at all surprised.

'Ume, Rupert Murdoch was right. Bloggers talking to each other is no substitute for quality journalism. But Murdoch and his kind come from a newspaper paradigm. I suspect that, for many of them, the internet means replacing newsprint with computer monitors. I belong to a different paradigm, one that works with energy, reactions and catalysts.'

He gave a sudden smile. 'The way I see it, we should be paying our audience to write their own newspaper! We should pay policemen to report on crime, and politicians and voters to write about politics. We should pay computer users to review hardware and software, and theater-goers to review plays and movies. The better their stories are, the more people who read them, the more we should pay. They are the energy, we'll be the catalyst – giving them the means to reach a global audience, regardless of location and language, and rewarding them for their effort and courage...'

I was still grappling with this when Ume cut in. 'Sorry, Shan – I still don't see how this project can be sustained when your money runs out. Which will happen even faster than I thought, if you're paying citizen journalists.'

'My apologies, Ume. You're right – I can't sustain this project indefinitely. And you're doubly right when you say there's only so much advertising to go around. But I'm not aiming to get a piece of the advertising pie, I intend to get nearly all of it...'

There was a collective in-breath from the group. All except Jim, who smiled at us like someone who knows how the joke ends.

Shan smiled too. 'The simple fact is that more readers equals more advertisers. If we can get everyone to read our publication, we can get everyone to advertise in it. My plan is to capture ALL the news audiences, no matter where they are, what their interests, or what language they speak. And ALL the advertisers.'

There was a silence as we digested his words, and as he waited for our reactions. I wondered what he'd say if I suggested that he should pay patients to design their own drugs? If we were hearing this from anyone other than Shan Gupta, I for one would be heading out the door to see the sights of Istanbul about now. But I reminded myself that this was a man who saw opportunity long before others, and who was prepared to put vast sums of money where his mouth was. Even more important, Jim Wallace shared his vision, so I stayed. So did the others.

'Excuse me, Shan...'

'Go ahead Russ.'

'I agree that the big thing today is quality. Not only in news coverage, but in everything. But... we are also talking quantity here, aren't we? Unless I have misunderstood, you are planning to set up the world's biggest news-gathering and dissemination structure – using amateur reporters. And your success... your financial viability... depends on achieving extremely high quality and extremely large quantity, and then giving away the end result?'

Bloody good question. Wish I'd thought of it myself. Shan looked pleased.

'Precisely, Russ! That's exactly how I see it! Except that we're not really giving anything away – we're buying media share and selling it to advertisers. But I think your central point is… how do we achieve quality and quantity using untrained journalists? And I freely confess the mechanics of actually doing that were beyond me, which is why I turned to Jim Wallace. I knew that, if anyone can work it out, he can. And he has! Please Jim, would you tell everyone what you told me?'

We all knew Jim Wallace to be a media visionary and a masterful teacher, but the next hour blew us away. With nothing but his voice and his hands he described the assignment Shan had given him, the way he'd set about the task, and what he found. Nobody interrupted. Nobody asked questions. Nobody needed to. He'd thought of everything.

What Jim had done was the equivalent of Andrew Wiles' solving of Fermat's Last Theorem. Just like Wiles, Jim brought a number of seemingly unrelated tools to bear on the problem – in Jim's case ranging from frequent-flier miles and trade-exchange vouchers, to computerized credibility algorithms and semi-automated translation. He'd assembled these pieces into a surprisingly lean and elegant structure, drawing on decades of media experience, finished off with exquisite attention to the detail of what he called the 'three R's' – resources, revenues and responsibilities.

The climax to Jim's presentation was the answer to a question we hadn't even asked – if the content of the new publication was coming from citizen journalists, what were we doing here? Jim's answer was that we'd be like the judges on one of those big-budget TV talent shows. They aren't expected to sing, dance, cook, design clothes or tell jokes, and in most cases they don't even decide on the winners, the viewers do. But the judges' credentials and opinions must be – if not beyond reproach – at least well-informed and entertaining. They add so much value that most people can't imagine the show without them.

In short, as senior editors we wouldn't write the news – we'd predict and interpret it, and package and present it to a huge audience who may not know very much about the subject, but who weren't afraid to say what they thought. We'd be the catalysts, just like Shan said.

Suddenly a lot of things made sense. There were many fine journalists out there, but each of us in this room had a reputation for sticking our necks out, and for being right most of the time. Just as important, none of us was stereotyped by our nationality – we were all reporters without boundaries.

And each of us had developed our talent for edgy reporting in spite of the corporate straitjackets we wore. Which was what made Jim's proposal so irresistible. Simply put, his idea was to set us free – to go wherever we wanted, talk to whomever we wished, and engage with a global audience in pretty much anyway we liked.

'Look, with Shan's backing and money I can do for news what Wikipedia have done for knowledge. But that's not enough for me. It's too... neutral. Anonymous. I want a publication with a persona, a life-force. We need to be recognizably human, with opinions and ideas, strengths and even weaknesses. I want you guys to be that persona.'

When Jim finished there was a long silence. It felt stupid to applaud, but the blinding brilliance of his vision had created a pressure in the room which had to be released. I felt like crying, or yelling, either of which would have been even more stupid than clapping. It was José who got it exactly right.

'Sooo... what was the question again?'

When order was finally restored, and another round of drinks handed out, Shan brought us back to the nitty-gritty.

'For me, having come this far, the issue is simple. If we don't do this, somebody else will. Once someone has seen the future – the way Jim has – it's just a matter of time until it becomes the present. So we have a choice. Do we, in this room, make it happen? Or do we follow it on the news?'

There were no takers, so he continued.

'I know that every other major news organization will latch onto Jim's ideas, as soon as they hear them. Which is why we need to offer the full-strength formula right from the beginning. And, as Jim said, that means we need each of you.'

He reached into a satchel and brought out a bunch of A4-sized manila envelopes, which he began to hand out. 'I realize that I'm asking you to invest your careers in this idea, so I've prepared a detailed business plan for you to look at. You'll also find a written offer of three years of work at three times your present income, paid yearly in advance. And there's a bonus of a further three times present income at the end of this term, whether you stay or not. In other words, I'm offering twelve years' income for three years of work.'

We'd already crunched the numbers.

Jim broke the awed silence that followed. 'Guys, I think I need to issue a disclaimer at this point. I wrote most of the business plan, but the financial offer – that's all Shan's work. I'm afraid my imagination didn't stretch that far!'

He waited for the laughter to subside. There was a lot of nervous energy in the room. I was picturing myself in an Aston Martin DBS. Triple salary paid yearly in advance. Jesus! I wondered what the tax rate in Turkey was.

Jim kept going. 'After I handed my report to Shan, I had a sneaking suspicion he might ask me to take it on, so I gave it a lot of thought. So when he approached me, I had a lot of questions lined up. By the time we'd finished talking, there was only one he hadn't answered. That was whether I could have you guys on my team.'

He looked pretty serious. 'Like you, I like the sound of the money, but I'm not exactly suffering where I am. For me to do this, I need you all. If we're going to get ahead of the news, and the industry, I need a team of mavericks to help me break the mold...'

'Excuse me, Jim. What is a maverick? Is it like a millionaire?' The soft-spoken Enoch brought the house down. I still don't know if he was joking or serious.

We spent the rest of the day and evening together, talking through every element of the plan. After a while we moved to a restaurant across the street, where the food and wine flowed – although I noticed the bottled water went down even faster. This was serious business.

I can't pinpoint the moment when the decision was made. It's more like we reached a stage where we could no longer picture doing anything else with our future. We started talking about 'when' rather than 'if'. That left only one thing.

'So what's it called, Jim?' I asked.

'What?'

'Our new baby.'

'Oh, right. I've proposed "The World Online" to Shan.'

'TWO?'

'To Shan.'

'No, Jimboy. The acronym. T–W–O.'

'Ah. I guess that would make you the TWO wit...'

'Don't say it. Twit for short?'

'Hey, if the acronym fits...'

Nairobi, Kenya
08:30 Sunday 2 January

Elroy Hardman broke his stride when they reached the swimming pool, glanced back at the house to make sure they were out of earshot of his wife and kids, and glared at his political attaché. 'Who dreamed this up, Ben? We're an embassy, not a fucking fortress...'

He smiled wryly as he realized the irony of what he had just said. 'Well, OK, we are a fucking fortress. But there's a big difference between deterring terrorist action, and challenging your host government to a pissing match. Damn!'

'I gather it was proposed by the WHO, ambassador. Do you want to communicate your views to Washington, or should I talk to them first?'

Ambassador Hardman and Ben Berzack had not worked together for long, but the young head of mission had quickly learned that his battle-hardened deputy was highly adept at managing the byzantine politics of the State Department. Hardman understood immediately what Berzack was hinting at. If an ambassador queried a directive but was told to go ahead anyway, there was no court of appeal. But if a subordinate queried it, the ambassador might have another shot.

Hardman was always careful to give credit where it was due – one of the traits that had brought him to the ambassadorial residence in Nairobi's plush Muthaiga district. 'Yeah, good thinking, Ben. By the time you call they'll probably have heard from some of the other embassies, and have thought twice about this hare-brained scheme. Mind you it's... what... midnight in DC?'

'Yes. But they said they'd be standing by. I... we have to call in the next hour.'

'Okay. Go ahead and call, then.'

'And what about our staff? If they know we're storing ARVs...' Once again Berzack's apparently innocent question was loaded.

'Right again, Ben. It's going to be tough to pull this off without the staff knowing. Maybe better to make an announcement, if it comes to that. Damn, I really hope it doesn't.'

'At the same time, sir, a lot of staff, especially the Kenyan nationals, will be worried about their own health. Those who are taking ARVs, I mean. If you made an announcement, you could tell them that they'll be provided for.'

The ambassador absent mindedly slapped a rolled up Sunday newspaper against his leg. There was no mention in the paper of the Indian bombings which happened just five hours earlier, but the online media were full of it.

'I wonder if we can give that assurance, Ben? It could easily look like we grabbed the drugs for our own use. To protect our people, at the cost of the host population. I'm told the ARVs are the only thing keeping this region from meltdown. I can't imagine who could possibly do something like this...'

After a lifetime in the diplomatic service, Berzack was not easily rattled. 'Should we be reviewing our exit strategies, ambassador?'

'Yar. Quickly and quietly, Ben. I'm afraid the turds are airborne and heading toward the fan, even as we speak.'

Over Pakistan
13:30 Sunday 2 January

I jumped when I felt a someone touch my arm. 'Miss? Miss!' It took me a moment to recognize the sari babe. Across the Gulfstream I could see blue sky and haze through a window, but next to me the shutter was down.

'I'm sorry to wake you, miss, but we will be landing in Delhi in an hour. If you have your breakfast now, you will have time to get ready before we land.'

She must have thrown out my first breakfast – or given it to the pilots. 'How long have I been asleep?'

'Nearly three hours, miss.' I saw no recrimination in her eyes, just concern that I should be fed by the time we landed. I wondered whether Shan would be open to an offer, so I could take her home to Emily. Damn, but money is corrupting!

If I wasn't fully awake, that changed when I put the first forkful of food in my mouth. It was a kind of pancake, as advertised, slightly crumbly and neutral in flavor – nothing like the pikelets I was raised on. But this neutrality didn't extend to the contents of two little porcelain pots of curried vegetable stew and scrambled eggs with fresh herbs. Not a muted note, nor a hint of reheating anywhere. The aerial waitress – Dolly – offered coffee before I could ask, and didn't blink when I asked for espresso. As breakfasts go it wasn't good, it was spectacular!

Getting ready before we landed meant using the bathroom with its full-sized shower and enough space to swing a cat – or a pair of jeans – without breaking anything. So this was how the other half lived. Well, the other half dozen.

As the Gulfstream rolled to a stop in Delhi and the stairs were lowered, a smiling official came on board to stamp my passport (the dream continues!) closely followed by another respectful pilot in Maurya livery who escorted me to a black Bell JetRanger parked nearby. Then we were airborne again, skimming over the northern plains of India, heading toward the pale mountains lining the horizon.

It must have taken an hour but it felt like a few minutes before the white Himalayas were filling the windshield and we were flying between the mountains, then circling what looked like a modern alpine castle. The contrast between this crystal scene and the smoggy plains of north India could not have been greater, but before I could take it in we were shrouded in a cloud of powdered snow and, moments later, settled on a helipad. As the blizzard raised by our downdraft cleared Shan himself appeared at the door, tugging it open and letting in a blast of cold air.

'Welcome to Shimla!' He had to shout to be heard above the fading shriek of the helicopter's engines. As soon as we were far enough from the chopper to speak normally he paused and handed me a delicate and beautifully embroidered shawl. 'I thought you might not be prepared for the cold – we're above seven thousand feet here. Wrap this around you.'

I thought the gesture was more symbolic than practical, but I was amazed to find the flimsy shawl warmed me almost immediately. He was waiting for my reaction and smiled boyishly when I duly registered surprise. 'It's made from the hair of Pashmina goats, which are unique to the Himalayas. Please keep it as a souvenir of your first visit to Shimla.'

'I'm trying hard to be blasé about the executive jets and helicopters, Shan.' I looked at him sternly. 'Just so long as you know how much I'm suffering!' He laughed, but then I remembered why I was there. 'I'm sorry, Shan, I shouldn't be joking at a time like this…'

'That's alright, Gipsy. I'm glad you got the opportunity to enjoy some of our toys. Let's get inside.' I followed him along a path through some trees and shrubs, and then I saw the building. It was even more impressive from the ground.

'This is really something, Shan. How did you land up here?'

'During the British occupation this was the summer residence of the governor, Lord Kitchener. It burned down, and was rebuilt as a small luxury hotel by a friend of mine. It was meant to be the jewel in the crown of his group of hotels but unfortunately it never made money, so he was open to my offer. It suits us very well.'

As we covered the last few yards Shan pointed out a turreted roof rising above the forest a couple of miles to our right. 'That's the official summer residence of the president of India. She's my neighbor.'

The inside was all marble and bright oriental carpets, with fires in several hearths. Very cozy. Two women in black silk saris just like Dolly's, and a man in a similar tunic with elaborate embroidery that suggested rank, greeted us with bows and hands pressed together, then the man led us to an enclosed terrace where a huge buffet was laid out.

Shan paused. 'I normally have lunch with my staff on a Sunday afternoon – it gives us an opportunity to enjoy our surroundings and to talk shop. Please join me.' I didn't ask why everyone was working on a Sunday afternoon – for many Indian companies it's a normal working day.

The steward led us past empty tables and seated us in a corner. Through the double-glazing I could see serried ranks of white mountains fading to infinity. A black eagle rode an air current just a few yards away, scanning the forest below. The bird was so close I could see when it blinked.

Shan explained the buffet was a traditional Kashmiri banquet or wazawan. I wasn't really hungry after my late breakfast on the Gulfstream but I'm a sucker for anything new so I asked if I could have a 'tiny taste' of everything. It was a good choice, because he served up a procession of extraordinary morsels while we talked, accompanied by a spicy green tea. After the first plate arrived I asked Shan how serious the sabotage was for Maurya.

'It's very serious. Our Chandigarh plant is where we make active pharmaceutical ingredient which we supply to other plants in our own group and also to companies producing finished medications all over the world.' He passed me a leather folder. 'I've had some information compiled for you. To save your stringers some time.'

I riffled through it. Some glossy company blurb and a few sheets of data. I saw a table of drug types, with annual production in kilograms and dollars, and another with the number of staff employed in different categories at the Chandigarh plant. There was also a short obit on the seven people who died in the blast, with photographs showing four men and three women staring gravely into the camera.

'This is very useful, thank you. What about the other factories? The ones in Hyderabad?'

'I don't have the same detail on them, of course. But they also make API. They are our major competitors. Between us we produce most of the generic API in India, and we supply a large part of the global demand for certain molecules.'

It was a while since I'd heard the reference to 'molecules' so I skipped a beat while I reminded myself that making drugs begins by synthesizing the designer-molecules which make them work.

'So… who else is in the business of… synthesizing these molecules?'

'Well, the originators of course, for proprietary drugs. Big pharma. They're mostly in North America and Europe. For generics there are the Chinese, and a few producers in south east Asia and elsewhere. The Chinese are by far the biggest producers of API by volume, although they have difficulty meeting quality standards for the international market.'

'Okay… So which of them planted these bombs?'

He smiled and shook his head. 'I don't think it was any of them. I mean… I can't bring myself to believe that big pharma would do it, because they really don't have anything to gain. Of course they don't like us, because we reverse-engineer their drugs and cut into their profits, but… blowing us up won't change anything. Another company will step into the gap, and in due course we'll just rebuild our factories and carry on.'

'So the Chinese will step into the gap, and make a lot of money? Doesn't that give them a motive?'

'Well… not really. It's not like there are two or three big companies in China who may have colluded to do this – there are thousands of them. None can be sure they'll take our place.'

'But collectively… couldn't this be a national strategy to take this business away from you… permanently? Wouldn't that drive you… the three of you… out of business?'

Shan looked surprised, then snorted. 'Well… yes, I suppose it would, in a manner of speaking. Both us and them, in a nuclear firestorm.'

'What! What are you talking about?'

'Ah, Gipsy, this is… not my area of expertise.'

I picked up the clue. 'Okay. Just for background then?'

'Well, hypothetically, the Indian national intelligence service may have phoned me to ask if this sabotage could be interpreted as an act of war by China, or Pakistan.'

'Whoa! War? Pakistan?'

'Oh absolutely. Whenever there's any kind of terrorism in India, it's always blamed on Pakistan. It's a tradition around here. Ever since partition. But there's no earthly reason why Pakistan would do this, much less China. Remember our three countries all have nuclear weapons, very large armies, and very excitable populations. Between us we account for about a third of the population of the earth. The last thing any of us would do is sabotage our competitors.'

'Okay. So… you told your spook what?'

'My spook?'

'Spook… spy… the intelligence guy who called you?'

'Oh, right. Hypothetical spook, remember? I would have told him what I just told you. That it really makes no sense. If the Chinese refuse to sell us API, for our own finished drugs, it will look a lot like an admission of guilt, and our… spooks… would take a very dim view of that. I'm pretty sure the Chinese will be falling over themselves to help us in our hour of need.'

'What about blackmail? Extortion?'

'No, we haven't received any threats or demands.'

'Maybe the demand is still coming? You pay us a lot of money, or we'll do it again.'

He looked thoughtful, then shook his head. 'It wouldn't really make sense to blow up three factories... three different companies. Easier to just blow up one, and threaten the others.'

'Unless they plan to blackmail someone else... some other industry. Say, for example, the computer industry. If we can do this to pharma, we can do it to you. Pay up!'

Shan laughed. 'You're good at this, Gipsy. I hadn't thought of that one. Maybe I'll have another chat to my... spook. Hypothetically, of course.'

'You're welcome. It's the least I can do for letting me play with your nice shiny jet. So... have you put a figure to the damage? I mean, both repair of the damage and loss of business?'

'Not yet. It will take some time. But it's many crore..'

'Crore?'

'Yes, sorry, it's how we count. A crore is ten million. One crore rupee is about two hundred and fifty thousand dollars. I'd guess the repairs in Chandigarh will cost somewhere around a hundred crore – 25 million dollars – but that's really a bit of a thumb-suck.'

'Jesus, that's a big number. What about loss of income?'

'That's not easy either... we don't know how long it will take us to restore API production. It depends how much we have to pay the Chinese and others to get API for our own products. My guess is that it won't be much more than it costs to make it ourselves, so it shouldn't affect the profitability of our downstream operation.'

'That's some good news, at least.'

'Yes. The truth is that I'm relieved. This could have been so much worse. If the plant had been in production, that bomb would have killed hundreds of people, not seven. We are very protective about our people, as you know.'

'Do you think it's a coincidence that the bombing took place while the factory was closed?'

'No, I'm sure it's deliberate. Normally the plant is in continuous operation. We shut down only four times a year. It's the same for most API manufacturers – it's the most economical way to operate. That's another reason why it can't be the Pakistanis. They go for big body counts, like railway stations and markets.'

'Do any of you have any idea how this was done? The kind of bomb, how it was planted and so on?'

'Sorry, I can't help you with that. The police will tell us in due course, I'm sure. I only know it destroyed the chemical reaction chambers. They are the heart of the API production process. Whoever did this knew what they were doing. That's the hardest part of the plant to replace.'

'What kind of molecules did you produce?' I caught the gleam in his eye, and an involuntary glance at the closed folder in front of me. Right question.

'We produce quite a wide range. The biggest by volume are ARVs, of course.'

'Oh yeah... of course!'

It must have been the suddenness of this trip, jetlag, being untimely ripped from my bed, whatever. It felt like I'd been sleepwalking. Not the best way to impress your boss. Shan's name was synonymous with antiretrovirals. He had been one of the first to thumb his nose at the originators of the most important ARVs, back in the nineties. He not only reverse-engineered their drugs but he started shipping his copies to Africa at cost price, or less.

At the time Indian patent law didn't protect finished products, only the processes used to make them. This policy served India well, providing their population with affordable drugs and supporting a billion-dollar generic drug industry. For a long time the Indian government simply ignored the howls of protest from western pharma and their paid-for politicians, who appeared to value intellectual property rights more than the right to life. It isn't easy to bully a nation of a billion people.

Shan's offer to ship ARVs at cost was the first domino to be nudged over in a long line which ultimately led to the roll-out of ARVs − both proprietary and generic − to millions of people who previously could not afford them. As a result he became significantly richer and more famous, and he was even nominated for a Nobel Peace Prize. Personally I thought he should have won it − even before he made me quite a bit richer and more famous myself. If Shan noticed my embarrassment at overlooking the obvious, he didn't let on.

'We mainly produced API for nucleoside reverse transcription inhibitors. NRTIs. Our competitors in Hyderabad focused on non-NRTIs. So between us we cover... covered most first line ARVs. Volume is everything in this business − it's much more cost efficient for each of us to focus on a class of drug than to compete across the whole range.'

It flashed through my mind to ask whether this amounted to collusion, but then a far bigger thought intruded. 'Hang on a sec, Shan. Are you saying this sabotage has destroyed India's capacity to supply first-line antiretrovirals?'

'Well, the active ingredients at any rate, yes.'

Jesus! If I was still in my bed next to Em sleeping off the alcoholic assault on my liver, now would be a good time to wake up... 'But you... India... supply most of the world's generic ARVs, don't you?'

'Yes − over 60 percent of the finished drugs, and about 90 percent of the molecules.'

'Jesus, Shan!'

He said nothing, watching with a sad smile as the enormity of the situation sank into my addled brain. I made a big effort to get my shit together. I'd been thinking the story was about who and why the plants were bombed, when in fact it was about...

'Okay – tell me what this means for supply of ARVs.' I hadn't thought to wear my headset while interviewing my boss, but now I pulled my handheld out of my purse and held it up for Shan to see. He nodded, so I pressed the record button.

'I think it depends very much on the Chinese, and how quickly they can spool up their production. Also on the state of ARV stockpiles around the world.'

'Do you think the Chinese can do it in time... make up the shortfall?'

'I think they'll react quite quickly – hopefully they'll meet our needs within a few weeks. I certainly hope so, because I don't think we can restore our own API production in less than... oh, five or six months. It's difficult to replace chemical reactors – you can't buy them off the shelf.'

'And the global reserves of ARVs?'

'There's quite a lot of product out there, particularly in major hospitals and AIDS clinics in the most affected countries. But it's vital that their medical communities hear that there may be a hiatus in the supply, so they use their resources appropriately...'

'Appropriately...?' I knew that you can't stop antiretroviral treatment without risking a dramatic decline in the patient's health, and the development of drug-resistance. Once started, ARVs must be continued for life, without interruption.

'Yes. Delaying the initiation of ARV therapy for new patients, prescribing the drugs they have most of...'

'Oh, right.'

I suddenly realized the tables around us had been quietly filling up with other staff. As I looked around now I caught the eyes of a few people, all of whom smiled and clasped their hands in greeting. I returned the smiles but was too self-conscious to do the prayer thing.

Shan rose and held out his hand to me. 'Come, let me introduce you to some of my colleagues. And then I imagine you need to communicate with your office? A quiet space to work?'

As the story rattled around in my brain I could feel the warm hands of Indian men and women shaking mine, read in their brown eyes that if I was important enough to have lunch with Shan Gupta, then it really was a pleasure to meet me. Then Shan and I were walking through the building, and he was saying he was planning to fly down to Chandigarh in an hour or so.

'It's only 15 minutes away. I need to commiserate with the families and see how bad the damage is, now that the dust has settled. You're very welcome to join me. Or if you prefer I can get you to Delhi or Bombay to connect with an outbound flight?'

I didn't give him an immediate answer, but while I was waiting for my laptop to boot up I reminded myself what I'd been hired to do. Get ahead of the story. I couldn't see how Chandigarh would help me do that. To see what happened next, I'd have to go where the ARVs were no longer going.

Istanbul, Turkey
12:00 Sunday 2 January

Zvonimira Jelena was expecting Gipsy North's story when it appeared on her monitor. The World Online's content manager usually handled copy from the senior editors herself, leaving her team of moderators to deal with posts from tens of thousands of stringers.

Jelena was in her early 50s. She was born in Croatia but raised in many countries, thanks to her father's work installing steam turbines in power stations. As a result she grew up speaking six languages like a native, and had since acquired functional literacy in another five – one of the key requirements for her present job. She finished her schooling while her father was working in Montreal, Canada, and she joined the Montreal Star as a junior sub-editor at a time when computerized newspaper editing and page-makeup was in its infancy. She had been involved ever since in getting news ready for publication – first in newspapers, then television, and for most of the past decade, online.

In print-media, sub-editors trimmed stories to fit the areas of the page not already sold to advertisers – there was some truth to the old joke that a reporters' job was simply to keep the advertisements from meeting in the middle! The front page was always the last to be finalized, so that late-breaking news could be given prominence. Television news was similar – editing scripts and video clips to fit the time allowed, and keeping your options open until the last minute.

But online newspapers like TWO were different. Stories could be added, modified or moved around at any time, and length was limited only by the material available and the expected attention span of readers – or users, as they were now called.

The vast majority of TWO's content was sent in by stringers in the form of written copy, digital photos or video clips. Every submission was reviewed within minutes by one of Jelena's moderators – who would have been called 'copy-tasters' in the old days – who categorized each one on the basis of language, news-type, rank and risk.

Hard-news stories – which were supposedly factual – were forwarded to one of a dozen companies around the world for editing, translation and sometimes legal opinion, before being sent back to TWO's page-makeup department on the second floor. There they were converted to HTML, the computer language of the internet, and queued for posting. It only remained for Jelena to paste the story to an appropriate location. Once posted, the position of stories changed according to the hit-rates and user-ratings, with more popular and credible stories moving automatically to more prominent positions.

Although stories were posted in the contributor's language, users could read them in any language they liked, thanks to the miracles of automatic translation. However high-ranked material was sent for pre-publication translation into a dozen of the most popular internet languages.

Processing thousands of stories a day, and keeping the average time from submission to publication below thirty minutes, was an extraordinary – and extraordinarily expensive – feat, but what truly energized TWO was the fact that its citizen journalists were paid.

Payment was not in cash but in 'stringettes', a play on the newspaper term for a part-time correspondent. But the name 'stringettes' actually came from a classic Monty Python sketch, in which a manic ad-man named Adrian Wapcaplet – played by John Cleese – brainstormed ways to sell 122,000 miles of string which had been mistakenly cut into three-inch lengths. TWO's marketing team – whose meetings often descended into Wapcapletese – were ridiculously proud that a use had finally been found for 'stringettes.'

TWO's stringers accumulated stringettes in much the same way that airline passengers collected frequent-flier miles, and they were entitled to exchange them for any of the goods or services sold by the site's advertisers – a process which gave accountants and tax collectors nightmares, but which was hugely popular among both stringers and advertisers. Regular contributors whose stories attracted higher ratings were promoted, getting more stringettes for each contribution.

The first thing that Jelena's moderators looked for in any contribution was opinion. Op-ed stories were treated differently to hard news. The term op-ed was a hangover from the newspaper world, where it meant the page 'opposite the editorial page', and not 'opinion editorials' as widely believed. Anyone could submit their opinion on anything to TWO, and millions did, but these posts were generally sent without editing to the chat forums – better known as the 'TWO Cents' pages – where they attracted lively discussion, but no stringettes.

However, a few of the best op-eds from contributors were rescued from TWO Cents and found their way into print, alongside the articles written by the e-paper's senior editors. TWO's weekly news digest appeared in a dozen languages to cater for the shrinking but still very influential breed of people who couldn't or wouldn't read the news on an electronic device. The slim magazines were distributed free in airports, hotels and coffee shops around the world and had proved to be one of TWO's most powerful marketing tools.

Within seconds of receiving Gipsy North's story from Shimla, Jelena forwarded a copy to the English sub-editors in Seattle for proofing – even experienced journalists produced typos or wrote in British English when they were under pressure – while she extracted the first couple of paragraphs for a teaser on TWO's portal, or front page.

She had barely finished the teaser when the body of the story reappeared in her queue. Intelligent software had linked many of the words in North's article to other stories, so users could find out more about AIDS, ARVs, Chandigarh, Maurya and Dr Gupta.

Nine minutes after Gipsy North's copy first appeared in her in-box, Zvonmira Jelena posted the teaser to the English portal. A click on the headline or 'full story' link would take users to the body of the story, making it instantly accessible to millions.. Within another twenty minutes the story would be translated into all twelve of TWO's standard languages, and posted to their respective portals, expanding the potential readership to more than a hundred million users.

As she watched, the hit-counter at the foot of her screen began to spool up.

Washington DC
05:00 Sunday 2 January

'Come in Vince.' Delgado saw no reason to apologize for asking her senior adviser to spend the first night of the new year working when she was prepared to do the same. 'What news from the trenches?'

'The ambassadors are... not happy, madam secretary. I think they are genuinely worried about the safety of their embassies when word gets out that they're stashing ARVs.'

The secretary of state grunted impatiently. 'But... haven't we been clear? It's only for a day or two. They tell their host governments that we have intelligence leading us to believe there's a high risk their ARV reserves may also be sabotaged, and that we'll hand the drugs back as soon as it's safe to do so.'

'I'm sure the ambassadors understand, madam secretary. A couple of them have even told me they support the principle behind it...'

'So what's the problem? Is it difficult to get our hands on the drugs?'

'No, that's pretty easy. There's always someone – from the CDC or one of the agencies – who is directly involved in the distribution of ARVs, and who effectively has carte blanche to move them around. I understand that most of the missions have already figured out their strategy. They're just waiting on a green light from you. But they're worried about what happens next.'

'Meaning?'

'They're afraid the local military or police will shoot first and ask questions later. As you know, in many countries HIV prevalence is highest in the armed forces. They could easily see this as a threat to their survival, and not bother to check in with the politicians...'

'I don't know, Vince. It seems unlikely that they will move so quickly, especially if we play open cards with everyone from the beginning. Or at least, as soon as the ARVs are in our hands. Any word from the risk-assessment analysts?'

'They're still working on it, madam secretary. Their first take tends to support what the ambassadors are saying. Or at least, what their deputies are saying.'

A ghost of a smile passed over the secretary's face, and then disappeared.

'Okay. Well, I'm not happy about it myself, but I just got off the phone with the president and we're going to stick our necks out on this one. He says it's time to demonstrate that our military strength is not only there to protect Americans, but vulnerable people everywhere. It's our time to take some risks. Diplomatic and physical.'

The adviser recognized the change in tone, and clicked his ballpoint pen in readiness to take instructions from his boss. She didn't notice.

'Tell the ambassadors to move on the acquisition of the drugs, and to put their marines on full alert immediately. But tell them not to do anything which they can't defend later on the basis that it was a humanitarian imperative. Above all, don't hurt anyone. Unless there's a full-scale attack on their embassy, of course. Keep me in the loop, Vince. At least every hour.'

Before he could respond there was a brief rap on the door and Delgado's personal assistant came in without waiting for an invitation. 'Sorry madam secretary, but I thought you would want to see this immediately.'

'What is it, Harry?'

He handed her a single sheet of paper. 'It's a story which has just been posted on The World Online, Ma'am.'

Delgado took the page and read the first few lines, then looked up at her adviser. He wasn't sure what her expression meant. It might have been relief.

'Vince, ignore what I just said. The word is out on the ARVs.' She swiveled her chair to stare for a moment at the collection of photographs above her bookshelf, as she usually did when she was thinking. Then she turned back.

'Okay. Vince, set up a tele-conference with all the ambassadors in an hour. Harry, get the secretary of Defense on the line – I need to see if he can join the conference. Oh, and Vince, tell the ambassadors to dust off their emergency evacuation plans.'

'If they haven't already done so,' he murmured.

The secretary stared at him blankly for a moment, her mind still working down a checklist, visible only to her. Then she caught up with his comment and smiled grimly. 'Yes, we've probably just skipped a step... Okay gentlemen, let's get to it.'

London, UK
12:00 Sunday 2 January

Ernest Wintermeyer looked suitably grave as he faced the cameras in the BBC World studio and followed the story on his teleprompter.

'In our lead story this noon, the bombing of three commercial pharmaceutical laboratories in India early this morning has effectively crippled the global production of antiretroviral drugs, the mainstay of the fight against HIV/AIDS. The World Online quotes Indian pharmaceuticals manufacturer Dr Shan Gupta, who owns one of the laboratories destroyed in the attacks, as saying the blasts were clearly intended to interrupt the supply of first-line generic antiretrovirals. He said the countries most likely to be affected are in Africa, South East Asia, Latin America and the Caribbean. And in the latest twist to this story, TWO reported moments ago that a United Nations warehouse near Stockholm was extensively damaged by fire last night. The fire is believed to have begun at exactly the same time as the bombs went off in India. TWO's health editor Gipsy North has pointed out that the warehouse is used to store antiretrovirals which are destined for the same countries.'

Wintermeyer paused as instructed by his teleprompter and turned to his fellow anchor, Leslie Shaw, his face lined with concern. 'This is terrible, Leslie. What do we know about the implications for AIDS patients, particularly in the third world?'

Shaw gave a grim smile, which offered reassurance and sympathy at the same time. 'Ernie, this must be an extremely worrying time for everyone who depends on ARVs, and for the medical personnel who have dedicated themselves to fighting the AIDS pandemic.'

She turned to face the camera. 'Although we have not managed to locate Dr Gupta since he first exposed the link between the sabotage and antiretroviral drugs, The World Online quotes him as saying it will take months to fully restore production, and doctors around the world need to adjust the way they prescribe ARVs to make their supplies last as long as possible.'

Shaw lifted a hand to her ear. 'I've just been told our UN correspondent June Reddy is standing by in New York with the director of the United Nations Joint Secretariat for HIV and AIDS, Dr Ibrahim Mazzer. June?'

Reddy's face appeared on the monitor behind Shaw and then filled the screen. 'Thank you Leslie. As you said, I'm talking to the director of UNAIDS.' She turned to the Egyptian who was standing next to her, bundled up against the cold and looking as though he would rather be in bed rather than standing on a freezing Manhattan sidewalk before dawn.

'Dr Mazzer, can you confirm that your warehouse in Sweden has been damaged by fire?'

'There has been an event of some kind at the UN storage facility, yes, but I have very few details as yet.'

'And can you confirm these events in India and Sweden targeted the production and distribution of antiretrovirals?'

'No, absolutely not. It is possible that the Indian plants produced some of the ingredients for antiretrovirals, and that ARVs were stored in our warehouse, but I'm sure you'll find these factories and our warehouse have many other products in common, such as painkillers and antibiotics. There is a very real danger to jumping to conclusions, as I'm sure you are aware.'

Reddy was not easily put off. 'Can you say to what extent the flow of ARVs may be affected?'

'I don't think that treatment for any disease will be affected at all. Remember these events happened...' he glanced at his watch 'not even twelve hours ago. It will take several days before we have all the data, and can make a proper determination.'

'Dr Mazzer, do you have any idea who could be behind these blasts, or what their motives might be?'

'We have no information on the sabotage in India. As for our warehouse, it was more of a fire, so it could have been a malfunctioning gas cylinder, or some kind of spontaneous chemical reaction. Also we received no warning, and we cannot see what such an action could achieve. The conspiracy theory being promoted by The World Online makes no sense at all.'

'What does this mean for the medical community, and for people who are receiving antiretrovirals?'

'I don't think anyone who is receiving chronic medication of any kind should be concerned, whether they are living with HIV, diabetes, hypertension, tuberculosis or anything else.'

Mazzer turned to look directly at the camera. 'Remember the pharmaceutical industry is one of the largest in the world. Whatever happened in India... it has not affected the originators of these medications in Europe and the USA, nor the hundreds of generic-drug manufacturers all over the world.'

Reddy recognized a stonewall when she heard one, but she tried one more shot. 'So you would not agree with the report from TWO which quotes Dr Gupta as saying the blasts have crippled global production of ARVs?'

Mazzer smiled thinly. 'I fear that Dr Gupta may have been misquoted by The World Online, or perhaps has been influenced by the fact that he owns that publication.'

'Are you saying that he deliberately exaggerated to encourage users to visit his website?'

'I wouldn't go that far, no. Maybe their reporter was throwing around some ideas with her employer, and his speculation was misinterpreted as fact.'

'Thank you Dr Mazzer – we'll have to leave it there. From UNAIDS in New York this is June Reddy. Back to you in London, Leslie and Ernie.'

Istanbul, Turkey
15:00 Sunday 2 January

'Jim? Zvonimira.'

'Hi Vonnie.'

'I thought you might like to look at the hit-rate on Gipsy's story, especially from countries with significant AIDS epidemics. I've put together a graphic showing the increase in hits since the story broke.'

'Just a sec… Okay, here it is. Jesus, that's impressive! Those are huge numbers! We've obviously stirred up something…'

'Yes. And I noticed the hit-rate went up after the latest round of TV newscasts – the networks had no choice but to mention us. We've also recorded a record number of click-throughs from other news sites, so we'll be generating good revenue from those.'

'That's great, Vonnie. Shan will be pleased.'

The content manager laughed. 'Just as long as we're right!'

'Oh, I'm not worried about that. Shan knows what's going on in the drug industry. And if he's wrong… well, it's his money.'

'No, I wasn't thinking of the accuracy of the story. I meant whether we were right to publish it…'

'Oh?'

'Yes, this increase in hit-rates… what if it's a sign of panic among people who rely on ARVs?'

'What makes you think that, Vonnie?'

'You might want to look in on TWO Cents…'

'Is it also going crazy?'

'Yes, but it's not only the number of posts, it's what they are saying. There are a lot of people who aren't buying the line from the UN that there's nothing to worry about. Some of the posters are doctors in organizations like MSF and the Red Cross who are saying they'll run out of ARVs in a few days.'

'Okay. Drop a line to Gip in case she hasn't picked it up – she's on a flight to Johannesburg.'

'Johannesburg? She's not coming back here?'

'No she decided to go to South Africa. It's the epicenter of the AIDS epidemic and the main consumer of ARVs. Lots of AIDS organizations have offices there.'

'Okay, I'll let her know.'

Pignon, Haiti
09:00 Sunday 2 January

It was raining hard as the army truck scrabbled for grip on the slippery and deeply rutted road leading to a cluster of buildings on the brow of the hill. The unarmed man at the gate was not there to keep people out of the clinic but to direct them to the right place – the counseling and testing center for first-time visitors; the consulting rooms, dispensary and food bank for returning patients; and the hospice and morgue for those visiting terminally ill relatives, or collecting their remains.

The guard waved down the truck to ask their business but the driver ignored him and drove into the compound, sliding to a halt in front of the main building. Immediately a dozen men in dirty army fatigues jumped down from the canvas-covered back of the truck, rifles at their chests, and pushed their way through the crowded verandahs and into the various entrances. A moment later they emerged with half a dozen nurses and the single doctor on duty.

A man who appeared to be their leader, although he wore no badges of rank, was leaning against the worn wooden parapet of the verandah waiting for them.

'Who is in charge?' he asked in French when the staff were assembled in front of him.

The doctor raised his hand a little, unsure of what was happening. Although unnerved by the rough entrance of the soldiers he did not fear for his life or those of the nurses. This humble clinic was literally a life-saver for thousands of families living in the surrounding highlands. In the fractured politics of Haiti, the doctors and nurses of Hands of Care were perhaps the only people respected by everyone.

'Where is Legrande?' asked the officer in a conversational tone.

'He's out of the country at the moment,' the doctor replied. 'I am Dr Ferry, his assistant. How can I help you?'

'Bon. We are taking over the clinic.'

'What? You can't do that. We are here with the permission of the government. Who are you?'

'Surely you know, doctor?'

Dr Ferry did, in fact, have a pretty good idea. Haiti's recent history was essentially a record of the struggle between various elected governments and the remnants of a national army disbanded in 1995, which refused to lay down arms. This militia controlled large parts of the country outside of the capital, Port-au-Prince, and mostly lived in a state of uneasy peace with the legitimate authorities.

'The FLRN – the Cannibal Army?'

'Bravo!'

'But Dr Legrande has met with your leaders, and they agreed we could operate here..'

'Doctor – did I say anything about you not continuing your work? We are here to make sure you are not interrupted.'

'But why do we need protection? Who would interrupt us? I don't understand.'

'Ah, I see you have not heard the news. There will be no more antiretroviral drugs for some time. It seems the companies that produce your tablets can no longer get the... essence... from India.'

The doctor's first reaction was to laugh, but he realized this might be a mistake and choked it off. It sounded almost like a cry of surprise. 'But surely... sir... that's impossible. I mean there are a lot of drugs, made by many different companies..'

'Ah yes, but they all get this... principe actif... from India, and those factories were destroyed yesterday evening. Also the United Nations reserves in Sweden. Poof! It seems we will have to make do with what we have for some time to come.'

'Well that won't be very long – we usually keep about a week's supply of ARVs. Our vehicle brings in supplies every Thursday from Port-au-Prince...'

'And today is Sunday. I don't think it's very likely that your delivery will arrive this week, doctor.'

'But... sir...'

'You can call me Major.'

'Major, this is a catastrophe. We have many hundreds of people who depend on us, both here and in Port de Paix.'

'Well, doctor, we may need to find ways of... how shall we say... stretching your supplies a little, until the situation is restored to normal.'

'What do you mean, "stretch"?'

'It's quite simple. We'll tell you who to treat, and who will be taking a little holiday from their medicines.'

'Major, you can't take a holiday from these medicines. It just takes a week or two and... then the drugs don't work any more. After that you need different drugs, which are very hard to find.'

'What is your stock of those second-line drugs, doctor?'

The term 'second-line' was the giveaway. Ferry knew he had to stall, to protect his very small and precious supply of second-line ARVs.

'Actually, major, we don't have any – normally they come in on a Thursday and we dispense them to the patients who need them the following day...'

Without warning the officer stepped forward and slapped the doctor on the side of his face, hard. The sound was as shocking as the pain, and several nurses screamed.

'Doctor, in my line of business we also dispense medicine. Most people find it distasteful but it... always... cures the problem. We are especially good at curing forgetfulness.'

He held up his right hand, palm upwards. 'This... is the weakest of our medicines. Sometimes to cure a particularly bad case, we must use our medicine on someone else...' He paused and glanced at the nurses. His meaning was lost on nobody.

'Do not lie to me again,' he said quietly.

38

PHARMAGEDDON

New York
11:00 Sunday 2 January

If Maryam Kapur was tired after the long-haul flights from Karachi's Quaid-E-Azam to London's Heathrow and on to New York's JFK, she didn't show it. The secretary general was driven directly from the airport to her office at UN Plaza for the eleven o'clock briefing by UNAIDS executive director Ibrahim Mazzer, to prepare her for the emergency stakeholder meeting the following afternoon.

Mazzer began by briefing her on the arrangements for the next day's meeting, then he responded to her request for an update on the epidemic by handing her a printed table of figures, which he explained in his accented but accurate English. The Egyptian wasn't sure how much she would remember from previous briefings, so he took it from the top.

'Five years ago there were roughly 33 million people living with HIV. Today that figure is approaching 36 million – an increase of a little over eight percent.'

Kapur was tracing the data on the table with her pen, and merely nodded to show she was listening.

'But as you will see from the regional data, SG, that modest increase in global data masks a major shift in the locus of infection...'

The secretary general's pen moved to another row, paused over a number, then flicked back and forth between two columns. 'If I'm reading this correctly, Dr Mazzer, prevalence has actually fallen... quite substantially... everywhere except southern Africa?'

'That's correct.'

'You told me previously that southern Africa was running against the trend, but... my god! I had no idea the situation had gone this far!'

'These are the latest surveillance data, SG. We only finished compiling them last week, and I'm afraid the numbers were far worse than we expected. We were expecting... hoping that prevalence in southern Africa would have begun to decline, as it has in other regions, but instead it's showing an accelerating trend.'

'So southern Africa now accounts for, what, nearly 30 percent of global HIV infections?'

'I'm afraid so. Up from 20 percent five years ago. From 6.6 million to 10.6...'

'And the rest of Africa... there are so many figures here it's hard to see the patterns.'

'My apologies, SG. If you exclude the five countries of southern Africa, the pool of infection in the rest of sub-Saharan Africa has remained steady at a little over 15 million people.'

'And the rest of the world? Is this a decrease from 11 million to 9.75 million people?'

'It is. If you exclude sub-Saharan Africa, global prevalence has actually declined by more than 11 percent. But if you include everyone, it's increased by 8.2 percent.'

Kapur put down her pen and stared at the UNAIDS head. 'Dr Mazzer, the obvious question is... why? Why is it different in southern Africa? Are they not getting the same interventions as everyone else?'

'They are, SG. In fact Botswana and Namibia have been an example to other countries, with everyone who needs ARVs actually receiving them. About a third of those infected have reached the point where they need the medications...'

'And South Africa?'

'They came off a very low base of antiretroviral use, as you know. They're currently treating about a fifth of those living with HIV, and the proportion is increasing steadily. But... the figures don't tell the whole story.'

'Go on.'

'There are still many doubts and suspicions about antiretrovirals among their people. A lot of them buy into conspiracy theories – the drugs will make them sterile, or kill them sooner. Many patients only take them when they are desperate, and then stop taking them as soon as they feel better.'

Kapur shook her head in dismay. 'Surely they're told how important it is to take the drugs consistently?'

'Of course, and they're informed that the drugs may no longer work if they interrupt their treatment. But there are so many people... such strong folklore... telling them their illness is not dangerous, but the drugs are. That it's all a plot by big pharma...'

'I suppose this dates back to former South African president Mbeki?'

'Yes, although Mbeki was merely adopting Peter Duesberg's theories. It's been extremely difficult to develop the same momentum we've achieved in other countries...'

'Is the medical establishment in South Africa fully behind the program?'

Mazzer shrugged. 'The physicians, yes. But we aren't so sure about the nursing staff. They have protocols, of course, but we have concerns about the way in they are monitored and enforced in South Africa.'

'Presumably if patients aren't taking their medications consistently, we will see an increase in newly infected people with drug-resistant strains of the virus?'

'Not really, SG. At least, not in the short term. As you know, the average period from infection to the appearance of symptoms is around seven years...'

'Ah, of course. If someone is infected with a drug resistant virus today, it will be years before we know it.'

'Just so. There are exceptions, of course, but it's only when we have data from a large cohort of patients that we can draw conclusions about what happened seven or eight years ago.'

'And what are the data telling us right now?'

'Well, Botswana established universal first-line treatment nearly a decade ago, and we're beginning to see an increase in drug resistance today. Within the next 12 months we may need to start all new patients on second-line formulations.'

Kapur appeared lost in thought for a moment, then focused again on Mazzer. 'I assume the South Africans have seen these figures? How did they react?'

'Unfortunately they have a real problem with the data. They are saying a 60 percent increase in prevalence over the past five years proves that ARVs aren't working... or that they are making the epidemic worse. Some are saying that perhaps Mbeki was right all along.'

'But... why is their HIV prevalence rising, when it's steady or falling everywhere else?'

'Well, there's an interplay of factors. When you give ARVs to everyone who needs them, prevalence tends to rise because people are no longer dying at the same rate...'

'Yes, I understand this. New infections increase prevalence, deaths reduce prevalence. If you reduce the number of deaths without reducing new infections, prevalence will go up.'

'Exactly! However, in most countries we've seen a decline in new infections which has been greater than the decline in mortality, so the pool of infection has remained steady or fallen. But this trend hasn't been followed in southern Africa.'

'So you're saying that new infections are not decreasing in South Africa? Are you attributing this to concurrency?' Kapur knew that research showed that Africans typically had no more sexual partners than anyone else, but their practice of maintaining several concurrent relationships, as opposed to the 'serial monogamy' model popular in the rest of the world, provided an ideal environment for the spread of HIV.

'We think that's a key factor, yes.'

'But concurrency isn't unique to southern Africa, is it? Why is the trend there so different to the rest of the continent?'

'We don't know, SG. We can only speculate that South Africans have been slower than others to... modify their behavior.'

'I suppose it doesn't help to have a president with multiple wives and mistresses...'

'No indeed. Unfortunately they react quite badly to being told by foreigners that their culture poses a threat to their survival. This kind of message can come from their own leaders – which is... unlikely, under the circumstances.'

Once again Kapur retreated into her thoughts for a moment, tapping her pen on the sheet of paper in front of her before she focused again on the UNAIDS head.

'Dr Mazzer, I was under the impression that antiretrovirals significantly reduce the risk of infecting others. Surely the roll-out of ARVs in South Africa should have reduced the rate of new infections?'

'They do, SG, but this effect has tended to be... misunderstood. The problem is that people are at their most infectious within a couple of weeks of becoming infected themselves. At that point they don't even know they are infected, let alone start taking antiretrovirals.'

Kapur shook her head at the irony. 'So... when can we expect to see the end of the epidemic?'

Mazzer gave a short laugh at the unexpected question. 'Well, there's no cure, so the only way to eradicate the virus is to wait until everyone who is infected... dies.'

'Hopefully from something other than AIDS?'

'Indeed. We can only compute an end-date to the epidemic when there are no new infections, and when we know how long people with HIV will survive. With appropriate treatment, of course.'

'In other words, from the time of the last new infection, it could be... decades... before the virus ceases to exist.'

'In the absence of a cure it will be decades, yes.'

'What is the typical survival rate at present?'

'For a stable patient, about nine years from when they start antiretrovirals...'

'So if you add the period from when they are first infected until they start treatment, that's an average of 16 years from infection to death.'

'Yes, although these numbers are a poor indicator of individual life expectancy. Some people die within weeks of infection while others live for decades, even without treatment. In practical terms we expect more than half of those living with HIV today to die from causes unrelated to HIV.'

'You're talking about developed nations?'

'No, life expectancy is typically lower in third-world countries anyway, so that... lowers the bar somewhat.'

'And new infections?'

'The only conclusion we can draw from the data you have in front of you, SG, is that new infections have fallen – dramatically – over the past five years. Everywhere except southern Africa.'

'How dramatically?'

Kapur was surprised to see a fleeting smile on the Egyptian's face. 'If it were not for the latest figures from southern Africa, and now the latest threat to the supply of antiretrovirals, I would be asking you to announce that the end is in sight.'

'What are you saying?'

'It appears that in most countries, new HIV infections are now... quite rare.'

'But... that's wonderful news!'

'Indeed it is, SG. For most of the world.'

Kapur read the conflicting emotions on her colleague's face, and nodded slowly. 'One road for Africa, another for the rest of the world. Again.'

Mazzer nodded too. 'And now we have this... sabotage... to contend with.'

'Yes. Tell me doctor, what are our prospects of restoring the supply of ARVs before present stocks are depleted?'

'We simply don't know as yet, SG. We know how much production capacity has been lost, but we have no idea how much spare capacity there is around the world. Needless to say Jean Folbert's team and mine are working around the clock to find the answers...'

'Very well. Let me ask you this – what will happen if we cannot restore supply before existing stocks are depleted?'

'Then we are looking at a large-scale treatment interruption, SG. Once again we can't predict exactly what it means, because it's never happened, but we know that after a couple of weeks without antiretrovirals, viral load increases sharply in most patients, and drug-resistant strains emerge....'

'Which means those patients will only respond to second-line medications?'

'Many of them, yes...'

'And there's no way to separate those who can safely resume first-line medications from those who cannot?'

'Not when we're talking about hundreds of thousands of people, possibly millions. We would need to start everyone on second-line medications.'

'So we need to know how soon each country will deplete their stocks of first-line ARVs, and whether we can restore production before then?'

Mazzer nodded. 'And we need to know immediately. If we find that large-scale treatment interruptions are unavoidable, we need to focus on producing second-line drugs. Naturally this will have profound implications for... well, everyone.'

The two UN executives sat staring at each other, sharing a common thought. Finally Mazzer put it into words. 'And we'll need to ask ourselves who gains from all of this, and whether they will attempt to disrupt our work again.'

New York
12:00 Sunday 2 January

The sound of his feet pounding on the treadmill and his heavy breathing made it difficult to hear the news at noon on CNN, but when Baldwin caught the reference to the UN he climbed off the machine and moved closer to the TV. And when he heard that a UN warehouse in Sweden had been sabotaged he headed for the showers.

In the six months he'd been living in New York, Baldwin had been able to schedule his time pretty much as he pleased. At first he'd stuck to the routine he'd followed for more than 20 years in the military, but after a while he discovered that he was most productive in the early morning, when he would usually have been running or pushing weights like everyone else. He also found that if he worked out in the middle of the day, he got more work done in the afternoon and evening. In addition to the daily workouts, he got in at least three hours of endurance training every Sunday, either in Central Park or, if the weather was bad, on a treadmill in the gym.

Working away from his fellow officers meant there was no pressure to fill his weekends with golf, cookouts and meeting eligible girls, and Baldwin hadn't gotten around to making many friends in New York. It wasn't that he was antisocial, exactly, but he found the freedom of living alone to be... liberating. Much the same could be said about his work. The Director himself told Baldwin there was no users' manual for his assignment as the ODNI's liaison officer at the United Nations. There would be nobody to tell him what to do.

'I want you to write the manual, colonel. Find the best way to safeguard US security and intelligence interests as they relate to the UN. Bring a pair of fresh eyes to this.'

In the six months he'd been living in mid-town Manhattan, Lieutenant Colonel Arthur Baldwin had done exactly that – written a detailed proposal on how certain aspects of the complex relationship between the USA and UN could be modified to fall in line with the goal of the Office of the Director of National Intelligence, which was to integrate foreign, military and domestic intelligence in defense of the homeland and of United States interests abroad.

Baldwin knew his proposal, once it had been vetted and spun by countless securocrats, would be merged with similar documents from the departments of state, treasury, trade and others, to give shape to the so-called 'new beginning' jointly announced by president Thomas and secretary general Kapur shortly after the president's inauguration.

Ten days ago Baldwin submitted the first draft of his proposal and he was now waiting for further orders – either to re-work some or all of the document, or to report for a new assignment. But for the moment he felt... directionless – and he was enjoying the feeling!

Baldwin's first call was to Frances Dumont, the UN chief security officer, who was already at her desk. Although she sounded pleased to hear from him she said she had not yet been cleared to discuss the issue, and he knew better than to press her. She promised to call back when she could.

His next call was to his boss at his home in Virginia. As he expected, the deputy director told him to gather as much information as he could on the situation and report back. He sounded pleased that Baldwin was taking the initiative.

Baldwin's third call was to the headquarters of the Centers for Disease Control and Prevention in Atlanta, who patched him through to their deputy director. He didn't sound very surprised to be hearing from the ODNI. He told the colonel that the man he needed to talk to was professor Paul

Stanislav, the CDC's chief HIV epidemiologist, who just happened to be in New York for the holidays.

A call to Stanislav on his cellphone found the epidemiologist at a Soho bookstore, where he was looking for rare books to add to his collection. He said he would be happy to have lunch with the colonel at the bookstore's coffee shop. Baldwin spent a few minutes downloading as much information as he could about the AIDS pandemic, and about the bombings that had interrupted his holiday weekend, before heading out in search of a taxi.

Just as he was giving the driver the address of the Housing Works Bookstore he got a call from Dumont, asking if they could meet at 14:30, which meant keeping his lunch with Stanislav very short. When he arrived at the bookstore in Crosby Street he learned it not only had a superb collection of collectible books, but devoted all its profits to homeless people living with HIV.

Paul Stanislav looked more like a reclusive software developer than a top epidemiologist. The thirty-something professor was wearing distressed jeans and a woolen jumper with the sleeves pulled up. He sported a stubble-beard and his long sandy hair was drawn back into a pony tail.

'I guess I should be pissed at being called to a meeting when I'm finally getting some R and R but…. Jesus… when I saw the news! What do you need, colonel?'

'Well prof, right now I don't know whether these bombings have any implications for US security, but if they do I need to be on top of it so I was hoping you could give me some background. I know very little about AIDS, but I need to get up to speed, fast.'

Stanislav looked at Baldwin thoughtfully. 'How do you want it?'

'Straight up, no spin. I was reading this…' Baldwin held up a copy of UNAIDS' annual report which he'd downloaded from the internet and scanned in the taxi. 'Maybe you could settle one thing for me first – HIV, AIDS?'

The epidemiologist smiled. 'Okay, that's a good place to start. Just cause and effect. HIV is the virus, and AIDS is the resulting illness. It's like saying Staphylococcus aureus and zits. One causes the other. We say someone is HIV positive or living with HIV from the day they're infected, but we only say they have AIDS when the virus has damaged their immune system so much that it's obvious there's something wrong. It can take years for HIV infection to advance to AIDS and most people have no idea they are infected during this time, unless they're tested.'

'Epidemic and pandemic?'

'The same thing. A pandemic is just a widespread epidemic. But, way I see it, we don't call it an epidemic until it's widespread, so it's a pointless distinction.'

'Okay, thanks. I see nearly three quarters of this epidemic – of people living with HIV – are in Africa. Why?'

'Three reasons, I'd say.' He counted them off on his fingers. 'First, we're pretty sure the virus originated there. Second, sexual practices in that part of the world seem to favor transmission. And third, we've done all the wrong things to control it in Africa.'

It was Baldwin's turn to smile. 'Talk about an answer that raises more questions...'

'Hey, what can I tell you? You want me to go through them in turn...?'

'Please.'

'Okay, but I should warn you that, when it comes to AIDS, there's almost nothing that everyone agrees on. Still, we're pretty sure the virus jumped species from apes to humans, maybe sixty, a hundred years ago. Apes carry a very similar disease – called SIV, simian immunodeficiency virus – but it doesn't kill them...'

'So how did it get into humans?'

'The conventional wisdom is that some guy cut himself while slaughtering a chimp for the pot. They call it "bush meat" out there. It's possible the guy got some chimp blood into his own bloodstream.'

'And this SIV kills humans?'

'Not necessarily. We've found people – pygmy tribes – who've been hunting and eating chimps forever. And sure enough they have traces of chimp viruses in their blood, but it doesn't make them sick. My guess is something else was needed to transform SIV into HIV. Something involving medical science.'

'Like what?'

'Well, they did this experiment at the University of Kansas. Took a weak virus which could be given to monkeys without much of a problem, and made it into a much stronger bug that gave those monkeys AIDS.'

'You don't say. How?'

'It's a trick called serial passaging. It... shit, it's like a relay race. If you pass the virus quickly from one host to another, and another, and if your timing is right, the bug gets stronger.'

'So you're saying that someone, somewhere, did this serial passaging thing before we were born?'

Stanislav smiled. 'Yeah. Not deliberately, but... well, if you look at the timing of the epidemic, it's probable that HIV was created around the time we were learning about vaccines and blood transfusions, say fifty or sixty years ago. At the time medics often used one syringe to treat thousands of people, and they harvested blood for transfusions from people who had recently received a transfusion themselves.'

'So they were transferring blood from one person to another... and there's your relay race?'

'Could be. Also the way they did smallpox vaccinations back then – they scraped the blisters on the skin of people who'd recently been vaccinated, and used the gunk from inside those lesions to inoculate the next guy...'

'You're joking!'

'I wish! A lot of things we did back then seem crazy by modern standards.'

'So, prof, you're saying that AIDS could have been created by doctors…'

Stanislav nodded slowly. 'Yeah, epidemiologists like me, sure. But in mitigation of sentence, your honor, we did it while successfully saving millions of people from diseases like smallpox and polio. Of course there are people who say we created HIV deliberately.'

'Really?'

'Yeah, sure, to control population growth in Africa, or to kill homosexuals – that kind of shit. Some say it was a deliberate project run by the US army. Listen, I like a conspiracy theory as much as the next guy, but it's all crap. I mean, even back then they'd have known that releasing a dangerous virus into a population could end up wiping out everyone, including them. Still, there are some people around who believe it.'

Baldwin made a note on his pad. 'Okay. So the virus jumped from apes to humans, maybe with some help from medics. Then what? How did it kill millions of people?'

'Well, let me just say that AIDS doesn't kill anyone. Not directly, anyway. What it does is weaken their resistance to other infections, so diseases they'd normally shake off end up killing them.'

'Right. I knew that.'

'Okay. In Africa there are a lot of people with weak immune systems – you know, from malnutrition, malaria, tuberculosis, whatever. And they are exposed to a lot of bugs because they don't have good water, food, safe ways to dispose of sewage. So they get more infections, and they die more often from them.'

'So… it would be easy to miss AIDS, because it's not like the people were dying from anything new…'

'Yeah. Hey, you're good at this! They were just dying more often from the same old diseases. So HIV spread for years – decades – in central Africa without anyone noticing. They may have had their suspicions, but it's not like they knew what to look for, or there were any tests they could use. Also there was a war going on in that part of the world – remember Idi Amin?'

'Sure. So how did they spot it?'

'Actually we identified it first here in the USA, in our gay community. We noticed that there's a rare form of cancer called Kaposi's Sarcoma which often manifests in AIDS patients. What we didn't know is they were also seeing a lot of Kaposi's in southern Uganda. Then a doctor at the Uganda Cancer Institute – David Serwadda – made the connection and… bam! Overnight we realized the epidemic was much bigger in Africa than here.'

'So the epidemic started in Africa and was transferred to the gay community here in the US?'

'Yeah, probably through Haiti. Back then everyone blamed it on Haitians, and they got pretty pissed off, but turns out there's good evidence that it was carried from the Congo to Haiti, and then from Haiti to the gay community right here.'

'Through anal sex?'

'Well, yeah. Maybe. I mean we're pretty sure anal sex is riskier than vaginal sex, but we know for sure that screwing multiple partners is how it spreads, regardless of the hole you stick your dick into. Some of those guys had more than a hundred partners in a year!'

Baldwin grunted and shook his head, but didn't look up from his note taking. Stanislav ladled sugar into his espresso, stirred and swallowed it in one gulp, then caught the eye of a waiter and signaled for a refill before turning back to Baldwin who was sipping his own flat white.

'Funny thing about this bug – the deadliest epidemic in human history – is that it's 100 percent preventable, and pretty much everyone knows how to prevent it! It's almost like some people have a death wish. I think it was Robin Williams who said that God gave man a brain and a penis, but not enough blood to operate both at the same time!'

Baldwin spluttered into his drink, put it down quickly and swabbed at his mouth with a napkin as the epidemiologist continued.

'I mean if everyone had a single sexual partner for life, and nobody shared a needle, that would be the end of it. New infections just wouldn't happen.'

'But needles... injecting drug use isn't an issue in Africa, is it?' He patted the UNAIDS report, to show he'd done his homework.

'Naah, it's pretty much all heterosexual sex out there. In places like eastern Europe and south east Asia they share a lot of needles, and the rate of transmission is huge, but the bug seldom spreads outside the circle of users, their partners and kids. In places like that we hardly ever see a prevalence over one percent.'

'What about prostitution?'

'Well, sure! We used to think prostitution was the key to everything – prostitutes are infected with HIV, pass it on to their clients. And it's true, but once again the bug doesn't seem to spread outside of the guys who go with working girls and their immediate families. Except in Africa...'

'Which is because...?'

'Well, like I said, there's nothing about AIDS that everyone agrees on, but we're pretty sure now that the answer lies in concurrent partnerships. Sexual concurrence.'

Baldwin frowned at the unfamiliar term. 'What – like polygamy?'

'Yeah, but more often it's informal. Wife, mistress, mistress number two...'

'I've seen that in the Caribbean. Women have kids with different fathers, who still come calling.'

'Exactly. Which is why the Caribbean has a similar epidemic to Africa – we call it a generalized epidemic, where it's not confined to specific groups like people who go with prostitutes or share needles. In generalized epidemics we see a lot more women infected – even more than men.'

'So… are you saying that men in Africa and the Caribbean have more sexual partners than… others?'

'Hell no, amigo! We've got a pile of surveys that tell us the average African guy gets laid no more often than anyone else. But they keep doing it with the same group of women. Concurrence.'

'So… someone in this circle gets infected, and… suddenly they're all infected?'

'Hey, listen colonel, if you are thinking of a change of career…'

Baldwin laughed. 'Hey listen professor, how about you call me Art?'

Stanislav offered his hand. 'As long as you call me Paul.'

After they'd shaken hands Baldwin leaned back, and looked surreptitiously at his watch. 'So it's really about behavior patterns?'

'That's right, Art. And in Africa we find some behaviors which are pretty dangerous, when you have a bug like HIV on the loose…'

'Like concurrency.'

'Yeah, but a lot of other things too. Girls having sex with older men in return for school fees or phones. Tribes where the headman deflowers all the virgins, or where widows are obliged to have sex with their brothers-in-law. Ritual circumcisions, tattoos, body piercing, where the same blade is used for everyone…'

'Jesus!'

'It's a long list. And there's a lot of sexual abuse of children and rape… but the thing that's really driving the epidemic is those concurrent sexual partnerships.'

'But what about condoms?'

'Yeah, what about them? Look, from the guy's perspective, these are his regular partners – so why use condoms? As for raping kids, one theory is that they do it because it's seen as safe sex, and another is that it's a way to cleanse themselves of the virus. Either way the whole point is not to wear a condom.'

Baldwin blew between his teeth, and shook his head. Stanislav continued.

'And then there's the official response to the epidemic – which for a long time was a total fuck-up.' The epidemiologist hesitated. 'Hey Art, this is another long discussion. How are you for time?'

'Almost out. Can we do the headlines?'

'Sure, I'll try. Problem one – denial. For a long time African leaders had a hard time accepting that HIV existed at all, or that it was transmitted by sex, or that condoms could prevent infection, or that ARVs were effective, or that their customs were making things worse. Some of them disagreed, but in Africa nobody wants to speak out, break ranks, because loyalty is a big thing.'

Baldwin nodded. This much was obvious from the news.

'Problem two – inertia. African politicians take a long time to be convinced of anything, and longer still to act. It's often a case of one step forward, two steps back. Then you have corruption. It's really hard to get anything done – even humanitarian stuff – without turning a blind eye to self-enrichment by those in power.'

Another nod from Baldwin as he took notes.

'And problem three – machismo. Real men don't wear condoms. Real men don't talk about sex, especially to women and children. Real men spit on those living with HIV – after all, "they brought it on themselves!" It's amazing how many of these guys blame their women for infecting them, even when they're screwing three other women on the side.'

Stanislav spooned sugar into his second espresso and downed it, while Baldwin swallowed the last of his own coffee.

'Listen, Art, I'm not suggesting any one of this happens only in Africa. But… it all comes together there. It reaches a critical mass.'

Baldwin pulled a wry face to show he was listening as he wrote, but said nothing.

'And then there's us.'

'Us?'

'The west. The north. Developed countries. We've also fucked up, big time. Even though we knew condoms were the best way to prevent infection, our Bible-thumping politicians said abstinence and faithfulness were the way to go. We couldn't bring ourselves to give condoms to schoolkids, so we gave them bullshit instead…'

Baldwin looked up, as though he wanted to say something, but then thought better of it. Stanislav continued.

'Then there are ARVs. Long after we had them here in the US, the drug companies were holding out for prices which they knew bloody well they couldn't afford in Africa, Latin America, south east Asia. The suits were full of crap like: "even if they have the drugs, they don't have the means to administer them." But then we saw some projects in Haiti and Cape Town which showed ARVs could be used very effectively, even in low-income countries. India and Brazil began issuing compulsory licenses to make generic drugs, and pharma found themselves being dragged into court in South Africa – and losing. So finally they rolled over.'

Baldwin looked at his watch and began to collect his papers. 'So how was it resolved?'

'Well, the biggest actor in all of this was the US government…'

Baldwin froze. 'Oh?'

'Yeah. Our administration was backing pharma big time, trying to prevent the third world from making generics. There was some pretty bad stuff going on behind the scenes – people being beaten up, threats of trade sanctions. But after pharma saw the light in 2003, Bush launched the biggest AIDS program in history to buy ARVs from big pharma and dish them out to the third world. Fifteen billion dollars over five years. And in 2008 Congress voted to triple that amount.'

'Could this have anything to do with the bombings?'

Stanislav nodded slowly. 'I'd be surprised if it didn't.'

***

'Come in, Art. I hope I haven't spoiled your Sunday by making you wait?'

'Frankie, you know I'm always at your disposal. And I was able to use the time.'

Frances Dumont was dressed in a business suit, as usual. Her office in the UN building was as impersonal as an office-furniture showroom. Baldwin had met the UN chief security officer many times over the past six months but he knew very little about her – and the French-Canadian gave no sign that she was interested in what he did in his own time. Still, he enjoyed working with her, and they had slipped into nicknames very soon after meeting. She didn't waste any time on small talk. As usual.

'I've been given the green light to share with you, although I probably can't tell you anything you don't know already.'

'Try me.'

'Okay. We know that four devices were detonated simultaneously...' she looked at her watch, 'nearly 20 hours ago. Three in India and one in our warehouse outside Stockholm.'

'So you haven't heard about the one in Iceland?'

'What?'

Baldwin smiled. 'Yeah. There's a research laboratory in Reykjavik which is developing a new class of antiretrovirals. It's been approved by the FDA and the WHO but they haven't reached production yet.'

'What happened?'

'They got lucky. It seems a group of cellphone transmitters were shut down for routine maintenance. Middle of the night. This place – Vikmed – was also closed over the holidays but one of their company executives heard about the bombings in India and... well, when he couldn't reach his security guards because their phones weren't working, he called the Reykjavik police and asked them to check on the lab. When he said he was worried about a possible bomb they followed their standard protocol for bomb threats which includes...'

'Shutting down the cellular network! Of course.'

'Yes. Or keeping them shut down, in this case. When they sent their bomb-squad to the laboratory they found a device.'

'That's great news. Is it in the public domain?'

'No. The authorities in Iceland have agreed to keep it under wraps. But I thought it would be useful information for you guys.'

Dumont was nodding thoughtfully. 'I hope they are more successful in keeping it quiet than we were with Stockholm.'

Baldwin pulled a face. 'Yeah, everyone is a reporter these days.' Then he smiled. 'Okay. So I've showed you mine…'

She grinned and pretended to rip open her blouse. 'Well, I've been instructed to give you full access…'

When they'd finished laughing, she continued. 'All we know about Stockholm is that at the same time as the Indian blasts – which was two am in Sweden – an incendiary device was triggered in the drug cage. That's a secure area inside the warehouse. It caused a fire which destroyed everything inside the cage, but left the rest of the warehouse intact. Nobody was injured and the automatic sprinkler system put the fire out before the local fire brigade arrived.'

'Any leads?'

'Only circumstantial. Pointing to a couple of security guards employed by the company that does our security in Stockholm.'

'Did the guards have access to this… cage? Where you stored the drugs?'

'No. But they might have got hold of a key.'

'And how big is the security detail?'

'Normally it's four. But it seems that one person didn't report for duty – sleeping off his celebrations on Friday night, probably. And another guy spent most of his shift sleeping. He's the shift leader, normally a very reliable fellow. They're giving him a blood test to see if he was drugged. The other two are missing.'

'Those two – how long had they been working there?'

'The Swedish guy for several years, but the German was quite new. About five months.'

'Sounds like a contract job, doesn't it?'

Dumont shook her head. 'I can't believe we didn't see this coming. It seems… so obvious now. How vulnerable the ARV pipeline really is. It was so easy for them.'

'Hindsight is always twenty-twenty.' Immediately Baldwin regretted the cliché, but Dumont didn't react, so he continued. 'I'm going to have a look at the Reykjavik laboratory tonight – see if I can get a handle on who might be behind it… what it all means. And then I'd like to go on to Stockholm, if that's okay with you. You're welcome to join me…'

'No, thanks Art. I need to be here. But there's no problem about access, as I said. Will you keep me in the loop?'

'Sure. Same for you?'

'Absolutely.'

PHARMAGEDDON

Johannesburg, South Africa
01:00 Monday 3 January

What a way to spend a Sunday! Breakfast on Shan's Gulfstream, lunch at his headquarters in Shimla, dinner on a commercial flight to Johannesburg!

The South African Airways A340-600 was in the air for more than eight hours, but flying west meant it was still – just – Sunday when we landed, back in the same time-zone in which I'd woken that morning. I'd spent more than seventeen of the past twenty hours in the air. It felt like the longest and most bizarre dream of my life, and being cooped up in the first-class cabin of the Airbus meant I had plenty of laptop time to follow the unfolding nightmare.

First came the bombshell from a regular stringer in Stockholm, 'Blogsson', that a UN warehouse had been sabotaged at the same time as the Indian plants. I didn't need to be told what that meant – I'd visited that warehouse a year earlier with my friend Nikki Kershaw while writing a story on UNAIDS' ARV procurement and distribution network. I knew their central purchasing service had saved many millions of dollars – and almost as many lives – in impoverished countries.

Vonnie's concern at the undercurrent of panic on our chat forums had been right on the money – before I landed in Jo'burg there were reports of raids on a rural AIDS clinic in the Haitian highlands, and at a government drug dispensary in the city of Imphal, north eastern India. These were both areas where the epidemic was particularly bad, and also where there were long-standing military insurgencies. I knew that men in uniform are not only prime candidates for HIV infection, but also the most likely to do whatever it takes to survive.

I felt certain the only reason we weren't getting similar news from Africa was that it was the dead of night, and that the morning would bring unwelcome news – especially from the southern end of the continent, which had not only the world's biggest AIDS-epidemic but also some of its highest crime-rates. And a lot of men in uniform.

On the plane I wrote an op-ed which I called 'After Pharmageddon, Judgment Day.' What can I tell you – the word 'pharmageddon' just popped into my jet-lagged brain.

'Evil' doesn't simply mean 'bad', it means immoral. The word belongs to people who see the suffering of others as incidental to their quest to get whatever they want – a matter of inconvenience rather than a troubled conscience.

The sneak attacks which have crippled the global production of generic antiretroviral drugs are quintessentially evil because they threaten the survival of millions of people who have nothing the bombers could possibly want, and who can do nothing to help themselves. Clearly, for the terrorists, these people are simply pawns in some kind of bizarre game, a means to some– as yet undefined – end.

Whoever did this is evil. And anyone who finds merit in their actions deserves the same epithet.

Edmund Burke famously said that all that is necessary for the triumph of evil is that good men do nothing. So what should good men and women do about the sabotage in India and Sweden? We should shout out that those responsible are not fit to walk among us. We should reassure those who depend on these medications that we will not rest until their future supply is assured, and those responsible have been stopped.

School biology tells us how the human immune system reacts to viral invasions. Unfortunately HIV – the virus that causes AIDS – has the ability to dodge this response, and then to weaken the immune system itself to the point that almost any infection becomes life-threatening.

Strangely enough the AIDS epidemic does the same thing to society as the virus does to our bodies – it tricks us into indifference and inaction, probably because of its association with social taboos. As a result every step in the war against AIDS has been a desperate struggle to persuade people to overcome their prejudice and preconceptions, and calmly stare the beast in the face.

The AIDS epidemic demands that we talk to our kids from an early age about sex; that we make condoms available to everyone; that we work with prostitutes, intravenous drug users and men who have sex with other men; and that we drop our assumption that people living with HIV somehow deserve it. The epidemic demands that we help AIDS patients to live, instead of ignoring them to death.

Three decades into the AIDS epidemic we know these strategies work and, thankfully, so do an increasing number of people in positions of power. While the epidemic is unparalleled in history, so is the scale and scope of the global response. AIDS is no longer considered a life-threatening disease in most of the world, and people who are successfully medicated are no longer considered infectious.

There have also been giant leaps in preventing new infections. Transmission of the virus to new-born babies has almost been eradicated. Countries which are working with, not against, prostitutes, injecting drug users and gay men have turned a torrent of new infections into a trickle. Countries which are equipping their children to protect themselves with knowledge, condoms and institutional protection are at last able to imagine an AIDS-free future.

The fifth secretary general of the UN, Javier Perez de Cuellar, said the measure of any civilization is how it treats its weakest members. His successors have honored him by ensuring those who are defenseless against this virus receive sophisticated and expensive drugs, not excuses. It is a perfect expression of civilization, and the antithesis of evil. It may well be mankind's highest achievement.

Which makes four bombs, strategically placed to undo this great work, our lowest.

Yesterday the world witnessed pure evil. Today is judgment day. It is time to choose sides. There is no space, there is no time, for anyone to do, or to say, nothing.

By the time I hit the 'send' button I was collecting a lot of material from my earlier spray of emails, for example the one from Folbert at the WHO quoting Macbeth: 'A tale told by an idiot, full of sound and fury, signifying nothing.' At the time it didn't occur that he was probably talking about me, rather than the bombers.

On the blogs everyone was blaming everyone else. But it did help me to construct some scenarios for the editorial conference that Jim had scheduled for that afternoon. I certainly wasn't stuck for ideas.

But by the time we landed at Johannesburg's O R Tambo the scenarios were blending into the breaking news in my jetlagged brain, and it was all I could do to recognize my name on a board held by the Michelangelo Hotel's chauffeur – and I don't even remember checking in.

Reykjavik, Iceland
04:00 Monday 3 January

Baldwin spent most of the five-hour flight monitoring the latest developments on what the media were now calling 'pharmageddon', and researching Iceland. He was surprised to learn the island was ranked as the most developed country in the world along with Norway, and was also one of the most egalitarian.

There's only one problem, he thought. All that ice! But then he read that the winter temperatures in Reykjavik seldom dropped much below freezing, thanks to a relatively warm ocean, and he decided he would keep an open mind. An hour later the Icelandair Dreamliner fluffed out her skirts and settled on the runway at Keflavik. Only a few passengers disembarked from the plane, which was en route to Frankfurt.

Baldwin wasn't expecting to be met at 4 am but as he exited the airbridge he saw a graying woman who looked like she should have been waiting for a grandchild, except that she was airside of passport control and was holding a placard with his name on it. She introduced herself as Eva Arnarrson, liaison officer for the Vikingasveitin or counter-terrorism unit.

'I imagine you would like to go directly to the laboratory, colonel?'

'Thank you... Mrs Arnarrson?'

'You can call me Inspector, but I would prefer Eva. Or aunty. Most of my colleagues call me that.'

Baldwin laughed and followed her as she swiftly negotiated his way through immigration and customs, and to a waiting Volvo in the car park. In ten minutes they were heading towards the Vikmed Laboratory on the outskirts of Reykjavik, twenty minutes away.

During the drive Baldwin confirmed the combination of good luck and good police work which saved Vikmed's laboratory. A clutch of cellphone towers owned by Siminn and Vodaphone had been shut down after midnight for routine maintenance. Executives at Vikmed's parent company in Chicago, alarmed by the news out of India, called the Reykjavik police on a landline at around 2am – an hour after the Indian blasts – to say they couldn't reach their security staff, and were worried about a possible bomb.

Following standard procedure the duty officer contacted Siminn and Vodaphone and instructed them not to turn on the towers until further notice. A search by the bomb squad found a device which would have been powerful enough to flatten the entire building, and to kill anyone inside.

Baldwin was amazed to find the laboratory brightly lit and crowded with cops at four thirty in the morning, a day after the bomb was found. Aunty Eva was greeted with hugs by everyone from constable to commissioner. Only later did Baldwin learn that she was the widow of a much-loved former chief of police who dropped dead at his desk from a cerebral hemorrhage. Until his untimely death his wife had been a kind of mother figure to the island's close-knit law enforcement community. Six months after his death they missed having her around so much they asked whether she would consider joining them as a liaison officer. It turned out she was missing them just as badly.

Inside the laboratory Baldwin was shown the explosive device, defused but still in place, and introduced to the head of the Icelandic Intelligence Service Per Johannson, commissioner of police Stefan Erikkson and others. They made him very welcome, and spoke English to each other so he would not feel excluded. He began to warm to these people. A steaming concoction of coffee, caraway seeds and vodka certainly helped.

Once the ice was thoroughly melted Baldwin told the group why he was there.

'Well Arthur,' Erikkson didn't ask for titles and didn't use them. 'The cellphone which was rigged to the detonator was locally bought, from a department store, and the SIM card was the prepaid type anyone can buy over the counter. They were purchased about a month ago, by someone who paid cash. There were two inbound calls, both from a European pre-paid card, on Friday morning and eight more on Saturday night. The first was at eleven, and the rest were at ten minute intervals. The first two were almost certainly to test communications. The rest, of course, were not connected.'

'Eleven pm was the same time as the devices in India and Sweden were triggered?'

'Yes.'

'What are the chances of tracing the owner of this phone?'

'Not as bad as it would be in a bigger country. But it might be someone who was asked to do it for a stranger – a child, or an old person.'

'And the European card?'

'We're waiting to hear from the German police. We understand the calls were placed from Stuttgart.'

Baldwin made a note. 'And what about the explosive?'

'It is military grade. We should know very soon where it was made – my guess is the former Soviet Union. It must have been smuggled in, possibly on a fishing boat.'

It was all pointing to a sophisticated international operation, rather than the work of one or two fanatics. 'So that leaves us with expertise and access...'

'That's right. And I have most of my staff working on that right now.'

'Forced entry? Guards? Staff? Security video?'

Erikkson smiled at the questions. 'I can save you some time, Arthur. We have been unable to locate a security guard who was on duty during the day-shift yesterday. We are afraid he may have left the island last night.'

'What do we know about him?'

'He's a contract worker from Germany. Stern. Johan Stern. He's been working at Vikmed for the past five months. According to the security company he has a clean record.'

'This security company...'

'Yes, Arthur. It's the same one that provides security for the UN warehouse in Stockholm. A multinational company. It seems unlikely that their management is involved in something like this, but some of their staff could have been... planted or persuaded.'

'Would this guard have access to the inside of the laboratory?'

'Only in an emergency, in which case he would have to break a seal to a cabinet containing a key, and an alarm would be automatically triggered. But if he had a duplicate key he could have entered undetected, except for the CCTV.'

'And the video tapes?'

'The recording for Saturday is missing. Or rather, it is blank. It is not a tape – they use a hard-drive system, and it appears someone erased a section of the recording. Unfortunately it is possible for anyone with physical access to the security console to do that. It seems the administrator's password was common knowledge among the guards.'

Erikkson must have caught – or imagined – a fleeting expression on Baldwin's face, because he gave an embarrassed laugh. 'There is very little crime in Iceland, Colonel. I'm afraid it can make some of us... complacent.'

'I assume Stern wasn't working alone during that shift?'

'No, there was another guard. There should have been two more, but... they were on a skeleton staff for the New Year weekend. Another weakness in their protocol, I'm afraid. The second man is an Icelander, Guðmundur Bergen. It seems he... went to sleep. He welcomed the New Year the night before, and Stern said he would cover for him. Guðmundur volunteered for a polygraph today, and we are pretty sure he is... not involved. We are also awaiting the results of a blood test to see if he was drugged.'

Something about the way Erikkson spoke attracted Baldwin's attention. 'Do you know this second guard. Bergen?' He saw at once his intuition had been right.

Erikkson gave a small nod. 'He is my nephew. My sister's son. He's a university student, and this is his way of earning money while allowing him to study on the job. I was with him during the celebrations on Friday night. It will make no difference to our enquiry, I assure you. His interrogation was... is... being done by Per's men.'

The Icelandic Intelligence Service chief took this as his cue. 'Colonel Baldwin, our theory at this stage is that Stern was probably working alone, and left the country before the bomb was due to detonate. But we are exploring all possibilities. We are checking airport and harbor records and tapes. Fortunately there are not too many tourists at this time of year, so it narrows the field.'

Baldwin looked back at Erikkson. 'I understand two men disappeared after the Stockholm device was detonated. One was a German, also with about five months on the job, and the other was a Swede, with several years of experience. The local man hasn't been found. Yet.'

The police chief looked down at his hands, and nodded. Baldwin scanned the group sitting around the table in the laboratory canteen. 'Does anyone have any theories as to the motives, or who is behind this sabotage?'

There was a pause while they looked at each other to see who would speak first. Attention gravitated to a young woman sitting at the far end of the table. Baldwin had been introduced, but could not remember her name.

Per Johannson cleared his throat. 'Chief Inspector Einarson... Katrin... was sharing a theory with us when you arrived.'

'I was saying that if I wanted to blow up targets in several countries I wouldn't use my own people. Regardless of the nature of my organization. I would hire a contractor. Mercenaries. That would make it much harder to trace back to me. Much less risky than attempting to train my own followers.'

Baldwin nodded approvingly. 'I would do the same. The problem with using believers – whatever they believe in – is that they are not necessarily good soldiers. The fact that they may be willing to take great risks or even give their lives for the cause makes it harder to stop them, but easier to trace them. Contractors are far more difficult, and unfortunately there are a number of, ah, people, that take on such work.'

Baldwin was expecting the young woman to look pleased at his endorsement of her theory, but she nodded gravely. 'Yes, that's what we were thinking. I mean our security think-tank. We met last evening to brainstorm these attacks. Except that we thought of another advantage for... believers. They are cheap. I believe mercenaries are quite expensive.'

Johannson must have seen Baldwin's embarrassment. 'Katrin lectures in security studies at the University of Iceland, as well as being a senior detective.' He smiled. 'Many of us wear several hats. It keeps our heads warm!'

Baldwin just managed to stop himself from apologizing to the young woman for patronizing her. He reminded himself again not to take anything in Iceland at face value. Instead he ploughed on.

'May I ask – is there anything in this situation which does NOT fit this theory – that a contractor was hired to infiltrate a man onto the Vikmed security staff, and to plant a bomb with a cellphone trigger?'

This time there were no takers.

'And is there anything which leads you to believe that anyone who is still in Iceland could have been part of this conspiracy?' All he got were shaking heads.

'What about the nature of the work done here? The kind of pharmaceuticals?'

A young man with a beard and unkempt gingery hair spoke up. 'That's my department, colonel. I'm the chief research biochemist here, Dr Alan Walker.'

'What can you tell me, doctor?'

'Well, we do developmental work here. Biogenetic analysis of organic compounds – like folk medicines and herbs – to determine their active constituents and test them in vitro. Then we design processes to synthesize the molecules we want, and we support clinical trials. Finally we design industrial equipment to mass produce active pharmaceutical ingredient...'

'The same kind of materials they produced at those factories in India?'

'Well... yes and no. They produce the API on a large scale. We develop the kind of processes and equipment they use to do that. We are developing a new generation of ARVs here, as you probably know.'

'Why would someone want to stop you?'

Walker shook his head. 'I'm not sure... we've completed the clinical trials phase on this drug, but we're still several months away from full-scale production.'

'And when you do go into production? What are the implications of this new drug?'

'For patients, or the pharmaceutical industry?'

'Both.'

'Okay. For patients – it will be a big deal. The drug works in cases that are resistant to all other medications, and it doesn't need to be used in combination. Side effects are minimal, whereas they can be pretty severe with some ARVs. And our dosage form is an injectable, once a week. Which makes compliance a lot easier to monitor. It really is a huge step forward in the treatment of AIDS.'

'And the industry?'

'I don't think it worries our competitors too much. Our drug will be very expensive, so there's no incentive to replace existing regimens with our injectable. Also, our dosage form will be a better fit in a first-world setting, where a weekly injection is less of a logistical challenge than it would be in a third-world setting. We don't see an immediate application in most of Africa, for example.'

'Why will the drug be expensive?'

'Oh, partly because our parent company invested hundreds of millions developing it, but also because the production process is very sophisticated. The equipment to produce it at a commercial scale will be some of the most expensive apparatus ever used in the industry.'

'And how much of a setback would it have been if the bombs had gone off?'

'Well… that's the strange thing. It would have set us back a few weeks. Couple of months, at worst. But you can't un-invent something. It wouldn't have affected the final outcome – we'll still make this drug in the end.'

'So all it would have done is to buy time. For somebody.'

'Yes, it would simply be a matter of replacing the equipment and re-establishing the cultures but not…' Walker's voice trailed off and his face lost its ruddy flush.

'What is it?'

Walker was out of his chair and heading into an adjacent office. Baldwin followed, as did most of the Icelanders. They found the scientist seated at a computer terminal. For a long moment the only sound was the clatter of keys as Walker hammered at the keyboard.

'Oh Jesus,' he whispered. 'They've hacked into our records. It's all gone.'

Erikkson pulled up a chair next to Walker, and spoke softly. 'What is it Alan?'

The biochemist stared at the monitor for a moment longer, then swiveled in his chair to look at the people crowded into the tiny room. 'I… can't believe I didn't check this earlier. It simply didn't occur to me.'

Nobody spoke. Walker rubbed at his hair impatiently. 'Aaargh! All the data from our research… is gone. We'll have to do it again. This is really going to slow us down.'

Erikkson put a hand on Walker's arm. 'Please, Alan. Explain it to us non-scientists.'

Walker stared blankly at the police commissioner. 'The output of our work here is... figures. Data. Terabytes of data which are meaningless to anyone except us. But they're the data we need to design the production process — temperature readings, pressure, times, volumes for each constituent, every reaction. It's very slow work. There's no way around it, but it only needs to be done once.' He shook his head dazedly. 'Unless you lose the data. In which case you go back to the beginning. This is... years of work.'

Baldwin spoke, keeping his own voice soft. 'Surely you have backups?'

Walker turned to look at the American. 'Of course. Three levels of backup, two of them off-site — one at our head office in Chicago, and one at a secure online data repository.' He turned back to his monitor. 'But I can see them all from here. They're all... blank.'

As Erikkson probed gently, it emerged that the backup system was designed to protect the data from physical damage — even if the whole laboratory were to be obliterated their records would be safe — and from data corruption, by storing copies in three different locations.

And while the backups were protected by a firewall from internet hacking, they were not secure against someone with physical access to this terminal and a password. Even the password could be overcome, given enough time and skill. The researchers had simply not anticipated that anyone would want to erase the data, or that anyone with the necessary skill and intention would have access to this computer.

Katrin Einarson asked about the possibility of retrieving the deleted data from the storage media, but nobody believed that anyone who went to such lengths to delete them would have neglected to use scrubbing software to remove all traces. Still, it was something to try.

'But surely you keep copies on CD-ROM, or some similar media?' she persisted.

Walker shook his head impatiently. 'No, writing the data to any portable medium is considered too risky. It can be stolen or copied. There aren't any ports or devices for removable media in our computers.'

The group moved back to the canteen and a fresh round of spiked tea was served while they chewed over the implications of the data loss. Baldwin asked if the bombing of the plant could have been planned as a diversion, to hide the loss of data, but Walker pointed out it would only have been a matter of hours before the scrubbing of their hard-drives was discovered, even if the bombs had been detonated.

When Katrin Einarson suggested the blasts might have been intended as a publicity stunt, Baldwin's first reaction was to laugh, but the sober nodding of the rest of the assemblage stopped him. In the end they concluded that it was entirely possible the perpetrators wanted to make sure their action could not be concealed — a simple assault on their computer storage system could easily have been hushed up by the company, whereas a massive explosion in the industrial quarter of Reykjavik would inevitably lead to a public inquiry.

But why was it important to be seen to attack Vikmed? And was the sabotage in India also designed to prevent a cover-up? The question led to a renewed commitment by all present to keep a lid on this information, although secrecy was becoming increasingly difficult in these days when anyone and everyone was supplementing their income by reporting the news.

Two hours later, after a breakfast with enough cholesterol to shorten everyone's life by at least a year – and even though it was still five hours before sunrise – the gathering broke up and Aunty Eva drove Baldwin back to the airport to catch the next flight to Frankfurt, to make a connection to Stockholm.

Durban, South Africa
08:00 Monday 3 January

King Edward VIII Hospital in Durban is a huge, sprawling campus of buildings built over three quarters of a century, ranging from the original four-storey red-brick edifice, to rows of prefabricated wooden wards erected just a few years ago to cope with the growing tidal wave of humanity that arrive every day looking for help.

KEH is the largest hospital in the biggest city in South Africa's most populous province – the province with the highest HIV prevalence in the country with the world's biggest AIDS epidemic. In other words, this hospital is ground zero for the global AIDS epidemic.

When HIV infections exploded in the 1990s, KEH – like everyone else – was caught napping. Suddenly most of the medical cases they saw were manifesting one or another of the symptoms associated with AIDS, leading the hospital's head of medicine to tell a gathering of Rotarians that 'we used to see the occasional case of AIDS – now we don't see anything else.' His audience knew that this was hyperbole, because KEH was already infamous as a referral center for stabbings and gunshot wounds which, during the same period, escalated almost as fast as HIV infections, but far more visibly.

The nineties were a time of great instability in this part of South Africa, as opposing political factions made their feelings known to each other in the most brutal way. Researchers later came to believe that, while government focused on establishing a new political order they fatally neglected the business of public health. Indeed, some researchers speculated that returning political exiles unknowingly imported the virus from Zambia, Tanzania and other countries that had been their homes during the closing years of apartheid. With political salvation they brought with them the seeds of destruction.

As political killings diminished around the turn of the century they were replaced by the casualties of crime, as the have-nots finally gave up waiting for the politicians to hand over the keys to a new house and a BMW and decided instead to help themselves. And while the carnage of crime filled the emergency rooms, AIDS filled the medical wards and unleashed a torrent of people who wanted to find out if they, too, had the virus. During the first decade of the new century the number of people coming forward for HIV testing and treatment doubled, redoubled and doubled again.

This Monday morning was no exception.

The voluntary counseling and testing center – the point of first contact between the hospital and people who suspected they were infected – had the usual long queues, although today there were more young men than women, a reversal of the usual situation.

While the news of the destruction of ARV plants in India the previous day was the subject of much discussion in the nurses' station and the doctor's lounge, nobody had told them to do anything different so they opened the doors of the VCT center as usual, about 20 minutes after the official opening time of 8am.

Without a word a group of young men rose from the queue and barged into the center, producing hand-guns and knives and shouting at the nurses to get down on the floor, like a bad movie of a bank robbery. From the cacophony of yelling the nurses were able to make out a common thread: 'Give us the ARVs!'

Nurses in South Africa are a formidable bunch. Often the most qualified, and frequently the best-paid members of their extended families, at home they are expected to behave with deference to all the men of the household, but at work they are unquestionably In Charge.

The senior nurse pushed through her colleagues, raising her voice even higher than the wired youths. 'Be quiet!' she yelled, and for an instant they were. 'There are no ARVs here! We do not treat people here – we test them! If you want to be tested, get in the queue like everybody else!'

The other nurses squealed with joy at the sister's brave words, but their joy turned to screams of terror as the young men resumed their yelling and began trashing furniture and equipment. After a few seconds of mayhem one of the thugs fired a shot into the ceiling, and the others quietened. The shooter approached the senior nurse.

'Sister, where are the ARVs?' he said in a stage whisper.

'They are not here…' she began. In a flash he held the gun to her head. Her courage deserted her and she turned pale. The line between threats and murder is easily breached in South Africa.

'Ayee – I can tell you – we send everyone who tests positive to the HIV clinic in Block E,' she pointed to her right. 'They test them there for CD4, to see if they need ARVs, and if they qualify they collect their medications from the pharmacy.'

'Ja, so where is this pharmacy?'

'It is there – in the main building, next to casualty.'

The youth turned to his colleagues. 'Let's go,' he commanded. 'But get their phones.' Immediately the gang collected mobile phones from each of the nurses. One was slapped when she said she did not have a phone – an unlikely occurrence in South Africa – and finally produced a small Samsung.

The gang rushed for the door and across the courtyard to the main building – all subterfuge abandoned, guns drawn and yelling as they ran into the casualty reception area, and straight into the arms of a large group of policemen who, alerted by the noise, were waiting with their own guns drawn.

A great deal of screaming ensued as patients in the packed waiting room stampeded towards the exits until a huge voice rose above the din. 'Everyone… stand still!' And they did – patients, the youths and the policemen. For a moment the scene looked like a still photograph.

'Put down your guns or you will all die this morning,' said the same voice, from a police officer clearly in charge of the others. 'Now!' he bellowed, and the thugs complied, schooled in the choreography of defeat by Hollywood.

'But… we want ARVs,' said the gang leader, as though this explained everything.

'Well, you're in luck,' said the officer. 'It is the policy of the prison service to give ARVs to prisoners. Oh, no, what am I thinking? There are no ARVs anymore. Well, at least you will get three meals a day until you die.' Then, turning to his colleagues, 'On second thoughts, men, collect their weapons and let them go – we have more important things to do. Sergeant Sithole, go into the pharmacy and collect the ARVs. Ngomezulu – bring round the vehicle.'

'Yes sir!' the men echoed.

A keening sound emerged from the press of patients, a wail from an emaciated young woman with a baby tied to her back with a blanket. 'But, sir, what about us. We are here for ARVs…'

The officer turned to her. 'Sorry my sister. Come back tomorrow,' he said in the universal language of dismissal. 'Maybe you will be lucky.'

Through the hatchway to the pharmacy came a sudden cry and the sound of something hard meeting flesh and bone. A moment later the sergeant returned to the group. 'Sir, they only have a very small amount of ARVs here – the pharmacist says they draw their stocks from the government dispensary in Sydney road.'

'Are you sure, sergeant?'

'Yes sir. He knows we will come back.'

'Right. Take what they have and let's go.'

The government dispensary is only a five-minute drive from the hospital. The building is the distribution point for drugs and medical supplies to every government hospital in the district. Many of the drugs would be worth a considerable sum on the street, so the installation is as secure as any prison or bank vault, with electrified fences and armed guards.

However, when the police director's black Mercedes and the police bus arrived they had no difficulty persuading the private security guards to let them in, or the frightened officials inside to stand back while they took away cartons of antiretrovirals 'for safekeeping'.

When chief storeman Vincent Veersamy asked for a receipt he was told one would be forwarded to him. Like everyone else he was aware of the sabotage of ARV plants in India, but he was in no position to argue with a senior police officer and 20 men.

What Veersamy could do, however, was to tell his story to The World Online. This story should be worth plenty of stringettes, maybe enough to buy one of the latest generation iPhones – the one with a high resolution video camera, which was perfect for surreptitious recording of news-clips for TWO.

As he clicked the send-button on his desk-top computer, Veerasamy was unaware that one of the nurses at KEH was doing the same thing on her cellphone, which she'd recovered from one of the disarmed and embarrassed thugs, or that one of the police constables would follow suit in the next half hour, as soon as he'd finished unloading cartons of ARVs at the police director's home. Of course none of them knew that hundreds of similar stories were being posted from hospitals and government dispensaries around South Africa, and in many other third-world countries.

Johannesburg, South Africa
10:00 Monday 3 January

Oh jeee-zus! I hadn't set an alarm, or asked for a wake up call. The heavy drapes kept the room dark, the double glazing shut out the drone of traffic, and I'd slept through till ten.

Well, shit, so what? Then I realized that I hadn't brushed my teeth before I crawled into bed. God, I must honk like a sailor on shore leave! I staggered through to the bathroom to reduce my yuk factor, only to find I didn't have a toothbrush. The Michelangelo sent up a free Oral B, closely followed by a groaning and incredibly expensive breakfast trolley. My own fault for asking for a 'bit of everything'.

Suitably reborn I called Em. She looked and sounded bright and happy. Kenan the barbarian, as we had nicknamed her ripped but soft-spoken nurse-aide, had just finished getting her dressed and ready for the day, so we minutely compared the details of our ablutions, clothes and breakfast. As usual we each decided we'd prefer to be in the other's... well, maybe not shoes, considering Emily had no use for them.

Listening to her easy laughter and seeing her sitting in the day-room in Fenerbahçe, with its wonderful views over the marina to the west and the Princess Islands to the south, I felt... full. I'll never forget when I first pushed her buggy into that room and told her to open her eyes. For a time she didn't say anything, but when the silence grew I walked around to face her – and found her face soaked with tears. It took me a moment to realize they were happy tears. And another moment to understand that she didn't need to say any more. Or couldn't.

She'd arrived ghostly and exhausted the previous night but now, after a good sleep and a bit of a cry, she was reborn, and her face was a picture as she steered her buggy across the room and out onto the deck, soaking up the view and the unfamiliar sounds and scents.

When Emily insisted she wanted to relocate from the Cotswolds to Istanbul I'd found this villa with no stairs and four bedrooms so her friends could come and hang out for as long as they wanted. Using the internet Em recruited Kenan, as well as a general factotum (she said butler was way too elitist!), a cook and night nurse, using her laptop and her growing mastery of Turkish.

All of our staff spoke perfect English, fortunately for me. Em had an incredible capacity for languages, even if her willful tongue could no longer shape them, while I struggle in anything other than Strine and its various dialects. Weird that I make a living from words, but there you are.

Em's first day in Fenerbahçe ended with Jim's arrival, clutching a chilled bottle of Veuve Cliquot. He had known her much longer than he'd known me, and they were as close as a brother and sister. Maybe closer.

'Jim, I owe you,' she said, when she thought I was out of earshot. Jim was also used to the way she spoke, since her MS had lurched southwards, and they chatted on the phone several times a week. He could have emailed her but he preferred to talk, even though it was a slow business and his career redefined the meaning of busy.

'Emily, you owe me nothing,' he said, understanding her perfectly. 'Gip deserves everything she's got. Except maybe you. Nobody should be that lucky.'

They sat smiling at each other, their eyes bright with tears. Not joy or sadness, just… understanding. I was bawling my eyes out in the study, but I made sure neither of them saw. I guess we all knew this would be Emily's last home. But we also knew she would be in beautiful surroundings, and among people who loved her, until the end.

Johannesburg, South Africa
12:00 Monday 3 January

Miu Andersson turned out to be in her late forties, about five-five, square figure, short gingery hair streaked with grey, bright blue eyes and a sprinkling of freckles across her nose and cheeks.

She took me on 'the scenic route' through UNICEF's open-plan offices, stopping to introduce me to several colleagues before we arrived at the top-floor cafeteria. The glass walls of the modern building gave an impressive

view over the capital city of Tshwane – which everyone still called Pretoria
– and the seat of government, the Union Buildings, not far away. Above us
a glass roof showed pillars of cloud building up to one of the impressive
electrical storms which add spice to many summer afternoons on the South
African highveld.

'It's quiet here – at least until lunch starts in an hour,' she explained, then
she hooked a thumb at the ceiling. 'Unless it starts to hail. Coffee? How
about iced tea? They make a good one here.' As we shared a pitcher of iced
honey-bush tea I confirmed that Miu was the link between the UN's central
drug-purchasing service and the ministries of health in the five countries of
southern Africa. Even though her area of specialization was children's
rights.

'How did you get from children's rights to AIDS drugs?' Always ask –
you never know what you'll find.

She smiled. 'It's not a big jump, really. So many children's rights are
threatened by AIDS, mainly because the people who are supposed to look
after their rights are getting sick and dying from AIDS...'

'So you have to persuade the governments to keep those adults alive –
for the children's sake?'

'That's right. Well, to be precise, we keep reminding them that they are
duty bound to do it, because they are all signatories to the Convention on
the Rights of the Child. And it's not just a matter of keeping them alive. As
you know AIDS doesn't kill parents right away – first they get sick, then
they discover they have AIDS, which brings...'

'An avalanche of shit?'

Miu laughed, showing a perfect set of white teeth. 'Exactly! They're
stigmatized, can't get work, can't afford medical care, have to borrow
money, sell everything, take the kids out of school, swallow weird herbs.'

I nodded. I'd written plenty of stories on the collapse of families and
communities as their productive members were mowed down by the virus.
'So how is it going?'

'Well, we were just beginning to believe that universal access was
achievable in South Africa...' She broke off, pursed her lips and shook her
head. 'It really is too bad. This is the wealthiest country in Africa, yet it
took so much... so long... to persuade them to make ARVs available to
everyone. And now... this!'

On an impulse I reached over and put my hand on hers. She put her other
hand on top of mine, patted it and gave me a grateful look.

'But is it really that bad, Miu? Surely if the supply of ARVs can be
restored in a few weeks, this'll all blow over?'

She shook her head impatiently. 'I'm not sure we have weeks.'

'What do you mean?'

'The police are stripping hospital and government dispensaries. Your
own site has a list of them. Treatment has stopped completely...'

'Yeah, but surely they can be re-supplied? The pharmaceutical companies must have ARVs ready for distribution, and ingredients to keep making them for a while...?'

'I don't think it's that simple. If you put the ARVs back into government pharmacies they'll just vanish again. And it's not only ARVs...'

'What do you mean?'

'The police are taking every kind of drug they can find. Right now government doctors can't treat anything – pneumonia, TB, diarrhea, fever, pain. They are writing prescriptions to private pharmacies but I'm sure you've heard they've also closed their doors until government assures them they will be protected. I...'

I saw her think twice about what she was going to say next. 'What is it?'

She just shook her head and took a sip of iced tea. I knew the signs.

'You want to go off the record?'

Miu looked relieved. 'You'll have to get this elsewhere, Gipsy. We can't afford to lose our credibility with the government. I... saw a memo this morning from the commissioner of police to the private pharmacies, saying the only way he can guarantee their safety is if they hand over all their ARVs. Voluntarily.'

'Are you kidding me? Did he say why? Or what they would do with them?'

She shrugged. 'He's not denying they've taken all the drugs from hospitals, but he's saying the ARVs were being targeted by criminals, so his men are holding them for safekeeping. The implication is that they'll be returned in due course, but he didn't say so directly. And of course they've not given the hospitals any paperwork – no court orders or government instructions, no receipts.'

I'd seen the analysis that Zvonmira was putting together at TWO as new reports came in – a table showing every incident of ARV looting around the world. Hundreds of raids had been reported across Africa this morning alone. A few were said to be the work of gangsters or insurgents of some kind, but far more were attributed to the police and army.

Miu continued. 'I heard the pharmacists are planning to do what the commissioner is demanding. Better to be without ARVs than closed down altogether.'

I had an overwhelming sense of unreality. It was simply bizarre that a government could tolerate the looting and effective closure of their hospitals and pharmacies. Maybe I was being affected by the black storm clouds which I could see through the skylight above us, muttering and flickering. Miu stared back at me with a 'what can I say?' expression.

'So, getting back to the government hospitals...?' I prompted, hoping she would understand this also meant 'getting back on the record.'

'Yes. I'd think it will take them a week or two to restock their pharmacies with everything except ARVs. Hopefully the private pharmacies will share their stocks of antibiotics and other meds in the meanwhile. Or we're going to see a lot of avoidable deaths.'

'And what's going to happen to AIDS patients?'

'Well, you know the medical prognosis better than I do, Gipsy. I'm more concerned at what this will do to health care generally. A lot of doctors are saying there's no point coming to work if they have no drugs. And patients will stay away, too. The question is whether they'll ever come back.'

'Who – the doctors or the patients?'

'Both. Everyone here knows that most illness is AIDS related. Without ARVs the number of people falling ill from opportunistic infections will increase at an incredible rate, and they'll be difficult to treat. And, well, Africans are strange that way – if they don't think they can be cured, they just give up and wait to die. Some think it's a curse, or judgment day.'

Judgment day again! This business about waiting to die sounded a bit far fetched, but I had to respect the UNICEF officer's experience and obvious sincerity. Maybe try a different tack.

'Listen Miu, I know South Africa is host to a lot of medical trials relating to AIDS. I've reviewed as many studies as I can find, but I can't see anything on large-scale treatment interruptions. Do you know of any data?'

She nodded, then shook her head. 'Not primary research, no, but we've been funding a meta-analysis of structured treatment interruptions. They were all small-scale, but there've been quite a few of them in the last decade. The report isn't finished but this morning I spoke to the guy who's doing it. He says it's impossible to predict with any accuracy what'll happen when hundreds of thousands of people stop taking the drugs at the same time.'

'Why would it be any different to what happens in smaller groups?' I had a pretty good idea of the answer, but I needed to hear it from her.

'Oh, lots of reasons. A big one is psychological. With structured interruptions, which are done for research purposes, there are medical staff working with every patient to monitor their condition. You make sure they understand what can happen – for example their medications may need to be changed afterwards, because their old ones probably won't work. And of course every patient knows they'll get treatment afterwards. But with this… pharmageddon of yours…'

'Whoa! It isn't my pharmageddon!'

She laughed and flicked my arm. 'I know, I know! But you gave it that name, didn't you? Anyway, it's completely different to a controlled study. The patients aren't prepared. They don't know when – or if – their treatment will start again. There aren't enough doctors in the world to monitor their condition, or test them for drug resistance. And when ARVs become available again… that's when it'll get really crazy!'

'How so?'

'Well, obviously we can't screen two million people to see who's developed drug resistance, like in a clinical trial. We'll have to put everybody on a standard second-line cocktail and wait to see who gets better and who doesn't.'

'So you're saying that everyone should be put on second-line drugs?'

'I can't see it working any other way, can you? If we put them on a first-line regimen again and they don't respond, they'll be dead before we can get back to them.'

'So… you're saying there's not much point in restoring the supply of the existing first-line drugs?'

'Not unless this looting of drugs can be reversed in the next day or two, no. And of course there'll be a rise in incidence.'

'How do you mean?' Again, I knew what was coming, but I needed her words.

She gave me a confused glance. 'Well... when you stop taking ARVs the virus multiplies rapidly in your system, and you become much more infectious. There'll be a spike in new infections, and a rise in prevalence…'

'Assuming treatment is restored soon,' I prompted.

'Yes. Otherwise there will be…' I watched her computing the scenario, and the shock creeping into her face. 'Herregud! It would be as if every person with HIV is in their most infectious phase, all at the same time. It would be catastrophic!'

I tried to take the edge off it. 'Except that most of their sexual partners are already infected, so there is a limit to the number of new infections, surely?'

It helped a bit. 'Yes, but still…' Then I saw the penny drop. 'Oh, is that what you meant? When you asked about research into large scale treatment interruptions?'

'Yes. Someone needs to think it through in detail. Crunch the numbers. Plot scenarios on a timeline…'

'You're right, Gipsy. I'll see what I can organize.'

'Great. Promise you'll share the preliminary results with me?'

She smiled again. 'How many of those stringettes will you give me?'

'Enough to make your dreams come true.' It was the wrong thing to say. I watched the distress flash across her face. 'Oh god, I'm sorry Miu. Most people have easy dreams, like a date with Brad Pitt. A better future for all the world's children is… a little harder.'

'It really is fucked up, isn't it?' She stared at me, but I knew she was seeing something else. Welcome to my nightmare. I had to ask. 'So… what do you think? Is there a solution?'

The UNICEF officer was looking at her hands, shaking her head slowly. 'If there is…'

'Tell me what you see.'

After a moment she looked up at me, and smiled sadly. 'An old Vietnam war movie. Oliver Stone, Stanley Kubrick. Hundreds of army helicopters flying out of the sunrise. But instead of soldiers with guns, they are carrying doctors with ARVs. But it's… more George Clooney than Jean-Claude van Damme.'

I caught another look in her eyes. 'In other words, we need a miracle?'

She nodded, and said something that was drowned out by the sudden roar of hail-stones on the glass roof above our heads.

Johannesburg, South Africa
14:00 Monday 3 January

Enoch was waiting for me when I got back to the Michelangelo. We'd arranged to have lunch before the editorial conference. Over a draught beer and German sausages for him and a salad Niçoise and a glass of sauvignon blanc for me I told him about my interview with the UNICEF adviser, and asked how he'd spent his morning.

'I went to Chris Hani Hospital in Soweto. I grew up near there, Gipsy – it was called Baragwanath Hospital back then. It was the biggest hospital in Africa. But now it's like… going to a school during the holidays. Almost deserted. I found a few doctors treating people for injuries, and a few patients in the intensive-care wards. The ones who couldn't leave. But most of the doctors have stayed away. They have no medicines to treat their patients.'

'Yeah, I heard.'

'Outside there was a huge crowd of students, toyi toying.'

'Doing what?'

'Dancing. It's like a political dance. They chant and dance. They use it when they are celebrating or protesting…'

'What are they protesting?'

He shook his head. 'It's not a protest. They are celebrating. Celebrating the end of ARVs.'

'What?'

'They are saying those bombs were an act of god. Saving us from the poison. White man's poison.'

'Enoch, please tell me you're having me on!'

'They made up a song. About a fire that makes us stronger. That delivers us from evil. The burning bush…'

I was beyond speechless. 'But… I was just checking the forums. I didn't see anything like that.'

He raised his eyebrows. 'What are they saying? In other countries?'

'Not much… some looting. People being turned away from hospitals. Desperation. Definitely no celebrations.'

'Ayee. South Africans… we're a bit different! A few years ago the people in our squatter camps attacked foreigners… Africans from other countries… and drove them out. Even though their countries welcomed us when we were fighting apartheid. And this business of ARVs – we are the only country that resisted them.'

'So, Enoch, do you think this… celebration in Soweto is an aberration, or something we might see elsewhere?'

He looked serious. 'That crowd was political. It was organized by the Youth League. When you listen to them, you hear the words of our future politicians. They really do believe ARVs are poisoning the people, and they are convinced this… event… is proof of that. That it shows president Mbeki was right all along, and everybody else was wrong. I know how it must look to you, but… don't you believe in things that nobody else does?'

I laughed. 'You mean like – money can buy happiness? Crime does pay?'

He laughed too. Or maybe it was a sob. 'Hau! You would make a good South African!'

***

We have our editorial conferences on Mondays at 3pm Istanbul time, which is the same as Johannesburg. That's seven in the morning in New York, and ten at night in Tokyo. And if you're unlucky enough to be in California, or in New Zealand, it will definitely mess with your sleep. But at least we can do it from anywhere there's broadband. Like a hotel bedroom.

I watched as the faces of my colleagues appeared in the little squares on my computer monitor, like chess-pieces, wishing each other happy new year. Enoch was in the hotel room with me, but using his own laptop.

'OK, we're all here, let's get to it.' Jim looked all business but I recognized the undertone of excitement in his voice.

'I don't need to tell you all that Gip's pharmageddon story is… huge. Or that we're right where we like to be – at the head of the cavalry. Of course that also means we'll be the first to see our asses unless we're careful, so we need to keep our shit together.'

The editorial team were very still. Usually there's a lot of bull flying around, but this story impacted on all our beats – politics, economics, military, even sport and the arts, since so many of their stars were living with HIV. Jim was obviously thinking the same.

'We're going to need to pace ourselves, boys and girls. This story is very broad, and it could be with us for a while. Right now we need to look at scenarios and decide which horses to put our money on. But before we do, is there anything new?' He meant any breaking news which hadn't made it onto our radar yet.

'I may have something, boss.'

'Yeah Linus?'

'I've heard on the grapevine that the UN approached the American government a couple of hours after the bombings to get hold of as many ARVs as they could, and to store them in US embassies.'

'They what?' I was so surprised I couldn't help myself.

'Ja, Gipsy, it looks like they understood right away that some people would try to grab the drugs, so they asked the US to use their embassies to keep them safe. They have extraterritoriality status, of course, and they've been very well protected since the first Al Qaeda attacks in '98.'

Something was wrong with this picture. If the UN anticipated a scramble for ARVs, why didn't they ask the media to play down the fact that these particular drugs were the common denominator in the bombings? And why didn't they ask Shan and his colleagues in Hyderabad to do the same?

'So what happened?' Russ asked.

'Ach, nothing much. I don't know whether the US government thought seriously about doing it, but as soon as Gipsy broke the story it was too late.'

'Linus, are you saying our story – my story – prevented the Americans from safeguarding the drugs?'

In his little square on my computer screen Linus looked surprised. 'Oh no, Gipsy. If we didn't break the news, somebody else would have. It must have been obvious to a lot of people what those factories had in common.' He hesitated a moment. 'I hope you don't mind though, I borrowed your word for my story. Pharmageddon.'

Jim chuckled. 'You're not the only one to follow Gip's lead, Linus. I hear several of the cable channels and wire services are using it.'

Oh great, I'd baptized a fucking global disaster! I still felt unsettled about Linus' news about the UN and the American embassies, but Jim pressed on.

'Okay, scenarios?'

This was always Jim's next question. It's how we work. To get ahead of the competition we have to anticipate what's coming instead of simply reacting to what's happened. And to do that we construct scenarios.

'Well, I'm thinking Al Qaeda.' Linus was on a roll.

'Let's hear it, Linus.'

'Ja, well I was throwing this around with some guys who… well, let's just say they spend a lot of time thinking about AQ. They have a theory that these bombings are their way of attacking the US and western governments.'

'Go on.'

'Okay, it goes like this. The USA is a major producer of ARVs, and American companies even make money from copies of their drugs. The American government is by far the biggest buyer of ARVs through their foreign aid program. They buy the drugs and give them to countries that can't afford to buy their own. They don't only buy American-made drugs – most of the generic ARVs are also paid for by American taxpayers. My contact was saying – even if it's made in India there should be an American flag stamped on every pill.'

'I'm sure the same could be said for lots of other products which are designed in America, bought by Americans, but made somewhere in Asia.'

'You're right boss, but there's more. Some of the guys were saying AQ sees AIDS as the will of Allah – that God wants people with AIDS to die and that Americans, with all their drugs are… you know… interfering with the will of God.'

I saw a lot of eyes grow wider on my screen, and a few heads shaking. I ticked off one item on my own list. Jim prompted again. 'So AQ's motive would be…'

'To stop America messing with the will of God. And making money from the misery of others.'

The team sat in stunned silence as they tried this theory on for size. Finally Georghe spoke up. 'My problem with that scenario is that Al Qaeda risks killing many thousands of people – mostly in countries they have no argument with – just to score a point against America.'

'No, Georghe – they've only killed a few cleaners and guards.' Mandy Jones cut in, surprising us all with her vehemence. 'It would be God killing people with AIDS, not Al Qaeda. I think Linus… your guys are on to something.'

Jim read the mood. 'OK, this is a strong possibility then. Linus, do you need someone to share the load?'

'Well, if Mandy could help with the religious angle it would be a big help. Not my thing.'

It took just a few seconds to allocate responsibilities and then Jim asked for more scenarios.

'I'm thinking white supremacists.'

'Take us through that, Russ.'

'It seems like Africans – black people – are by far the worst affected by AIDS. If you are crazy enough to want to kill blacks, disrupting the production of generic ARVs would be a good way.'

The thing about the little lenses set into our laptops is that you can't see what people are looking at. But I'd guess we were all looking at Enoch, our only African colleague, who was nodding and looking glum. I resisted the temptation to turn and look at him across the room.

Russ continued. 'I also think it would be a mistake to underestimate the willingness of these white supremacist groups – neo-Nazis, Ku Klux Klan or whoever – to kill. A lot of people thought they were responsible for the bombing of the federal building in Oklahoma City, which was the biggest act of terror in the USA before nine-eleven.'

'But…'

'Yeah Ume?'

'Russ, I thought the Oklahoma City bombing was the work of just one or two men?'

'Uh huh, Timothy McVeigh and Terry Nichols. But there was evidence that others were involved – possibly neo-Nazis and even Islamist terrorists. The court refused to hear that evidence. In fact this scenario could easily overlap with Linus' theory on AQ.'

'God help us if white supremacists have linked up to Islamic terrorists,' Jim cut in. 'But I agree we need to look into it, Russ. Will you take that on?'

That settled, Jim asked yet again for scenarios. I had the sense that Jim had something specific in mind and was pushing on until someone presented it.

'Oi! Can I play too?'

'What position do you want to play, José?' This was José and Jim's usual game.

'I prefer to watch this game on TV, vagão.' We certainly needed some levity, and our sports editor frequently provided it. I saw some of my associates stretching and easing their frown lines.

'Please go ahead, José.'

'How about the Americans?'

The levity evaporated. I put a third tick on my list.

José continued. 'You may not know this, but my own government was the first to commit itself to universal access to ARVs, and the first to issue compulsory licenses for generic ARVs...'

'Compulsory licenses?'

'Yes – our government overruled the patents on those drugs, so we could make affordable generics. And in the process we met Satan himself. He wore the face of the big pharmaceutical companies, and his body was the US government.'

José leaned close to his laptop. The lens in his computer struggled to focus, and he spoke in a low voice. 'We heard a rumor that pharma was blackmailing George Bush, saying they funded his election campaign and now it was payback time.' He imitated an American accent. 'If you can't stop Brazil and India copying our drugs, Mr President, then you'll just have to buy our drugs yerself and give 'em away for nothing.'

Georghe cut in. 'I heard another story – that big pharma were almost bankrupt, so they leaned on Bush to bail them out, by purchasing vast quantities of ARVs with public money.'

'I also heard that one, companheiro. Either way George Bush got Congress to fork out billions of dollars for AIDS drugs. That's a fact.'

I thought for a moment that my connection had broken, because none of the faces on my screen were moving. Then I saw José's mouth move again.

'Today the Americans have a new president, who has inherited a situation where vast amounts of money go to foreign generic-drug producers. And there's no end to it, because the epidemic isn't getting any smaller. It's just a big hole that they are pouring tax dollars into. So, somewhere between the White House and pharma, they decide to... end it.'

I was expecting shock from my colleagues but most of them looked... thoughtful. We were all fairly cynical about pharma, even though one of them paid our salaries. The exception was Jim. Despite the tiny image on my screen I could see he was pale and his eyes were round. We all knew he was a close friend of the new president.

'Jesus – it's just... unthinkable. But... what's your take on this, Georghe?'

Our politics editor didn't look up from his doodling, and made no attempt at levity. 'Well, Jim, it's theoretically possible, of course. It could have originated in the administration, as a way of getting out of a funding black hole, or it might have come from pharma themselves. Keeping the money at home by blowing up their foreign competitors. It's possible, but I wouldn't describe it as likely.'

Once again the connection was silent, apart from a few sighs and mutterings.

I decided to throw in my two cents. 'If pharma or the US administration did it, then it would be business, rather than ideology. So they'd target critical equipment, rather than people – they'd pick a time when there are as few people around as possible, like when a factory is closed for the holidays.' I saw the shock on Jim's face as he saw the logic, and a small nod from Georghe. José looked vindicated.

Then I added: 'Still... it doesn't necessarily support José's big pharma scenario.'

'Aaargh. Why don't you just push a knife into my heart, Gipsy?'

'Sorry, Jay. I actually asked Shan whether the bombs could have been planted by the originators of the drugs and he said there was no point. They'd know that other generic manufacturers would take up the slack, and I doubt they are into empty gestures. But the "funding black hole" scenario is interesting...'

'Gip, do you seriously think the American government would do something... like this? Place so many lives in jeopardy? Lives that they've spent billions to save, until now?'

'Jim, until yesterday I wouldn't have thought that anyone could do this at all. But somebody did. Now we just have to write a name in the blank space.'

'Yeah, fair enough. Who takes the lead on this one? Gip?'

'Jim, I'd really prefer to focus on what happens here in Africa, rather than in Washington. Effects, rather than the causes. Any chance that Georghe could run with the yankee-slash-pharma conspiracy theory?'

'Georghe – how do you feel about that?'

'Sure, Jim. I love conspiracies. But chief, can you... talk to your friend in the White House?'

Our executive editor was obviously distressed but he responded without hesitation. 'That's exactly what I'm going to do, Georghe. Any more theories?'

I took them through the idea which I'd thrown at Shan over lunch in Shimla – that the bombings may simply have been a demonstration, a precursor to blackmailing other industries or even governments. Georghe agreed to look into it as well. Then Jim started to wrap up.

'Okay folks. Let's get together again same time tomorrow to see what we've got. Any last thoughts, anyone?'

'Jim, I have one more scenario.' Enoch's interjection seemed to surprise Jim, but he recovered quickly. I couldn't help turning to look at Enoch, sitting at the hotel desk while I sat propped up on the bed. Our graying education editor looked at his hands for a moment, and then said in a low voice: 'It could be my own government.'

This one was not on my list, and it looked like my colleagues were beyond surprise. I'd had a sneaking suspicion at lunch that Enoch was working up to something like this.

'Please go on, Enoch,' was all Jim said.

'This is difficult, Jim, but listening to the other scenarios, perhaps it is no harder to believe.' Enoch paused. Nobody said anything. With a deep sigh, he continued.

'Before we had these drugs, these ARVs, many people died. Every week we buried someone. But HIV prevalence reached some kind of stability, a plateau. We thought we had reached the turning point, and it would go down. But then we got ARVs, and suddenly the number of people living with this virus was going up again. It seemed like the more we used these drugs, the more people we came to know were living with this virus.'

I saw Georghe's head come up, but he obviously decided to hold his question. Enoch continued.

'For several years around 20 percent of our adults were HIV positive. Now it's over 30 percent. I read somewhere that at this rate, in five years more than half of our adults could be living with the virus. That's... a majority of the voters. And half of all our parents.'

Enoch's voice was rising. 'Africans are now in the power of whoever controls those drugs. They hold the power of life and death over us. We are becoming a nation, a region, of... slaves! It is... the one thing we cannot do. Again.'

'Jesus H Christ,' Jim breathed. 'Enoch... are you saying your leaders would rather... what are you saying exactly?'

Enoch swung his head from side to side, like he was trying to evade a persistent fly. He looked a little crazy.

'Truly, Jim, I do not understand why these drugs seem to be making things worse. But what I do know is that after today, nothing will be the same again. Right now they are celebrating the end of ARVs in Soweto. Celebrating!'

'Phew, man. That's just... incredible.' Jim looked stunned. 'Tell you what, Enoch, can you tease this thing out a little before we talk again tomorrow?'

Another minute and the meeting was over.

New York
15:00 Monday 3 January

'Excellencies, ladies and gentlemen, thank you for making the effort to be here.' Maryam Kapur looked over an audience of more than a hundred assembled in the UN auditorium. She recognized executives from a dozen pharmaceutical companies, diplomats and bureaucrats from at least thirty countries, and executives from half a dozen UN agencies and at least twice as many international NGOs and donor agencies. Ibrahim Mazzer and Jean Folbert shared the top table with her.

'I realize many of you had to adjust your diaries at just a few hour's notice, and some have traveled long distances for this meeting, and I take this as confirmation that you regard this issue with the same urgency and gravity as we do. I trust you all received the documentation prepared by UNAIDS and the WHO, and have had time to review it?' There were nods and murmurs from the audience. 'I will ask Dr Mazzer to summarize the issues which bring us together this afternoon.'

Mazzer stood, and nodded to a technician in the projection booth at the back. The lights dimmed and an image appeared on a screen in the corner of the auditorium to his left. It showed a map of the world, with bar graphs superimposed over each region.

'I'm sure you have all seen these figures before. This slide shows the HIV prevalence in each of nineteen regions around the world, together with the number of people who are infected.'

He pointed a laser device at the screen and a bright red dot moved across the map.

'You can see how much worse the situation is in sub-Saharan Africa than anywhere else. Nearly three quarters of the people living with HIV are located in this region, and almost 30 percent of the world total are in the five southernmost countries of Africa.' He nodded to the projectionist, and a different set of bar-graphs appeared over the same map.

'These graphs show the current distribution of antiretroviral drugs in each region, broken down into generics and originator drugs. As you can see consumption of ARVs is proportionately lower in sub-Saharan Africa. Seventy three percent of those living with HIV are in this region, but they consume 67 percent of the ARVs. However this ratio is considerably better than it was just a few years ago.'

Mazzer scanned the audience, wondering whether he should elaborate on the huge advances made toward the goal of universal treatment, but decided to stick to his notes.

'What is more striking, perhaps, is the difference in the type of drugs consumed in rich and poor nations. As you can see, about 95 percent of the ARVs used in developing and transitional countries are generics, while in developed countries – principally north America and western Europe –

more than two thirds of the drugs consumed are from the originators.' He nodded again at the projectionist.

'This slide shows ARV consumption divided into first-line and later-generation medications. As you can see the developing world still overwhelmingly uses first-line drugs, while in high-income countries more than half of all AIDS patients are now using second- or third-line regimens. The reason for this is that patients in developed countries have typically been taking ARVs for much longer than those in the rest of the world, so more of them have developed resistance to their initial combinations.'

Mazzer looked around again to see if there were any questions. He was half expecting someone to raise the myth that originator and second-line drugs were somehow 'better' than generics or first-line, and were thus reserved for richer nations, or to point out that many patients in Africa never got the chance to advance to later-generation meds, but simply died when their first-line therapy stopped working. However there were no hands or voices raised so he nodded at the projectionist and the lights came up.

'Our understanding is that nearly all of the active pharmaceutical ingredient for first-line generics comes from India... or at least they did until Saturday night. The drugs destroyed in our warehouse in Stockholm were mainly first-line generic medications, destined for Africa, south-east Asia and eastern Europe. Most of Latin America and the Caribbean is now supplied by Brazil, who also get most of their active ingredient from India.'

Mazzer saw a hand raised in the middle of the audience. It was the British deputy minister for international development, Evan Jones. 'Ibrahim, forgive me if I'm jumping the gun, but I understand the terrorists haven't touched the originators who invented these drugs, nor the many pharmaceutical factories around the world that formulate the finished medications. Surely it's possible for them to... take up the slack?'

'Thank you Evan. Before we ask the pharmaceutical industry to respond directly to your question, I want to give you some idea of the scale of the... slack... to which you refer. Nearly all first-line ARV dosage forms today are fixed-dose combinations, three active ingredients formulated into one dosage form – usually a tablet or capsule – taken once a day. About nine million people are taking ARVs, and about 7.5 million are on this kind of pill. That's nearly three billion doses a year, or more than two hundred million doses each month.

'The pills are usually packaged in thirties, or a month's supply, which means 7.6 million packs are dispensed each month. A single package of drugs is about 200 cubic centimeters, or 5,000 packs to a cubic meter. So the consumption in sub-Saharan Africa alone is equivalent to 1,200 cubic meters – or 37 shipping containers. Every month.'

There was a silence in the auditorium. Mazzer continued.

'As you've pointed out, Evan, a considerable portion of the global production capacity is unaffected by Saturday's sabotage. But our initial estimate is that nine-tenths of the global production of active ingredient for first line ARVs was destroyed on Saturday night. So the question we are asking today is... can the companies who make the other ten percent increase their production ten-fold? In a month?'

'In a month!' Mazzer's last words triggered a chorus of disbelief from the audience.

'Yes, I'm afraid so. If we are to maintain first-line ARV regimens, we have to ensure an unbroken supply to patients. I'm sure you're all aware that, if their treatment is interrupted, we need to abandon first-line therapies and switch to second-line drugs. This morning we polled a number of manufacturers and we believe the undelivered reserve of first-line drugs is sufficient for about one month. This reserve is made up of stock which is ready for shipping, or already in transit, along with finished drugs that can still be produced until the producers run out of active ingredient.

'The other significant reserve is made up of drugs which are already in pharmacies and dispensaries around the world – especially in public hospitals in sub-Saharan Africa. But as you know from media reports, some of those ARVs have been... removed from the supply pipeline... and we are concerned this trend may spread to other countries. Our approach has always been to hope for the best but plan for the worst, so we believe it would be prudent to ignore in-country reserves in our planning.'

Mazzer drew a deep breath. 'In some countries, patients who were due to renew their prescriptions today... went home empty-handed. In other words, their treatment has already been interrupted. With each passing day the number of patients whose treatment is interrupted will grow. In a month, everyone who depends on those hospitals and clinics will be without ARVs. As you know, there is no practical way to test hundreds of thousands of people for drug resistance, so once we reach that stage we must assume that none of those patients will respond to first-line medications, and they will all need second-line drugs.'

'Dr Mazzer – I don't think that's possible.' A graying man in the front row, whom everybody recognized as the chief executive of one of the largest pharmaceutical companies in the world, was shaking his head slowly.

'Please continue, Mr Hohner.'

'Well, doctor, as you've just pointed out, the quantities of first-line drugs now being manufactured and distributed, particularly to Africa, are simply... enormous. And second-line ARVs – protease inhibitor based drugs – are much more expensive, and complex to administer. And we still need vast quantities of NRTIs to formulate those medications...'

'I'm sorry, NRTIs?'

Hohner swiveled in his seat to see his questioner. It was a woman two rows back. 'Yes, both first- and second-line ARVs are formulated with a base of NRTIs. Nucleoside reverse transcription inhibitors. First-line medications combine these with non-NRTIs, while second-line drugs combine them with a protease inhibitor. Our colleagues in India were making almost all of the NRTIs consumed around the world – even by our own company. It isn't... it hasn't been economically viable for us to make our own.'

'What are you saying?' The woman looked horrified. 'Are you saying that you also relied on those factories in India?'

Hohner didn't answer, but turned back to face Mazzer, looking as though he wished he were somewhere else.

'Mr Hohner?'

'Yes, I'm afraid so. It's common practice to subcontract certain components. Of course we test every batch for quality, so we can guarantee the quality of our medications. But I'm... I'm not sure we can even maintain our existing levels of production in the next couple of weeks, let alone increase supply. Of either first- or second-line medications.'

A quick poll of the audience confirmed the same was true of other pharmaceutical companies, all of whom had been buying active ingredients for at least one component of their first-line regimens from India. Further discussion produced a consensus that it would take at least two weeks for them to spool up their API production to meet this shortfall, but increasing production ten-fold would be impossible.

Maryam Kapur sensed that the meeting was losing direction, and took charge again.

'So, ladies and gentlemen, are we agreed there is no way to avoid an interruption in the supply of first-line ARVs?'

'No, I think we must qualify that...' The voice came from Brazil's ambassador to the UN.

'Excellency Da Costa?'

'Thank you madam secretary general. As I understand it, most of the countries where ARVs have been seized – where they are no longer being dispensed to the general public – are among the largest consumers of these drugs. It seems likely that any further deliveries of these medications to them will be... diverted. In other words, continued supply to those countries will not help those whose treatment has been interrupted.'

Kapur spoke over a rising murmur from the audience. 'What are you suggesting, excellency?'

'Madam, I am questioning the wisdom of continuing deliveries of ARVs to those countries until they have restored treatment in their hospitals...'

'You are advocating genocide! I will not sit here and listen to this!' The ambassador from South Africa had risen to his feet. He was trembling with rage.

'I agree, madam secretary general, this is unthinkable...' The Nigerian ambassador had also risen. 'We are not lambs to be led to the slaughter...'

Kapur was also on her feet. By now there were five angry African ambassadors, all shouting their indignation. The secretary general fixed them with a stony gaze, but said nothing until they resumed their seats, glaring around them. Then she spoke. 'Nobody is cutting off Africa, and I cannot believe his excellency Da Costa meant that we should. Mr Da Costa, would you care to clarify your statement?'

Da Costa looked shaken by the reaction to his comment. 'Madam, I am certainly not proposing that we withhold drugs from African patients. On the contrary. My point was simply that if any government is unable to deliver ARVs to the people who need them, for... logistical reasons, then it would be pointless to deliver fresh stocks to them, until they have overcome those problems. In the meanwhile the drugs should be delivered to countries that can use them. In this way fewer countries will face treatment-interruptions, or need to abandon first-line treatment.'

Half a dozen hands shot up in the audience.

Kapur deferred to the South African ambassador. 'Excellency Gumede?'

'Thank you, madam secretary general. The South African police have secured ARVs in our public hospitals as a preventative measure, to keep them out of the clutches of gangsters. There is no truth whatsoever to the claim that patients are being turned away from hospitals empty-handed.'

The secretary general kept her voice even. 'Thank you, excellency. That is very good news. I'm sure we all agree that our task is to use all the available drugs as treat as many patients as possible, for as long as possible. The key problem, as I see it, is that we do not know how big the national reserves are, so we are unable to calculate the date by which fresh supplies of ARVs must be available.'

There was a murmur of agreement from the audience. Kapur continued.

'What if we were to agree that all ambassadors will supply UNAIDS with an estimate of their national reserves of ARVs within 24 hours so that we can ensure an equitable distribution of the undelivered reserve? These estimates must be verifiable, of course...'

'No, no, no!' Once again the South African ambassador was on his feet. 'Madam, that is unacceptable. We demand that supplies continue as before, until there are no more ARVs in the pipeline.' The other African ambassadors were nodding. 'How we use those drugs is an internal matter. We are a sovereign nation – we cannot be expected to account for ourselves like schoolchildren.'

The ambassador for Namibia was also on his feet. 'If this is your demand, madam, then we report that we have no ARVs. We have run out. We need to be re-supplied immediately.'

Once again Kapur stared silently at the handful of ambassadors who were now on their feet, willing them to return to their seats. Unfortunately the tactic did not work this time and after a few more minutes of heckling the ambassadors walked out of the meeting. As the door closed behind them an uncomfortable silence fell over the rest of the audience. Finally the Thai ambassador raised his hand.

'Excellency Talent?'

'Thank you, secretary general. Dr Mazzer had made it very clear that the world is facing a crisis. It is also obvious that this crisis needs central management, and that the United Nations is the appropriate body to play this role. I do not believe it is unreasonable for every nation to provide the UN with an estimation of their reserves of ARVs, both first and second-line, within the next... well, shall we say three days? Any nation which does not supply this information, or which does not submit to UN verification of their reserves, and also to verification that patients in public hospitals are, in fact, being treated, should not be re-supplied.'

Once again there was a murmur of agreement and a nodding of heads.

'Thank you, excellency. But how do we enforce this? We have no authority over the drugs which are in the pipeline. We have no mandate from the Security Council in this matter.'

'Madame, if I may?' The director general of the World Health Organization spoke for the first time.

'Please go ahead, Dr Folbert.'

'Most of the generic ARVs in the pipeline have been ordered by the UN, or by a donor nation, for delivery to our central purchasing facility in Stockholm. The normal practice is to allocate those drugs to countries that need them, subject to availability. The question of which country needs the drugs most, and of what constitutes "availability", is left to us to decide. Of course we have no control over direct sales by pharma to individual governments but... they have discretion over who they sell to.'

Kapur stared at the head of the WHO. 'What are you suggesting, Dr Folbert?'

'Madame, I am saying the policy articulated by his excellency the ambassador of Thailand is both practical and enforceable, as long as our colleagues from donor nations and the major pharmaceutical companies agree to go along with it.'

She turned to the audience. 'May I ask whether the representatives of pharma agree with this proposition?' They did. As did the ambassadors from the USA, UK and European Union, among other donor nations.

'SG?'

'Yes Dr Mazzer?'

'This decision will certainly help us to allocate the ARVs which are presently in the pipeline, but it offers no guidance as to how to recover our capacity to produce these drugs.'

'Do you have a proposal?'

'I do. I believe we will find that nearly every country has at least a month's reserves of ARVs. Together with the undelivered reserve, this gives us roughly two months before those countries run out of first-line generics. The central question is whether we can restore production of active ingredient in that time? If the answer is no, then we need to begin work right now to increase production of second-line drugs, which will work even if there is a global treatment interruption.'

'Dr Mazzer, how long do we have in that event? Before patients start dying?'

Mazzer looked surprised. 'Oh, I think any discussion of mortality is... premature, SG. If nobody is left without medications for a month, or perhaps even two, I believe the death rate will be insignificant – as long as they move on to the next generation of drugs, of course.'

Kapur noticed another hand in the audience. 'Yes sir. Forgive me but I do not know your name.'

'Thank you madam secretary general. I'm Paul Stanislav from the CDC. I have a logistical concern about restoring treatment after a general treatment-interruption. When ARVs are made available again, all the patients will turn up for treatment. Simultaneously. Many will be extremely ill by then. Depending on the location and duration of the treatment interruption, we could be talking about millions of people demanding drugs, all at the same time. It'll be a logistical nightmare – a recipe for disaster.'

'Do you have a suggestion, Mr Stanislav?'

'Well ma'am, just that we need to avoid treatment-interruptions at all costs. There's no question at all in my mind that we must go for broke. We must ensure an uninterrupted supply of first-line ARVs, or die trying! It's that important.'

The SG noticed both Mazzer and Folbert nodding, along with others in the audience.

'So how can we ensure an unbroken supply? Especially when small-scale interruptions have already begun in some countries. Anyone?'

Kapur saw another hand in the audience. 'Yes madam. Again I apologize for not knowing your name.'

'My name is Nicola Kershaw, ma'am. I'm head of drug procurement for UNAIDS. I'd like to make two points. The first is that we can conserve a lot of first-line ARVs by substituting second-line drugs in those countries which have fully functioning public health systems...'

'But my dear...'

Kapur was surprised by the interjection from the UNAIDS director. 'Dr Mazzer?'

'Forgive me, SG, but Nikki... Dr Kershaw... is suggesting taking thousands of patients off a perfectly effective drug regime. There are significant practical and medical implications...'

'Dr Kershaw?'

'Actually ma'am I'm suggesting that patients in high-income, low-prevalence countries like the EU and USA should be allowed to volunteer to switch to new-generation drugs. In effect to donate their first-line drugs to low-income countries. I believe that a great many will do so, as a gesture of solidarity to people in less privileged circumstances.'

'That is a very interesting proposal, Dr Kershaw. You said you wanted to make two points?'

'Yes, thank you ma'am. The other point is that we haven't mentioned China as yet. The Chinese produce more active pharmaceutical ingredient than everyone else put together. It's true there have been problems with quality, and also true that no single Chinese manufacturer can produce the kind of volumes we need. But they are a huge resource, and one which we must exploit.'

'Another excellent point. Thank you Dr Kershaw. I received apologies from the Chinese ambassador who cannot be with us this afternoon. Do we have a representative of the Chinese pharmaceutical industry?' A hand was raised. 'Yes sir. Please tell us your name.'

'Thank you madam secretary general. My name is Yingjie. I am the chairman of Dynasty Pharma in Shanghai. We already produce API for several NRTIs and NNRTIs – the first line drugs. We do not have the reactor volumes to produce the quantities that are required, but I am sure that we can subcontract to other companies and meet your shortfall. Very quickly.'

The secretary general glanced at Mazzer and Folbert and was surprised to see they were not applauding or even smiling, but simply looking at the Chinese industrialist. A few members of the audience looked like they wanted to break into song, but also picked up on the neutral reaction from the two agency heads. Maryam Kapur was too experienced to put her colleagues on the spot in a meeting like this, so she played for time.

'That is very interesting, Mr Yingjie. I am sure that Dr Mazzer and Dr Kershaw will follow up with you immediately after this meeting. Are there any other potential sources of active pharmaceutical ingredient?' She looked at Mazzer.

'There are, SG. And we have a team under Dr Kershaw already canvassing every potential supplier around the world. We have been looking into other possibilities, too, such as the new injectable drug which has been approved by the FDA and is being prepared for commercial production in Iceland.'

Kapur nodded. 'Ah, yes, I…' Kapur caught herself before making a reference to the thwarted sabotage, which was not yet public knowledge. 'Please continue.'

'Unfortunately this new drug is still many months away from entering the market, and there are factors relating to production and administration which make it unsuitable for large-scale application in the developing world.'

Kapur saw another hand in the audience, and recognized the owner. 'Yes, Dr Gupta. My sympathies for the setback you suffered in Chandigarh.'

'Thank you, madam secretary general. We may be down, but we are not out. I believe Professor Stanislav is correct in saying that recovering from a large scale treatment-interruption will pose huge… unprecedented challenges. But we should take note that those issues relate to our current pill-a-day treatment regimens. The new injectable drug to which Dr Mazzer has just referred could go a long way to overcoming these challenges.'

'Dr Gupta, forgive me, but I'm not sure I see the relevance. Dr Mazzer said the new drug is still many months away from production…' The secretary general's Pakistani accent was noticeably stronger as she addressed her neighbor from India, even though his own voice was made in England.

'Madam secretary general, this new drug is already approved for use. The delay in commercial production is simply a matter of logistics and technology. With respect, these are matters which we are able to do much faster in India. If the originators licensed us to produce their drug, we could produce sufficient quantities within three months to administer them across Africa. Using a high-pressure aerosol gun, a doctor can inject several hundred people an hour, which is vastly better than trying to restore a pill-a-day regime to five or six million people.'

'But Dr Gupta, how would you produce this drug? Your factory has been destroyed.'

'Ah, I'm sorry madam, I should have explained. It is public knowledge that this new-generation molecule is engineered in an entirely different way to existing ARVs. You… um… grow it, rather than baking it. I have a large bio-pharmaceutics laboratory in Shimla and I would be happy to suspend the experimental work we are doing there and convert it to commercial production.'

There was a palpable sense of excitement in the room. Hohner raised his hand. He didn't look the least bit excited.

'Madam, I must sound a note of caution here. As Dr Gupta is aware, my company owns the patent on this injectable. It is important to understand that it has not yet been used outside of clinical trials, and we have not yet perfected the production methodology. It is also very expensive to produce. It was never envisaged for use on a massive scale, or in a low-income setting.'

Kapur turned on him. 'But Mr Hohner, I'm sure you would agree that nobody envisaged finding themselves in a situation where millions of people are at risk…'

The discussion was obviously not going the way that Hohner wanted it to, so he stalled. 'I will certainly take this idea to my board, madam, and to my research team, to see whether there is any possibility… but please do not count on this idea to… save the world.'

Within ten minutes the meeting had dispersed, with everyone needing to be somewhere else. Nikki Kershaw left with Dr Yingjie, while Shan Gupta and Kurt Hohner went looking for a place to talk in private. Maryam Kapur found herself alone again with her two agency heads.

'Dr Mazzer – I have the impression we stirred up a few hornets' nests this afternoon?'

He smiled grimly. 'Yes, SG, they are hornets we know very well.'

'The Chinese drug companies?'

'Well, it's true they have hundreds of plants which produce API, but they have an equal number of problems. A few years back the head of their own regulatory agency – the equivalent of America's FDA – was executed by the Chinese government for taking bribes and granting licenses illegally. In 2005 they approved more than 11,000 drugs while the FDA approved 80. Some of these Chinese plants flood the global market with counterfeit brand-name drugs, which sometimes have no API in them at all.'

'Does that mean they cannot make the API we need?'

'No, I'm sure they can. But they are notorious for variable drug quality. You can test one batch and it's fine, but the next one turns out to be placebo.'

'But surely with appropriate oversight…?'

'Yes, indeed. I know that Nikki is looking at this. There are a few Chinese producers which are regular suppliers of quality API and finished medications. But most of their producers are small operations, and will be working at full capacity. With the others it's… like a game of chance.'

'And what about this new generation drug, in Iceland? Mr Hohner did not look very pleased about Dr Gupta's offer.'

'SG, I think that's the understatement of the year. Hohner would happily kill Gupta with his bare hands, if he could. Maurya have been reverse-engineering his drugs for years, and Gupta made Hohner and his colleagues look like avaricious psychopaths when he sold generic ARVs at cost price. His offer today… well, it's like a thief asking you to hand over the keys to your vault for safe-keeping.'

'But is there no chance Dr Gupta can do what he said – produce this new drug in three months? Surely that would give us a valuable safety-net, in case there are treatment interruptions?'

'Well, it would be a good answer, if it were possible. But…' Kapur saw Mazzer and Folbert exchange looks. Folbert cleared his throat.

'Madame, shortly before this meeting I received an update from Iceland. It seems the attempted sabotage was not altogether unsuccessful, after all. The bomb may have failed to detonate, but the saboteurs erased a huge body of technical data on the new drug. It has set back the development process by many months. Even with this data, I doubt that Maurya could have begun commercial production in three months. But without the data, there is no chance. None at all.'

The secretary general took the news in her stride. 'That's a pity. What is your view on the proceedings this afternoon, Dr Folbert?'

'I think it was very productive, madame. The protocol proposed by Da Costa and Talent is extremely useful. It provides a strong incentive to countries to maintain universal treatment, or to restore it before any serious damage is done.'

'Do you have the capacity to verify which countries are dispensing ARVs?'

'Mais oui, madame. We have officers in every country, and we're in touch with medical institutions and NGOs. Verification, at least, is no problem.'

'And how will you process the drugs which are... in the pipeline?'

'I believe we should continue as before – send them to Stockholm, where we will arrange for their onward dissemination. With increased security, of course. And we will simply withhold shipments to those countries which do not conform to the new protocol, if there are any.'

The secretary general took a step back so she could face the two men squarely. 'Gentlemen, if there are any countries that do not – or cannot – restore universal treatment, how do we answer to accusations that we are contributing to genocide, by withholding drugs?'

Folbert didn't hesitate. 'But madame, there is no case to answer. It is their governments who are withholding ARVs, not us. If they resume and maintain treatment, we will replenish their stocks. It is that simple.'

'Dr Mazzer?'

'Jean is right, SG. Controlling the supply of the reserve inventory is the only leverage we have to... persuade... those governments to restore universal treatment.'

'And if our leverage works? If they all restore treatment, what then?'

'Then, SG, we have two months. After which the fate of Africa is in the hands of the Chinese. And Allah!'

Johannesburg
01:00 Tuesday 4 January

I was still awake when I got a text from my spy at Maryam Kapur's emergency meeting in New York, outlining what happened. I called her right back.

'Hey Nik, can you talk?'

'Hey Gip! Yeah, I'm in a taxi heading back to the office. It's too cold to walk. Where are you?'

'In Johannesburg. Where it's too hot to sleep without airconditioning! Listen, thanks for the info from that meeting. I've already posted most of it, and also passed it on to Bettina.'

'I hoped you would. Who knows what her bosses tell her?'

Nikki Kershaw and I had been good mates since we attended medical school together in London, back in the nineties. Although our careers took us in different directions, we stayed in touch and made a point of attending the same medical conferences – particularly when they were held in interesting cities. And while we danced the conference-shuffle during the day, I'm sorry to say our evenings often descended into somewhat questionable behavior. One of our regular partners-in-crime at these conferences was Dr Bettina Shabangu, who had recently been appointed director general in South Africa's department of health.

'Yeah, I'm going to see her tomorrow. So tell me, Nik, are the Chinese going to save the day?'

'Time will tell. We'll place a huge order for API – and then test the shit out of every molecule they send us.'

'First- or second-line?'

'Both, babe. We're going to order enough to go either way, or both ways.'

'That sounds familiar!'

Nikki had a wonderful laugh. I was sorry we didn't have a video link. 'Wash your mouth out with soap! That was a long time ago.'

'So tell me about my boss.'

'Oh yeah, that was fun, Gip. He tried to get Kurt Hohner to hand over the recipe for his new generation ARV. Said he could make it in his research lab in Shimla. Kurt was not amused…'

'Could it work? I mean, you should see his headquarters – it's like something out of a James Bond flick. I didn't see any laboratories, but then I didn't stay long.'

'Not a chance. It was a clever offer, but there's something your boss doesn't know…'

'I'm all ears!'

'Okay, hang on a sec.' I heard her telling the taxi driver to ride around the block, then she came back on the phone, speaking in a low voice. 'There was a bomb at Vikmed. Kurt Hohner's laboratory in Reykjavik. But it didn't go off.'

'Jesus! Are you serious?' I found myself speaking softly too.

'Deadly. Should have been triggered by a phone call at the same time as the other bombs, but the local network was down.'

'Fuuuuck! This is hot! Did they catch whoever planted the bomb?'

'Dunno, girl. You may have to do some work yourself.'

I blew a wonderful raspberry, spattering my computer with spit.

'You always could do great tricks with that tongue of yours, Gip!'

'Thank you, Nik. You're still doing good work with yours. So – how does a non-exploding bomb affect Shan's offer to Kurt Hohner?'

'Oh, it doesn't. But whoever planted it also managed to destroy all their research data. It's set them back by yonks.'

'Holy crap! So… without this data, there's no chance of anyone making this drug anytime soon?'

'That's right. Listen, I've got to go. But you be careful out there. It could get a little weird.'

'Weird? In South Africa? Surely not!'

I took her laugh to bed with me, but not before I'd blown the lid off the Vikmed story.

***

Getting into bed was easy but getting to sleep wasn't, which was unusual for me, so I let my thoughts go where they wanted, which turned out to be my first day at TWO – barely two weeks after that first meeting between Jim's 'dream team' and Shan Gupta.

I'd spent some of that time sitting in my solicitor's – sorry, my lawyer's – office as she paged through Shan's offer, shook her head and muttered things like 'some people have all the luck'. And of course I spent a difficult half-hour in my boss's office at The Economist explaining that all good things come to an end, and asking if I could take my accumulated leave in lieu of notice. I also spent quite a bit of time with Emily. No dice without her. Fortunately she was incredibly supportive, as usual. My rock.

When I walked into the TWO building as a fully-fledged employee I was amazed at the transformation. The name was up on automatic glass doors. A uniformed concierge handed me a visitor's pass. The fourth floor was carpeted, partitioned, furnished. No decorations yet, nobody sitting at the reception desk – I just walked into Jim's office. Classy but functional, with that huge wall monitor at one end and picture windows down two sides.

'Gip!' he said, coming out from behind the table with a huge smile and giving me a hug. 'Welcome to your new home! Well… your virtual home, I guess. What can I get you?

As we sat drinking Turkish coffee, Jim showed me some of his new toys. He picked up a remote, pressed a button and some magic happened to the windows, dimming the bright morning outside without obliterating it altogether. Which made it much easier to see the finer detail on the huge multi-function monitor which gave him dozens of windows on the world, allowing him to view as many TV channels and web-pages as he liked at the same time, moving them around and adjusting their size to suit their content or his interest.

'We'll also use this setup for our news conferences – you'll get the same software on your laptops, so we can all see each other. You'll be able to connect through LAN cables, WiFi, cellular or satellite – whatever is available – so you'll never be away from the office. Best that money can buy, I'm told.'

'Beats the shit out of anything I've seen before.'

'Yeah, and check this out.' The central part of the screen merged into a single window, displaying a huge satellite image from Google Earth, showing the eastern Mediterranean and Middle East. Jim moved his finger on a trackpad and the image zoomed in to the crowded coastline of the Bosporus towards the Golden Horn and Karaköy, and then to the roof of a building with a cluster of satellite dishes and aerials, an area dotted with tables, umbrellas and potted trees, and a helipad .

'That's us – and our informal meeting space on the roof,' he continued. 'Right now these are Google's regular images but we're negotiating for semi-live coverage in exchange for links to our own news service, like this…' a blue exclamation point appeared on the screen, directly over the image of our building. As he moved the cursor over this icon a panel popped up headed 'Headquarters of The World Online (TWO)' followed by a list of links inviting users to read the latest news, or find out more about the magazine's history, policies and personnel.

'For the moment there'll be two ways to find our stories online – one is geographic, like this...' the bird's eye view of the building was instantly replaced by a map of the world, peppered with bright blue exclamation points. 'Every one of those markers is a news story originating from that place. Or they will be, once our stringers have written them...' he tore his eyes off the monitor to give me a wicked leer. 'Then there's thematic coverage...' another jab on the remote, another image – the TWO portal, beautifully designed with links to politics, finance, environment, health, technology, sport, the arts and so on.

I was impressed. 'Wow – you've been busy! And I thought we were just starting out.'

Jim laughed. 'Well, yeah, Shan has had a bunch of guys working on the technology, design and so on. All I had to do was tell them what I wanted. But there's more good stuff to see... finished your coffee?'

The next room was a large open-plan office, furnished with a dozen or so computer workstations. 'This is our ECO – editorial coordination office. When you want to know anything about anything, you'll speak to your editorial coordinator, who'll be sitting here. You'll have one on duty at all times. They'll work only for you, and they'll delegate research, monitor inputs from stringers and so on. Free you up to be wherever you need to be.'

'Why here, Jim? Couldn't we locate our coordinators anywhere?'

'Yeah, we could. But they are also my point of contact with your beat. I can talk to them, they can talk to each other, so we all know what's going on at any time. Our HR consultants have a short list of people for you to interview, but you can have anyone you want. And our people are assembling a global database of hot-shot researchers for each beat.'

'Impressive.' It really was. 'Next you'll tell me that these guys can whisper in my ear while I'm conducting interviews.'

Jim looked at me, deadpan. Then I caught the twinkle. 'We've already ordered headsets which work with cellular or satellite technology, just like your laptops, handhelds and mini-cams. They are pretty much invisible when worn...'

We moved on, and passed a string of smaller offices, all unfurnished. 'Your office is down here Gip,' we paused outside a glass door with my name embedded somehow in a chunk of glass: Dr Gipsy North. Health Editor.

Jim opened the door but didn't go in. 'My secretary has found a decorator – just tell him what you want. Unless you have the time to do it yourself.' Jim knew I didn't, so he didn't wait for an answer. 'Look, it isn't a huge office Gip but, frankly, I don't expect you to be here much. It's really so you have somewhere to hang your pictures, make phone calls, while you're in town...' he looked at me closely. 'Unless you want to be based here?'

'Well, actually Emily is quite open to the idea. But… you know, it takes time to sort things out. You hinted that I don't need to relocate right away…?'

'Sure, take your time. It's just that you may have more time to get Em settled now, rather than later when it gets… busy.'

We went down a flight of stairs and found a huge open plan area, dotted with what looked like a hundred workstations. 'This is the content office, where copy is assessed and referred for editing and translation. Then it comes back to the page-makeup department which takes up the second floor. It's all controlled by the duty content manager who will be over there,' he pointed to a glass door at the far end of the room.'

'What's on the other floors?'

'Computer servers and communications equipment on the first floor and generators in the basement. But our primary servers will be in at least five other locations around the world, to reduce intercontinental traffic and manage risk.'

'Risk?'

'Sure, power failures, hardware failures. And maybe political risk – there will always be someone who doesn't like what we're saying.'

'What about languages? You said translation…'

'Yeah. We'll carry news in the language it's sent to us. Of course automatic translation means it can be read in pretty much any language, but high grade news will be translated into a panel of languages, and we'll have dedicated portals for them. Within a month or two we should be up to ten…' he closed his eyes and stabbed at the air, like he was pointing at countries on a map of the world. 'English, Spanish, Portuguese, French, German, Russian, Arabic, Hindi, Japanese and standard Chinese. We may consider other portals later, depending on demand. Translation should take about fifteen minutes for the average story.'

'Holy crap, Jim – how many people are you hiring?'

'Altogether? We'll probably be up to four hundred or so by the end of the year. But that's not counting contractors – we'll keep a few thousand people busy at any given time. As for stringers – well, the sky's the limit.'

'Jesus – I know that Shan is rolling in cash, but… we're going to need it!'

Jim chuckled. 'What did I tell you Gip? Blank check.'

Pretoria, South Africa
09:00 Tuesday 4 January

'Gipsy! Why has it taken you so long to come back to us?' After running the gauntlet of growling chihuahuas, at least the alpha bitch behaved like the old friend she was, giving me a big hug and a peck on both cheeks.

Bettina Shabangu was every bit the career woman, slim and beautifully turned out in a dark green tailored suit with discreet silver jewelry. I'd watched and applauded as she soared through the ranks of South Africa's NGO community until she was offered a senior post in the department of health. Then, when her boss compounded his incompetence by being caught with his fingers in the cookie jar, she was the obvious choice to succeed him as director general, the top job in the government health service.

'Yeah, well it seems like this is the only way I'll get to see you, since you stopped coming to the conferences.'

'Ayeee, I know! I really miss seeing everyone. But I have to expose younger people to the latest information – broaden their horizons.'

'Younger? You must be joking – you're just a baby yourself.'

She shrieked with laughter, and I guessed not many people who came into this office dared tease her like I did. I knew she'd accepted the top job in the ministry of health with some misgivings, since she didn't agree with many of her government's policies. We'd talked about it often enough in restaurants and nightclubs over a bottle of wine. Or two. But it was largely thanks to her determination that the nation with the biggest AIDS epidemic finally began to roll out antiretrovirals with the same kind of enthusiasm its neighbors. Unfortunately it came too late for hundreds of thousands of people, but late was a lot better than never for those now receiving the life-prolonging meds.

She was looking at me thoughtfully. 'Oh Gipsy, it's so good to see you. It reminds me of... better times. When we thought we could save the world.'

I sensed a real pain in her words, so I took her hand. 'Bettina, the way I hear it, you've been doing a pretty good job of saving at least a part it.'

I wasn't ready for her reaction. Her face seemed to melt like ice cream in a microwave, and I could see she was fighting back tears. She looked... vulnerable. No, more like violated! For a long moment she couldn't talk, and I put my arm across her shoulders. Finally she shook her head and retreated behind her desk, gesturing to me to sit across from her. When she spoke again her voice was strong, and I sensed embarrassment behind her smile.

'So Dr North, what can I do for you?'

'Well Dr Shabangu, I was hoping you'd tell me what the fuck is going on?' For a split second my heart lurched as I wondered whether I'd presumed too much about our friendship, but she gave another shriek of delight.

'Aaah Gipsy! Two steps forward, one step back. This one is a really big step back. But listen, I'm going to have to be careful. Everyone will know that you've come to see me today. Can you still dance the quick-step?'

Aha! An old joke. I'd once told Bettina that reporting sensitive news was like dancing the quick-step, meaning both you and your informant had to be light on your feet and totally in synch or you're likely to get tripped up, stepped on, or worse. In short it meant protecting your source – making it seem like information came from someone else – and Bettina and I had done it a few times over the years. So far we hadn't been caught.

'Of course, Betts, but let me tell you what I've got already. Your public hospitals and clinics have been cleaned out by the cops. Not even an aspirin left. Pretty much every AIDS patient who pitched up at a clinic yesterday went home with nothing. So did every medical patient, regardless of their illness. Your doctors are staying away. Only your trauma centers are operational – to some extent. Your police commissioner has told private pharmacies and hospitals to hand over their stocks of ARVs, and it looks like they might. Your boss, Colin Makeba, has said nothing to the media. Your ambassador to the UN walked out when they said they'd only send ARVs to countries where universal treatment is continuing.'

She nodded grimly, but said nothing.

'The way I see it, girl, you've got a window of opportunity here. If you somehow get the ARVs back into your hospitals, and if you give the UN a tally of your stocks, you'll be fine... you can carry on like nothing happened.'

She just looked at me, and I just looked at her.

'But if you don't... by the end of the week... the backlog of patients, the mind-set of doctors, and cops – you'll have a real treatment interruption on your hands. After a month it'll be total, because every patient will have run out of their meds. Your only hope will be that you can get second-line ARVs for everyone. If you don't, after a couple of months a shit-load of people will start dying and then... well, there's no easy way back.'

Finally she drew a long, unsteady breath. 'Oh Gipsy. It all sounds so easy. That's what the minister said when I told him exactly what you just said. It all sounds so easy. It's what he always says when he has no argument, but he's not going to take your advice anyway. There was nobody else in the room so you mustn't use that.'

'I won't. But Jesus, is he serious? What's happening in his head?'

Again she looked like she was fighting back tears. 'I don't know what to do. Will it help if I resign? Or should I stay and try to change things from inside?'

'Bettina, what if you go on record? Confirm everything. Say that if the cops don't take the ARVs back to the hospitals today, there's no turning back, no way to avoid putting countless lives at risk. Getting into a trap you can't get out of. I'm sure they'll fire your ass, but it might... make them reconsider. It would give the international community a lot of ammunition. It could save a lot of lives.'

She looked at me thoughtfully. 'We don't like pressure, here in Africa. If people tell us to do something, we usually do the opposite. You can persuade us behind closed doors, sometimes. But the moment you go public, then you can be sure we won't do what you say. We just don't bow to public pressure. It's not our way.'

'Okay. So what would work? Today?'

'That's the problem. We also don't like to do things quickly. Decision making is done by committees...'

'Shit Betts. The cops moved quickly enough. It'll be a lot easier to return the drugs today than it will tomorrow, and by the end of the week it'll be bloody nearly impossible.'

She let out a huge sigh. 'Ja, that's true.'

'Did the cops act on political instructions? When they grabbed all the drugs?'

'I don't know. I suppose politicians must be involved, but…'

'But what?'

'Well, it's not easy to know if the police are acting in their own interests, or whether it was an official decision.'

'Why is that important?'

'Because if it's not official, then it's not done for the people. Someone, or some group, are strengthening their personal positions. Giving themselves leverage. Power.'

'But surely the president can call them to order? Tell them to send back the drugs?'

'Uh uh. It isn't… that easy.'

'Why not?'

'If they acted without his instructions when they took the drugs, they won't listen when he tells them to give them back. And he won't say anything, publicly, because then everyone will know that he's lost control.'

'You've got to be kidding! Seriously?'

'This isn't Britain or America, Gipsy. Or Australia.'

'Is there any way the president can turn it around?'

'Only through a lot of negotiation. Behind closed doors. Give them something in return for the drugs.'

'Which will take a lot of time. Time you don't have, Bettina.'

'I know. But what can I do?'

'You mean, what can WE do? I obviously can't leave you hanging all by yourself, girl.'

This time there was no fighting the tears. It took some time, and some tea served by a secretary who looked at me as though I was abusing her boss, but finally Bettina cleared her diary for the rest of the morning and we got down to some serious thinking.

South Africa came late to democracy, but when they finally sloughed off the dead skin of apartheid they did so in style, with a model constitution and an election which was both peaceful and joyful. And when founding president Nelson Mandela reached the end of his first term of office he gave the world – and particularly developing nations – a lesson in dignity, as he made way for younger blood.

In the fight against AIDS, South Africa once again came late to the party but when they did, true to form, it was in grand style. In just a couple of years they developed the largest antiretroviral treatment program in the world, and the human carnage is at last abating.

Faced now with the greatest challenge yet to their survival as a nation, in the form of the unexplained attack on the global supply of these drugs, the South African government has once more given the world a lesson – this time in decisive action. By sending their police to secure the nation's reserves of ARVs, within hours of the bombings, the South African government effectively slammed the door in the face of gangsters who would without question have used these drugs as their ticket to unimaginable wealth and power.

Happily, South Africa's example was followed by a number of African states, who have also successfully secured their precious stockpiles of life-saving medications.

Today's statement by the director general in South Africa's department of health, Dr Bettina Shabangu, that supplies of ARVs will be delivered under police escort to public health facilities from tomorrow, and that regular hospital services will be restored immediately, leaves South Africa's critics scraping egg off their faces.

Dr Shabangu had hard words for UN bureaucrats who yesterday threatened to withhold further shipments of drugs to countries that declined to explain their actions, or to account for the ARVs already in their possession.

'It's just horribly inappropriate. In South Africa we manufacture most of our own ARVs, so this is just empty posturing on their part. But it's far more sinister for other countries which acted immediately to prevent the theft of their drugs, and now find themselves being threatened with genocide by the UN!'

Confidential discussions at the UN suggest there is, in fact, no cause for panic. The world has sufficient stores of ARVs for at least two months, and Chinese pharma – the world's largest producers of pharmaceuticals – have said they can step up production in good time to meet demand.

All that is needed is for cool heads to prevail and this crisis will pass, like many before it.

PHARMAGEDDON

Near Stockholm, Sweden
12:00 Tuesday 4 January

'I'm not sure what I'm doing here,' Baldwin admitted. 'At one level these bombings are so obvious – what the perpetrators did, and how they did it. Yet we don't have the slightest idea who's behind it, or what they hoped to gain from it. And I have no idea where to look for the answers. This seemed as good a place as any.'

'We'd like to know as well, Colonel. And any friend of Director Dumont is welcome here.' Stefan Einarson was the director of the UN emergency supply depot near Stockholm, which served a cluster of UN agencies including the WHO, UNAIDS and UNICEF.

Baldwin was surprised that Frankie had introduced him as a friend rather than a business associate, but he covered his feelings well. 'That's kind of you.'

'What would you like to see?'

'How about the scene of the explosion?'

From the outside the warehouse building appeared undamaged, and the reception and office areas gave no sign of the sabotage just two days earlier. But as soon as Einarson opened the door to the warehouse itself Baldwin noticed the unmistakable odor of an extinguished fire, overlaid with a sour chemical smell which made his eyes smart.

Einarson noticed. 'We don't know if that is the smell of burned drugs or the packaging. But the warehouse has been fully ventilated, so I believe it is safe.'

The Swede led the way through rows of steel racks, thirty feet high and mostly filled with boxes on pallets. 'We have a very big range of materials here – tents, mosquito-nets, water purification equipment, mobile kitchens, election-monitoring kits, educational toys, protective suits for biological or chemical hazards, emergency food rations…'

They came to a large area in one corner of the warehouse secured by heavy chain-link fencing from floor to ceiling. The wire mesh was blackened but intact, as were the walls and the steel roof, high above. The concrete floor had been cleared, and a stack of about 50 steel barrels stood against one wall, while a large pile of trash – including charred remnants of wooden pallets, twisted steel racking and packing materials – had been pushed against the other wall.

'This is where we keep pharmaceuticals. Or it was. After the fire was put out they hosed everything down with high-pressure jets and pumped the contaminated water into those drums. That…' he pointed at the pile of sodden junk 'is all that is left of the containers and racking system.'

'Who is "they"?'

'Stockholm bio-hazard unit. It is a unit within our fire brigade.'

'Did they put out the fire?'

'No, it was already out by the time they arrived. We have a very good automatic fire control system – it covered everything with foam. The fire was out within 10 minutes, but it was enough to destroy everything in this area.'

'So there was no explosion?'

'No, just the fire. Very hot. And very quick. Let me show you the recording.'

The men walked back to Einarson's office where he turned on a TV monitor, and inserted a DVD into a machine. Two camera angles showed pallets packed with cartons, each roughly four feet cubed, stacked in a steel racking system just like the rest of the warehouse. Without warning there was a huge bloom of light, and in an instant the entire area was burning. In another moment foam began to cascade from unseen nozzles above and, just as the Swede had said, in ten minutes it was all over.

Baldwin was transfixed by the image. 'Oh man, that's fast! It wouldn't have happened any quicker if the whole area was soaked in gasoline!'

'Our bomb squad said some kind of incendiary ribbon must have been spooled between the pallets. It would have taken them hours to lay it out.'

'Surely it would have been visible if anyone had inspected those pallets?'

'It seems likely, yes, but there was nobody here over the new year weekend – except for the security staff – and they do not have access to that area. I do not think it is possible that the device was planted before Saturday, because people were collecting and delivering stock to the cage…'

'And the security recordings from Saturday?'

'The DVD from the day shift is missing. If the guards had a key to the cage… the drug storage area… they would have had twelve hours to work, without being disturbed. The cage was closed when the next shift came on duty.'

'Could the guards have disabled the automatic fire system if they wanted to?'

Einarson took his eyes off the video monitor to look at the American. 'Yes… they have access to the master valve. That's an interesting point. Either they didn't think of it, or they didn't want the fire to spread outside the cage.' Neither man believed that the saboteurs had overlooked the fire control system.

'Mr Einarson, when we first spoke you told me that two guards from Saturday's shift are missing – a German and a Swede?'

'Yes. We still have not found them. But we… I… do not believe the local man was involved. He is an older man – a grandfather – who has worked for our security contractors since he retired from his regular work four years ago. He was well respected by everyone. Of course the police have spoken to his family, and there appears to be no reason why Tomas would involve himself in anything like this. We are afraid he may have been taken by the other man. The German, Erich Von Klemperer.'

Baldwin saw no reason to press Einarson to clarify what he meant by 'taken'. But before he could say anything, the Swede continued, his voice soft and introspective. 'We are all aware it could have been much worse, if it happened on a working day. So much worse.'

'Sir, the German police have names and photographs of the missing guards from Reykjavik and Stockholm. I don't know what the chances are of finding them but, even if they do, I doubt they'll know who ordered the sabotage.'

'So you're saying we're no closer to establishing a motive, or figuring out whether there are any implications for homeland security?' Baldwin could hear muted traffic sounds behind the deputy director's voice, and guessed his boss was being driven somewhere. He knew it was nine in the morning in DC.

'Yes sir, it looks that way. And from what we know about the Indian bombings, it looks like those devices were planted by contractors as well.'

'Do you have any thoughts on how we can establish a motive, colonel?'

'Well sir, maybe the answer lies in what the saboteurs didn't do...'

'Like what?'

'Well, they didn't try to kill people. In fact, it looks like they tried hard not to hurt anyone. It seems those who died were just... unlucky. In the wrong place at the wrong time. And the device in the UN warehouse was planted in such a way that it only destroyed pharmaceuticals, but left everything else untouched. It would have been easier to plant a bomb.'

'Okay, but what does this tell us?'

'It's almost as if they're sending a message that their fight isn't with the UN, or pharma, or any particular country. Just with people living with AIDS.'

'But why...?'

'Whoever did this, they really wanted to stop the flow of antiretroviral drugs. I mean, they REALLY want to do it, not just show they can plant bombs in different countries. For me, the most significant fact in all of this is the destruction of that research data in Reykjavik, because it tells us they want to interfere with the treatment of AIDS patients in the long term...'

'Fair enough, but who fits that profile?'

'So far I've thought of two kinds of people, sir. The epidemic is much worse in Africa than anywhere else, and these drugs are the only thing keeping millions of Africans alive.'

There was no response from the deputy director, although Baldwin could still hear traffic noises in the background. 'Sir?'

'I'm still here, colonel. I'm just trying to imagine what kind of animal would want to kill millions of Africans.'

'Yes sir. The other kind of person is the one who is paying for these drugs.'

'What?'

'Well, sir, from what I understand the epidemic is not getting any better in Africa. So whoever is paying for antiretrovirals will have to carry on paying... for a long time.'

'Jesus, colonel! Who IS paying for them?'

'Sir, that would be us – the United States government. We donate the drugs to countries that can't afford them. The next biggest purchasers are the governments of the southern African countries – South Africa, Botswana and Namibia – who are able to buy their own ARVs. In fact South Africa manufacture most of the ARVs used in their region.'

'But they weren't sabotaged...'

'No sir, but they depend on the active ingredient from India, just like all the other ARV factories around the world.'

Once again there was a long silence on the phone. Baldwin could hear the line was open, although the sound of traffic had disappeared. He heard a low voice in the background and the sound of a closing car door before the deputy director spoke again.

'Sorry Art, just getting some privacy. I'm sure you understand the implications of what you're saying?'

'I think so sir. It's possible that the perpetrator may be a white supremacist organization, possibly based in the US or involving US citizens. Or it could be one of our own government agencies.'

'Exactly. I take it that you've talked to nobody else about this?'

'No sir. Only you.'

'Good. Do you have any ideas on how to narrow it down? Or at least to cross US interests off the list?'

'Only one, sir. Whoever it is, it seems they are very good at covering their tracks. Although it's early days, we may never find them by simply investigating what they've done. It's just too well planned. I believe we need to take the initiative. Force them to act... to show themselves.'

'Show themselves! Art, you could be talking about the CIA, or one of our special military groups.'

'Yes sir. Or it could be someone else.'

'Fuck! Well, I suppose this is why they pay us the big bucks. Do you have a specific plan in mind?'

The deputy director of national intelligence listened carefully while Baldwin outlined his idea, and then authorized him to put all the elements in place before checking in for a final go-ahead.

Johannesburg, South Africa
15:00 Tuesday 4 January

'Great story from Bettina, Gip.'

I was expecting this, but still I felt guilty about the piece I'd posted a few minutes earlier. Our executive editor wouldn't take kindly to me writing fiction dressed up as fact, even if the scam saved thousands of lives. Then again, maybe he would approve. I didn't feel like finding out, though.

'Yeah, thanks Jim. We've got stringers lined up all over to see what happens tomorrow.'

'Great! Okay people – you know the drill. New news?'

'Jim, you first. Did you talk to your friend in Washington?'

'Yeah, Georghe. He took my call. He sounded pretty rattled by the bombings. Said he couldn't believe that all our work... the US government's work... on AIDS could be undone so easily. I told him it's been suggested that someone in his administration may be behind it. Tried the funding black hole scenario on him. He said it simply didn't scan – the USA gets more out of Africa... you know minerals, oil, stuff like that... than they put in. ARVs are just a way of making friends and protecting our interests. In fact he's going to ask Congress to release cash faster than originally planned, to restore the production of ARVs.'

'Well that doesn't exactly strengthen our conspiracy theory.' Georghe sounded almost disappointed. 'Did you try the big-pharma-kills-the-generics scenario?'

'I did. He laughed. Said big pharma were still making money hand-over-fist on ARVs. The last thing they'd want to do is kill the goose. Course it was all off the record.'

'Jim, you know this man...'

'Yeah, Georghe. And I'm sure he's leveling with me. I'm not saying we should kill that scenario, or even the possibility that he's involved. But to my mind it's pretty far fetched. What did you dig up on it?'

'Not much, chief. At least not on the government involvement angle. Spoke to a few congressmen and they weren't really worried about the financial black hole. One guy said that after the banking bail-out of '08 this was peanuts. Another said the AIDS program was a lot cheaper than a war – less than the price of one warship, and much better at keeping the peace...'

'What about pharma?'

'Yes, funny thing. A lot of people said they wouldn't put it past pharma, but nobody could think of a reason why they would do it. As your first friend said, Jim, they are still making a lot of money out of AIDS, even though the generics have muscled in on their action.'

'So where do we go with this, Georghe?'

'I'm not sure we can do a lot with the black hole angle, Jim. But big pharma is an obvious suspect in the public mind – maybe we should do some interviews, print some denials, just to lay it to rest. Maybe some fleas will jump out in the process.'

'Okay. Perhaps pump it up with some vox pop on Gip's story about Kurt Hohner refusing Shan's offer to fast-track that new drug?'

Vox pop is journo-speak for vox populi – the voice of the people – which means getting our stringers to ask people how they feel about something. Since we had no difficulty putting stringers on any street, anywhere in the world, it was one of our most popular tools. It cost a lot of stringettes – which cut into advertising revenue – but our sugar-daddy wasn't complaining. I had a sneaking suspicion that Kurt Hohner would never speak to me again but... you never can tell. If everyone reads what you write, people have a way of overcoming their reluctance to talk to you.

With the details sorted, Jim turned to Linus and Mandy for a progress report on the Al Qaeda angle.

'Jim, I spoke to a few Islamic scholars today. They thought I was out of my mind at first, but as we talked they started to buy into the idea that AQ may be thinking that western drug companies and taxpayers are blocking the will of Allah.'

'Mandy, surely if someone is making drugs to keep people alive, that's also the will of Allah?'

'Well, sure. But you must remember that AQ is famous, or maybe I should say infamous, for re-interpreting the Koran so that it supports their fight with the infidel in general, and the USA in particular.'

'Okay, but would AQ hire contractors to do the bombings? Doesn't seem their style.'

'No. My contacts said absolutely not. You can't be a holy warrior and then pay someone to fight your battles. But we haven't proved yet that it was contractors... have we? Linus?'

'No, it's just a strong theory. I was talking to some guys today and they also liked the AQ scenario very much. But they put a different slant on it. For them it was about non-Muslims behaving badly.' Linus smiled at the confused faces of his colleagues.

'They say the HIV epidemic is tiny in Muslim countries, compared to Christian and Hindu populations. What if the bombings were intended to make the world recognize this fact? Send a message that Muslims behave better than Christians...?'

'Jesus!'

'You can say that again, boss!'

Jim pulled a face at Linus' snappy comeback. 'Well, from what the two of you say it sounds like the AQ scenario has legs. What do we do with it? Linus?'

'I think we should write it up, boss. Interviews and op-ed. I've got quite a lot of on-the-record material. Mandy has too. It's a good story. If nothing else it'll drive the religious forums crazy.'

'Excellent. Let's go with that. Russ, what about the white supremacist thing?'

'Okay, I spoke to a few people today. Some whose run around in white hoods with burning crosses, and some who prefer jackboots and swastikas. It seems they are all extremely happy that these bombings threaten the lives of blacks and homosexuals. They said things like – if we didn't do it, we should have. But I couldn't find anybody who thinks they actually have the initiative or the capacity to do it, or the money to pay others. White supremacy hasn't been a money-spinner for a long time, especially since apartheid came to an end.'

'But Russ, I was checking the forums and there are a lot of rednecks cheering their heads off.'

'Yeah, Jim, that's what I'm saying. They're as happy as... what does Gipsy say? Oh yes, pigs in shit!' That diverted us all for a moment, but soon Russ picked it up again. 'One more thing, these guys have no argument with the pharmaceutical industry. On either side of the Atlantic. It's the kind of equity they put their pensions in, so they'll be financially secure in their old age as they doze in front of the fire with a shotgun across their knees.'

'What about on a possible link with Islamic extremists?'

'No, I think we can rule that out, Jim. I was told that after 9/11...' he looked down at a note, and read from it: 'the rednecks didn't want to have anything to do with the rag-heads.'

'That's a good line! So where do we go with this, Russ?'

Our economics editor shrugged. 'The same as the others I suppose. I have some material I can use...'

'I have a suggestion, Jim.'

'Yeah, Gip?'

'I think all of these scenarios are interesting, but none of them will get anyone to cream their jeans. How about if we write outlines of each scenario, with lots of links, and get users to argue for and against, and do their own detective work? We may not get final answers, but everyone will have a ball. Let's turn the news into a reality show.'

The others thought this was a great idea – although it seemed alarmingly obvious to me.

Jim was careful not to overlook Enoch like he nearly had the previous day. 'Enoch, how do you see your scenario fitting into Gip's pharmageddon fantasy feature?'

Enoch wasn't in my room today, but it felt like he was smiling at me from his little window on my computer monitor. 'Actually, I think it's perfect, Jim. We don't have enough dialogue between ordinary Africans. Our leaders talk to each other but we only hear what they want us to, and we don't read newspapers from other African countries. So South Africans have no idea what Malawians or Ethiopians or Senegalese are saying or thinking.'

'Okay, but let's start at the beginning. Take us through that scenario of yours in more detail.'

Enoch didn't waste any time revisiting the near total shut-down of South Africa's public health system, or describing the bizarre celebrations which began outside the giant hospital in Soweto, because by now it had been extensively covered by everyone. Instead he told us that opinion was divided on the underlying reasons for the celebrations – some said they were arranged by the South African government to deflect possible riots by

AIDS patients, fearing for their lives, while others said they were a spontaneous expression of public mistrust in ARVs. The government itself said nothing – until I dropped Bettina's and my concoction into the whirlpool, just a few minutes ago.

Enoch chose his words carefully. 'I still believe my government may be behind the sabotage, Jim. My problem is that I have no hard evidence to support this. It is… well, it's mainly intuition. Based on a lot of small things – rumors, popular misconceptions and so on – which I would feel foolish presenting as evidence. In fact I was planning to ask you to ignore my outburst yesterday, but then I heard Gipsy's suggestion of a special forum for conspiracy theories – which would be perfect! I would be very comfortable writing a short motivator for this particular theory, and then to let our users take it from there.'

Georghe asked Enoch how the failed attack on the Vikmed factory fitted into his scenario, and Enoch admitted he couldn't explain it. 'But that doesn't mean there isn't a reason – it just means we don't know what it is yet.'

Jim cut in. 'Gip, what's your take on this?'

'Well, the South African government has done some pretty weird shit over the years, so I can't say it's impossible, Jim. I remember the Virodene incident in the late 90s, when they funded research into an industrial solvent as a cure for AIDS. But imagine for a moment that they really did blow up these places, and they were found out…' I let that sink in for a second. I could see shaking heads. 'Exactly. A giant leap backwards to the dark ages. International isolation. Another North Korea.'

'Gipsy, I'm sorry my girl, but I don't believe they are concerned about western opinion.' I was surprised to see how animated Enoch had become. 'Ten years ago we would never have believed that Robert Mugabe would steal every white-owned farm in Zimbabwe. And when he did, the west said exactly the same thing – a return to the dark ages, isolation. But African leaders didn't say a word against him, for many years! And yes, let's talk about Virodene. Even though the world laughed at us, it was later tested in Tanzania and it is still manufactured in Namibia. Africans don't easily let go of an idea. If the world laughs at them, they become even more determined…'

'No no, I'm sorry Enoch! I really didn't mean to say your scenario is impossible. Even though it's completely off the wall, I'm kinda getting into it. I think we should put it out there, so people can throw roses and rotten tomatoes at it. What have we got to lose?'

Johannesburg, South Africa
05:00 Wednesday 5 January

It was already light outside, although government out-patient clinics weren't due to open for another three hours. Longer, if you take into account the way things work in Africa.

I risked another of the Michelangelo's breakfast trolleys, but this time Bettina was there to help me get through it. It had been just like old times, solving the problems of the world – with the help of several bottles of Rustenberg Peter Barlow '99, the most expensive South African wine in the hotel's cellar, but a bargain compared to anything comparable from the old world.

I'm not sure whether Bettina jumped at the idea of a pajama party because she wanted company or because she wouldn't feel safe at home. I know she told her husband to take their kids to his brother's place for the night, so their house would be empty. South Africa can be a violent place, especially if you mess with the police.

Our editorial concoction won pride of place on national prime time TV, just as we'd hoped, so the kite was well and truly flying. Bettina turned off her official cellphone, keeping only her private phone so she could say good night to Ephraim and her kids. After that call her handset remained blessedly silent.

Nikki phoned from the St Regis in New York – and then it really was just like old times. When she heard about our breakfast trolley she called down to the hotel kitchen, which accepted the challenge and sent her a breakfast trolley – in the middle of dinner service. With a cute butler to pour latte-art onto her coffee. I got Nik to take a photo of her trolley, so I could write a little fluff on the experience for our lifestyle page.

Bettina had been rambling on about how great it was to have friends around at difficult times. Nikki tried to lighten it up. 'Hey guys, do you remember our motto from the Barcelona AIDS conference?'

'Jesus, Nik. Do you think we're elephants?'

'No, it was much lighter than that.'

Bettina picked up the clue. 'Oh, I remember! If we lift each other up, we can fly!'

We all guffawed at the memory, which stemmed from a silly school demonstration of the limits of logic. I could picture every detail of the tacky hotel room in Barcelona where we tried to lift each other up, ending up in a hysterical heap on the floor instead.

It happened in July 2002, in the middle of a wonderful conference which exploded the myth that ARVs were only for the first world. The following decade was good for all of us – a time in which we'd often lifted each other up, and in which many of our dreams had come true.

I looked at the others, Bettina sprawled over a chair nibbling at a croissant, Nikki on the other side of the world, staring smiling into her coffee cup, both lost in the memory of those years.

'So... will we fly today?'

Bettina licked the flakes of pastry off her fingers, in quick succession. 'Let's see if the newspapers have arrived.'

I phoned down to the concierge and they sent up the morning papers, in three languages. All reported Bettina's statement, all said attempts to reach her had failed. Two said police and ministerial spokespersons had declined to comment. In another paper a police spokesman said they'd have to wait and see what happened in the morning. I fired up my laptop and found echoes of our story from several other African countries. All waiting for the sun to rise.

Needless to say we'd spent hours chewing over the looting of ARVs, trying to figure out whether it was an idea which simply occurred to the cops, or whether it had been ordered by someone at the center. We even wondered whether the cops in high-prevalence countries could be part of a syndicate which ordered the bombings. After all, if ARVs are freely available, nobody will pay for them, but the moment they become scarce people will give everything they have to stay alive. The sabotage could make a lot of people very rich.

It was a nice theory – and I made a note to include it on the conspiracies forum – but in the end we decided the looting probably began with one corrupt politician or cop and snowballed as others heard about it and 'scrambled to make eggs', as Bettina charmingly put it. Actually we were desperately hoping this was how it happened, because the lack of central coordination meant we just might be able to trick some cops into returning their loot. With a bit of luck the rest would follow suit, believing the game was up, the supply of ARVs was about to be restored, and they would all be hailed as saviors. Or something like that.

In Istanbul, Nerisha and my other editorial coordinators had lined up hundreds of stringers in dozens of countries to monitor the major hospitals. It was already nine o'clock in India but still no word from the north-eastern states of Manipur and Nagaland – not that I was particularly optimistic, since the looting of AIDS clinics in that mountainous region had been attributed to 'insurgents' rather than the army or police.

As we scanned the online news and counted down to the opening of hospitals in eastern and southern Africa, the sleepless night finally trumped the coffee and adrenalin, and I started to zone out. I could feel Emily stroking my arm and hair. It felt good, but she became more insistent, murmuring my name. I opened my eyes and it was Bettina, not Em. Beaming at me. 'It's working, Gipsy! They're bringing back the ARVs!'

I sat up. Bettina was dressed for the office, looking fresh, her smile brilliant. 'We did it!' I was hugging her, Nikki was beaming from my laptop, and the sun was shining brilliantly outside.

It started at a district hospital in Kisumu, western Kenya, where the police arrived with a van-load of drugs and guns drawn to protect their bounty against imaginary bandits. A TWO stringer, Lakeman, reported the solemn handover by the chief of police to the hospital superintendent, in turgid prose. Within minutes our stringers everywhere were posting similar stories, and to lock it in I posted an op-ed calling it a triumph of good over evil, a classic example of the law enforcers protecting the most vulnerable members of society.

Corny. But it's hard to be original when you've just dodged a nuke.

A little later Bettina called from her office to invite me on a walkabout of AIDS clinics, so I leapt into the shower and began dressing. But suddenly I found my heart was racing and I broke out in a cold sweat. I was overcome by nausea and lost my expensive breakfast – and what seemed like pints of coffee – leaving me weak and shaking. I called Bettina back and told her I must have eaten a bad egg, pushed the 'do not disturb' button on the nightstand and crawled into bed.

Johannesburg, South Africa
15:00 Wednesday 5 January

'It's bizarre, Gipsy. My minister is behaving like it never happened.'

I'd called Bettina to apologize again for fading on her earlier in the day, and to find out how her boss had reacted to her unauthorized public statement.

'What... no medals? Not even an honorable mention?'

'Oh no. If you do something they don't like – and it works out – they won't say anything. They want the world to think they supported you, or even that it was their idea. It's okay, as long as it works.'

'I suppose it's better than asking for permission and being turned down, then doing it anyway...'

'Oh ja – he would fire me for that, even if I succeeded.'

'Seriously?'

'Ja, but not right away. He would invent another reason.'

'It sounds like you can be crooked or incompetent, but you can't be disobedient?'

'That's so true.' There was so much sadness in her voice. I guessed it was a reaction to the sleepless night and the adrenalin rush this morning – I was still feeling pretty hammered myself, and I'd slept most of the morning.

'How do you put up with it, Bettina?'

She let out a long breath. 'It comes with the job, Gipsy. I knew what it would be like before I accepted this post. I can't pretend to be innocent now.'

'So how is it going in the hospitals? Any problems?'

'Eish, there are plenty of problems, but nothing too serious. About half of them received some drugs today – sometimes the wrong medications – but it will be better tomorrow. Some pharmacists went with the police to identify what they needed...'

'Oh wow, that's pretty weird! Where were the drugs?'

'Mostly at the home of a senior policeman, or a politician.'

'Unbelievable! Well, I suppose we should just be happy that they're giving them back. What about the patients and doctors at the hospitals? Did they all pitch up today?'

'Not all. But we are hoping it will be business as usual tomorrow. I've authorized the delivery of fresh stocks of ARVs from the manufacturer to some hospitals, now that I'm sure they won't be stolen.'

It may be business as usual in Bettina's world, but I felt like someone had ripped my guts out and stuffed them back in random order, and I couldn't decide who to blame – post-traumatic stress or room service. But if treatment resumed in earnest the next morning, the longest anyone would be without ARVs was three days – hopefully short enough to avoid resistance. I desperately wanted to believe this story was moving from news to history, but my gut simply wasn't buying it.

'So Betts… will you submit an inventory of your national reserve of ARVs to the UN?' There was a short silence on the line, and for a moment I thought we might have been disconnected. 'Bettina?'

'Sorry, Gipsy. I have a visitor waiting…'

Something wasn't right here. 'What's the matter, girl? Do you want to go off the record?'

Another long sigh. 'Aah Gipsy. I can't…'

'Don't keep me in suspense, girl. You know I won't tell anyone. What gives?'

'Well, there's good news and bad news. But…'

'It could only have come from you, so I can't use it?'

'Yes.'

'So let's start with the good news.'

'My minister told me to go ahead and submit an inventory to UNAIDS…'

'Good news? That's incredible news! My god! You must be over the moon!'

She certainly didn't sound overjoyed. 'It's good news, yes. But…'

'Okay, let's hear it. What's the bad news?'

'Well, the minister also said that he wasn't really worried about the UN, because our major supplier, Nguni Pharm, has enough active ingredient to keep us going for months. Long enough to wait for new supplies from China or India…'

'Are you kidding me? That's not bad news! That's fantastic!' I knew South Africa made their own ARVs with active ingredient from India. I was bracing myself for Bettina to unleash one of her shrieks, then admit she'd been razzing me. So when she spoke in the same unhappy tone, I didn't absorb what she said at first.

'… we normally export half of our ARVs to our neighboring countries. But now the minister wants us to keep it all.'

'Oh… shit! That's not good. But…' Something was wrong with this picture. 'Hang on, Bettina. How does he know how much API your factories have, when you didn't know yourself?'

There was a long pause. 'You swear this is off the record, Gipsy?'

'Cross my heart.'

'He's involved in Nguni Pharm. He's a part owner – a shareholder. Through a proxy, of course. We have a lot of that in South Africa…'

I must have said something to Bettina, but all I remember is that my head flooded with questions. Minister Colin Makeba was making money from the purchase of ARVs by his own ministry. Maybe this explained why he stood with his arms folded while existing stocks were looted from hospitals – he stood to make a fortune by re-supplying them. And he had known all along that his country had sufficient reserves of ARVs to ride out an interruption in the global supply. How did this play into Enoch's theory that the South African government was responsible for the sabotage? But what was this about withholding exports to neighboring countries? Was Makeba, or his government, trying to build up some leverage over them? Or drive prices up?

'Gipsy?'

'Sorry Bettina, I was just having a melt-down. What the fuck's going on, girl?'

'I wish I knew. Really.' She sounded a touch less tense, probably relieved that she'd shared her secret. 'He told me not to ask Nguni Pharm for details about raw materials, or to include undelivered ARVs in the national inventory for the UN – just what we had in hospitals before the looting. I don't think he meant to tell me about their API, it just slipped out.'

'Holy crap. What are you going to do… what are WE going to do?'

We talked it over, and agreed the only thing she could do was confront her boss. To put her neck on the chopping block, once again. I couldn't even imagine the courage it took. She said she wouldn't be able to see Colin Makeba until the next afternoon, because he was attending a cabinet meeting in Cape Town.

'Maybe that's a good thing. Give you an opportunity to catch up on your sleep, and to think about what you're going to say when you see him?'

She didn't sound convinced. 'I suppose so. But… can I spend the night with you again? It was such a big help, having you and Nikki to talk to last night. I felt so much… safer.'

'No worries, girl. I'm sure Ephraim and the kids won't mind spending another night with your brother-in-law.'

'No, they had a great time – I don't think they missed me at all!'

'Excellent! So let the good times roll!'

Bangkok, Thailand
10:00 Thursday 6 January

Staff at the check-in desk of British Airways at Bangkok International Airport are accustomed to processing one or two unaccompanied minors on each flight. It is a painstaking process because children can't be held responsible for their actions in the same way adults can – like presenting themselves at a departure gate at the right time – but also because it would be a disaster if a child went missing, or landed up in the wrong city like misdirected baggage. It's an expensive and fraught business, heavy on human resource and often involving anxious moments – for example when a child says they don't know the adult who meets them at their destination. Or when nobody arrives.

Senior check-in controller Jamie Smythe frowned as she scanned the bookings schedule for the Thursday night flight to London. On this flight there were no fewer than twelve unaccompanied minors. This was a logistical nightmare for ground staff at both ends of the flight, and she didn't envy the cabin crew or the other passengers in economy class, since unaccompanied children had to be paired up with an unsuspecting woman passenger once seated, and the younger ones often became fractious or weepy.

Smythe picked up her phone and pressed the key for the regional manager's office. 'Dick, I've got twelve UMs on this evening's flight to London – can you send me another three girls to handle them?' The accepted ratio was three kids to one staff member, and Smythe had only one available. She wasn't surprised by his reaction.

'Oh come on Dick – of course I can't handle that number without additional staff. You know the risks better than I do. And it's a full flight.'

He asked her whether she could give more warning next time. 'Dick, please don't talk to me like a novice – you know full well that we don't see the bookings until the morning of the flight.' He promised to do what he could, and rang off.

Within a minute the phone rang, and he was back on the line. Smythe was dumbstruck as he told her that he'd checked the bookings for the next few days, and the number of unaccompanied minors increased with every flight. The regional manager promised to put some extra staff on overtime until the situation returned to normal.

However later in the day he called again, to say he'd heard from London that a similar trend had been seen in many of BA's destinations. They'd had one of their passenger-trend analysts look at the phenomenon and she found other intercontinental airlines were seeing the same thing. Finally she'd looked at the countries involved, connected it to the news which dominated every newspaper, and concluded that families in countries with significant HIV epidemics were sending their children to stay with relatives in first-world countries.

When the news was passed up the line to the airline's CEO he telephoned the director of a charity for which he was a patron – an organization helping children affected by HIV/AIDS. The director was gobsmacked. Then he began to connect the dots.

'You know Edward, I'd bet these children are the tip of an iceberg. I wouldn't be surprised if, for every unaccompanied child, you will have nine or ten adults – or mothers traveling with children – who are running to countries with strong health infrastructures.'

'Good god, Brian, do you mean to tell me that all of these people are HIV positive?'

'Not the children, no, although the odd one might be. But there's a good chance that adults traveling with children are infected. I'd do the same in their shoes. The richer parents will escape with their children to a country where they are more likely to find antiretrovirals, while poorer parents will send their kids to live with relatives, knowing that they themselves will probably be dead in a few months.'

'I see. Can you think of any implications for the airline?'

'Not offhand, no. HIV isn't transmissible in normal situations, of course, so there's no risk to other passengers or crew. But I daresay the Ministry of Health would be interested in this, since it could represent a significant drain on the national health system. And I would suspect that a lot of these people are entering on tourist visas, with no intention of leaving.'

'Right – I get the picture. Thanks old man.' The CEO rang off.

Within an hour, both the Ministry of Health and the Ministry of the Interior, which controlled immigration, had delegated people to look into the issue and come back with recommendations. They also passed the word to the Americans, Canadians, Australians and to the EU. Within a day, embassies in almost every developing nation were demanding proof of HIV status from visa applicants, in contravention of several UN agreements on the right to confidentiality.

'I don't care,' muttered Britain's minister of health to a cabinet colleague over lunch. 'There's no way we can allow them to export their problem to us. It's a horror – but it's their horror, not ours.'

Chandigarh
10:30 Thursday 6 January

'Welcome to India, colonel Baldwin. Is this your first visit?'

Baldwin shook Gupta's hand. The industrialist was much smaller than he was expecting – not only a head shorter than the American but fine boned, like a scaled down model of a much taller man. And Gupta's eyes held no hint of the belligerence or fear which Baldwin expected to see in smaller men – especially when confronted by someone who looked like a heavyweight boxer – only an easy warmth.

'It is. I'm not sure what I was expecting. It's cooler than I thought it would be, and your drivers certainly hoot a lot!' Baldwin had arrived in Delhi the previous evening and spent the night at the Imperial Hotel on Janpath before catching an early flight to Chandigarh. The transfers to and from Indira Gandhi International in the hotel's cream Mahindra SUVs were not something he'd soon forget.

Gupta laughed – a spontaneous and infectious sound. Baldwin found himself laughing too.

'Ah yes, our drivers. We like to hoot! Did you notice how many of our trucks have a sign on the back saying "horn please"?'

'No – I was too busy trying to figure out what the rules of the road are here, and to recall if my estate was in order.'

'Rules of the road? I didn't know we had any! But the good news is that road accidents are much less common, and generally much less severe, than in your own country colonel. It looks like chaos but somehow it works. But I'm forgetting my manners – allow me to introduce my colleague, Dr Shyam Chaturvedi. He's the director of our API plant. Or what's left of it.'

Gupta's companion stepped forward to take Baldwin's hand. He was no taller than his boss, but much older with a pleasant scrunched up face, wreathed in smiles. He murmured a greeting, wagging his head slightly from side to side, and then stepped back. Gupta made no attempt to introduce the rest of his entourage, whom Baldwin assumed were bodyguards, drivers and secretaries. Two were talking softly on cellphones. When one caught his eye he smiled and nodded respectfully, but no more.

'My people will take care of your luggage, colonel. Do you need anything, or would you like to go directly to the... scene?'

'That'd be great, thank you.'

The group headed for the exit. Baldwin noticed the minders walked ahead and on either side of Gupta, Chaturvedi and himself, effectively clearing a path for the three principals but without being obvious about it. A casual observer would notice nothing unusual, nor would their eyes be drawn to Gupta as a man surrounded by bodyguards. Baldwin scanned the busy airport concourse and saw that nobody was taking any interest in them. They were effectively invisible. Very professional and discreet.

Outside a chauffeur in a black uniform opened the door of a Toyota Landcruiser. The unmarked vehicle looked no different to the other SUVs which appeared to be the vehicle of choice for hotels, businesses and wealthy individuals. Gupta ushered Baldwin into the back and climbed in next to him while Chaturvedi took the front seat. Baldwin noticed that the minders disbursed into several nearby vehicles, in different makes and colors, also with no distinguishing logos or accessories. The casual observer would see nothing to link them to Gupta. As the driver pulled off he saw one of the cars moving ahead, while another pulled into the traffic two cars behind them. It was certainly not an obvious convoy.

'I must compliment you on your security. Very discreet and professional.' As he delivered the kudos, Baldwin was surprised to see a fleeting look of disappointment pass across Gupta's face.

'Ah, you noticed them. My head of security will be disappointed. He prefers our guests to think we're alone, not surrounded by a dozen caretakers.'

Baldwin was impressed – he'd only seen five men and two women, not a dozen. But he wasn't here to review Gupta's personal security. 'So gentlemen, I understand this attack on your plant was completely unexpected. No threats, demands, warnings... nothing of that kind?'

Gupta glanced at Chaturvedi, who was swiveled around in the front seat, before replying. 'That's right. No warning at all.'

'In the Stockholm bombing and the failed attempt in Reykjavik it seems the devices were planted by security guards from an earlier shift. Do you have any insights as to who planted the bomb in your plant?'

Again Gupta glanced at his plant manager. This time Chaturvedi responded. Baldwin had to strain to hear his soft voice above the growl of the Toyota's diesel engine. His Indian accent was very pronounced, but his use of English was perfect. 'It could have been placed by a technician. Several of them have failed to return to work. It would be easy to bring explosives into the plant during a break.'

'Are they Indians? The technicians who are not accounted for?'

'Yes. We have two men from Europe installing control gear, and a Japanese supervising the installation of the reactors. They haven't disappeared, though – they're in the same hotel where you're staying tonight.'

'Reactors?'

'Yes. Chemical reactors. They're the apparatus we use to synthesize pharmaceutical molecules. The active ingredients in drugs. It usually involves a series of chemical reactions. We have some of the biggest reactors in the world here, and we're always installing new models, or upgrading the ones we have, so we can produce more complex API and do it faster and at lower cost.'

'And you have no reason to suspect any of these foreigners?'

Chaturvedi's friendly grandfather face didn't change but his voice grew stronger. 'Colonel Baldwin, we have no reason to suspect anyone at all. Some of the technicians haven't come back to work after the explosion, and we can't locate them. For all we know they may have heard about the explosion and decided to look for work elsewhere.'

Baldwin decided to back off.

'Gentlemen, I don't have any jurisdiction here. I'm not trying to solve the case or apportion blame – I'm sure your police are perfectly capable of doing that. But I would like to get a sense of whether there are international factors at play, and what they might be, so that we can anticipate and prevent another attack of this kind.'

Gupta responded – this time without looking at Chaturvedi. 'Colonel, as I said when you first called, you can count on the complete cooperation of everyone at Maurya. Naturally in the last couple of days we've talked a lot about possible motives, but really none stand out...'

'I've been reading the various conspiracy theories which are posted at The World Online, but I'd be grateful if you could share your own ideas.'

'Oh yes, it's been fascinating to see how many interpretations can be applied to the bare facts of the sabotage. I admit I've spent hours reading those posts at TWO. It really is addictive – and a little bizarre. It's almost like we've become part of a giant video game!'

'Any of those theories stand out for you?'

'Well, yes and no. They all seem to be possible, to some degree. My own view is that the sabotage of the UN warehouse in Sweden shows the perpetrators are not only targeting us – the Indian pharmaceutical industry – but rather the entire supply chain for antiretrovirals. I agree with the person who wrote that we were simply the most vulnerable link in the supply chain. We gave the saboteurs the best bang for their buck.'

Baldwin returned Gupta's wry smile. 'And the attempted sabotage in Reykjavik?'

'That simply confirms the saboteurs aren't targeting generic producers alone, or limiting themselves to first-line ARVs…'

'Yes, I've heard that second-line drugs have been affected as well. Don't they use the same active ingredients which you made here?'

Gupta looked impressed. 'Quite right! Two of the three active ingredients in both first- and second-line combination drugs are NRTIs – only the third molecule is different. But global consumption of second-line drugs is very much smaller than first-line, so we expect the originator companies will be able to restore second-line production without much difficulty.'

'But they won't be able to make enough to replace first-line treatment with second-line?'

'Well, no, but if they decide to do that in all high-prevalence countries, the industry will have much more time to rebuild its capacity.'

Gupta noticed the uncertainty on Baldwin's face, so he explained. 'I'm sure you know that drug-resistance develops very quickly if ARV treatment is interrupted?' The American nodded. 'Well, if treatment IS interrupted – deliberately or otherwise – most patients can go a couple of months before their health declines significantly. As long as they progress to the next generation of drugs when their treatment resumes, they should be fine.'

'Okay, I get it. If they want to maintain first-line therapy, they have to restock hospitals before they run out in, what, two months?'

'Yes, about that.'

'But if they decide to switch everyone to second-line drugs, they only need to send them in… four months?'

'Correct. Perhaps even more – we don't really know for sure. But it will definitely give the pharmaceutical industry more time to get itself sorted out.'

'Is that enough time for you?'

Gupta hesitated slightly before answering. 'Theoretically, perhaps. But in practical terms, the Chinese will have increased their production of NRTIs by then, so it's a moot point.'

'So what will you do here?'

'We're not sure yet, colonel. Of course we'll resume production of all the other molecules which we made before the bomb went off, but as for antiretrovirals – we're waiting to see what happens next.'

'What happens next?'

'Yes. Perhaps you've been wondering why anyone would bother to sabotage laboratories and warehouses around the world, when all it achieves is a brief hiatus in the pharmaceutical industry, and in a few hospitals around the world, with no clear winners or losers?'

'Yes. In fact I was going to ask for your thoughts on that.'

'Certainly – here they are. I don't think the saboteurs are finished yet. Our view is that they have something else planned. What we do here...' Gupta pointed out the window '...will depend on what they do.'

Baldwin turned to look where the Indian industrialist had pointed, and found himself staring at the damaged shell of a large modern building, surrounded by scaffolding and swarming with construction workers. A sign next to the entrance read 'Welcome to Maurya Pharmaceuticals, Chandigarh.'

Chaturvedi led Gupta and Baldwin on a short tour of the badly damaged laboratory. 'Unfortunately the bomb destroyed all of our chemical reactors, and they are not easy to replace. At least, not in a hurry. Restoring the building is relatively easy.'

'What about your product – your API? Did the blast destroy stuff you'd made already?'

Chaturvedi shook his head. 'No, our dispatch area was empty. We shipped everything before we closed down for the holidays.'

'What do you make of the fact that the bombings took place when all the plants – and the warehouse in Stockholm – were closed down?'

Gupta answered. 'Do you mean – did they want to spare lives, or was it easier to place the bombs when there was nobody around? I think it might be the latter. After all, killing a lot of critical staff would certainly have made it much harder for us to recover. It takes far longer to train people than it does to build reactors.'

Chaturvedi picked up the thread again. 'But it also means the bombers still have leverage. They could return to attack our people...'

Baldwin let out a low whistle. 'Damn, that's worrying. But doesn't that imply some kind of threat? Some ultimatum? Stop producing NRTIs, or we'll kill your people!'

Gupta nodded. 'It is worrying. And it's another reason why we're not publicly committing ourselves to anything. At least, not yet.'

'So what are your immediate plans?'

'We've ordered new equipment to replace what we've lost here, of course. In the meanwhile we're continuing to produce some active ingredient in the research laboratory attached to our headquarters near Shimla, which is not far from here. But our capacity there is quite limited.'

'It's a small facility?'

'No, it's actually quite big. About the same floor area as this one. But it's equipped for research, rather than production, and we recently refurbished it to focus on biopharmaceuticals – essentially living compounds, rather than chemical molecules.'

'Like those at Vikmed?'

'Yes, exactly. In fact I offered to help them – to get their injectable to large-scale production quickly, so it can be used in Africa. But Kurt Hohner wasn't impressed. And anyway, it looks like the treatment interruption there has been averted for the moment.'

'You said you refurbished your laboratory in Shimla. How was it set up before that?'

'Well... more conventionally...' Gupta was obviously not certain how to answer the question.

'What if you were to find you still had equipment – reactors, like those which were destroyed here in Chandigarh – kept in storage, from before the refurbishing took place?'

'I... I'm not sure what you're getting at, colonel.'

Suddenly Dr Chatuvedi's grandfather face broke into a broad smile, and he murmured a couple of words in Hindi. Gupta turned on him in surprise, but then his face changed and he looked back at Baldwin and bellowed one of his trademark laughs.

'Ah hah! This should be interesting! Well, Dr Chaturvedi's wife has prepared some lunch for us and then, if you wish, we could take the helicopter to Shimla and poke around in our store-rooms. You never know what we may... come up with!'

Baldwin was smiling too. 'Looking forward to it!'

New York
11:00 Thursday 6 January

'You may recall, ma'am, that you authorized me to share any information we had on the sabotage of our warehouse in Stockholm with the US intelligence community?' Francis Dumont was explaining the background to the meeting she'd requested with secretary general Maryam Kapur, UNAIDS executive director Ibrahim Mazzer and his head of drug procurement, Nicola Kershaw.

'Yes I remember, Ms Dumont.'

'Well, our point of contact is colonel Arthur Baldwin, from the Office of the Director of National Intelligence. He's monitoring the various investigations to see whether there are any security implications for the US and, I guess, for anyone else. He's been to Reykjavik and Stockholm, and he's currently in India...'

'I didn't realize the ODNI conducted their own investigations?'

'Oh, no ma'am. I believe he's simply observing, on behalf of the director.'

Kapur raised an eyebrow, but didn't comment further. 'Please go on.'

'Colonel Baldwin called me last night to brief me on his progress so far. The bottom line is that he doesn't believe anyone is going to identify the perpetrators, anytime soon. Evidently none of the investigating bodies even have a good theory as to who might be responsible – or at least a better theory than those which are being thrown around in the public domain.'

'So Ms Dumont – what can we do for the DNI? Or what can they do for us?'

'Well ma'am, colonel Baldwin says that until we know who was behind the bombings, we'll have no idea what they might do next. And he believes the only way to find out who they are, before they strike again, is to force them to reveal themselves. He's come up with a plan with Dr Gupta – they want UNAIDS to announce that Maurya are converting their research laboratory in Shimla to produce active ingredients for ARVs, and that it will begin production very soon.'

Maryam Kapur glanced at Mazzer and Kershaw. Mazzer took this as his cue to speak. 'Are you saying this is simply a fabrication – a bluff?'

'Yes. They figure the bombers, whoever they are, will do whatever they can to stop Maurya. But they won't have the initiative – they'll have to react, rather than choosing the time and place, and there's a much better chance they'll make a mistake.'

'But Ms Dumont,' Mazzer was looking incredulous. 'This would be extremely dangerous…'

'I know, doctor! But Baldwin tells me that the Maurya research lab is in a remote area in the Himalayas, and they are convinced they can catch anyone who tries to sabotage them. He says the Indian government is willing to commit strategic resources to catching these people…'

'No, my dear, you misunderstand me. I'm not talking about danger to Maurya, but danger to millions of people who depend on ARVs…'

'Oh, I'm sorry, I… don't follow.'

Mazzer's incredulity was slowly turning into anger. 'Let me spell it out for you then, Ms Dumont. Once word gets out that the ARV crisis is over – or even that it's less serious than we thought – how do you think all those who are presently engaged in resolving it will react?'

Dumont recognized a rhetorical question when she heard one, so she merely shook her head.

'I'll tell you! They will slow down, or opt out of the rescue plan altogether. Go back to what they were doing before this… pharmageddon. A lot of pharmaceutical companies are giving up profitable work in order to help us avert a humanitarian disaster which could be beyond anything we can imagine.'

'But… what if we told them what's really going on?' As she uttered the words, Francis Dumont wished she could take them back, or alternatively that the floor would open and swallow her up before her face turned bright pink.

Mazzer's own face grew dark. 'How can we? For all we know, the saboteurs could be one of these companies! Or word of this could leak out to the perpetrators. The whole idea is horribly misconceived – I cannot believe an intelligent man like Dr Gupta would go along with it.'

'Ibrahim, maybe we don't have the full story here.' Nikki Kershaw put her hand on her boss' arm. 'Let's say for argument sake that we... let it slip that Maurya are about to resume production. Not full scale, not enough to warrant a reduction to our orders with the Chinese, or to abandon any other aspect of our recovery strategy, but enough to significantly increase our confidence that disaster can be averted.'

Mazzer was not looking convinced, but Kershaw kept going. 'We could even say we're planning to increase the UN stockpile of ARVs from one to three months, so we're less vulnerable in future. It's something we've been talking about anyway, and it would explain why we'd keep the pressure on the other API manufacturers.'

Maryam Kapur held up a hand. 'I'm sorry, but I want to go back a step. It sounds like this colonel Baldwin is doing a great deal more than observing foreign investigations. Surely we need to know why this initiative is coming from the Director of National Intelligence and not the CIA? Unless...' She stared at the other three in turn. 'Unless they think the CIA may have been involved! Is that a possibility?'

Francis Dumont saw an opportunity to redeem herself. 'Ma'am, there are many theories floating around on public forums, like the one at The World Online. One is that the US government did it – through one of their agencies – to bring an end to what they're calling the funding black hole. American taxpayers providing chronic medication to an ever-increasing number of Africans, forever. But the US president has categorically denied it, and is asking congress to actually increase funding to help restore the status quo.'

The secretary general looked thoughtful, and her chief security officer kept going. 'Dr Mazzer is right, of course. If we go along with this plan, we can't tell anyone. Whatever we decide, it must not go outside of this room.'

Kapur nodded, as if she'd come to a conclusion. 'I have several thoughts on this matter. The first is that, until we know who is responsible for these attacks, we are all vulnerable. We need answers, and we need them quickly. If conventional investigations are leading nowhere, unconventional measures may be needed.'

She focused on Mazzer. 'I share you concerns, Ibrahim, but I haven't heard a better idea, and we must be careful not to reject anything until we've looked at it carefully. Of course, if we decline to... participate, there's nothing stopping the ODNI and Maurya going ahead without us. At least if we are involved, we can negotiate a modicum of control.'

Mazzer was nodding, his earlier outburst forgotten, and Kapur continued.

'What about sending Dr Kershaw to meet with Gupta and Baldwin to help refine their plan – to give it the best chance of success, with the least risks – and then to report back to us? Just as long as they agree they will shut down this project instantly if it threatens our recovery program in any way.'

Johannesburg
21:00 Thursday 6 January

'You're going where?'

'To Shimla. To meet your boss.'

'Hey, that's great, Nik. Make sure he gives you one of his souvenir shawls – and ask for a ride in his chopper. Tell him I told you all about it.'

Nikki was on video, so I saw her wicked leer. 'I'd love to get hold of his chopper! But I wasn't planning to tell him that we're friends – unless you already have?'

'Oh, no, I suppose you're right.' If Shan learned that Nikki and I were mates he'd know she was my deep throat in the UN. 'But he's very well informed – you may find he knows already.'

'I'll let you know, Gip. But listen, I have to leave for JFK to catch my flight…'

'Okay but… will we be able to chat later – when Bettina gets here?' I'd already told Nikki that Bettina was coming over to the hotel again to update us, but I'd said nothing about minister Colin Makeba's involvement in Nguni Pharm, or his factory's secret stash of API. If I had, it might get back to Bettina – better that she tell Nikki herself, which was very likely after a couple of glasses of wine.

'Oh sure. I'll have an hour to kill in the departure lounge. I tried to call Betts earlier but I couldn't get through. I wanted to let her know that we got her inventory of ARVs – just under the wire! I'm dying to hear what's going on in their hospitals. Will you call me when she arrives?'

After we rang off I sat for a while thinking about Shimla, and wondering whether Nikki would be given the same red-carpet treatment I got. I knew she'd be jugging the many balls involved in getting first-line ARVs flowing again, and perhaps trying to broker a deal between Kurt Hohner and Shan Gupta to get the new generation drug into large-scale production. My muse was cut short when Bettina came crashing in with an overnight bag, looking very pleased with herself.

It turned out her minister had no idea how much API they had at Nguni Pharm, even though he was a major – albeit secret – shareholder in the company. Bettina told me he 'wasn't much of a reader' and relied on verbal briefings on most issues, so he'd not read the routine reports sent to him and simply assumed they were flush with stock because 'it's a very well run business.'

After worrying about it all morning, Bettina said raising the issue with Makeba had turned out to be easy – he'd been in a celebratory mood as she briefed him on the restoration of medical services around the country, and no less jovial as she handed him an inventory of ARVs, prior to the looting, which he'd authorized for immediate release to UNAIDS.

When Bettina told her boss she'd ordered fresh stocks of ARVs from Nguni Pharm, for hospitals that were due for replenishment, he had merely nodded his endorsement of her decision. Then, when she added how relieved she was that the factory had generous reserves of API, he shrugged and said he'd simply assumed this was the case, and asked Bettina to get up-to-date figures from Nguni on their reserves, 'for planning purposes'.

To crown it all, it seemed Makeba's instruction not to export antiretrovirals to neighboring countries had been based on yet another misconception – he hadn't realized that looted ARVs were being returned to hospitals in those countries too, so naturally he thought that sending them fresh stocks would simply add to the already well-stocked garages of the powerful. Today he waved away her concerns about an embargo as simply a misunderstanding.

I asked Bettina whether the minister grasped the irony of his position – he'd proposed an embargo of ARVs to neighboring states for precisely the same reason that the UN had threatened South Africa with the same sanction. Her deadpan response was that the minister was 'quite unspoiled by stupidity.'

By now we were laughing so loudly that an embarrassed manager arrived at the door to ask us to tone it down, because the people in the next room were trying to sleep!

'We need champagne!' I bellowed at the man, who returned ten minutes later with a bottle of Piper-Heidsieck. We called Nikki so she could hear the cork being popped and be jealous, but she smugly reminded us that they had pretty good champagne in the first-class lounge at JFK and on the Emirates flight, so our ambush fell flat – even though our bubbly didn't.

Johannesburg
15:00 Friday 7 January

Once again I said goodbye to Bettina as she left for her office. I hadn't argued when she hinted that she'd like to sleep over, even though there seemed to be no risk for her or her family – it was great to have company. If Bettina was kept awake by my snoring, she bore it stoically. According to Em I make more noise than an outback Landie. Not that Emily has ever been in the Australian outback – or in a Landrover with no exhaust – as far as I know. The English and Irish value quietude. And carry earplugs.

Giving a sisterly hug to Bettina made me miss Emily terribly, so as soon as I was alone I voiped her and spent a happy hour filling in the gaps in what she'd read online. If Em was jealous of my life, or of the people in it, she gave absolutely no indication – and I held nothing back in telling her all about them.

I found myself promising her that I'd book my return flight to Istanbul, and then actually doing it while she giggled incomprehensibly out of my laptop. The quickest connection was Swissair to Zurich, then back to Istanbul, departing Jo'burg at seven that night. Yay!

The day flew by as I tied up all the loose ends to this story and spent an hour in a hairdresser in the giant Sandton City shopping mall, to which the Michelangelo Hotel is attached. By 3pm I was about to ask the concierge to arrange a car to the airport when my phone rang.

'Gipsy?'

'Bettina? What's wrong?'

'Oh Gipsy! You're not going to believe…'

'What? Tell me, girl!'

'Those ARVs – from Nguni Pharm? The new batch I ordered for our hospitals?'

The concrete mixer in my belly was back, and churning up to maximum speed. 'Yeah, I remember. What about them?'

'There's something wrong with them, some kind of toxicity. Contamination. Patients who take them are reacting… vomiting…'

'Jesus, Bettina! How many people are affected? And how do you know it's those ARVs? I thought you only ordered them yesterday?'

'Yes, but some of the hospitals were so desperate they had vehicles standing by to collect them at the factory, and started dispensing them immediately. Patients always take the first dose in the doctor's rooms, and they react within half an hour – nausea followed by diarrhea. We're admitting and re-hydrating them but it'll be hours – days – before we can analyze the medications and know what's causing this…'

'Oh Christ, Bettina. But it's only one batch of ARVs, right?'

Bettina didn't reply immediately. My heart skidded to a halt. 'Bettina?'

Finally she spoke, and I could hear she was in tears. '…it makes no difference.'

I wanted to be strong for her, but gentle. Strong and gentle. 'Bettina, girl. What makes no difference?'

Again the pause. What wasn't she telling me?

'It's started again.'

'What? What's started? Bettina?'

'The police. The looting. They must have heard the latest drugs were bad, or that there will be no more. It's going on right now.'

I'd shut down my laptop, but it was open now and logging on through the hotel's Wi-Fi. I needed to alert our stringers – we couldn't afford to miss this – but something inside me was praying that Bettina was delusional. Or exaggerating. Or I was dreaming.

'Gipsy?' Her voice was very small.

'Yeah girl?'

'Can you… not say anything? I mean on your website? Can you keep this quiet?'

'Oh god, Bettina. I don't know how to… you know how we work. Most of our news comes from stringers – they post it directly. I… can't control it. That's the whole point of TWO. Nobody can stop the news getting out. We've got hundreds of stringers all over South Africa. It's probably already there – on our site. I'm just checking …'

And it was. The system was working. The genie was out of the bottle. If there was anyone in this country who didn't know already that ARVs were being cleared out of government hospitals – again – they soon would. As I told Bettina what I was reading, I heard her ragged breathing. She sounded beyond grief. Beyond despair.

'Bettina – if I can write something that will help, I'll do it. We sorted it out once before, girl.'

'Oh, Gipsy. I don't see how we can… really. The minister called. He told me I mustn't issue any statements to the press without clearing it with him first.'

'Bettina, let's work through this together. I bet you we can think of something.'

We tried. I cancelled my flight. We roped in Nikki, who was waiting for her connection to Delhi in Dubai. We gave it our best shot.

By the next day – Saturday – the dispensing of antiretrovirals in public health centers throughout South Africa had stopped. By Monday the pressure was back on private hospitals and pharmacies to turn over their remaining stocks of ARVs to their local police.

One piece of good news was that most private pharmacists had seen this coming, and placed their precious stocks of ARVs out of reach. But this meant they couldn't be openly dispensed, which in turn gave a huge boost to the black market.

Another ray of hope was the fact that South Africa's neighboring countries had not yet received any of the contaminated drugs and, for the most part, their newly restored treatment programs kept going. UNAIDS locked it down by promising an immediate shipment of new ARVs to take the pressure off.

In South Africa the renewed looting was met with a blast of condemnation from the media, international community and the medical establishment, but silence from the minister, director general, and – bizarrely – from most AIDS patients, who seemed oblivious to the fact that, with every day that passed, tens of thousands more people were being left without the drugs which kept them alive.

PART II

Johannesburg, Saturday 8 January

After we took off from Johannesburg's Lanseria airport I found myself thinking about the irony of my situation. Instead of flying north on Swissair to Istanbul, celebrating a happy ending to this story, I was heading south on a chartered KingAir to the coastal city of East London to see for myself where it all went wrong. I'd decided to splurge Shan's money on the charter so I could get back quickly if I scored an interview with minister of health Colin Makeba.

Weekends aren't a good time to set up a meeting with South Africa's top politicians. It's not that they disappear, exactly – most of their endless round of consultations, celebrations and funerals take place on Saturdays and Sundays. The problem is that their gatekeepers are nowhere to be found, and your chance of getting to see the lion without being jumped on by his fleas is zero.

Bettina gave me all the parasites' numbers, of course, but they weren't answering. When the minister's most senior bureaucrat herself tried to set me up to meet him, she was told he was fully committed. In other words, he didn't want to see me. We hit the same brick wall when I tried to schedule interviews with other politicians, all the way up to the president.

When I finally made contact with Makeba's personal assistant he told me the best he could offer me was a slot the following Friday at 7,30am. We both knew what that meant – hang around until His Lordship feels like seeing you – but my choices were limited so I took it. I thought of camping out in the minister's waiting room but, frankly, I had better things to do, so I pleaded with the maggot to see if he could get me in earlier, and got on with my checklist.

Top of my list was to marshal our troops for a vox-pop – hundreds of stringers asking thousands of people for their thoughts on what South Africa was doing. Or rather, not doing. Our citizen journalists canvassed a huge range of opinion across the region and around the world, covering every conceivable demographic. Most of their interviews were on cellphone video, from which my researchers snipped and clipped together a very snappy overview, with links to some op-ed from yours truly and, as always, unlimited opinion from the blogosphere.

Of course this feature was only one dish on the Pharmageddon smorgasbord. The conspiracy forums were still the hot favorites, giving every kind of crank an opportunity to blow hot air out of every orifice, and every Mother Grundy a chance to spray their nauseating air-freshener back. For those looking for facts rather than fantasies, my team pulled together backgrounders on every aspect of the epidemic, the people involved and the events of the past week. And naturally I tried to guess where it was all going, in a spray of op-eds.

The Pharmageddon feature broke every record we kept, including hit-rates, unique visitors, and web-feeds for those who didn't want to miss a thing. In fact our coverage became a major news story in its own right. If CNN's live coverage of the first Gulf War opened a real-time window into war, TWO turned a complex global crisis into an interactive game, with real victims and villains. And everyone wanted to play.

We weren't surprised to get posts saying the South African government was looking for ways to restrict public access to our site but, if they did, they soon realized it's a lot easier said than done – especially if you don't want to bring the biggest economy in Africa to its knees.

Nor were we surprised to see a surge of newly registered stringers saying that South African hospitals were fully functional, ARVs were being dispensed, and those who said otherwise were trying to discredit the government. I could almost hear the whoops of joy from our regular stringers as they peppered these turkeys with video of deserted hospitals, worried medics and desperate patients.

If the issue hadn't been so serious, it would have been fun. Hell, for a large slice of humanity it WAS fun. I could only imagine how Shan felt, watching his vision of truth for the common man take shape.

***

'I'm not happy about talking to you, Dr North, but it seems better than the alternative.' Pieter Ferreira was the plant manager at Nguni Pharmaceuticals, South Africa's ARV factory.

I'm old friends with the let's-play-hard-to-get gambit, so I countered with my best disappointed-cute pout. It often works with intellectually-arrested heterosexual men, but it didn't seem to make much difference to Ferreira so I played it straight. 'What do you mean about the alternative?'

He dragged his face into a humorless smile. 'Having my staff acting like cops, sniffing around for clues and asking each other a lot of questions, just so they can get some of your frequent flier miles. It really... fucks with our operation, if you'll excuse the French.'

I guessed Nerisha had been stirring up a hornet's nest by offering double stringettes for this story. 'I'm truly sorry you've had a problem with your ARVs, Mr Ferreira, but...'

'But you can't leave it alone. I know. The whole world wants to know what happened. That's why I'm talking to you, and why I've told my staff that you're here. So they can leave it alone, and get on with their jobs. In return I'd be grateful if you could arrange not to dish out your frequent flier miles on this story... to remove the incentive?'

He left it hanging. I didn't feel like stroking this prick so I just gave a non-committal smile and shrug as if to say, whatever you want. 'So tell me what happened?'

'Well, you may not believe this, but we've never had a case of contamination, in nearly ten years of production.'

'Could it have happened during the delivery process? Between here and the hospitals?'

He gave another humorless grin. I wished he wouldn't – it didn't suit his face. 'I really hope it did. We'd be off the hook.'

'If you were a terrorist, and you wanted to do this, how would you go about it?'

The grin changed. The new one had a touch of reality about it. 'Funny, I was expecting the police to ask me that, but they didn't. At least not yet.'

'Well, how would you?'

'Ag, the simplest way would be to doctor a few blister-packs of tablets ahead of time, and then swap them for the originals while they're being shipped...'

'But then the batch numbers wouldn't match, would they?'

'No, you're right. But they do match – at least the packs we've seen so far do. So the terrorists either have some very fancy equipment or they somehow got their contaminants in here.' He waved his hand towards the deserted factory floor, visible through a large window in his office. While he was escorting me to his office he'd explained that the factory was closed until they knew the source of the contamination.

'Would it be difficult?'

'If you're inside, and if you know what you're doing, no. Dead easy. A handful of chemicals chucked into a bin of one of the inert ingredients...'

'Have you tested the bins?'

He nodded. 'Waiting for the results. But they may not show anything. Most of the bins were sterilized after the last batch of ARVs. But we've sent samples of the contaminated ARVs to Europe for analysis – they may be able to tell us how it was done.'

'But not by whom?'

'Ja, that's the question, isn't it? I read what happened in those other countries, and I think ours could have been done by the same people. Or at least in the same way – by planting someone in our security company.'

Now that Ferreira had played out his little game, he was much more animated.

'We were also closed over Christmas and New Year, just like those guys, so our guards had the place to themselves. Our CCTV tapes seem to be okay, but they could've been changed. The cops are analyzing them to see if they were actually recorded at the time they were supposed to be.'

'Obviously you've spoken to your security company...?'

'Oh ja, of course. They didn't tell me much, but I know the cops are focusing on them. I asked if there were any guards on duty who were new to the company, and they said they were all regular staff...' He caught himself.

'But you thought they were lying?'

His eyes answered. 'No, I can't say. It's for the police to find out.'

Time for a different tack. Or rather, attack. 'How much API do you still have, Mr Ferreira?' I saw his pupils contract. 'How many doses of your ARVs can you make before you run out?' Bull's-eye!

He looked at me for a moment, then lurched forward on his tilting office chair and reached for a folder on his desk. He opened it, found the page he wanted and stared at it, but I could tell he was thinking, not reading. He knew that I knew that he knew!

'We have very limited stores of active ingredient, unfortunately. Maybe enough for another ten days of consumption by the public health services. But of course we can't use it until we know it's free of contaminants.'

I would have liked to ask who owned his factory, but I was pretty sure that would raise the alarm bells. So I got some background on the company's history and their plans for the future, turned down Ferreira's offer of tea and a tour, and headed back to the airport.

In the taxi I tried to pull it together. Even though Bettina was convinced there was no secret stash of API, Ferreira's eyes had betrayed him. Did this mean the minister had managed to fool Bettina, or that the minister was himself being fooled by Ferreira? Or was I mis-reading the plant manager's reaction? Maybe there was something else going on?

My thoughts were going round in pointless circles until I boarded the KingAir. We'd just got airborne when Shan called.

***

'I wanted to give you some news,' he said after we'd got through the courtesies.

'I'm sorry Dr Gupta – if you want coverage from TWO you'll have to get your jet to fly me to Delhi, and a chopper to Shimla, and then a great meal…'

He gave his trademark laugh. 'When you hear this news you'll be begging to come back to Shimla…'

'I don't need to hear your news – I'm begging anyway. Can I bring my skis this time?'

'Well, maybe you should hear the news first…'

I gave an exaggerated sigh. 'Oh, okay then. I suppose I can give you a few minutes.'

'We've just finished a feasibility study, looking at the possibility of converting our research lab here in Shimla into a production facility. I thought you may be interested?'

'I'm interested!'

'We found several de-commissioned chemical reactors. Equipment that we mothballed a couple of years ago when we decided to concentrate our research on bio-engineered molecules. I didn't know we had them.'

'Which means you can make active ingredients for ARVs?'

'Indeed it does!'

'How much?'

'Probably 20 percent of what we were making in Chandigarh – maybe 25, when we reach full capacity.'

'And how soon?'

'We're hoping to start production within two weeks.'

'Jesus – that's wonderful, Shan. I assume you'll be producing the same API as before, NRTIs?'

'Yes, but…' There was a pause on the line. I wished we had a video link, so I could see his expression. 'We've had Dr Kershaw here from UNAIDS, talking through our options. Now that we know there'll be a treatment interruption in South Africa, they've decided to use our NRTIs as a base for protease-inhibitor based ARVs. Second-line drugs.'

I was surprised to feel the lurch in my stomach. The treatment interruption wasn't a figment of my imagination – it was real! But the good news was that Nikki and Shan had already come up with some answers.

'Where will you get the PIs from?'

'Dr Kershaw tells me the originators can increase production – build up sufficient reserves for a recovery campaign in southern Africa in six to eight weeks.'

'Oh Jesus…' I don't know what I was expecting to hear. From a medical point of view, this sounded fine, but practically speaking the idea of kissing it better after a couple of months off seemed ludicrous. I think Shan took my reaction as a prayer of thanks, rather than a profane expression of doubt.

We talked for another half hour. It was obvious he was on top of the international recovery plan following Nikki's visit, and it was equally obvious that she was doing a wonderful job in getting all the global ducks in a row.

Of course it was hardly surprising that they were scrambling to save the day at the bottom of Africa. Of the nine million people depending on ARVs, two million were right here! Dreadful as it sounded, the interruption of first-line treatment in the epicenter meant there were enough to go around in the rest of the world. But it also meant this region was flying without a safety net. If they didn't have second-line ARVs within a couple of months, and get them to everyone who needed them, people would start dying.

Shimla, Sunday 9 January

His first thought when he opened the door to the dimly lit security control room was that there was no place for him to stand. The small room was usually occupied by a couple of men watching the bank of CCTV monitors on the left, and a supervisor at his desk against the wall on the right. Now, however, an extra table had been dragged to the middle of the room and six large men stood around it, studying a map illuminated by a desk-lamp.

As Shan Gupta appeared at the door the men instantly straightened up, stepping aside to make space. His security officers snapped to attention and saluted, while two men in Indian army uniform braced up in the British Army style. Arthur Baldwin simply smiled and stepped forward to shake Gupta's hand.

Gupta had already been introduced to the army men – a major and a captain from India's elite counter-terrorism force the National Security Guards, better known as the Black Cats after their preferred operational garb of black nomex coveralls and balaclavas. He greeted them in Hindi, switching immediately to English as a courtesy to Baldwin.

'Gentlemen, I popped in to check whether you have everything you need?' He glanced at the Maurya security chief, who gave a small nod of affirmation.

'We're all delighted by the RISAT images,' Baldwin said, gesturing to a large plasma monitor on the rear wall, currently split into two images. He didn't say that the major had just been confiding his amazement at the speed with which Gupta had been able to cut through India's Byzantine bureaucracy to mobilize the Black Cats and get the satellite imagery needed for the trap they were laying.

Gupta moved past the men to take a closer look at the monitor, showing two magnifications of an infra-red image from India's Radar Imaging Satellite, one covering an area of a hundred square kilometers while the other covered the immediate environs of the Maurya headquarters.

Most of the small-scale image was made up of a featureless dark blue, reflecting the uniform icy cold of snow-covered forests and pastures, interrupted by an occasional speck of yellow or orange as the high-resolution camera 600 kilometers above them registered a warmer building or vehicle. Near the lower edge of the screen was a large irregular splodge of yellow, sprinkled with spots of orange and red – the city of Shimla, clinging to the slopes of the Himalayan foothills.

The large-scale image was similar, but the shape of the Maurya complex was clearly visible in pale gold in the center, with red plumes marking the outlets of exhausts from its oil-fired boilers and diesel generators. A much smaller square some distance away showed the position of the guard-post at the entrance to the Maurya compound.

As Gupta watched an approaching vehicle stopped at the guard-house, its engine compartment glowing red while the rest of the car varied from orange to green. Three orange oblongs emerged from the guardhouse and moved around the vehicle, like white blood cells attacking an invader on a microscope slide. In this case, however, the invader obviously passed their test because it was allowed to continue towards the main buildings.

'What d'you suppose that is?' The men all turned to look where Gupta pointed. Some distance from the building – perhaps a kilometer away – a pale golden oval was moving slowly through the midnight blue of the forest.

The Black Cats major leaned across to a console and adjusted a setting, and the balance of colors shifted on both monitors. The ghostly oval was now orange, and more clearly defined, while the featureless inky blue of the forest became more detailed – a Rorschach pattern of pale blue and turquoise.

'It's an animal, sir. You can tell from its size and the speed. It's probably a stray cow or horse – wild animals like musk deer or tahrs are better insulated, so you don't see them at the default setting. It's very cold out for domestic animals – I don't think its chances of survival are very good...' The major was staring intently at the monitor, as if looking for something.

'Ah yes... see here, these shapes are probably predators.' He pointed at faint outlines in pale green against the pale blue. He adjusted the contrast again, and the shapes changed color to gold, and became more distinct. As the men watched, they moved toward the larger animal, now showing in a flame red. 'They're most likely snow leopards, given the size of their prey. Their coats are better suited to the conditions, so they show up as being cooler. I think we're about to see a kill.'

The major muttered a few low words in Hindi to his fellow officer, who in turn gestured to the Maurya security personnel, and they moved away leaving Baldwin, Gupta and the major to watch as nature took its course, silently observed from space.

Baldwin saw that the two Maurya guards were carefully scanning the CCTV monitors while their supervisor was checking in with the guard-posts. The Black Cat captain was watching the Maurya guards at work. He was impressed at their professionalism – they'd obviously realized that a moment of distraction meant their defenses were down.

If Gupta noticed their actions he gave no indication, but when the hunt was over, and the large animal lay cooling in the forest while ghostly yellow predators gnawed at it, he called the group back to the table.

'I thought you should know that our intention to resume production of API in the laboratory here in this complex is now in the public domain – I told Gipsy North all about it, just a few minutes ago.'

There was a moment of silence in the room as each man thought in his own way about the fact that they had just painted a huge bulls-eye on this location, and sent an invitation to the unknown terrorists to try to stop them.

'Cry havoc.' Baldwin mumbled, under his breath.

Shan Gupta completed his sentence. 'And let slip the dogs of war.'

Johannesburg, Monday 10 January

I was sitting on the lawn in front of a university building talking to a charming and beautiful professor about an invention her team had made, which was going to revolutionize the world's supply of energy. Her extraordinary amber eyes shone as she described their breakthrough. It all seemed terribly obvious, even to a scientific midget like me, and I found myself whooping along with her at the thought of what an unending supply of clean, cheap power could do for us all.

The professor was starting to answer my question about how they planned to implement their new technology – which REALLY interested me – when a bell started ringing. She smiled and said she was scheduled to give a lecture but – with her eyes buried deep in mine – would I mind waiting until she was done? But there was something about the bell... it wasn't really a bell at all. It was a phone. It was my phone. I could swear the professor gave me a look of genuine regret as I realized she was a figment of my dream world and opened my eyes.

'Dr North?' It was woman's voice that I didn't recognize. The pitch of her voice was exactly like my dream professor's, but her accent was African.

'We'd like to meet with you, Dr North. We want to talk to you – to tell you what's really happening with these ARVs. We must meet right away. We can pick you up at your hotel.'

She said her name was Thandi, but wouldn't put a name to the 'we'. I had to go immediately because 'we' had just finished a meeting, and they wanted to talk to me. In a couple of hours they would've disbursed and the opportunity would be gone. They were not far away – no more than 20 minutes. I was free to do an audio-recording of the interview, but no video.

Normally I would have told her to go to hell, and gone back to the golden-eyed professor with the British version of the same voice, but we badly needed to open up Pharmageddon. The decider was when she compromised on her offer to pick me up, and said I could follow her in my own car.

I phoned the office and told my editorial coordinator on duty, Jaynee, that I needed real-time monitoring and backup. South Africa was one of a dozen countries where we kept a private security service on retainer. Tracking and panic alerts were built into every piece of equipment we carried. Once alerted, I was assured the cavalry would be only minutes away if I needed them.

All the same, my pulse was racing as I sat in my rented Lexus outside the Michelangelo, with the engine idling. After a couple of minutes a dark-blue BMW pulled up next to me and the tinted passenger window scrolled down to reveal the smiling face of a middle-aged woman, leaning across an empty passenger seat.

'Dr North? I'm Thandi. Please follow me.' I did, reading her license plate number over to Jaynee, who in turn watched my progress on her monitor. She sounded a lot less worried than I felt, and was delighted when I told her so.

'Nothing's going to happen to you Gipseee,' she said in her gorgeous Indonesian accent. 'You are heading south on Rivonia and you're about to cross Grayston Drive – if you look to your left you'll see a white Land Cruiser parked two cars back from the corner. That's one of three which have been assigned to follow you, but they will provide more vehicles if you go to a high-risk area.'

Instead of crossing Grayston we turned east, so I drove right past the white Cruiser, incongruous in an area littered with up-market SUVs. 'Thanks Jaynee, I see it.'

The car's GPS was now showing Alexandra Township a couple of kilometers ahead. 'What happens if we go into a shanty town? A motor like that will stick out like a sore thumb.' I didn't really want to know, but I liked having a friendly voice in my ear.

'One minute Gipseee.' I could hear Jaynee's fingers rattling on her keyboard. There was a pause, then a light giggle. 'Oh, they say they use different vehicles, depending on where you go, but they also say you'd be surprised at the kind of cars you find in squatter camps!'

Sure enough we made a right then a left, directly toward the township, one of the city's most famous ghettos. Nelson Mandela lived there when he first arrived in Johannesburg, but this was also the place where xenophobic pogroms broke out in 2008, triggering a national refugee crisis.

As we drove down 9th Road Thandi's BMW pulled into a bus stop and she climbed out, as I stopped behind her. I could see she was a woman of substance – in several senses – as she waddled up to my window.

'Dr North, do you know where we are?'

'Yeah, my GPS tells me this is Alexandra Township?'

'That's right. I thought you might be worried about coming here in the middle of the night, particularly as a white woman. In fact you should be worried!' She smiled broadly. 'But we are going to a church which is right next to the entrance to the township – I wanted to tell you so you don't worry.'

'Thanks, Thandi. And please call me Gipsy.'

She reached into the car and shook my hand as a man would. 'It's a pleasure. Please follow me – we're nearly there.'

As we pulled away I checked with Jaynee that she had overheard everything. 'Yes, Gipseee. And we have video.'

'Well done, Jaynee! That's impressive.' I looked around but the streets were empty.

Within a minute I was parked outside a small red-brick church, alongside a few other cars. An old man with a stick signaled that he would look after my car. I handed him a coin, even though I knew anyone who tried to break into it would get the surprise of their life, with god-knows how many real guards watching us.

I followed Thandi into the church, which was deserted and lit by only a single light near the door. We walked into our shadows until we reached the altar, where my large companion bobbed and crossed herself, then opened the door to what I imagined was the sacristy. It was, and it was crowded with people, sitting and standing in a circle, in total silence. My impression was of a mixed crowd of men and women, young and old, reasonably well dressed, all black. As someone closed the door behind me a short man in his forties stepped forward and offered his hand.

'Dr North, I am Eric Ngubane and these...' he gestured to the group, 'are the committee of our local IFP branch.'

I knew the Inkatha Freedom Party was a conservative political party with strong ties to the hereditary leaders of South Africa's largest tribe, the Zulu. Most of their supporters lived in the province of KwaZulu-Natal – or KZN – but they also had a following in Johannesburg, where millions of Zulus lived and worked. In the country's first democratic elections in 1993 the IFP won a slim majority in their home province – the only one of the country's nine provinces to elude the African National Congress, which scored nearly two thirds of the seats in the national Parliament.

Like the IFP, the ANC denied any tribal affiliations, but everyone knew they were dominated by members of the second-largest tribe, the Xhosa, including Nelson Mandela, Oliver Tambo and Walter Sisulu. But all that changed in 2008 when the ANC elected Josias Shezi – a Zulu traditionalist – to replace their (Xhosa) leader, Thabo Mbeki.

Shezi was a controversial figure – a man with limited education and an undisclosed number of wives, who had been found innocent of charges of rape three years earlier but, in the process, admitted to having unprotected sex with a young woman he knew to be HIV-positive – and then taking a shower to reduce his risk of infection!

Until a year earlier Shezi had not only served the nation as deputy president, but also chair of their AIDS council and a moral regeneration movement! However, he was sacked when his financial adviser was found guilty of corruption, implicating Shezi in the process. In time similar charges were brought against Shezi, too, but they were dropped by the state prosecutors shortly before he led the ruling party into the national elections of 2009.

Shezi's court appearances and campaign rallies drew huge crowds, many wearing t-shirts or carrying banners proclaiming him to be '100 percent Zulu boy'. This meant the IFP was opposing a ruling party which, while not exactly Zulu dominated, was clearly no longer indifferent to Zulu interests, and the IFP was all but wiped out in the 2009 poll.

Ngubane handed me a business card, one hand cradling the other in the traditional sign of respect. It identified him as Pastor E E Ngubane, chairperson of the Alexandra branch of the IFP.

'You are safe with us, doctor. I hope your bodyguards are able to get some sleep.'

This was so unexpected that I guffawed. 'Hey, the next sound you hear will be a dozen guards committing seppuku!'

His face creased. 'Sepoo...?'

'Oh, sorry, it's Japanese ritual suicide. When their warriors are dishonored, they kill themselves by sticking a sword into their stomachs. Very painful.'

The silent group erupted into a mixture of wails of horror and laughter, deafening in the confines of the small sacristy. Ngubane mimicked plunging a blade in his round belly and bent backwards, roaring with laughter.

'Oh no, doctor. They mustn't kill themselves. We didn't see them – but we know how it is with foreigners when they come to dangerous Alexandra. So we assume that you are being tracked.'

'So it isn't dangerous here?'

He became serious. 'Oh, it can be. The tsotsis like to take your car, and your phone, and you – but you are with us, so you are safe.'

'No worries, Mr Ngubane...'

'But you would rather be sleeping. I understand. We are grateful to you for donating your dreams to us, and we will make a long story short.'

He gestured to an empty chair in the crowded circle. I was interested to note that women received no special consideration in the allocation of seats, nor did the older members of the group. Thandi squeezed into the circle of standers while Ngubane sat down opposite me.

'Doctor, in our culture we should tell you all about ourselves, and ask about your life and your family. But, considering the time, it may be better if we forget our manners.'

I wanted to make a joke about Australian 'culture' but I doubted they had any beer and it wouldn't be much fun without it, so I let it slide and just smiled back.

'When we heard you were here in Johannesburg we wanted to speak to you because you... you have spoken to us, since the beginning of this thing. We look for your name on our cellphones so we can understand what is happening.'

'Thank you. That's good to hear.'

'You are not afraid to speak the truth, so we want to tell you the truth. So you can tell others.'

'That's why I'm here.'

He looked around, maybe to see if there were any last minute dissenters, but there were none.

'We are all Zulus here. The IFP is a home for Zulus who believe in traditional values. We welcome other ethnic groups, and we still have a few white and Indian members, but the other tribes do not feel comfortable among us.'

As Ngubane spoke, the group murmured and clicked their tongues. After a while I was waiting for the hallelujahs.

'Unfortunately the Zulu people are suffering with this four letters.'

'Four letters?'

'Oh yes, H-I-V-AIDS. We are told that half of our people have this disease, even if they feel fine.'

'I'm sorry.' Dunno why I said that, it just seemed right at the time. He acknowledged my sympathy by closing his eyes for a moment.

'We have been told that these four letters affect Zulus much more than the Xhosa, or the Sotho, the Tswana, or anyone else.'

He seemed to be waiting for me to say something.

'I read somewhere that KZN is the worst-affected province.'

There was a kind of collective sigh from the audience, then Ngubane spoke again.

'Doctor, we think that the Xhosas are trying to kill us.'

I heard the words, but they made no sense. I looked around the group to see if they were suppressing laughter, but every face was serious.

'Oh?'

'They have stopped these ARVs to kill us, because we are the ones with the four letters.'

'But… I'm sorry. I don't understand.'

He looked disappointed.

'This problem in our hospitals, and with the United Nations. It is all done by those Xhosas. They have taken the ARVs so they can look after themselves. And so that we will die.'

It occurred to me that I had no idea to which tribe the minister of health, Colin Makeba, belonged. Nor my good friend Bettina Shabangu.

'Why, Mr Ngubane? Why would they do that?'

'Because we are the biggest tribe. And we are the strongest. They want to make us small and weak.'

'Mr Ngubane, your president is a Zulu…'

'Yes, but… when they sing, he dances. They chose him because he is weak. His only job is to be a Zulu. To take votes away from us. The true leaders are hiding behind him. And they are Xhosa.'

For the second time since this saga began I wondered whether I was, in fact, still dreaming. This was just too far off the wall. Mind you, the Nazis tried to recruit King George, who wasn't the brightest light on the Christmas tree. And everyone believed that George W Bush was merely a bumbling front-man for the troika of Cheney, Rumsfeld and Ashcroft.

We talked it out, and after what seemed like a few minutes I saw sunlight outside and heard the sounds of cars and people. I noticed that the group had also thinned down to a dozen or so, all seated now. At some point a cup of lukewarm sweet milky tea was pressed into my hand – it was about the last drink on earth I would have asked for but it tasted wonderful, as did the slab of white bread covered with thick butter and jam that came with it.

At the end I had to admit to myself that the facts fit, even if the evidence was purely circumstantial. This little group certainly had the facts at their fingertips. Zulus made up almost a quarter of the nation of fifty million. The next biggest tribe, the Xhosa, numbered close to nine million, but none of the remaining tribes reached half that number.

Official data did not separate HIV prevalence – or AIDS deaths – into ethnic groups, but they gave numbers for each province. A young man in the group, who said he was a university lecturer, produced a map which showed how closely ethnic distribution coincided with provincial boundaries. Another map showed that HIV prevalence in the Eastern Cape – the 'homeland' of the Xhosa – was around half that in KZN. There was no doubting that, unless ARV treatment was restored, it would be catastrophic for the Zulu people.

The young man's voice carried the imprint of expensive schooling. 'The boers kept the tribes separate, each tribe in their so-called homeland. I am too young to remember that time but as you can see we are still a nation of separation, not integration.'

'I thought the ANC tried to do away with... all that.' This drew a round of hissing and tongue-clicking from the remnants of the group, who continued to hang on every word.

'No, Dr North,' Ngubane said. 'The history of South Africa has always been about ethnicity, and it still is. The ANC just manages to fool most of the people, most of the time.'

'So you believe your government planted bombs in India and Sweden... to kill Zulus?'

Ngubane shrugged. 'Who else could it be?'

'But... they're risking so many lives around the world...'

'Yes, but they're all fine now, aren't they? The only countries that are not okay are our neighbors and us, because our governments HAVE CHOSEN not to comply with UN demands.'

A woman murmured something to the political pastor, and he turned back to me. 'Yes, and our government HAS CHOSEN not to control the police, who stole the ARVs from our hospitals. These are the actions of our government, which is controlled by members of all the tribes except the Zulu, who are worst affected by these four letters.'

Ngubane said something about Mbeki's attempts to stall the introduction of ARVs, and I zoned out for a moment, thinking through the research I'd need to do before going to print. Most of the information – such as the tribes to which the most powerful politicians belonged – was readily available. The historical perspective was already in our archives. I wondered who to approach in government for their side of the...

'Mr Ngubane, is there someone in government who you believe masterminded this plan?'

For the first time he looked unsettled. 'No, I cannot say for sure. We do not think it was any of the party structures, because it is too hard to keep secrets. But the fact that government has not acted to stop this behavior shows that it involves many top people.'

'Some kind of inner circle?'

'Yes, something like that.'

'And what are you hoping will happen when your views are made public?'

'We want them to stop! We want these drugs back in our hospitals. We want our people to speak up, to say they will not accept this kind of behavior. And we want the international community to say the same.'

'What makes you think they will stop? Reverse their actions?'

He looked surprised. 'But... their plan can only work if it looks like we are helpless, as a nation. Victims of international terrorism. If you show that it started here... if this plot is exposed... it cannot possibly succeed. Millions of lives depend on this, Dr North.'

Oh fuck, doncha hate it when the survival of millions depend on you?

***

'Hope we didn't get you out of bed, Gipsy?'

I held up my middle finger, and slowly moved it toward the video lens at the top of my screen until my rectangle on the screen was finger-colored – which got the round of hurfs I was looking for. I had, in fact, spent most of the morning in bed with the do-not-disturb light keeping the Michelangelo's housekeepers and switchboard at bay, while their double-glazing and drapes did the same for the day outside. What can I tell you – I need my sleep.

Enoch must have spilled the beans because he had to hammer on the door to wake me up when I didn't appear for our pre-conference lunch. With the lens still covered I pushed out my tongue at him, as he sat across the room, and he made an 'I surrender' gesture which of course the others saw and enjoyed.

I whipped my finger away and stared hard at the lens. 'So how are YOUR hit-rates doing?' There were bellows of 'touché' and 'ouch' from the gang. They all knew the hit-rate on the new 'Xhosa-nostra' page which I'd posted to the conspiracies page before breakfast was simply off the charts.

'Okay, let's get too it.' Jim called the meeting to order.

'As Gip has modestly reminded us – we're riding the wave, folks. I've had a note from our marketing people to tell me there's a feeding frenzy among advertisers trying to get a slot on the Pharmageddon forum. Mainly the corporate social investment types and the drug companies, to say they are working tirelessly and yadda yadda. They know the world's looking, and they want to be seen.'

I saw Enoch's reaction, and wondered if my own face showed the same revulsion that the philanthropy business – and our own medium – should be exploiting the horror which was hanging over the world. But then again, that's what news is.

'At the same time, guys, a word from an old surfer – waves are fickle things. We've got other users and other stories, so we've got to keep it together. So, breaking news?'

I had something. 'Jim, I just got a call from the minister of health's lackey – it seems the man has suddenly found a slot in the minister's diary, so he can see me tomorrow.

Our executive editor's expression said he wasn't at all sorry that I was hogging the limelight, but then it switched to concern.

'Ah, that's great Gip. Just be... careful, woncha?'

I didn't make light of that. 'I will.'

'Do you need anything from us?'

'Actually, It'd be really helpful if we could run through some scenarios – help me prepare for the interview, if that's okay?'

'Sure. What are you looking for?'

'Well, it's about this Xhosa-nostra thing.' I couldn't do the click with the side of the tongue which locals did when they said 'Xhosa' so I pronounced it like the Spanish for 'thing' – cosa. 'I've been doing some checking, and I confirmed this with Enoch over lunch. The police here are drawn from all the tribes and ethnic groups. Enoch says there are probably a lot more Zulus in the police than Xhosas. So it's hard to square their looting of ARVs with some anti-Zulu conspiracy.'

'Gipsy, who is the top cop?' Georghe wanted to know.

'His name is...' I checked my notes, 'Henry Chamu. The national commissioner.'

'And he's a Zulu,' Enoch put in. 'Just like our president.'

'Okay, so it's unlikely either of them are part of a conspiracy against their own people. In which case this Xhosa-nostra is outside of government...'

'If the Xhosa-nostra exists, Georghe.' Enoch had no trouble with the 'X' click, or adding a slightly reproachful tone to his voice. 'As I told Gipsy at lunch, I would be very surprised if it does...'

'Out of curiosity, Enoch, what tribe do you come from?' Somehow the question was okay coming from Ume.

'I am from the Tembu clan of the Xhosa, Ume. The same as Nelson Mandela.'

'Okay, so you would have a better sense than most of whether such a thing is possible.'

The old man was quite unruffled. 'There have been rumors for many years about some kind of Xhosa cabal – it surfaces in the media from time to time – but there's never been any proof. It's probably driven by resentment or jealousy, at how well my people have done in public life.'

'Okay people, let's try to help Gip with this. Assuming for a moment that this group exists, and that they're outside government, how would they get the cops to play ball?'

'Maybe they didn't, boss.'

'How's that, Linus?'

'Well, if something doesn't make sense, we should check our assumptions. We're assuming the looting of the drugs was part of some grand-plan. But what if it came as a surprise to the conspirators?'

'Good point...'

'Or...' José cut in. 'Or it could be that the cops are ... fantoche?' Words failed him, but he bounced his shoulders up and down, and wagged his head from side to side.

'Puppets?' I don't know if Mandy recognized the charade or the Portuguese.

'Está bem! Maybe the police involvement came as a surprise to the perpetrators, like Linus says, or maybe they didn't care who took the drugs – as long as someone did.'

'That's it!' Russ hadn't said a word until now. 'Didn't you say these ARVs are made in South Africa, Gipsy?'

'Yes, in East London. I was at the factory yesterday...'

'Let me guess – that's in the Xhosa part of the country?'

I looked over at Enoch and he nodded sadly, looking like a soldier about to climb out of a trench at Gallipoli. 'Yes, in the middle of it...'

'And that's where the contaminated drugs came from?'

'That's right, Russ.'

'So, maybe the conspirators needed the hospitals to be emptied of ARVs so that orders would be placed for fresh supplies – for drugs that they knew would be contaminated. The contamination is enough to force the authorities to recall the drugs...'

I'd got that far in my own thinking. I needed the group to take it further. 'Fair enough, Russ, but why?'

'Because the police started returning the drugs, and they needed to stop that...'

'No, wait a sec, Russ. This doesn't scan, somehow. The perps needed someone to loot the hospitals so they would restock with contaminated drugs. But the reason for the contamination was to stop them from returning the looted drugs? It sounds too... circular.'

'Maybe not, Gipsy. Maybe it was planned from the beginning like that. The contamination was a safeguard... to make it impossible for whoever took the drugs to return them. By undermining their belief that their hospitals could be easily restocked.'

We stared at each other in the little squares on our computer monitors, both wondering why anyone would think those ARVs could be easily replaced when we, the mass media, were telling them the exact opposite?

Russ' frown of concentration was replaced by a beatific smile. 'They have a stockpile of ARVs. Uncontaminated ARVs. Whoever is behind this. And the police know it. Or some of them do.'

José vented one of his terrifying cackles. 'Exatemente! They have enough to... preserve... the Xhosas, while the Zulus die. That's why they don't care who took the old drugs, as long as someone did. Because the looted drugs are very little, compared to what they have hidden…'

'Maybe it's not the ARVs, but the active ingredients to make them?' I didn't mean to lead the discussion – it just slipped out.

'Even better, Gipsy! They can keep making drugs for their own people, long after they are no longer available to the Zulu!'

That's what I wanted! But Enoch couldn't contain himself any longer.

'José… Gipsy… I know how it looks, but there is too much wrong with this idea. You talk about the Xhosa and the Zulu as though they are the only tribes, when there are many. Are you saying the Xhosa are trying to kill everyone else, or only the Zulu? If it's only the Zulu, does it mean the other tribes are part of their conspiracy? And, by the way, if the Zulu think anyone is trying to kill them, they will not go quietly! They see themselves as warriors…'

Jim nodded, looking like he wanted to move on. 'Good points, Enoch. Anyone else?'

'Jim, a rider to Russ's idea of a secret stash of drugs… or active ingredients.'

'Go ahead, Georghe.'

'Well, if it's true, it would explain why Gumede – their ambassador at the UN – walked out of that emergency meeting at the UN, after it was suggested that everyone should submit an inventory – a verifiable inventory – of their national reserve of ARVs. He didn't want anyone discovering this stockpile.'

I was waiting for someone to ask the obvious question. It came from Linus, right on cue. 'Enoch, what tribe does Ambassador Gumede belong to?'

Enoch didn't look like he was enjoying himself at all. 'He's a Xhosa.'

Jim was definitely getting antsy now. 'Okay, so we have a mythical mountain of API supporting an imaginary cabal of Xhosas. Or vice versa. Has this been useful, Gip? I'd like to move forward…'

'Sure, Jim. But can I drop in one last thing? Just as I was leaving the meeting this morning, someone said they'd heard that the minister of health actually owns the ARV factory…' Okay, so I made that up. But I needed to source it from someone other than Bettina. A casual comment in a crowd would do.

'Oh, that's just incredible!' Mikaela was aghast. 'Next you'll tell us that the minister is a Xhosa!'

'Actually he is.' Enoch's face was a mask. Time to end this.

'Thanks, everyone. This'll give me a lot of ammo for the battle of Makeba tomorrow.'

***

'Enoch, what I don't understand is that you were the first to suggest that the perpetrators were right here in South Africa, but you don't like the Xhosa-nostra theory…'

He chuckled and shook his head, chewing on a wad of steak. There was nothing wrong with Enoch's appetite, and there was nothing wrong with my salad. I just didn't feel like eating it. But the sauvignon blanc was good. I continued.

'Also, why doesn't your government simply order the cops to return the ARVs? Unless… they've ordered them already, and the cops have just ignored them?'

Enoch swallowed. 'I don't think so, no. But the politicians are unlikely to give a direct order. It is not our way. They would discuss the situation with the national commissioner, who would point out difficulties. Or vice versa.'

'Vice versa?'

'Yes, it is possible to imagine a situation in which the commissioner wants to order his subordinates to return the drugs, but the politicians tell him not to.'

'You're a constant source of mystery and surprise to me, baba.'

He chuckled deeply. 'It is life that is mysterious and surprising, Gipsy, not me.'

'Okay, so mystify and surprise me. If it's not a Xhosa conspiracy, what else could it be?'

He put down his knife and fork and sat back, his eyes telling me he was ordering his thoughts.

'To understand this, you need to understand two… no, three issues.'

I gave him a twinkly and pulled my notebook toward me. He smiled at our pseudo role-play.

'The first thing is that South Africans do not trust ARVs. In their heart of hearts they worry about plots to enslave them, or poison them, or make them impotent. When they are desperate they take the drugs – after they have nothing to lose. But when they get better, their mistrust comes forward and they persuade themselves that they have recovered in spite of the drugs, not because of them, so they stop taking them.'

I nodded. 'So a lot of people die, even though they've been on ARVs?'

'That's right. We – all of us Africans – have a strong, maybe even an over-developed, sense of the supernatural. Fate. Spirits. Whatever you want to call it. So when ARVs are taken away from us we believe it is divine intervention. It is meant to be. We don't like to meddle with these forces. We accept the consequences – even if it means death.'

'So… you are suspicious of these drugs, and then something – fate, god, terrorists – confirms your feeling by taking the drugs away?'

'Yes. Many believe it is their ancestors who have intervened to save them from these drugs. It's a sign. The fact that nobody knows who is responsible for the bombs makes it even more convincing.'

'And the third issue?'

'No my girl, I'm still on the first one. Our government is positioned somewhere between the west and the rest of Africa. They try to balance the science and economics and all the other holy cows of the developed world with the traditions and perceptions of our people. These ARVs fall right into... that space. Science supports the drugs, but our ancestors do not.'

A thousand questions popped into my mind, but I didn't want to divert Enoch. 'Okay...'

'So from government's point of view, if they restore ARVs it looks like they are agents of the west, or big pharma. And it looks like they are not respecting the ancestors who intervened to save us...'

It was getting really hard to keep quiet, but I did. He must have seen it because he gave a knowing smile and held up his hand in a 'wait' gesture.

'On the other hand, if the government refuses to restore ARVs to the hospitals, they are seen to respect the supernatural forces and oppose any attempts to enslave their people. But, when people get sick and start to die, they will be blamed for being ignorant peasants. So they offer a way out. They spread the word that those who do NOT respect the will of their ancestors can find the drugs... elsewhere.'

'Where?'

'The police. City councilors. Off-duty nurses. Street traders...'

'In other words, the black market?'

'I suppose so, yes. But...'

'But Enoch, surely you can see how bizarre this is? Nobody was forced to take ARVs before, but at least if they wanted the drugs they could get them without paying, and in a medical setting where they could be tested...'

'Well, your idea of being "forced" may be different to mine, but I get your point. Still, I must tell you that this approach makes perfect sense to most South Africans. It is... respectful.'

I kept reminding myself that Enoch was a man who tapped into the soul of his nation, while I was an outsider. I remembered the incredulity I felt when Zimbabwe's Robert Mugabe told his thugs to confiscate white-owned farms. It was economic suicide, but they did it anyway – and their people kept re-electing Mugabe, even while the unmistakable stench of collapse grew stronger. Somehow what Enoch said made sense. Maybe it was the sauvignon blanc.

'Have we reached the second issue?'

'Yes, it's the ANC youth league celebrating the end of ARVs.'

'What about it?'

'Well, the youth league has a special place in our country. In our history. It was established in 1944 by Nelson Mandela, Oliver Tambo and Walter Sisulu, among others, specifically to take control of the parent organization, ANC, which they did. And they have more or less held onto that control ever since. The end of apartheid is generally traced to the uprising by the youth in Soweto in 1976.'

'So when the youth league celebrates the end of ARVs, the government craps in its pants?'

For a moment I thought I'd gone too far, but as always Enoch was an indulgent teacher. 'No, but they would certainly have expelled a lot of hot air!'

'So you're seriously suggesting that the government would hesitate to restore ARV treatment because... what? The kids don't want them to?'

'Yes, I'm suggesting exactly that. Remember the president owes his position to the support of the youth league, and the rest of the cabinet owe their positions to the president.'

'Jesus, that's bizarre! Let's commit national suicide because the kids don't like these drugs!'

The faintest sign of irritation crossed Enoch's face.

'Don't forget most of those kids are adults in their twenties or thirties. Leaders in waiting. Of course the government doesn't want to sacrifice millions of people with AIDS, but it must show respect for the views of the youth. That's where the alternative channels for the drugs come in.'

'Wow, Enoch, it really is hard to wrap my head around all this. Suddenly life in Australia seems so... simple.'

He laughed. 'I'm sure it would seem complicated to me.'

'I can't imagine what the third issue is.'

He pulled a glum face. 'Unfortunately I think you can. It's simple corruption.'

Ah! 'How's that?'

'Even if the police were not ordered to take those ARVs out of the hospitals, we know they did. And unfortunately we know that the line dividing the police from the criminals in our country is not... clear.'

That was putting it mildly, but this wasn't the time to discuss the endless exposés of police corruption which filled the local media.

'So...?'

'And I'm afraid there is also a culture of entitlement among our politicians.'

'You mean the gravy train?'

'We might say political decisions are made by balancing personal interest and public interest.'

'In other words your politicians lost no time climbing into bed with the cops...'

'I would not be surprised.'

'How can they sleep at night? Knowing that they are keeping life-saving drugs from people who need them?'

'They aren't keeping them from the people, they are selling them instead of giving them away.'

'But... what's the difference? If you're poor, it's the same thing!'

'They won't see it like that...'

'Who? The poor people or the fat-cats who are trying to make a quick buck?'

'Both. I know this must seem strange to you, Gipsy. And I'm not suggesting that poor people will be happy about this. But they will see it as fate. Something unexplained took the ARVs away, and now the only way to get them is to buy them on the street.'

'I guess that's where we come in?'

'What do you mean?'

'We turn the unexplained into the explained. We tell them what the cops and politicians are up to.'

'Do you think Makeba will admit these things to you tomorrow?'

'Oh, no, I'm sure he won't. I was thinking about our stringers. All we need to do is throw the stick, and they'll fetch it.'

And all I had to do was post this theory to the pharmageddon forum, and thousands of people would be scrambling to prove – and disprove – it. In the end the truth would come out. It always did.

'Ah yes, I see what you mean. This way of doing things is still new to an old dog like me.'

'And new to your cops and politicians. But they'll learn soon enough that the old saying "you can fool most of the people, most of the time" needs revision.'

Enoch suddenly looked serious.

'Please be careful, my girl. These men are not known for their... sense of humor.'

I laughed at his choice of words, but I didn't take his advice lightly.

Pretoria Tuesday 11 January

Minister of health Colin Makeba kept writing as I was shown into his office. Perhaps he thought I'd stand at the door like a small girl admitted to the headmaster's office, waiting for the Almighty's attention. I walked over to his desk, planning to sit down, but when I arrived I thought, fuck this for a lark and leaned over his desk, my head just a few inches from his.

'Good morning Mr Makeba.'

I got my money's worth – he started and reared back. I suppose he isn't used to people inside his personal space, especially when he doesn't have bodyguards around. But I was giving him the full 32-tooth routine, like we were old mates. Very confusing I'm sure. He recovered and gave me an uncertain smile, his eyes flicking to the empty office behind me.

'Ah, Dr North. You... gave me a fright.' He hesitated a second then held out his hand to me. I held out mine, but his desk was too wide for us to connect unless I leaned forward, or he got out of his chair. I didn't lean forward. Another hesitation and he rolled out of his chair and onto his feet, and we completed the ritual. His hand was round and flabby, like the rest of him, and he didn't close it around mine but used his thumb to briefly press my hand against his.

'I'm sorry, I didn't hear you come in. But you are welcome. Please sit down.'

I didn't point out that his secretary had knocked on his door and he'd called 'come'. I dropped into a chair. He was rummaging through some papers on his desk, no doubt looking for his crib-notes. He found a sheet of paper and peered at the top of the page, and then at me. I gave him another bright smile.

'Thank you for seeing me, Mr Makeba. I'm sorry your trip didn't materialize.'

'My what?'

'Your trip. Your secretary said you couldn't see me this week or next because you were traveling...'

'Oh. Yes. Well we thought it was important to see you...'

'We?'

'Myself. On behalf of the government. So we could find out...' his eyes flicked down to the page in front of him, 'why you have started this very dangerous rumor.'

Oh, this was going to be fun!

'Which rumor is that, Mr Makeba?' His expression hardened – maybe because I didn't blather something about being a responsible journalist who didn't start rumors, or that I wasn't calling him 'Mr Minister.' Who gives a shit?

He tried to get stern, fixing me with his slightly bloodshot brown eyes. 'The one where the Xhosa are trying to wipe out the Zulu by withholding antiretroviral drugs.'

I tried to look shocked. 'ARE you? Trying to wipe out the Zulu?'

Give the man his due, he didn't fall into the trap, but I could see him holding himself together. 'Dr North, how much do you know about the history of the ANC?'

I held up my notebook and pen. 'I'm always willing to learn.'

'I would have thought you'd do some learning before writing such dangerous nonsense.'

'Please tell me which parts I got wrong, Mr Makeba.'

'All of them.'

'Okay, so the Zulu are not the largest ethnic group?'

'Yes they are...'

'They don't have the highest HIV prevalence?'

'We don't know that.'

I gave him a 'oh come on' half smile.

'Dr North, we know that prevalence is highest in KwaZulu-Natal, so it is possible that it is higher among the Zulu people as a whole. Our surveys do not record tribal affiliation.'

'What about Mandela, Tambo, Sisulu, Mbeki... and you?'

He stared at me a moment longer, than smiled slightly. 'Maybe I should rephrase what I said. There are points in your story which are correct, but that doesn't mean there's any truth to the rumor itself. We had no part in the sabotage of those factories in India. Nor in the contamination of the drugs from Nguni Pharmaceuticals. We are not trying to keep these drugs from anyone, including the Zulu people.'

I waited.

'There's no Xhosa-nostra, and the Xhosa people are not afraid of the Zulus.'

'Mr Makeba, why haven't you instructed the police to return the drugs they… confiscated from your public hospitals?'

Again his eyes flicked to the page in front of him.

'Well, firstly I don't issue instructions to the police. But my colleague the Minister of Safety and Security was acting at my request when he asked the police to remove those drugs and place them in safekeeping.'

'To keep them out of the hands of gangsters, so I've heard. But why are they not returning the ARVs? Nobody is being treated.'

'I think you must be mistaken. My information is that everyone who wants treatment is getting it. What has changed is that people are no longer willing to take those drugs.'

'Why not?'

'Because they are not working.'

'A couple of weeks ago you had the largest ARV program in the world, with nearly two million people on treatment. Now you have nothing. Why the sudden change of heart?'

'As I said, I don't agree that nobody is getting ARVs. But it's true there has been a change of heart, yes. We recently published the results of our latest HIV surveillance survey, and it showed that prevalence has risen sharply since we rolled out those drugs…'

'But surely you understand that this is because fewer people are dying from AIDS?'

'Dr North, we Africans are tired of white people coming here and telling us to do this and do that. It was white people who told us that HIV prevalence was an accurate measure of the epidemic, and that ARVs were the best way to fight this disease. Now you are telling us to be happy that prevalence is rising.'

It's not that I couldn't see it from his perspective, but – Jesus – this guy was in charge of the nation's health. I was sure countless people had tried to explain it to him and I had to fight the impulse to do it again.

'So a couple of million people saw your survey and decided not to take the ARVs?'

'Do you see queues at the AIDS clinics?'

'Why would they queue, when they know there are no nurses, no doctors and no drugs?'

'As I said before, you are mistaken. My information is that the nurses and doctors have been re-allocated to other sections because nobody is asking for their help at the AIDS clinics.'

Okay, moving along. 'Mr Makeba, why did the west... white people... encourage you to give these drugs to AIDS patients? If it wasn't to save lives?'

'To make money of course. We are spending – we WERE spending – millions of dollars on ARVs.'

'And the reason for setting up your own ARV manufacturing plant in South Africa?'

'To keep some of that money in the country, instead of importing everything.'

'Any other reasons?'

'No. Well, maybe to reduce our dependence on foreign suppliers. That was when we believed the drugs were necessary.'

'Is that the same reason that you were building up your reserves of ARVs?'

His eyes snapped into focus. 'Where did... you get that idea?'

'Just a rumor going around. Is it true?'

'I'm not involved in determining drug inventories – I'd have to consult my staff...'

'I'm not talking about your regular inventory, but a secret stockpile. Enough to last many months – years if you restrict the number of people who are treated.'

'Who told you... this nonsense?'

'Like I said Mr Makeba, it's a rumor. Is it true?'

'Well, if there was any such thing, we would hardly confirm it, would we?'

'Why not? It sounds like a good idea, to have a cushion in case there's a fall.'

He stared at me for a moment. 'What else do you want to ask me, Dr North?'

'Yes, I wanted to bounce another rumor off you. This one says that you're a major shareholder in Nguni Pharmaceuticals.'

Makeba's color darkened, he was looking left and right as though the answers were painted on the walls, and it sounded like he was struggling to speak. 'That's ridiculous! Where do you get this bullshit from?'

'Is it true?'

'I can't believe that you come in here, insult my country and question my honesty.'

'Mr Makeba, if you tell me it's not true then I will say that you denied it. Otherwise I must say you dodged the question.'

He wanted to throw me out, that's for sure. Well, to tear my head off, but it might be difficult to explain a headless ozzie in his office. I could see him trying to think his way out of the box he was in. His shoulders dropped, and his tone switched.

'Dr North – Gipsy – try to see this from our perspective. It doesn't matter what I answer. If you publish these allegations, everyone will believe they're true.'

'Which ones?'

'All of them. Well, it's too late on the Xhosa-nostra nonsense, but people have been talking about that for years anyway. But the allegation of a strategic reserve of API, and that I have a stake in Nguni Pharmaceuticals. Do you realize what people will think?'

I had a fair idea. 'Tell me.'

He really did look beaten. 'They will take it that I, as a Xhosa, have been making money from this Zulu disease, and now I am keeping the drugs away from them so they die. And giving the drugs to my Xhosa friends.'

'They might also suspect that your ambassador's rather... surprising... statement in New York recently was made because he couldn't commit South Africa to international verification of the extent of your ARV reserves.'

He nodded but said nothing, his eyes fixed on the sheet of paper in front of him. I felt strangely sorry for the man.

'Mr Makeba, I have the feeling that the truth is less damaging than the conclusions people will draw.'

He looked up, with something like hope in his eyes. 'Can we discuss this off the record?'

'I'm sorry. We have so much information already that we don't need off the record briefings. I can't commit to withholding information which could affect thousands of lives.'

He shook his head. 'It's millions of lives. If you publish these lies, it will be like setting fire to the country. The blood will be on your hands.'

'You've got to be kidding me! Your factory has been secretly stashing ARVs for months. Then you stand by with your arms folded while any cop who fancies a few boxes of ARVs helps himself. And your ambassador turns down a rescue plan for millions of your fellow citizens because he doesn't want the world to find out what you're up to. And now that the cat is about to be let out the bag, it's my fault?'

'How much money do you earn in a year, Gipsy?'

'A lot, Colin. What about you? When you add it all up?'

'Whatever you earn, I will pay you twice as much to drop this story.'

'That's a great deal of money, Colin. Shan Gupta has been very generous to me.'

'I'm sure he has. What would he say if I called him and told him what you're about to write?'

'I'd love to find out. I have his direct number right here.'

He seemed to bite his lip, and shook his head.

'Well, this has been fun Colin, but it's crunch time. What's it to be. Phone Shan? Confirm or deny that you have a controlling interest in Nguni and a hidden stash of ARVs? Tell me how you feel about Zulus? I'm taking calls on any of these topics.'

He was past desperation. I guessed his body was drenched in adrenalin. He was looking at me as though he was wondering how hard it would be to kill me before I could write my story. I wasn't feeling as butch as I sounded, by a long shot. I hoped that Nerisha was getting every word – the ace up my sleeve.

When he spoke his voice was soft. 'It's time for you to leave, Dr North. I believe you know the way out.'

I'd pushed my panic button before I reached the door, and Nerisha's voice was soft in my ear.

'I called them already, Gipsy. As you leave the building, three young white men in jeans will greet you like friends and walk with you to your car. One of them has ginger hair and a green T-shirt.'

By the time I got downstairs I was trembling, and my knees felt like jelly. Damn, that fat fuck wasn't the only one drenched in adrenalin and sweat.

'Hey Gipsy! Long time no see!' The ginger-haired guy and his mates were huge, and grinning broadly. In a second they were around me and supporting me under the arms as we scooted across the road and into the multi-level garage where I'd parked. Once we were out of sight they dropped the act.

'If you give me your keys Dr North, we've got a double who will drive your car. You'll be safer riding with us.'

A double? Wow, I wanted to see her. Then the door of a battered delivery van slid open, and I could see it was fitted with seats and harnesses like those worn by airline pilots.

'Jump in and we'll take you to a safe-house until we've assessed your situation. Watch your head.'

If this was fiction I'd be telling you that we were chased by men with sunglasses and black cars. But it didn't happen like that. We drove uneventfully to a suburban guesthouse where I was registered as the 'Mrs' part of Mr and Mrs Don Irwin. By the time I got into the room I was feeling faint with exhaustion.

Don – the ginger-haired guy – was the soul of professionalism, offering me a cellphone and laptop in case someone was trying to track me through my own, but Nerisha whispered in my ear that the techies on the second floor said they had remotely switched my equipment to 'satellite only' and to stop worrying. I did.

Don must have known I'd be starving once the adrenalin wore off, because he knocked on the door an hour later carrying a tray with a really good piece of barbecued barracuda, steamed vegetables and an icy bottle of sauvignon blanc.

I spent the evening writing up the interview. When it was done I stared at it for a while, thinking about what it might mean to Makeba and his country. But my reverie was more of a prayer for grace than a questioning of faith. Shan didn't invent the idea that everyone deserves the truth – he just made it possible. It's something I always believed in, and often wrote about. Makeba said what he said, and didn't say what he didn't say.

'Don't blame the messenger,' I snarled like a Hollywood hero, as I prodded the send button.

By midnight I was starving again, and ended up eating pizza and drinking beer with the guys. I learned something about the personal protection business, which sounded like fun. Don said my 'double' was watching TV in my room at the Michelangelo. He tried to break it gently that my double's name was Dirk, and he was some kind of martial arts star. He wasn't alone, though – he had a backup team in the next room, just in case. As to why they were there at all – it was the only way to find out if someone was actually after me. They had a way of patching calls from the hotel phone through to the guesthouse, but nobody called.

I told them that the primary motivation to harm me was gone – I'd posted my story. But that still left revenge. Don seemed to sober up suddenly.

'Revenge is long-term stuff, Gipsy. We can keep you safe for as long as we can keep you out of sight. Maybe you should think about leaving South Africa?'

'I am thinking about it.'

'And what about your friends? There's more than one way of taking revenge.'

My heart turned to ice! Bettina! I couldn't believe I hadn't thought about her earlier. That's why I hesitated before sending off my story – my subconscious had been trying to tell me that it could get Bettina into world of trouble. Makeba would be looking for the source of my 'rumors' about the ARV stash and his ownership of Nguni Pharm, and who better than my good mate, the head honcho in his own department?

The horror must have been written all over my face, because Don leaned forward and took my hand between his.

'What is it? What can we do?'

Suddenly I didn't feel very tough.

'I… don't know. It's a friend. A very good friend. She's in government.'

Don looked at his colleagues, whose faces were saying 'this-is-not-good'.

'How many people know that she's your friend?'

'Not many. I've visited her at her office in Pretoria. Oh… shit. Her staff may not know we're friends, but they know we've spent a lot of time together recently. She's got a family…'

'Gipsy, the details… if you want us to help, I'll have to know more.'

I started to tell him, but I hadn't got much beyond telling him Bettina's name when he was on his cellphone, speaking rapidly in Afrikaans. After a minute he was back with me.

'Okay, we're going to stake out her place. Just so we're there, if anything happens. Please carry on.'

I told Don about the story I'd just posted, and that Bettina would be suspected of being my source.

'When will the minister know what you've written?'

'He probably knows already.' Of course there was a remote possibility that my story had been lost in cyberspace, or delayed in the works. I grabbed Don's phone and logged onto TWO. There it was, and the hit counter was already close to seven digits, and the comments into the hundreds.

The three guys looked at each other for a moment, and one muttered something in Afrikaans. Don chuckled wryly. 'He says they are probably too chicken-shit to wake up the minister. But...that's a thought. Maybe it's the minister who needs protection, not your friend?'

'I don't care about Makeba. Whatever happens to him is because of what he's done. Dr Shabangu has only done good things for this country.'

'I hear you. Well, if you want we can extract her, and her family. But we need to move fast.'

'I must talk to her...'

'Okay, let's see what we can do.' He was back on his phone, and I gathered someone was going to knock on Bettina and Ephraim's door and hand a phone to her, so I could talk to her.

I could see Don listening as they approached the door and knocked. He looked over at me. 'No answer. They're going to look around.' He listened for another minute or so and then: 'Their car is gone and the house is empty.'

'Empty?'

'Ag, I mean there's nobody at home. But... hang on.' He spoke again into the phone and then disconnected. 'There's no sign of packing, rapid departure, anything like that. No dinner prepared or dirty dishes. I've told them to get out of the house. We... aren't supposed to be there.'

'So it looks like they... what? Went to a restaurant? Just haven't come home yet? Oh...'

'What is it?'

'They could be staying at her brother-in-law's house. They've done that before.'

We spent the rest of the night trying to trace Ephraim Shabangu's brother, without success.

Just before dawn we heard about the tragic car wreck that claimed the life of South Africa's director general of health, Dr Bettina Shabangu, and her husband and two children. Their car left the motorway between Pretoria and Johannesburg, landing in a concrete storm-water canal. They all died instantly. It looked like one of their front tires may have blown out.

Johannesburg Wednesday 12 January

My red-headed 'husband' strongly advised me not to hang around for the funeral, and so did my gray-headed boss. As usual the answer-to-everything from the nuns' at my convent-school – to ask Jesus – didn't-answer-anything, but Em was emphatic. 'Get out of there, lover. Come home.' Three votes against and two abstentions.

Waiting for my flight at O R Tambo International I had to keep busy, had to unscramble the egg somehow, so I phoned Shan, and tried to sound businesslike.

'I've been trying to get the results of the analysis of those contaminated ARVs from Nguni Pharmaceuticals. They're playing hard to get, but I thought you may know something.'

The video link caught his wry smile. 'I'm not surprised they are being difficult. Our molecule wasn't at fault, thank God, but we knew that already. We keep batch samples and we'd already checked – so it must have been one of the other ingredients. There are quite a few.'

'Can they narrow it down?'

He hesitated. 'I'm sure they can.'

I knew that look. 'Shan?'

He smiled again, a little sheepishly. 'Ah, can we call this… background?'

It was good to be able to give him something for a change. 'Sure, boss.'

'Well, we got hold of a sample of the contaminated drug, and we did our own analysis. I'm sure all their suppliers have done the same. But we all pretend we're waiting to be informed of the results from the official assay.'

'And?'

'We think the toxin was mixed into a binding agent.'

'Which tells you what?'

'That it almost certainly happened inside their plant. Which explains their reluctance to release the results.'

'What kind of toxin was it?'

'Oh, it's a simple compound which induces nausea and diarrhea. If you swallowed a spoonful you might die of dehydration, but in trace amounts it's not dangerous. Just uncomfortable'

'Is it fast acting?'

'Yes. Very.'

'So the patients would get no benefit from the ARVs they've just taken…'

'Very good, Dr North! The therapeutic ingredients are all slow-release, so they'd be purged from the system before there was any significant absorption.'

'And it looks like they went out of their way to avoid killing anyone... again.'

Shan was looking at me – or at least my image on his phone – like a proud brother. 'Yes. The same thought occurred to me. What do you suppose it means?'

It wasn't a new idea, but the Nguni contamination simply confirmed it somehow. 'Well, it's almost like they're trying to make a statement, prove a point, but without losing... honor. Or karma.'

'Yes...?' He was waiting for more.

My brain felt like mush. Did I really want to do this, after the worst day of my life? But then again, I had time to kill. 'Or they... shit, Shan, I don't know.'

'The bombers did such a good job of interrupting global production, they must have known there was a good chance that a lot of people could die. How do we reconcile that with a desire to hurt nobody?'

'Maybe they don't care about deaths from AIDS. Like that Al Qaeda scenario. It's god's will that they die. But it can't be Al Qaeda, because they certainly aren't shy about killing people.'

'True. Any other scenario that could explain a bomber who doesn't want to kill anyone?'

'Well, there's Enoch's theory. That some people – some Africans – believe ARVs just don't work. Or that they are harmful. And they arranged this interruption to prove it. In which case... their motives are to save lives, rather than take them. Bizarre, but possible I suppose.'

Shan was staring at me through his phone, his expression unreadable. Maybe the slightest twinkle in his eye. Like he was challenging me to go on. But go where?

I kept yapping. 'The only other people I can think of who would plant a bomb without trying to kill anyone are demolition people, like those guys who implode buildings. Then it's just business...'

'Just business?'

'Yeah. Maybe this was a purely commercial thing. They didn't plan for anyone to get killed. They were just looking for a piece of the action. Like the Chinese...'

'Although there's that little threat of nuclear war.'

'Oh, right. Well, whatever – from what I hear the Chinese aren't doing too well at filling the void. Quality assurance problems...'

'Yes. It's an old problem. And a good argument in their favor. If they planted the bombs, surely they'd have been ready and waiting to take up the slack.'

'How is your project going, Shan? Converting your research lab to production? Do you have any numbers I can use – projected output, dates, whatever?'

'Not yet. My people are still working on the process design and feasibility. It's a complex process.'

'When will you know for sure?'

'Sometime next week, I believe.'

'And if the answer is no?'

'Then we're back to the Chinese. Hoping they can make enough NRTIs for everyone – first and second-line drugs. Dr Kershaw from UNAIDS is here at the moment and she thinks they can do it, but it's going to be close.'

'We're assuming the South African government will dispense the second-line drugs, when they get them.'

'Yes, that's the big unknown.'

'And if they don't?'

'Dr Kershaw was saying the only way forward in that case would be some kind of UN intervention. But it would have to be on a massive scale. She's not very optimistic, after reading about your interview with Minister Makeba and hearing about Dr Shabangu's death.'

Hearing Bettina's name was like being punched in the stomach, and Shan must have read it in my face.

'Oh Gipsy, I'm so sorry. I'd forgotten that she was your friend. It's an absolute tragedy – especially for South Africa. She did so much to build their treatment program. I'll miss her greatly. And I know Dr Kershaw is very upset.'

I mumbled something, but I'd lost the thread of our discussion so I found an excuse to ring off, and headed for the free bar in the first class lounge.

***

For most of the flight and the layover in Rome I kept being sucked into frustrating dreams about writing a eulogy for Bettina's funeral. There were so many distractions, so much to do, so much to worry about, that I couldn't get on with it, couldn't think through it, couldn't get out of it. Everything was so complicated, and dangerous.

In my semi-wakeful moments I found myself daydreaming again about waking up next to Emily, to find the last ten days were all a dream. A dream in which I could remember every meal, every person I spoke to, everything I wrote. Em would insist I write a book about it, and maybe I would. After I'd phoned Bettina to wish her and her family a wonderful new year.

But there was that other possibility, too – the one where I wake up in Chippy to find The World Online was invented by my subconscious, not by an Indian billionaire. Could I start it myself? I doubted it – it would take someone with unlimited money and balls of steel. Perhaps I'd phone Shan Gupta, introduce myself, and tell him I had a dream…

Thanks to Shan's money TWO got off to a great start. It didn't take much to recruit stringers, and they soon gave form to Jim Wallace's vision. The first stage of the rocket that propelled us where-no-man-has-gone-before turned out to be the humble 'back page' – sports coverage! Nothing gets closet journalists into the open faster than a chance to report on their favorite game, and the 2010 football world cup in South Africa – and José's incredible op-eds – drew millions of new users to internet news.

Multinational corporations were swamped with requests from our stringers to advertise on TWO, so they could convert their stringettes into whatever they wanted – from Amazon and Orange, to Proctor & Gamble and the Open University. The increasing value of stringettes boosted the quantity and quality of posts from stringers, which of course pushed up our readership and our appeal to advertisers. Cycles are not always vicious.

The effect on the rest of the world's media was seismic. Hardest hit were the heavy hitters – the international print and electronic media. By the time they realized that TWO wasn't a joke, it was too late – they were caught in the reverse cycle of vanishing users and advertisers. Local media did better, mainly because they could carry local ads – cars, jobs, escorts – but their news pages were littered with credits for copy lifted from TWO.

From the beginning we allowed free syndication of our news, as long as it was credited, knowing it wouldn't be long before their readers and viewers realized they could get it quicker, cheaper, and in more detail, from the source. The old media found they were trapped into advertising for us!

At first a lot of politicians tried to ignore us, answering questions and giving statements only to the old media in the vain hope that someone would take their words at face value. But it made no difference, since there was always a TWO stringer waiting to convert their crap into stringettes – and to feed the rapacious hoards of users who loved to put every smelly factoid under their microscopes.

Our credibility algorithm was even more successful than Jim's predictions. Every story is held up to instant review by millions of users, who are invited to vote on accuracy and interest, as well as to offer their own thoughts on the subject. Sophisticated tracking of users' viewing, voting and commenting gives each a credibility weighting, which makes it virtually impossible to manipulate the ranking of stories. The end result is a user-driven bullshit boomerang, while credible, interesting news is just a click away.

Turkey's decision to host our truth-factory was tested very soon after we set up shop in Istanbul, when we began to get posts about Turkish army incursions into northern Iraq. Linus' investigative work left a lot of egg on a lot of faces in Ankara, but they made absolutely no move against us. Jim's take was that they realized there's no place for anyone to hide anymore, so they may as well score brownie-points for being 'the home of truth'. The Turks certainly made good use of our presence in selling their country as an enlightened Islamic state.

Shan and Jim were true to their word – as senior editors we had every tool and every benefit we could imagine, and some we couldn't. It may sound like they were begging us to spend money – actually it felt a lot like that – but nothing prepared us for the news of TWO's revenue. We'd been told not to concern ourselves with the balance sheet, so we were more than a little surprised when Jim raised it during a weekly news conference, not quite four months after launch.

'Guys, I thought you'd like to know that I was wrong in my projections of advertising support.' He managed to stay deadpan. 'In fact we've had to double the size of our marketing department to deal with all the enquiries we're getting, and our revenue line is where I hoped it would be after 18 months.'

'Jim – just as a matter of interest, did you and Shan agree on these projections?'

Jim knew that our economics editor could cut through crap better than anyone. 'No, Russ, we didn't see eye to eye on this. I'm talking about my projections. Shan's expectation was pretty much spot on!'

Suddenly a lot of us were visualizing a future beyond Shan's three-year horizon.

Istanbul Thursday 13 January

Istanbul looked different somehow, although I couldn't pin down the reason. What hadn't changed was the traffic – unfortunately 8am was the busiest time and it took me the best part of two hours to get from Ataturk to Fenerbahçe. But finally the white garage door swung up and I drove into our sanctuary.

Irem the night nurse had left but Kenan the barbarian, Helen the cook and Arda the factotum fussed around with my hand-luggage and offers of refreshment. Then I walked through to the day room and into the warmth of Emily's eyes, and at last I was home.

'G'day, mate.' Hugging isn't easy when you're in a wheelchair, even a state-of-the-art electric buggy, but it's never stopped us. And it's hard to fake an Ozzie accent when you can barely make sounds, but somehow Em managed that, too.

She used to speak so beautifully with a wild Irish accent and a crazy laugh, but speech control was the first to go as her immune system attacked her central nervous system, and her balance went next. If it was me sitting on that battery pack with wheels I'd spend my life worrying about which pony in my paddock was next for the knackers, but Em just made the most of what she had. And she had more than enough – so much, in fact, that she was always giving it away. People were drawn to Emily like a moths to a storm lantern.

'Why are you up so early?' It was my standard joke. She was always showered and dressed by the time Kenan arrived for the day shift, even though I kept telling her that she should enjoy being waited on. She was wearing a finely embroidered Indian kurta and salwaaz – tunic and pants – with a contrasting shawl.

Her eyes were filled with mischief. 'I thought Jamie and I'd go for a run along the beach.'

'Jamie?'

Suddenly I heard what sounded like a handful of gravel being thrown at a window and a yellow whirlwind appeared from the direction of the kitchen. Em's beloved companion dog always came when he heard his name, but now he was scrabbling for grip on the unfamiliar wooden floors. He was way too well mannered to jump on me, but he managed to convey that he really would if he were allowed, by burying his head between my knees and wagging his tail furiously.

'Jamie! When did you arrive?'

'I got here yesterday, daddy.' Emily spoke for him. Irish ventriloquism. 'The nice people at quarantine said I was special, so I didn't need to stay any longer.'

'That's great! Welcome home, big boy!' I could see the staff grinning from the kitchen door. 'How did he react when he saw you?'

'He said – why did you take me away from that holiday camp, you Irish bitch? Oh, hang on a sec. This is rather nice. Lots of people to feed me and tickle me. Hmm, and lots of space on the bed. Oh, OK, this'll do.'

I roared, and Jamie took this as an invitation to roll on his back so I could inspect his undercarriage and do some tickling. I caught Em's eyes on me.

'You must be exhausted, lover. Can Helen make you something?'

I'd had breakfast on the short leg from Rome so I declined and went to stand in the shower. By the time I turned off the tap I was practically asleep, and I don't really remember getting into bed. When I finally opened my eyes it was dark outside, and dead quiet. I turned over and found Em propped on one elbow, looking at me and smiling.

'How long…'

'About fourteen hours..'

'No, how long have you been staring at me?'

'About fourteen hours.'

I reached for her under the bedclothes and found she was naked. 'Uh oh!' She smiled. 'Uh oh.'

Even though Emily had practically no sense of balance, she was anything but disabled in bed. She said it was like fucking underwater, except you can breathe! And she kept in shape with daily exercises in our small but state-of-the-art gym, under the barbarian's supervision.

I threw off the duvet so I could get a look at her, starting with her naughty green eyes, pert nose and full mouth, down her beautifully formed neck and shoulders to her small breasts and rose colored nipples, now hard and puckered. I saw the gooseflesh form on her pale but perfect skin as I ran my hands down her stomach to the golden triangle and the soft, sweet hiding place beyond. I felt her quads tighten as she pulled her legs up and apart, to let me in.

In a second I was out of my t-shirt and knickers and she was exploring me, too. In a few minutes we were both grunting and groaning, and in another few – with some battery-powered assistance – we were wailing like banshees. When at last I felt her shudder and convulse, that was all I needed to send me over the top.

A little later I was lying behind her, my chin on her shoulder, her bum firm against my hips, my hands cradling her breasts.

'I missed you.'

'I know,' she said. 'You're supposed to.'

'Oh fuck – I can't imagine what Irem thought of us.'

I felt Em trembling with laughter. 'I gave her the night off. Said you'd look after me tonight. And you have! She put me to bed though. Without my jarmies.'

'Hmm. The end of innocence. Did you eat?'

'Mmmm. Pussy delight.'

'No calories in that. I'm starving. You?'

Turned out she hadn't eaten since lunch so I boiled up some pasta and we sat in the day room with a good Bordeaux and the lights dimmed so we could enjoy the bright jewels of light from Princess Islands and the yachts moored offshore, while I told her about the people I'd met and the strange things I'd seen. Just like always.

While they were happening, the events of the past ten days felt like scenes from a movie but now, as I recounted them, they became shockingly real. It was a discordant chant of horror, dread, confusion and disbelief, reaching a crescendo of sheer panic as I escaped from Colin Makeba's office. But when I got to the moment when I realized he would assume I got my information from Bettina, my vision dimmed and I felt light headed and nauseous. I scrambled for the bathroom but only succeeded in plastering the passageway with a mulch of pasta, tomato sauce and red wine. The remains of Bettina and her beautiful family.

Istanbul Saturday 15 January

It's not quite true to say the next thing I remember was waking up in hospital, but it's close enough. Memories aren't always useful. I lay there, drugged to the eyeballs, for a couple of days, but it could have been a few months for all I knew or cared. All I remember is a succession of tedious nightmares, separated by bad food and bed-baths. Actually I didn't mind the bed-baths. And Emily, sitting in her buggy by the bed. She didn't look too worried, just... there. That look you give someone which says: 'Hey, this is something, isn't it?'

Finally I was back home, again, clutching a bag full of medications that I had no intention of swallowing. Our staff looked pleased, again, and Emily looked amused. At least Jamie had the grace to look worried, although I suspected it might be because he'd sampled my artwork in the passageway and found it fell short of his usual culinary standards.

Em asked me to finish my story, and I did. We were both blubbering like schoolgirls as I passed on what I'd managed to drag out of the security guys, who talked to the paramedics who scraped the Shabangus out of their Audi.

Afterwards, as I lay on the couch with my head on Em's lap, staring into Jamie's bronze eyes, I was surprised and a little embarrassed to find that I felt okay. Also, it felt... real. I could feel Em's soft woolen trousers under my cheek, see specks of dust on the coffee table, and smell Jamie's dog-breath over the strange perfume of Istanbul. It wasn't a dream. I was there, in Fenerbahçe, in Istanbul. Safe. I sat up.

'I feel like I'm awake.'

'Good morning!'

'No, really. It's weird, but somehow the whole thing – going to Shimla, Jo'burg – at the time it all seemed so... unreal. It started off crazy and just went south from there. Off the scale.'

I looked into Em's green eyes and was surprised to find concern, for the first time. Then I understood.

'Don't worry, babe. I know Bettina has gone, and South Africa is in deep shit. I'm not... hiding from it. But I feel better. Really.'

***

A little later Jim arrived, unannounced and clutching a bottle of Cuban rum and a bag of limes and mint leaves. We supplied the sugar, ice and club soda, and spent the evening working on the perfect mojito. Eventually our learning curves and blood-alcohol levels converged, and Jim got to the point.

'Gip, I don't want to see you at the office for a while. You haven't taken any leave since we started TWO, and I want you to take a couple of weeks now.'

I caught Em's eye, and recognized the look of a conspirator. Then I surprised myself.

'Okay.'

'Okay?'

'Yeah, boss. I can't fight the three of you.'

Jamie didn't open his eyes, but flapped his tail to confirm his part in the evil plot. Jim looked unsettled by my easy capitulation, but I knew I needed to stand back for a while. To get some perspective.

'Okay then. I'll check in, to make sure you're not abusing my friends here.' He flicked his eyes at Emily and Jamie, but I saw the flash of angst as he realized his words could be taken as a reference to Bettina.

'But I have three conditions, Jimboy...'

'Ah, that's more like it. So give.'

'One, you promise not to pussyfoot around me. I cocked up, and Bettina and her family are dead. I'm not going to kill anyone else, and I'll be fine in a few days.'

I sensed a movement at my feet and found that Jamie had lifted his head to stare at me. That made three sets of round eyes, and a lot of stillness.

'Two, you don't argue if I stay on top of things from here. I won't scare the kids at work, but I want to monitor things online. And to write op-eds, if I feel so inclined.'

Jim didn't like that, and neither did Em, but they didn't say anything.

'And three, next time bring coconut cream and pineapple juice. I think we've nailed mojitos, so we may as well practice our piña coladas.'

Jim was smiling now. 'Anything else?'

'Damn right. We'll need another bottle of rum.'

***

Monitoring the unfolding drama in southern Africa was like watching a vast Hollywood epic being filmed. Scenes were being shot out of sequence, meaningless to anyone without a script until an editor finally assembled the pieces in the cutting room. I spent hours – days – sitting at my computer watching the river of posts, with each video, audio and text adding a pixel of light, color and emotion to an incomprehensible plot.

In South Africa I'd fluttered between confusion, elation, fear and anger, but it was theater emotion. Safe. Now, in Istanbul, I understood things much better but, after my meltdown last week, I felt… empty. No, that's not right – I felt dumbfounded. Stunned. The way I felt when I watched the re-election of George W Bush, after Michael Moore showed so clearly that the emperor had no clothes. Was it the same in Hitler's Germany, or Pol Pot's Cambodia? How can so many people ignore the obvious? Could it be that knowing the truth and behaving rationally don't necessarily go together?

The clips, bytes and tweets weren't all from South Africa, of course. Politicians, priests, public health specialists, economists, apologists, critics, Uncle Tom Cobley and all had something to say, regardless of where they were or how much they knew. TWO's bullshit boomerang proved its worth a million times over, keeping the big picture in view. Mind you, I picked up a few tasty morsels which had been dismissed by the early birds – as we call the news junkies who love to sift through new posts – and, with my editors' override, I brushed them off and restored their rank.

But it was all words. Talking heads. Reaction, without action. At first.

Just like Enoch said, the grapevine held the key. These information back-roads were built at a time when white journalists weren't listening, and black journalists weren't talking. But now our stringers were listening and talking, and every whisper found its way onto our pages.

At first the buzz was that ARVs had been 'withdrawn' from public hospitals because they were no good, and the epidemic was getting worse. But the good news was that government had arranged for 'better' ARVs, which would save the day. Hang in there, folks!

It was a good rumor because it tallied with what people saw, and it allayed their fears while requiring no action. It also tied in nicely with my story that Maurya were fast-tracking the production of active ingredients for second-line ARVs. If PI-based drugs were rolled out to government hospitals within the next couple of months, the blip in South Africa's AIDS deaths would be barely visible – especially after a little statistical massage.

For me the only dead pixel in this otherwise crystal picture was – why use the rumor mill? Why didn't the Government just say openly that they were planning to introduce second-line medications? The best I could come up with was that they were trying to save face. Or to buy time, while they chopped off a few heads following the secret stockpile fiasco.

Except that they weren't chopping off heads. The honorable minister of health denied everything, as did their ambassador to the UN, and – incredibly – the government closed ranks behind them. For their part, Nguni Pharm issued a public statement saying that, as an unlisted company, they were not required to reveal the identity of their shareholders, but minister Colin Makeba was not among them. Well, I knew that already – Bettina told me his equity was held by a proxy.

As for Bettina herself, the official line was that the death of the director general and her family was a tragic accident, but the buzz was that it was retribution by the west for her brave stand against their evil drugs. Never let the facts get in the way of a good story!

Meanwhile, according to Bettina's replacement, AIDS patients were simply going about their business, confident that international fears for their survival were misplaced. AIDS clinics around the country were deserted, but our stringers had no difficulty in finding ARVs for sale on the street, or in confirming there was a big demand for the looted drugs – even at extortionate black-market prices. The fact that many cops were ordering new cars, or buying bigger houses, didn't go unnoticed.

And of course the legend of the Xhosa-nostra was endlessly chewed over on our conspiracy pages. It was fascinating to watch the debate evolve from one-line declarations of support or opposition, to carefully researched historical and political treatises, either for or against. What they all had in common was a lack of hard evidence.

It didn't matter. Whether or not people believed in a secret cabal of tribal elders united against the Zulu, they certainly bought into the 'demographic adjustment' theory, and South African society began to disintegrate into its ethnic parts.

It began with small things – birds of a tribal feather flocking together during tea-breaks, or in work-groups or committees. Then there were reports – isolated at first – of people relocating from one township or suburb to another, or between farms, mines or companies, so they could be with their kin. As the days passed people began to talk openly about this township or farm being Zulu and that one being Xhosa.

The term 'Xhosa' also morphed from a clear tribal designation into an omnibus term meaning 'non-Zulu'. Disclaimers from the chiefs of other tribes such as the Sotho, Ndebele and Tswana made absolutely no difference. People believed what they wanted to believe, and used words to mean whatever they wanted them to mean.

I sat in my study, watching this river of news, trying to see where it was going. I tried out some of my ideas in op-eds, as did Georghe and the rest of the guys, while Enoch provided exquisite insight into the confusion and conflict of being South African. It made compelling copy, and the print-run on our airport mags had to be quadrupled as they were snapped up, particularly across Africa. Jim muttered that we were starting to carry way too much advertising, and that our marketing and finance people were becoming insufferably smug.

We were just adjusting to the Balkanization of southern Africa when another rumor bobbed to the surface in our pharmageddon forum, suggesting that the 'better' ARVs were destined for the non-Zulu areas of the country, leaving the Zulus to die! The geographic separation of the tribes, so the buzz went, was playing right into the Xhosa-nostra's hands, making it easy to control who was treated and who was fatally neglected.

The post struck a chord not only among our early birds, but among the hundreds of thousands of South Africans who were now following every word of the debate, and within a few days it acquired the ring of truth. At this point Zulu students at a university in Johannesburg staged a march to protest their anger at being 'targeted for destruction'. After a handful of them vandalized cars and buildings, the student representative council sent a delegation to 'allay their fears' but it turned into a brawl, and the riot police intervened. One of the leaders of the march – a Zulu student of social anthropology – was stabbed during the fracas, and died later in hospital.

That night, in a predominantly Zulu township to the west of Johannesburg, five men accused of being Xhosa informers were lynched by a street committee who placed burning automobile tires around their necks in the barbaric practice known as necklacing. Gangs of youths took their cue from the lynching and burned down twenty 'Xhosa shacks' in the same township. In one of them a woman, a small boy and a baby had been locked in by her boyfriend while he went drinking. In another, an invalid was unable to get out in time.

By the next morning the township was cleansed of non-Zulus, with several hundred taking refuge in the local police station and a thousand more simply disappearing into the night. When names were put to the dead it turned out that only one – the invalid – was actually Xhosa, the others being drawn from many tribes, including one Zulu.

That night president Josias Shezi addressed the nation on television. 'We saw the same thing happen in 2008, and we cannot allow it to happen again.' He announced the police would be deployed in full force to potential flashpoints, and that he was placing the army on full alert.

Shezi also took the opportunity to confirm rumors that 'better' ARVs were on the way for those who needed them, and to announce that the first province to receive them would be KwaZulu-Natal – the home of his own people, the Zulus.

Nobody was sure whether it was the carrot of the ARVs, or the stick of armed intervention, but the next few nights were quiet. Our stringers described how the calm was used by hundreds of thousands to pack up their homes and move to townships or provinces populated by their own kind. Within days, rumor had achieved what fifty years of apartheid failed to do – separate the nation into its tribal components.

The relocation of millions of its citizens devastated the biggest economy in Africa, particularly the economic heartland around Johannesburg which had always been an ethnic melting pot. Absenteeism brought industrial production almost to a halt, while consumers withdrew their patronage from stores, and their money from banks, which became associated with the other tribe.

Then came another post to the pharmageddon forum, saying that the plan all along had been to give the 'better' ARVs to the Zulu – but that 'better' actually meant 'toxic'! The new drugs, according to the post, were not designed to cure, but to kill!

The poster said the announcement by the Zulu president that his own people would get the toxic drugs was a masterstroke by the shadowy cabal who fed him their propaganda, and that the Xhosa-nostra's secret stash of API would sustain their tribe while the culling of the Zulu proceeded. And, for good measure, the poster added that Bettina Shabangu – herself of Zulu stock – had become aware of this plot and had been killed to prevent her from foiling it!

The latest rumor drew a blizzard of denial, with countless posts pointing out there was absolutely no evidence – or rational argument – to support such a bizarre theory. But it made no difference. All that a conspiracy theory needs in order to fly is that enough people want to believe it, and cannot be persuaded otherwise. Then fiction turns into fact.

Naturally there was an instant denial by the deputy minister of health, reinforced by the president himself, but overnight five AIDS clinics in KwaZulu were firebombed, sending an unmistakable message that the president was no longer trusted in his own province.

In Durban, campus demonstrations morphed into street riots, soon joined by Zulu tribesmen wearing traditional animal-skins and carrying sticks and spears. Buoyed by the collective bravado and more than a little alcoholic courage, one rabble marched on the local offices of the ruling African National Congress, where they chanted and stamped their feet in a terrifying display. A handgun fired into the air was enough to spook the frightened and outnumbered police assigned to monitor the march, who responded with a volley of shotgun fire. Unfortunately their weapons were loaded with buckshot, not the rubber bullets intended for riot control, and forty people were injured and two killed outright in what was instantly dubbed the Magagula Massacre, after the street where the 'massacre' took place.

Before the night was over, several police stations and the homes of a number of senior police officers were raided by armed gangs looking for – and finding – stashes of ARVs, then burning those buildings in retaliation for police brutality and 'disloyalty to the people'.

The following day emergency meetings were brokered between the police, students, traditional leaders and politicians by a group of church leaders. The discussions were never made public but they appeared to be successful because there were no further riots. What happened instead is that senior police, prisons and justice officials who were not Zulu quietly left the province, and were replaced by Zulus.

As the situation in South Africa careened toward the precipice, desperate diplomacy with their larger neighbors – Namibia, Botswana, Zimbabwe and Mozambique – persuaded them to pull back from the brink, and to declare they would restore universal ARV treatment immediately, and would look to the UN to re-supply their hospitals. However the tiny fetal nations of Swaziland and Lesotho could not be induced to leave the South African womb…

New York Wednesday 2 February

UN Secretary General Maryam Kapur was famously efficient as a chairperson – especially for internal meetings such as this – and less than a minute after calling the meeting to order she turned to Ibrahim Mazzer and asked for an update on ARV procurement.

Mazzer knew the heads of all UN agencies had been invited to the meeting but was not surprised to see a few had declined, and others had sent deputies in their stead. Nevertheless, alongside the more obvious agencies dealing with humanitarian and human-rights issues he recognized delegates from tourism, intellectual property, civil aviation, drugs and crime, food and agriculture, labor, trade, industrial development, the World Bank and the International Monetary Fund, pointing to the breadth and gravity of the issue.

'Thank you SG. Much of this information has already found its way into the public domain, so I will be brief. Four weeks ago, immediately after you convened the emergency meeting, we placed substantial orders with the Chinese for active pharmaceutical ingredients – API – for both first- and second-line antiretrovirals. In effect we ordered as much as each company said they could deliver of every type of molecule. If all of them had made good on those orders, we would by now have been in… aah… an interesting over-supply situation.'

Mazzer looked around to see if anyone would smile. Nobody did. The Egyptian picked up his spectacles in one hand, and a sheet of paper with the other.

'The first shipments began arriving at our depot in Bangkok within ten days of order, and every batch was quality-tested by two independent laboratories – one at the WHO and the other at a private research institute. There was a near-perfect correlation of their findings. To date, about one third of the API which was scheduled for delivery has been received and of that, about fifteen percent is of acceptable quality.'

A rumble of voices greeted this news. Mazzer spoke over them.

'The rejected batches included some with no measurable active ingredient, some were contaminated with other molecules, and some were of inconsistent concentration. The three companies that met our requirements have been given further orders, while the others have been given the option of submitting fresh batches for testing.'

Mazzer put down the paper and removed his reading glasses.

'I am sorry to say the acceptable API was not evenly spread across the range of molecules we need for combination medications. In other words, those we accepted are not useable without those we rejected. However, we did have some limited success in matching the good API with reserves of complementary molecules held by finished-drug manufacturers...'

He paused and looked around the table. 'The bottom line, colleagues, is that one month on, we have been able to facilitate the manufacture of only token quantities of combination drugs thus far.'

He glanced back at his notes. 'Naturally we've met with the originator companies and they are willing to overcome their... aah... reluctance to supply API to generic manufacturers, but there's a problem. Two problems, actually. The first, as Mr Hohner told us a month ago, is that big pharma was buying NRTI molecules from India when they were sabotaged, so they needed to make up their own shortfalls first. The other is that they can only increase production of API in the short term by suspending the production of other essential molecules. Which may be code for more profitable molecules – we can't be sure.'

Another ripple of reaction ran around the table.

'In the longer term, big pharma faces the same challenge as the Indian manufacturers, and indeed the Chinese. To increase the production of API they need the equipment – huge banks of very complex apparatus – and there are even fewer companies making this type of equipment than there are API manufacturers. It takes a long time to manufacture, install and commission this apparatus, and building up production of a new molecule can take weeks...'

Mazzer looked like he could go on in similar vein, but decided against it.

'However I imagine you are all more interested in the future than the past?' He got the reaction he was looking for.

'Firstly, you will all have read that Dr Gupta was hoping to convert a large research laboratory at Maurya's headquarters to API production? I am sorry to inform you that he was unsuccessful in this endeavor. My head of procurement...' he swiveled to gesture to Nikki Kershaw, who was sitting behind him, 'has been monitoring the situation, and she reports that the reactors he hoped to re-commission turned out to be unsuitable.'

Mazzer ignored the rumble of disappointment and ploughed on. 'Of course our original recovery plan was formulated before this offer came up, and we have been keeping the pressure on the Chinese and other API manufacturers, and today our best estimates are as follows.'

Once more the spectacles were parked on his nose and the paper lifted from the table.

'Within one month from today – that is, two months from the sabotage – we expect to have sufficient API to satisfy about two thirds of the pre-existing demand for first-line combinations, and most of the existing demand for PI-based drugs... second-line medications. After another 30 days we expect to reach 100 percent of first-line demand, and 120 percent for second-line drugs.'

Again he put down the paper, followed by the glasses.

'To explain what this means in terms of treatment on the ground, I would like to hand over to Jean.' Mazzer glanced at Kapur to indicate he was done.

'Thank you Dr Mazzer. Ladies and gentlemen, please hold your questions until we've heard from Dr Folbert.' She nodded toward the director general of the WHO.

Folbert leaned forward as Mazzer sat back.

'Merci madame. Like Ibrahim I will be brief. Following our meeting on the third of January, all countries supplied us with inventories of their ARV reserves. Our rough calculations at the last meeting proved to be almost correct – we found the global reserve of first-line ARVs was equal to 65 days. And of course we are now halfway through that period. Unfortunately three countries have not met the agreed protocol for re-supply – South Africa has refused to allow physical verification of their reserves and, together with Swaziland and Lesotho, they are not maintaining universal treatment.'

Folbert glared around the room to make sure he had everyone's attention.

'These three countries are home to nearly two million of the 7.5 million people who were receiving first-line ARVs. They are now committed to a large-scale treatment interruption, which means they have no option but to restore universal treatment using second-line drugs. Re-supplying them with first-line medications would be futile, since a large proportion of their patients will be resistant to those drugs.'

The Frenchman hesitated a second before continuing. 'I take no joy in pointing out that the unintended consequence of South Africa's... difficulty... is that the number of people who are continuing to receive first-line treatment has reduced from 7.5 to 5.5 million, and that the global reserve is sufficient to satisfy their needs until new stocks arrive, even allowing some margin for error.'

This time the ripple which ran through the group sounded like a sigh of relief. But Folbert held up his hand.

'At this point our major concern is for those two million in Southern Africa. In the past month we have had three independent teams working full-time to model the possible outcomes of a large scale involuntary treatment interruption, such as we are now witnessing there.'

Folbert nodded to an assistant and the lights dimmed, and a large screen at the furthest end of the table glowed with a brightly colored graph.

'The research teams broadly agree on what they call the simple biomedical model – that is, what is most likely to happen until ARV treatment is restored, in the absence of any non-medical factors. As you can see they anticipate an exponential curve in mortality, starting very gradually within three weeks of the treatment interruption, then rising more rapidly after three months, and reaching a peak somewhere between 12 and 18 months.'

Folbert pressed a button on a remote and a second curve appeared, branching off from the first.

'However, restoring universal treatment – with second-line medications – at any point will result in a leveling off in mortality within a week, and a decline within three weeks. Based on Ibrahim's projections, we expect to have sufficient second-line drugs available for universal treatment sometime in April. By mid-year we would expect daily AIDS deaths to be back within five percent of the pre-January figures.'

Once again he pressed a button, and the graph on the screen changed.

'The second graph reflects what our research teams have called the economic model, which takes into account the effects of declining health on productivity and earnings. Sick people can't work, and this line shows mortality among AIDS patients taking into account malnutrition and other compounding factors as their savings are used up.'

Folbert pressed a button and a second line appeared on the graph, rising above the first.

'This second line shows collateral mortality – the death rate among people who do not have AIDS, but who depend financially on people who do. We are particularly thinking of children and the elderly.'

Folbert looked around the table to make sure he had everyone's attention.

'We must remember that more than 90 percent of people with AIDS are aged between 20 and 50. They are typically family breadwinners, so their illness affects everyone in the household.' He pointed a laser device and a bright red dot appeared on the screen.

'As you can see the collateral mortality rate remains lower than the rate among AIDS patients for a while. This is the period during which families use up their savings, and sell their assets. Some children and old people will go hungry, of course, but we expect they will only start dying after about two months. Then the line begins to rise steeply, crossing the death rate for infected people at four months, and by twelve months we expect collateral mortality to be at least three times higher than deaths from AIDS.'

He glanced around the room. 'Not that we expect to go that long before treatment is restored, of course. It is simply... unthinkable.'

As he spoke the lights in the room brightened, and the image on the screen disappeared. Folbert continued.

'Then our teams looked at a third model, the socio-political model. As the name implies this considers the impact of various social and political phenomena such as civil unrest, sexual incontinence and ethnic cleansing. Frankly, this is where the teams started... to go a little crazy!'

His audience were as still and silent as a photograph.

'The worst-case scenarios, are very bad, I'm afraid, and our monitoring of the current situation in South Africa has led them to be... somewhat pessimistic in their predictions. In particular they were very alarmed by the ethnic separation of the country. Their fear is that this could trigger civil unrest, which would make it difficult to restore ARV treatment, even if the government is supportive and the drugs are available.'

Folbert looked like he wanted to expand on that theme, but changed his mind.

'Of course such a scenario moves out of the public health domain and into matters of national and international security. We have prepared a report along these lines which has already been given to the secretary general. Copies will be distributed at the end of this meeting. Essentially we have recommended a peacekeeping force to stabilize the region politically and militarily and to supervise the reintroduction of ARV treatment.'

Folbert leaned back in his seat, and for a long moment the room was silent. Most of those present were staring at their hands, or blankly ahead. Maryam Kapur broke the silence.

'Thank you, gentlemen, for your huge effort over the past month. I believe the world is in your debt. Do we have any questions for either Dr Mazzer or Dr Folbert, before we move on?'

There were no questions, but a spirited debate erupted over the wisdom of an armed intervention to 'save South Africa from itself' as one agency head put it. Kapur indulged the group for ten minutes before raising her hand.

'I'm sorry, colleagues, but a decision on a political intervention does not rest with us. Our role is to support the Security Council so they can make an informed decision, and I have already briefed the president of the Security Council and given Dr Folbert's report to him. He has taken the decision to call an emergency meeting tomorrow to discuss this issue.'

New York Thursday 3 February

The rotating presidency of the United Nations Security Council was in the hands of India, which had been elected as one of the two non-permanent members representing the Asian region on the fifteen-member UNSC a year earlier. Ambassador Divesh Dutta occupied the hot seat.

In terms of the UN Charter, members of the UNSC must always be available to meet at any time. None of the Southern African nations were current members of the council – the three seats reserved for Africa were held by Nigeria, Tanzania and Morocco – but the three southern-African states were invited to attend since their countries were under discussion.

After brief formalities Dutta invited Folbert to brief the Council, and the head of the WHO ran through his presentation from the previous day.

Dutta then deferred to the South African Ambassador, Aaron Gumede, who loudly renewed his government's 'anger and dismay at the unilateral decision by the UN to withhold ARV supplies – an action which has directly precipitated the crisis which we are here today to discuss.' The ambassadors for Lesotho and Swaziland spoke in similar vein.

Dutta was ready for this, and delegates were handed a fat folder of supporting documents but, more convincingly, sat through a compilation of video interviews with doctors and AIDS patients who confirmed that they were unable to deliver, or receive, ARV treatment in public hospitals. The three ambassadors made no response to the presentations but put on a show of disbelief, shaking their heads and muttering among themselves.

Finally the UNSC president tabled a draft resolution, proposing the deployment of a peace-keeping force to protect public hospitals in the four countries from armed aggressors, and to ensure the resumption of ARV treatment, within a month.

'Ladies and gentlemen, we are not suggesting that these countries are politically unstable, and we have no plans to meddle in the functioning or sovereignty of those countries in any way. The proposed mandate allows for intervention solely in the delivery of public health service provision, and expires as soon as the situation has been stabilized.'

Dutta looked at the ambassadors from the three southern African countries before continuing.

'The draft resolution offers an incentive to the host countries – they will not be asked to recover or account for drugs which may have been… removed… from public dispensaries. Instead, hospitals protected by UN troops will be directly supplied with second-line ARVs. In this way we believe we can limit AIDS-related mortality and the collateral deaths to which Dr Folbert referred, to almost negligible levels.'

The Swazi ambassador, Thomas Dlamini, signaled his desire to respond and Dutta yielded to him.

'Mr President, although we appreciate the offer to supply ARVs to our public health facilities, we do not accept the need for foreign armed forces on our soil. I speak for all of our countries when I say if these drugs are supplied to our governments, we can guarantee that they will be distributed to all who need them.'

Dutta waited for a response, and the hands of several members were raised. He recognized the British Ambassador, Lord Winthrop.

'Mr President, we have just heard compelling evidence that the South African government, and those of Swaziland and Lesotho, are either unwilling or unable to distribute the ARVs they already have. Although I have great respect for my friend Mr Dlamini I would suggest that his government is simply not able to make good on his promise. The British government will vote in favor of this resolution, and issues an impassioned appeal to the governments of all three countries to give their full support to this initiative. It appears they have everything to gain, and nothing to lose.'

Winthrop was followed by Philip Grogan for the United States.

'We're also broadly in agreement with the resolution, Chair, although we would like to see a clause which acknowledges that UN supervised hospitals and clinics would be foreign territory, much like an embassy or UN mission, for the duration of the mandate.'

The three ambassadors from southern Africa make a show of their disapproval of this idea.

Chinese ambassador Weng Shung was next.

'Mr President, the People's Republic of China has great respect for the sovereignty of these three nations, and respects their decisions in all domestic matters. We offer our sympathies and support to them in overcoming the challenges they are facing, and we will not agree to the deployment of foreign forces on their soil without their express invitation. Until such an invitation is forthcoming, China will veto any attempt to impose the will of foreign nations on them.'

The unbridled joy of the three ambassadors was in stark counterpoint to the stunned silence in the rest of the room.

Istanbul Friday 4 February

The call that took me back to South Africa came from a regular stringer in Cape Town. Thami Abrahams was one of an embryonic group of citizen journalists who had acquired semi-official status as TWO correspondents. He wrote under the alias Whineman, a conflation of his occasional work as an wine-maker and his talent for reporting the 'whining' of politicians. He was very well placed to do so because Cape Town is the seat of his country's parliament, and he'd become a fixture in the public gallery and corridors of that institution, regularly unearthing stories that had eluded the old media.

'Hey Gipsy, I was thinking it's time for another tour of the winelands.' Thami was a great guide to the hundreds of wineries around Cape Town, and he'd introduced me to some of the best wines I'd tasted anywhere. And believe me, this is a hard thing for an Australian to admit.

'Any excuse will do, BT!' Everyone called him BT, for Bra – or 'brother' – Thami. It stuck from his schooldays. 'So what's yours?'

'Oh that's easy. Wine is the only thing that takes away the pain of seeing my country coming apart at the seams.' There was an undercurrent of real pain in his voice.

'BT, are you alright?'

'Ja, Gipsy. It's no use complaining – nobody listens. But seriously, I think you should come and visit us, if you can. Something really big is about to happen.'

'Shouldn't you be telling Gheorghe? Or Enoch?'

'No, this is for you.'

'And I guess it has nothing to do with wine?'

A tiny pause. I couldn't see his face, but I knew he wasn't laughing. Then quite softly: 'No, this is really serious, Gipsy…'

'BT, you know how I love your part of the world, and even that dreadful stuff which passes for wine down there…'

'It's linked to pharmageddon.'

'Ah.' Actually, I was itching to see for myself what was going on in South Africa since they rejected the UN offer of a supervised reintroduction of second-line ARVs. But there was the small matter of my spat with the honorable minister of health, which had been churned over endlessly on our forums.

'Is Colin Makeba in Cape Town?'

'No, parliament isn't in session. All the ministers are at one of their strategy meetings at some luxury resort. You don't have to worry about him – I can promise you that.'

'I'd love to know how you can make a promise like that, BT.'

'You'll understand when you get here. This is… very sensitive, so I can't tell you more. Not even a hint. But if you can get here within 72 hours you'll see it for yourself. It won't be a wasted trip.'

'Okay BT, let me see what I can do. I'll get back to you.'

Cape Town Sunday 6 February

The approach to Cape Town International Airport is one of my favorite landings anywhere.

Twenty minutes before landing, the watercolor smears of the Karoo desert give way to a series of arid gray mountains and brilliant green valleys, decorated by vineyards and fruit orchards. On a clear day you can see vast wheat-fields stretching off to the north, filling the plain between the mountains and the icy blue Atlantic.

Passengers on the right of the plane, which by now is gliding silently to lose altitude, are treated to a view of Paarl mountain – the second largest granite outcrop in the world, named by the early settlers for the pearl it imitates when the light catches it at the right angle – while those on the left look over the green patchwork of the Franschhoek valley which holds not only some of the most expensive farmland in the country but also the Wemmershoek prison, from where Nelson Mandela was finally released.

A moment more and these pastoral scenes are yanked away and replaced by streets, houses and malls, and the Airbus banks hard left on final approach to the airport. But the left turn means passengers on the left are treated to a view of the university town of Stellenbosch, which is also the hub of the wine industry, while those on the right hit the jackpot – the sudden unveiling of Table Mountain and the great city and harbor cradled in its outflung arms which, until now, had only been visible to the pilots. There's nothing like it.

Whineman was waiting for me, looking a bit tense. He wasted no time in getting me to his battered 3-series BMW, and out of the airport complex. He avoided the freeway which could have taken us either west to Table Mountain and the city, or east to Stellenbosch and the winelands, but instead headed south and into a maze of small homes.

'Is everything OK, BT? Somebody chasing us?'

He chuckled. 'Ag no, Gipsy. It's just… a busy time. I want you to meet some people.'

'Some of your gangster friends?' When we'd last met, BT told me about his childhood in the badlands south of the airport, and how many of his friends were drawn into the violent gangs which ruled them.

He smiled, a little tightly. This was definitely not the Thami I knew, but I couldn't decide whether he was frightened, angry or excited.

'Ja, you could say that. But these are political gangsters, not drug dealers.'

He focused on driving, and I thought back to the wonderful day we spent touring some of the region's wineries, a few months earlier. In between teaching me about Cape wines he'd told me about the ethnic schisms which divide and define his country, and about his own group – the so-called colored people – who were forcibly removed by the apartheid government from their homes in the embrace of Table Mountain, and moved to the wind-swept flats around the present-day airport.

He explained that the coloreds, like the mestizos of Latin America, bore the genetic imprint of pretty much everyone who passed this way – the indigenous Khoikhoi or Bushmen, the early Dutch settlers, the slaves they imported from Malaysia and Indonesia in the 17th century, and the Bantu who migrated south in the past couple of centuries.

Unfortunately alcohol and drugs established a strong foothold in his community, spawning gangs and druglords. I'd seen something similar in the Caribbean, where many of the wealthiest members of society would be hard-pressed to explain their affluence, if anyone dared ask.

BT told me that, 'on the flats', every young man faced a critical decision – to go straight, or to go easy. Unfortunately either could end with a bullet, because the suburbs we were heading into were some of the most violent places on earth.

After a few minutes BT stopped his BMW outside a little house, in a row of others exactly like it. As we reached the front door it was thrown open by a huge man dressed in a black suit. At first I took him for a bodyguard or gang-boss, but then I saw the dog-collar of a Christian cleric hidden between the folds of his chin. Without a sound the giant grabbed BT in what looked like a wrestling hold, then just as suddenly let him go and turned to me. Just as I was deciding whether to run or surrender, a rather flushed BT introduced me.

'This is Dr Gipsy North, from The World Online.'

Goliath's face dropped into a look of mock amazement. 'Are you kidding me? THIS is the famous Dr Gipsy North?'

Before I could ask the giant what he was expecting, he loomed over me and I braced myself for the crunching of bones but he merely held his right hand out to me, palm upward. I didn't see any thorns that I could remove in order to save my life, but when I took his hand to shake he leaned forward with surprising grace and gently kissed my hand. I curtseyed, silently thanking the nuns for giving me at least one useful skill.

'Gipsy, any friend of Shan Gupta is... very welcome here.' The subscript was 'you're very safe here', which suited me just fine. I wanted this man on my side.

'Thank you... reverend?'

He reared back and turned again to BT who was grinning at this little pantomime, and looking a lot more like the old Thami Abrahams I knew. But then the mother of all fathers grabbed him again and pretended to bash his head in.

'Have. I. Taught. You. No. Manners? You forgot. To. Introduce me. To. The lady!'

Once more disentangled, but with his hair and clothing looking like he'd been set upon by a pack of cocker spaniels, BT completed his task.

'Gipsy, may I present the Reverend Dr William Abrahams, the chairman of the Cape Colored Alliance. And my big brother.'

BT told me later their school-teacher father died of TB when he was still a baby, and his mother followed suit – of alcoholic liver disease – a few days before his tenth birthday. He was taken in by his older half brother, Billy, who had been 'set free' by his own mother when he turned 16, and was making a living as a night-club bouncer, among other things. When BT's schooling was over he went to work as an apprentice wine-maker, and Billy announced he was enrolling at a catholic seminary.

Inside Billy's tiny living room I was introduced to a small gathering of men and women, all of whom seemed genuinely pleased to meet me. It transpired many of them had been involved in AIDS activism, working closely with the legendary Zachie Achmat of the Treatment Action Campaign, which had done so much to break down government resistance to antiretroviral treatment in South Africa.

Once the introductions were done, I tried to find out what BT was being so secretive about. 'So how are people making out here in the Cape? I mean in terms of ARVs?'

BT's mountainous brother was clearly the leader of this genteel gang, because everyone waited for him to answer.

'Gipsy, we're doing much better than the rest of the country. It's true the cops grabbed the ARVs out of our hospitals, but they only did it because we asked them to. To keep them away from the gangs. But they are keeping the clinics supplied, and nobody in this province is going without ARVs.'

'Nobody?'

He looked me in the eye. 'Everyone who was getting ARVs before, is getting them now. There's no treatment interruption in the Cape.'

I was amazed that BT hadn't written a word about this. But then I realized he would have been crazy to say anything – it would have been an invitation to… well, hang on a sec! If the cops were in on it, what about the politicians? I asked.

'We're all on the same side here, Gipsy.'

'Then… I'm confused.' I looked over at BT, who was looking just a touch pleased with himself.

'It's like Billy says, Gipsy. The local politicians are working with us, so are our cops. But if I'd written anything about this – if any of the media had – Pretoria would be all over us, trying to get us to hand over our ARVs. They must know that treatment is carrying on here, but they don't want people in the rest of the country to hear about it because it would make them look bad.'

'And a lot of people would come here to get treatment, I suppose?' It seemed like an obvious thing to say but, judging from the reaction in the group, it was a direct hit.

'It's just a matter of time before they come, Gipsy.' Billy's voice sounded like it was coming out of a deep cave. He must have delivered a sensational sermon. 'As soon as it becomes public knowledge that there are ARVs in Cape Town, we will be swamped.'

I had a lot of questions, and they had a lot of answers. The Western Cape province – known to all as 'the Cape' – had always been different to the rest of the country. It had a different climate, different landscape, and a much more cosmopolitan feel to it. The ethnic makeup of the Cape was also different, with a little over half its people being colored, against the 80 percent dominance of Africans in the rest of the country.

The Cape was the only one of South Africa's nine semi-autonomous provinces which was not controlled by the African National Congress – and it also had by far the lowest HIV prevalence, and by far the best response to the epidemic.

The Cape Colored Alliance turned out to be a bit like the Freemasons – a low-profile association of influential people, looking after each other. Since 'each other' meant the majority of the people of the Cape, this also meant looking after their province. Their influence was exercised through every facet of government service, the political parties, churches, trade unions, business and, as I had just learned, the media. I was left in no doubt that, in this part of the world, these men and women called the shots.

When BT heard of the looting of ARVs, he told Billy, who got on the phone to the police. His next calls were to the five men who controlled the drug-trade in the province.

'I told them – these are the Lord's drugs. They are out of bounds. I may have said a few other things. They listened.' His audience chuckled, the way that powerful people do.

'Then we told every doctor and nurse at every clinic to issue only a week's worth of ARVs at a time, so they don't have a lot of drugs lying around, and we also told them to tell their patients to say nothing to anyone about these ARVs. We said – if you tell anyone, we'll find out, and next week there will be nothing for you.'

'Has it worked?'

He shrugged. 'Ja, kind of. People whisper, you know. But they know it's a secret, so it hasn't got too far. The other thing we did was to go looking for suppliers of ARVs. The one thing that you can't teach any Capey is how to get drugs!'

This time the group erupted in laughter, and it seemed to be a cue to hand out a fresh round of beers, which were very welcome in the stifling heat of the tiny sitting room. I guessed it was a kind of compliment that I hadn't been asked if I wanted my frosty in a glass.

'So, Billy, are you getting fresh supplies of ARVs right now?'

'No, not yet. We could get stolen drugs but we turned those down. These are the Lord's drugs – we don't want to buy them from the devil. We've been talking to the drug manufacturers, and to some international organizations, just so they know we aren't in the same boat as the rest of the country.'

I could see he didn't want to be drawn on the exact details, but I felt sure he was talking about the UN. I made a note to check with Nikki.

'So how long can you last without fresh supplies?'

'About one more month. The private hospitals and pharmacies are working with us. Like I said, we're all on the same side.'

'This is just wonderful, Billy. But… I'm wondering why you invited me here. You obviously don't want me to write about this.'

Billy looked over at his brother with pride. 'Well done, boetie. You really didn't tell her anything.' BT beamed and Billy turned back to me.

'No Gipsy, we want you to witness and write about something else.'

I noticed the group was very still, all staring at me. I looked back at Billy. 'Let's hear it.'

'Tomorrow night we're going to close our borders with the rest of the country.'

'You're… what?'

'We're going to declare our independence from South Africa. We're going to secede.'

I'm glad now that I couldn't see myself. I must have looked like a nut case, just staring at Billy and the others. Wouldn't be surprised if my mouth was open. Oh god. I remember wondering why they invited me to hear this? I mean, it wasn't medical – this was major-league politics. Georghe would sell his mother to be here.

I must have said something, but all I remember is that BT described how they had canvassed the various political parties in the province, the police, the military, the hospitals, and had been amazed to find how receptive they all were to the idea. What sounded at first like a joke rapidly morphed into an inevitability. But everyone knew they had to move fast, or not at all.

Logistically it was not difficult. Most of the Cape is shielded from the rest of the country by a great arc of mountains – the same ones I'd admired earlier from the aircraft. Physically isolating the province meant cutting off a handful of road- and rail-passes over those mountains, as well as the roads along the narrow coastal plains to the east and north. Air and sea ports were easily controlled, especially since the chief of the navy – based at Simonstown – was a co-conspirator, as was the commander of the local air-force base at Langebaan.

They did not foresee a military response from the Pretoria-based government – at least not in the short-term. I drew a round of guffaws at the mere idea that anything could happen quickly. However, in time, an armed response of some kind was inevitable, as all the implications of the move sank in.

I was surprised to find that BT was doing most of the talking, and it dawned on me that his monumental brother may have the authority, but Whineman was the brains of the outfit.

'Our trump-card is the navy. We have four frigates in Simonstown, and they have 76mm guns which can stop tanks on either of the coastal approaches. And we can easily defend or sabotage the passes through the mountains.

'What about the airforce?' I didn't expect what seemed like a perfectly logical question to trigger a round of head-shaking and sneers from the group. BT looked embarrassed, but Billy silenced the others with a wave of his hand.

'Ag, I'm sorry Gipsy. It's a good question. I'm not sure if you know about the Gripen fighters our government bought? With the same money we could have introduced ARVs five years earlier. Well, we're laughing because there's nobody to fly those planes. The air-force doesn't have any pilots qualified to fly them – only three guys who are certified to train pilots but, guess what – all three are here in the Cape!' This time I joined in the laughter.

I could see BT was looking at his watch and trying to catch his brother's eye. Finally he did so and tapped the dial. Billy reacted immediately.

'Gipsy, we have to go to meeting. Final arrangements for tomorrow. We'll drop you off at the Mount Nelson and pick you up around noon tomorrow. Then we're driving up to a place called Three Sisters, in the Karoo. That's where history will be made.'

From Billy's little home in Manenberg, the Abrahams brothers drove me around the side of Table Mountain, pointing out landmarks as though we were out for a Sunday drive. We passed the hospital where the world's first heart transplant took place, and got a bird's eye view over the city, harbor and, out in Table Bay, the little island which had been home to Nelson Mandela for 27 years. A couple of minutes later they dropped me off at the Mount Nelson Hotel, a grand old pink landmark.

I was waiting for one of the brothers to ask me not to breathe a word of their plans, but they didn't. They didn't have to.

Three Sisters, Monday 7 February

Driving through the Karoo reminded me of the Australian outback. In the main city of Beaufort West the only thing I saw up close was the bathroom in a gas station – an urgent necessity after a six-hour drive from Cape Town. When I emerged BT and Billy were waiting at the car with a bucket of fried chicken, French fries and coke. My last meal was brunch at the Mount Nelson, eight hours earlier, so I suspended my usual resistance to force-fed fowl, re-heated oil and sugar-water, and tucked in while they told me that the doctor who conducted the first heart transplant at the hospital we passed yesterday was born right here.

An hour or so later, just as the sun was setting behind us, we turned onto an unmarked gravel road. A couple of hundred meters further on, hidden from the highway by a small hill, we found a group of military and police vehicles. A soldier carrying an automatic rifle flagged us down but, after a short exchange we were waved on and BT parked his BMW next to a large trailer, which turned out to be the command centre, where we were greeted with minimal formality.

Billy took a moment to introduce me to the officer in charge – an army major who was all business. The man greeted me civilly but I could see his mind was on the task at hand as he ushered us into the trailer which, blessedly, was air-conditioned. Inside we found two more men, one a provincial traffic policeman and the other an officer in the regular police service. Both seemed to have a lot of gold braid on their uniforms. Introductions over, the army major launched forth in Afrikaans but, at a word from Billy, switched mid-sentence to English.

'…so I said anyone who has a problem with what we are doing here can leave.'

'Did any go?' Billy asked.

The major remained deadpan. 'No, I told them if they wanted to go, they'd have to stay on the northern side of the border after we close it.'

The men snorted appreciatively, and the major continued.

'But they want to know how much force they must use… to stop people getting through.'

Billy responded immediately. 'No killing. Under no circumstances. Even if we get fired on. And don't shoot out their tires or do anything to disable their cars – they have to be able to turn around and go back to Colesberg. The word from Cape Town is to use the Casspirs as a barrier and a show of force.'

One of the cops spoke up. 'Reverend, you know that we'll all have to disobey direct orders – from Pretoria?'

'We've been through that, director…'

'Ja, I know, and I'm not arguing. My question is – what do we say to other officers who come from Colesberg or Bloemfontein and demand that we stand down?'

'The provincial commissioner raised that last night. The decision was for each force to say they are just supporting the others. So you refer any police to the major here, and he refers any army guys to you. You all say you are acting on orders from Cape Town, and that you can't make a decision here – their chiefs in Pretoria must sort it out with your chiefs in Cape Town.'

The men seemed okay with that – I guessed that buck-passing was old hat to them. The discussion dragged on, and soon slipped back into Afrikaans. After a while I caught BT's eye and gestured that I was going outside.

The night was warm, pitch black, and dripping with the smell of charred animals. I followed my nose and found thirty or so young men standing around a barbecue, with a single gas lantern providing the shadows. Somebody saw me coming and the group fell silent, then a guy in a police uniform of some kind came over to me.

'Good evening, ma'am. Do you want something to eat?'

'Thanks – but I was hoping somebody would offer me a drink.'

'Hey, are you Australian?'

I knew what was coming next, so I tried to dodge the bullet. 'Yeah, but a very bad one – I don't follow rugby or cricket…' In Oz this would be no laughing matter, but here it seemed to melt the ice.

Unfortunately there were no beers on offer but I was handed an icy can of grape juice and the guys started quizzing me about my home country. They seemed disappointed when I said I hadn't lived in Oz for nearly 20 years, but they soon got over it and asked instead about my work. It was interesting to discover that, out of a collection of army grunts and two flavors of cop, gathered in the middle of the desert at the bottom of Africa, all but one knew and used The World Online. It was equally interesting that not one of these men volunteered the reason they were here, or asked why I was there. Actually, I wasn't entirely sure myself.

After a while BT and Billy joined us, along with the officers, and the burned offerings were duly consumed. Fortunately there were some potatoes and corn on the cob, which were pretty good. I was trying to eat them off a paper plate when I was approached by a young man in army uniform.

'Dr North, I am Corporal Eric Zondi. I'm... a big follower of TWO.' He glanced around to see if anyone else was listening. 'I'm Jimmy9,' he murmured.

I get this all the time. TWO stringers come up to me and introduce themselves as though they are long-lost friends. The truth is that it's nearly always impossible to remember anything they've posted – but this time I did.

'Of course, Jimmy... I mean, Eric. I look out for your posts.'

I wasn't flattering him – he'd posted many stories about AIDS in the military, specifically the systematic victimization of HIV positive soldiers, in an attempt to drive them out of the force. All this bigotry achieved, of course, was to discourage others from being tested for the virus, and to force those who knew they were infected to say nothing, which is a far more dangerous situation than having them out in the open and treated. Jimmy9 exposed the truth in a series of posts which, although they needed quite a bit of editing, were detailed and compelling. I was pretty sure the army would love to find out who he was.

'Could I ask for your autograph, doctor?' He pulled out a copy of one of our print editions, and I remembered that I had included quotes from his posts in that issue.

'I'd be delighted, Eric. And please call me Gipsy. Would you like me to inscribe it to Eric, or Jimmy9?'

He looked around again. 'No, definitely Eric. We... don't get much privacy.'

I took the magazine, moved into the light coming from the trailer, and wrote above my – rather flattering – picture: 'To Eric, a fellow witness to history, with warm regards, Gipsy North.'

He took the magazine and read the inscription, his face wrinkled with doubt. 'But... if anyone sees this...'

'Eric, do you know what's happening tonight?'

'Ja, sure.' Suddenly his face cleared. 'Oh, right, I see. You mean tonight is history.'

'How do you feel about what you're doing here?'

'It's about time,' he said earnestly.

'Aren't you worried? About what the rest of the country might do?'

He shrugged. 'Ja, maybe. But life is cheap in South Africa. At least this makes it interesting.'

'Eric, there must be lots of your mates who support the Pretoria government. How will they feel about this?'

He looked at me a little surprised. 'But doc... Gipsy... I support the government. I grew up in an ANC family, my uncle is a member of the provincial parliament. But... this is different. This is about survival. What they're doing in Pretoria... it makes no sense.'

I remembered now just how clear-sighted his posts to TWO were, and told him so. I was sure I could see him beaming in the darkness.

'Eric, I hope you will write about tonight, and what happens after today... from the heart. I'll arrange to have you upgraded so you get some more of our magic string. If you like?'

The last bit was meant as a joke – who wouldn't like more stringettes? But he didn't laugh.

'Thank you... Gipsy. I wish I could buy more. Our rand will be worth nothing before long.'

It hadn't occurred to me to wonder what tonight's events would do to the already battered South African currency, but I realized now that our stringettes – which were pegged against the Euro – would be a great hedge. I made a note to ask BT how they planned to insulate an autonomous Cape against the financial collapse in the rest of the country. I felt sure he had an answer.

But when I did link up again with BT we got talking about military strategy instead.

'It's all about bluff, really. We're counting on people not wanting to hang around in the desert, in the middle of summer. But if they get serious about breaking down the roadblock we'll fall back to Beaufort West and blow up a couple of bridges. That'll slow them down a bit...'

'And if they keep coming?'

He shook his head. 'If they keep coming, we can't stop them. But the mountains can.'

'Which means sacrificing the Karoo?'

'Ja. It may come to that.'

'And the coastal routes?'

'No, like I said yesterday, we have the navy. And they have fucking big guns. We're hoping Pretoria will think very hard about taking them on. But... Gipsy, the truth is we're counting on them to wimp out. We're doing this thing to save lives – we don't want to start a war, which will end up killing a lot of people.'

Suddenly I knew why I was here. 'You want to know what I think will happen...' I said it under my breath, as the thought occurred, but I saw the confirmation written over BT's face, in the stark light of the gas lantern.

'Gipsy, we're committed to this. We think South Africa... South Africans... are going to turn against each other. But, if we're wrong, they'll turn on us. It's... a huge gamble. It all depends on the epidemic, and there's nobody who has a better perspective on AIDS than you.'

Still the question was unasked, but I thought I'd take a stab at it anyway.

'So it's all in the timing? Go too soon, and everyone will think you're crazy – including the people whose support you're counting on. Go too late, and you'll be swamped by people trying to get your ARVs, and there'll be nothing to protect?'

He nodded gravely. 'Exactly. So… how good is our timing?'

'Mmm, my sense is that you're in a kind of… calm before the storm. Most people are still hoping the rumors were right – that ARVs weren't helping, or were making things worse.'

'But… in the Cape we heard those same rumors, yet everyone is still taking their ARVs.'

'Yeah. So you're all waiting to hear whether patients who can't get their medications are going to die.'

BT's face was a picture of conflicting emotions. 'And are they?'

I thought back to my call to Miu Andersson at UNICEF last night. She'd been collecting unofficial data from her contacts in government hospitals, which pointed to a doubling of AIDS-related mortality every three weeks. But the actual numbers were still small, which meant the trend wouldn't be obvious to anyone who didn't have the figures. At least not yet.

'BT, I'd say you've got your timing just about right.'

He stared off into the blackness. Overhead the stars were brilliant. The sounds of the highway were muted behind the hill.

'Fuck, Gipsy, I can't believe we're gambling on… so many deaths. How did we get to this?'

***

At one in the morning the major ordered his sergeant to muster the men, and ten minutes later the vehicles were moving. It took only a few minutes to reach the highway, and a few more to a kind of picnic spot, where the road was wide enough for articulated trucks to turn around.

Approaching traffic would be alerted by police signs, then they'd see army troops with automatic weapons, and armored trucks drawn across the road. Generator-powered floodlights cast a brilliant light over the scene.

Although the scene would have panicked me, I learned that roadblocks like this were not unusual on this road, looking for traffic violations and contraband. This explained why the drivers of the first few trucks to arrive – there were very few cars at this time of night – looked relieved when they were simply told to turn around and go back because there 'was a problem on the road'.

The acid test soon arrived in the form of a minibus taxi. These 15-seaters are the mainstay of public transport in South Africa, and their drivers' tempers and bad driving are legendary. Their passengers, too, were not likely to be indifferent to the news that they couldn't get to their destination. However the sight of armed soldiers and the refusal of a traffic official to enter into discussion sent the first few back the way they had come. I noticed BT was taking video with his pocket camera.

I cornered Billy and BT. 'So what's the deal here, guys? When are we going to tell the world?'

Billy chuckled deep in his chest. 'Whenever you're ready, Gipsy! We want everyone to know. My boetie has written some stuff on what's happening here, but we're counting on you for the analysis.'

We moved back to their car where I checked over Whineman's carefully crafted story. I'd been working on one of my own at the Mount Nelson and in the car, so we were ready to roll. I hated to wake Jim at this ungodly hour but I knew he'd give me a mauling if I didn't, so I called him first, then Nerisha, so she could kick our stringers and researchers into gear.

Inside half an hour the world knew that South Africa – in a political sense at least – was coming apart at the seams.

The night became more interesting as frustrated motorists gathered in the darkness beyond our floodlights. After a while it occurred to me to wonder why no vehicles were approaching from the Cape Town side, and BT explained they were being turned back at Beaufort West, creating a no-man's land about 100 kilometers wide.

I could see the junta, as I thought of the field commanders of the three forces, watching the situation closely, but they weren't looking too worried. I walked over and asked what they thought would happen next. The major responded.

'We think they'll hang around until they hear the news on their radios. Then my guess is they'll head back north, to Colesberg or Bloemfontein. They may come over here and try a bit of begging and pleading – it won't get them anywhere.'

'And you're not worried about any kind of violence.'

'Ag no, ma'am. I've got a couple of heavy machine guns mounted up there...' he gestured to the top of the armored trucks, 'and they make a hell of a noise. If we even see a gun we'll fire off a few rounds into the desert, just to give them a fright... they'll shit in their pants.'

But it didn't come to that – at this road-block, or the other three which had been set up at the same time. By dawn there were no vehicles in sight, and we heard the traffic police were turning south-bound traffic back near Colesberg.

At 6am the news on radio and TV led with an interview with the premier of the Western Cape, saying the political parties had formed an alliance with the backing of the armed forces to 'isolate' the province for a period of one month.

'I wish to assure the nation that we did not take this step lightly, and we understand that it will have an impact on the national economy, and will disrupt many lives, and we apologize in advance for this. However we believe this step is necessary until we can negotiate an agreement with the other provinces on the movement of people, and secure guarantees that our provincial assets will not be confiscated by the national government, in the same way as they have confiscated life-saving drugs in their hospitals.'

The newscast included a clip from the national president, saying that there was obviously some kind of misunderstanding somewhere, and it was only a matter of time until it was sorted out. A bemused political analyst implied the whole thing was absurd.

Washington DC Wednesday 9 February

'Colonel, it seems like you've spent the past month chasing wild geese.' Baldwin didn't hear a question, so he didn't respond. The deputy director didn't look like he wanted an answer, either.

'You should know that I've received a note from the commander in chief of the Indian armed forces regarding your little operation in the Himalayas. He mentioned the fact that you tied up a company of Black Cats for the best part of a month, along with their radar imaging satellite, and kept a significant chunk of their military assets in that particular region on high alert.'

Baldwin was ready for the worst. He couldn't think of anything he would do differently if the same situation arose again, but the director of national intelligence was famous for expecting – and delivering – results, and his deputy danced to the same tune. Baldwin doubted that he'd be taken back into army intelligence, after this. Still, there was his brother-in-law's standing offer of a place in his home security company in Los Angeles. Some sunshine would be nice.

Then, unexpectedly, the director's expression softened.

'Fortunately the Indians were pretty gung-ho about the whole thing. Said it was a useful exercise, and they were impressed by your ability to cut through the administrative crap in their own backyard, and work with their people on the sting operation. Said he wished all military liaison wallahs were as easy to work with.'

Baldwin realized he'd been holding his breath. 'Thank you, sir.'

'Actually I called you in here to thank you, Art. I found the think-pieces you sent me very useful – they helped me to stay ahead of the agencies. Gotta do some butt kicking – seems like they don't have an original thought between them. This idea of yours may not have worked out, but it was a good one, and it made some good medicine with the Indians.'

'Thank you sir!' Baldwin wasn't planning to tell the director that most of what he'd written was a rehash of the ideas he found on TWO's pharmageddon forums. It was legitimate research, after all.

'Looking to the future, Art, I share your sense that, whatever happens next, it'll involve the UN. So I want you to get your head as far up their fat backsides as you can, and...' the man seemed to lose track of his own analogy.

'Keep my ear to the ground, sir?'

The image was so absurd that the deputy director lost his stony façade completely, and bellowed with laughter – a shocking sound closer to a scream than a guffaw. Baldwin half expected homeland security agents to burst in, guns drawn. But either they'd heard the deputy laughing before, or the room was soundproof, or they hoped that someone had stuck a knife in him at last.

'You go to it, Art! And keep me in the loop, 24/7, d'y'hear?'

Baldwin thought of asking the director whether he said to keep him in the 'poop' but thought better of it. No point pushing your luck.

'Aye sir.'

New York Friday 11 February

'Weng, you are of course aware of the recent events in South Africa?'

The Indian and Chinese ambassadors were having lunch at UN Plaza – a not infrequent occurrence, since both men had served as their countries' representatives at the UN for many years, and considered each other as friends.

In fact this friendship was widely regarded as one of the most important in the world, informally settling countless minor border incidents and facilitating the increasingly broad river of trade between the world's two most populous nations. Both governments used their friendship as a point of informal first contact. However their regular lunches had been somewhat strained since Weng's unexpected veto of the resolution for armed intervention in southern Africa, which had been supported by India.

The portly Weng swallowed his food and dabbed his lips with a napkin before answering Duttta. 'Are you referring to the secession of their Western Cape province?'

'Yes. Do you think it might be an opportunity to revisit the issue of a peacekeeping force in that country?'

'Divesh my friend, you know my government has committed itself to support the Pretoria government on this issue…'

'Of course, and I respect that. But I was wondering whether the secession issue may not pose a window of opportunity?'

'How so?'

'What if we propose the use of a peacekeeping force to resolve the secession issue? It is clear the secessionists are expecting some kind of military response to their move, and are prepared to respond in kind. This cannot be a good thing for South Africa.'

'I agree. But what role would a UN peacekeeping force play?'

'The underlying reason for the secession is the fact that the Cape is continuing to treat AIDS patients, and they fear a massive inflow of people who cannot get these drugs in the other provinces. But as you know the Pretoria government says ARV treatment is continuing – despite evidence to the contrary – and that there is no basis for this fear.'

'Yes, I understand their respective positions...'

'What if UN peacekeepers were to establish posts at the points of entry to the Cape province, and test everyone seeking to cross the border for HIV infection? They could allow those who test negative to pass through the border, and they could provide treatment to those who are positive.'

Weng stared thoughtfully at his Indian counterpart. Slowly his expression changed to a smile.

'Ah my friend, I am sure you have Chinese ancestry.'

Dutta inclined his head. 'From you, that is high praise, excellency. The question is whether you will be able to sell this to Beijing.'

'No, I think the question is whether you could sell it to Pretoria. If they have no objection, I can hardly imagine that my government will stand in their way.'

New York, Monday 14 February

'So these treatment camps... what would they look like?' South African ambassador Aaron Gumede was sprawled on the sofa in Dutta's office, his foot tapping to an internal beat.

'Tented encampments, run and provisioned by the UN, monitored by your government. When citizens ask for treatment, we will interview them in the presence of your monitors to find out why they cannot get ARVs from their local hospital or clinic. Your people can use this information to address any problems that may exist in your treatment program.'

'But I don't understand why they will be located at the entry points to the Western Cape.'

'Because they will not only treat people with AIDS, but will allow those who are not infected to pass through the border, which will allow normal trade and travel to resume. Perhaps this is all the people in Cape Town need, and they will drop this talk of secession.'

Gumede's expression was neutral. 'Divesh, why involve the UN? Why don't I suggest to my government that we set up these camps ourselves?'

'There's nothing preventing you from doing so of course, Aaron, but it will only work if both sides trust whoever is running the camps. If you send armed people to set up camps on their borders, they may interpret it differently.'

Gumede looked thoughtful. 'What if your... these camps are swamped by people demanding treatment? I mean, like any democracy we have opposition groupings who would not hesitate to exploit an opportunity like this to make my government look bad.'

'Ah, but all they would do is make themselves look bad. Everyone asking for treatment will, of course, be tested – for HIV infection, for viral load, and for drug resistance. Any attempt at... gerrymandering... will soon be uncovered.'

'And if a large number of genuine AIDS patients do turn up? I mean, they may think they will get better quality drugs from you than they do from our own hospitals.'

It was Dutta's turn to look thoughtful. 'I suppose that is a possibility, but it seems improbable that many thousands will undertake a long and expensive journey if they are medically stable.'

'Unfortunately we have a lot of poor people in South Africa. What will you do if they turn up at your camps, looking for food and shelter?'

'If they don't need treatment for AIDS, we will turn them away. We will only allow people to stay until they are stable, and can be sure that their treatment will continue when they get home.'

'But Divesh, what if they cannot be persuaded of this? Why can't you simply give them, say, a year's supply of drugs and send them home?'

Dutta knew his counterpart was fully aware that the life expectancy of someone leaving a treatment camp with a year's supply of ARVs would be very short.

'I don't think that idea would fly in the security council, Aaron.'

But Gumede wasn't finished. 'Maybe, but I can't see why these camps should be overseen by armed peacekeepers? Surely they should be run by the World Health Organization?'

'Ah, but we are dealing with perceptions as much as reality. And the perception is that your armed forces – your police – are responsible for denying ARVs to the general public…'

Gumede pulled himself upright on the sofa, shaking his head, and Dutta felt the deal slipping away.

'Aaron, I'm not taking sides on this. This plan is designed to reassure everyone… to play a constructive role in overcoming your problems. The WHO are afraid that men with guns – police, army, gangsters, whoever – will try to take their ARVs. The only way they will buy into this proposal is if the camps are recognized by your government as international territory, and defended by a neutral army, just like an embassy or UN building.'

Gumede shook his head slowly, but the interest was still in his eyes. 'Eish, they won't like this in Pretoria. How will it resolve the secession issue?'

'Well, it could go one of two ways. One is that very few people present themselves for treatment, proving that the Cape leaders have nothing to fear. The other is that many people turn up, giving your government the information you need to identify and fix any… bottlenecks in your ARV delivery systems. Either way, we remove the concern which led to this secession.'

Gumede was now nodding slowly, and Dutta pressed home his advantage.

'I can't imagine that anyone will want to live in a tent, in the desert, at the height of summer, when there's nothing stopping them going home.

We'd be happy to pay for transport to send these people home, once they are assured they will get treatment when they arrive.'

Gumede was on his feet now, pacing absent mindedly. 'If... hypothetically... we were to go ahead with your idea, we would insist on time limits.'

'What did you have in mind?'

'A month, two at the most?'

'Aaron, I'm sure you'd agree that any conditions must promote the chances of success. If very few people present for treatment, but we close down the camps too soon, the Cape will say it wasn't given a fair chance. If a lot of people arrive, it will take time for you to take corrective action so they are willing to go home.'

Gumede pursed his lips. 'How long are you suggesting?'

'I'd suggest a review date of six months from the day the camps open. If all three parties agree, then we close them down. After nine months if any two parties agree, the camps will be closed. After a year the camps will be closed unless any two parties disagree.'

'Divesh, this is a hard sell, but I'll see what my government says. Will you present these ideas to the Cape people and let me know how they react?'

The last thing Dutta wanted Gumede to know was that the plan actually came from the secessionists, specifically the fertile mind of Thami Abrahams. Instead he nodded sagely.

'Of course I will.'

New York Thursday 17 February

'Ladies and gentlemen, you have all been briefed on the negotiations between the secessionist alliance of the Cape and the government of South Africa. I'm deeply gratified to inform you that today, thanks to the far sightedness of both parties, we have an agreement to establish four treatment camps at the main entry points into the Western Cape province.'

The members of the Security Council nodded and smiled – this much they knew from the briefing papers they'd received before this special meeting. But Dutta wasn't finished.

'I must also advise you that we have received representations from the governments of Namibia, Botswana, Zimbabwe and Mozambique for similar camps to be set up on their borders with South Africa, in order to avoid an influx of people seeking medical treatment.' Suddenly the room was very still.

'These countries asked me to treat our negotiations in the strictest confidence, until they were concluded. I am delighted to advise that the South African government has agreed to a further six treatment camps near the main border posts to those countries.'

The surprise around the chamber was replaced by spontaneous applause, much of which was directed towards ambassador Gumede – who looked like a man receiving an oscar at the academy awards. When the applause had died down, the Chinese ambassador indicated his desire to respond.

'Mr president, I know I speak for the entire council when I offer my congratulations to you for this extraordinary accomplishment. You have reminded us, sir, of the rationale behind the establishment of the United Nations, and in particular this honorable council.'

Without a further word Weng rose heavily to his feet and began to clap slowly. In a moment the entire council followed suit, including the ambassadors for all the southern African nations. Dutta was embarrassed to find tears welling in his eyes. He raised his hands and gestured for everyone to sit, but it took several moments before they complied. His voice hoarse, the president of the security council continued.

'Thank you, from the bottom of my heart. However I beg you to recognize that this historic agreement is not the work of one person.' He briefly outlined some of the process that had led to the agreement and the contribution of key players – particularly the secretary general and the heads of the WHO and other UN agencies.

What Dutta did not say is that the UN had compiled damning video evidence of the collapse of ARV treatment in South Africa, and the government's failure to respond. When they came back to say they were not in favor of the security council proposal, Dutta showed him the video, and gave him a copy to send home. Gumede did not need to be told his government's choice was between public acclaim for approving the treatment camps, or watching these videos on prime time television and, very possibly, at The Hague when they were called to account for crimes against humanity.

As he finished sharing the credit, Dutta saw the hands of several more ambassadors raised, but he raised both of his own, palms outward, to indicate he had more to say.

'Before I recognize other members of this honorable council, I'd like to brief you on another agreement, or perhaps it should be described as an offer, which relates to the matter before us. My own government – the Government of India – has a special relationship with South Africa. Some members may not be aware that the largest population of Indians outside of India lives in South Africa, or that the social conscience of our founding father, Mohandas Karamchand Gandhi, was awakened in South Africa more than a century ago. And of course we are deeply troubled by the fact that the seeds of this crisis were sown by acts of sabotage in our country.'

Dutta could see he had the complete attention of the members.

'For these reasons I am authorized by my government to offer the services of the Indian army to establish and protect all of the proposed treatment camps, and further to offer Indian doctors and nurses to provide the necessary testing and treatment, under the supervision of the World

Health Organization. I may add that the necessary personnel and material have already been assembled and require only the mandate of this council and, of course, an invitation from South Africa, to proceed.'

This time it took no prompting for members of the security council to give a standing ovation to their president and his nation. Everyone in the room knew the greatest challenge facing any UNSC resolution for armed intervention in a conflict was logistical. Sending troops and equipment to foreign countries was a massively expensive undertaking, and few countries were happy to tie up more than a token number of troops abroad.

Early drafts of the proposal to establish treatment camps had been circulated, and members had spent many hours debating the two key assumptions on which the camps were based. The first was that each camp had to be capable of expanding at short notice to meet almost any level of demand, in order to avoid a dangerous overload situation. The second was that each camp must be capable of defending itself against most forms of attack.

To establish and defend each of the ten camps called for a battalion of nearly 1,000 soldiers, or three brigades in all. A fourth airborne brigade was divided between three bases inside South Africa so that reinforcements could reach any treatment camp in an hour. More than 5,000 support elements from engineers, drivers and helicopter crews to cooks, quartermasters and medics brought India's military commitment to more than 18,000 men and women, for at least a year. Even for the third largest standing army in the world, this was a major undertaking.

Their civilian commitment was no less impressive. Each camp would be staffed with an initial complement of 50 doctors and 500 nurses, of whom half would be on duty at any given time. Pharmacists, technicians, orderlies, morticians, caterers and administrators brought the overall number of civilians for the ten camps close to 10,000, with an equal number ready to be deployed from India at short notice.

***

'Jesus – five billion dollars! Does it come from the money they already pledged for ARV treatment?'

'Wouldn't be surprised, Gipsy. I heard that Dutta struck a deal with them. India would supply the people to set up and run the camps, if the US put in the money. Grogan couldn't wait to tell everyone, right after Dutta announced his government's offer.'

Nikki called just minutes after the Security Council meeting ended, to check whether I'd caught the news yet. I hadn't.

'Did Grogan say what the money would be used for?'

'I believe he said equipment, food, medical supplies…'

'ARVs?'

'Yeah, everything except the troops and medics. And the military stuff – the Indians are taking their own vehicles, helicopters, weapons, that kind of thing.'

'And what about the Chinese? Did they try to save face, after vetoing the original resolution?'

'Hell no, the Africans regard them as the real heroes. Without the Chinese veto, they might not have got any of this. I mean, it's really saved their bacon. It gives all their panicky AIDS patients somewhere to go, it reopens the border with the Cape...'

'And they don't have to lift a finger.'

She laughed. 'Well, I wouldn't have been quite that cynical!'

'Do you seriously think the South Africans will restore treatment in their hospitals? I mean, what's the point? First line-meds won't work any more, and they don't have second-line...'

'Oh, sorry Gipsy, I forgot to mention that the European Union offered to help them to kick-start second-line treatment. They'll do it in stages, starting with a few big hospitals, using limited stocks of ARVs, foreign doctors... until the system is running smoothly again.'

Progress, at last! South Africa, Swaziland and Lesotho may have been in free-fall, but this felt a lot like a parachute.

'Offered? Are the South Africans going to take them up on it?'

'Dunno, girl. You may have to do some work yourself.' Nikki made a show of protecting herself from raspberry juice.

We were back in Cape Town, and BT and Billy were closeted in a meeting with the rest of the coalition so they hadn't heard the news either. When I told them what Nikki told me, they looked like men rescued from certain death. I realized the whole thing had been a monstrous gamble, but it had paid off.

I spent another day talking to people around Cape Town to get their reaction. Their joy was no surprise – nobody liked the idea of military action – but what I didn't expect was that none of my informants seemed in any hurry to re-integrate with the rest of South Africa.

'Ag Gipsy, it's been coming for a long time. We've always been a bit different in the Cape, and over the last 20 years that difference has been growing. This ARV thing was just the last straw.'

We were sitting on the terrace of a winery which BT served as an 'itinerant winemaker', as he liked to call himself. But he was good at his job and the owner of the estate, a German industrialist, had offered him a permanent job, if he wanted it.

It was a beautiful spot, looking north towards Paarl mountain, with the slopes of the Simonsberg behind us – the very same view I'd seen from the air just a week earlier.

A pretty girl approached our table with a bottle in a bucket of ice, her smile fixed on BT.

'Mr Weiss asked me to give this to you with his compliments – it's from his private collection.' BT thanked her and solemnly inspected the bottle, which was an unusual botrytised wine. He told me this area had produced the first of this type of wine in the Cape, modeled after the Sauternes of France. I was expecting cloying sweetness but it turned out to be like lemon and honey, fresh and rich at the same time, with waves of almond nuttiness and a kind of floral perfume. It was exquisite.

BT was staring thoughtfully at his glass. 'Do you know how these wines, Sauternes, are made?' I didn't.

'The grapes are left to rot on the vine. If you're lucky they get the right kind of fungus, botrytis cinerea. The French call it pourriture noble, and the Germans edelfäule – noble rot. Then we pick them and make wine. And out of that horrible rotten mess we get this... heaven in a bottle.'

I could see he was in a reflective mood, so I just said it was magical. He looked at me, a slight smile on his face.

'Ja, Gipsy, I think magical is the right word. It's the right wine for today... to celebrate what's happened. My country had become so... rotten. But somehow we're making something magical out of it. Something sweet and fresh. I'm so glad you were here to see it happen.' He leaned forward and topped up my glass. 'And to taste this wine!'

It was definitely One Of Those Moments. The late afternoon sun over vineyards heavy with fruit, just weeks away from harvest, the angel wings of irrigation sprays in the distance, mountains ahead and to our right, and this alcoholic nectar going straight to my head.

I'm not sure how it happened but the next thing we were at a guesthouse in the Franchhoek valley, eating crayfish and drinking chardonnay. Then we were in the heated pool, sipping local cognac with espressos. And then we were in bed. It seemed the right thing to do – the only thing to do, after teasing the tail of the dragon and surviving.

BT was a gentle and considerate lover, taking his time to discover every part of my body, putting on a condom without being asked, and moving very gently until he could see I wanted him to go faster, deeper and harder. Later I challenged him to a return match, which was far more energetic and entertaining.

Durban Saturday 21 May

Max Cele's heart sank as he realized the taxi-rank marshal was heading his way. The man's nickname, Sipikile, meant 'nail' – supposedly a reference to his sexual prowess, but he seemed to enjoy bullying passengers and taxi-crews, more than chasing women.

'Cele! I see you!' The greeting was standard.

'I am here, brother.' As was the response.

'I came to tell you we are meeting tonight.'

'I am driving to Jo'burg tonight.'

'Not if you value your life, you aren't.'

'Hau! Who will stop me?' Cele, like most taxi drivers, wasn't intimidated easily.

'Nobody will stop you, brother, but when you come back you will find you are a stranger here. Tonight we pick sides.'

'What is this? Football?'

Sipikile gave a humorless smile. 'You know what it is. Tonight is the night. Nine o'clock.' With a meaningful look, the rank marshal moved on, bellowing the name of another driver.

Max wasn't happy about postponing his departure for Johannesburg. The Warwick Triangle taxi rank, where he stood, was the departure point for thousands of minibuses – known to all as taxis or combis – ferrying passengers between Durban and Johannesburg.

Since the rumors of a Xhosa plot to kill Zulus surfaced, business had been good for the combis which were the backbone of South Africa's public transport system. In common with the other long-distance drivers, Max had doubled his fares for the 360-mile run but nobody complained – at least not openly – and the huge demand for seats in both directions meant turnaround was very quick. In short, over the past few weeks, he had made a killing.

Max's nephew Mangaliso came over to say their taxi was loaded and waiting. Although the youngster was employed as his conductor, and had only an illicit driver's license, Max allowed the boy to drive on stretches of the highway where there were no police roadblocks so he could doze. In this way they had been operating virtually without a break for the past four months, and he had made as much money as he normally would in a couple of years.

However the flood of passengers had slowed to a trickle as everyone who wanted – or could afford – to retreat to their 'homeland' did so. Regular travelers were very scarce these days, and this evening it had taken more than an hour to fill his combi. Since it was now six pm, attending a meeting at nine – which actually meant ten or eleven, since punctuality wasn't a local strength – meant delaying his departure for at least six hours. Assuming the meeting only lasted an hour, which was very unlikely.

'Tell them we are broken down.'

The boy nodded and trotted off to give the bad news to the passengers. They'd be lucky to find a ride now, since all the local drivers would be attending this meeting, but Max didn't spend any time worrying about them. They were Xhosas, only useful for the money in their pockets. The rank was still regarded as neutral territory, but on the streets of Durban people suspected to be 'Xhosa' – or non-Zulu – were now openly taunted, spat upon and mugged.

The same was happening to Zulus in Pretoria, Bloemfontein, Port Elizabeth and countless other towns with non-Zulu majorities. Central Johannesburg was still relatively safe, since it had long been a melting-pot of tribes and nationalities, but each one of the hundreds of townships around the great city was now effectively reserved for either Zulus or non-Zulus, and woe betide anyone found in one of those dormitory suburbs who didn't speak the right language.

As Sipikile said, Max had a pretty good idea what the meeting was about. All the drivers knew it was only a matter of time until they were called upon to play a more active role in defending the Zulu nation against the aggression of the other tribes. Tonight would be the night. He wandered over to the dusty area that served as an impromptu football pitch and meeting place, bought a bottle of Carling Black Label beer from an informal trader, and began to chew over the possibilities with the other drivers.

At 9:43pm two black Mercedes and a black Range Rover pulled up, and a group of men joined the assembled drivers, now over 200 strong. Several of the newcomers were well-known political figures, representing both the ruling ANC and the opposition Inkatha parties. One was a senior police officer. Most of the rest were bodyguards. All were in casual street clothes. All were Zulus.

With minimal formalities the meeting was called to order. Sipho Bhengu, the chairman of the Durban branch of the ANC and provincial minister for law and order did the talking. He began, as always in such meetings, by describing the events which brought them together. Or his interpretation of them.

Max was not surprised to hear him say the conspiracy to marginalize Zulus dated back many years, and that a cabal of Xhosas had been manipulating the ANC since the death of the revered Zulu chief, Nobel laureate and founding leader of the ANC, Albert Lutuli, better known to Zulus as Mvumbi.

'We don't like to talk about this,' Bhengu said, his voice beginning to rise, 'but the Xhosa conspiracy goes back to Mvumbi's time. Even though he was elected president of the ANC, he was not shown our founding document, the Freedom Charter, before it was adopted at Kliptown in 1955. And Nelson Mandela did not consult Mvumbi before he launched the military wing, Umkhonto we Sizwe, despite what he said in his book. And to this day, nobody has explained the circumstances of the accident that took Mvumbi's life in 1967.'

These were indeed heresies – the kind of things muttered around a fire, or over a bucket of sorghum beer, but never by a senior member of the ANC, and never to a large group such as this, out in the open, where secrecy was impossible. The situation allowed for only two interpretations – it was political suicide or a political re-birth. Either way, bridges were burning and the taxi drivers, hard men all, were riveted.

'After Mvumbi we had Tambo, Mandela and Mbeki – all Xhosas – sitting in the big office at Lutuli House, our party's headquarters. It was only when we, the Zulus, mobilized against the manipulations and laziness of those Xhosas that a big man from the biggest tribe was again elected to lead the big party.'

Bhengu dropped his voice.

'Of course there were those who knew the gravy-train had reached the end of the line, so they ran away to form their own party, in time for the 2009 general elections, to see whether the voters would let them carry on gorging themselves at public expense. What happened? The rats got less than eight percent of the vote, while the elephant got more than 65 percent!'

The audience reacted as though iced water had been sprayed over them. The elephant was the royal Zulu symbol, a term usually reserved for the Zulu king. Burning bridges were everywhere. Bhengu's voice started climbing again.

'In the 2004 elections, the ANC under Xhosa leadership got less than 1.3 million votes in this province. But in 2009 we stood behind the ANC, under a Zulu leader, and we gave the party another million votes. But in every other province, the ANC lost votes! What this means, my brothers, is that it was our vote – the Zulu vote – that kept the ANC in power. Truly, it is now our party, running our country!

Bhengu waited for the murmurs of amazement at his crystal logic to subside.

'So of course the Xhosas are frightened! They know we are the strongest! They know we chose the president. They know we won the general elections. They know they cannot defeat us with their votes, because they are too few. They know there is only one way to regain control, and that is to make us smaller than they are. To turn us from an elephant into a mouse.'

The audience grunted in unison, a deep and frightening sound. Bhengu stopped suddenly, allowing the sounds of the city to wash over them. When he resumed his voice was enormous, frightening even the city into submission.

'They want to kill us, in our millions, my brothers! But they have failed to understand one thing. We have never forgotten who we are. Even before we are South Africans, before we are ANC, we are Zulus! We are warriors! Nobody threatens us, and remains standing! We will fight!'

Max found himself on his feet, adding his voice to the collective rage. Women street traders nearby began to ululate, an ancient sound which quickened men's pulses and washed away any doubts. Among men already stirred to action it had the same effect as the Scottish bagpipes, or the Yankee bugle.

The politician looked grave. After a moment he gestured to the men to sit. 'Brothers, if you have any doubts…'

'No chief, we are with you!' one man yelled out. The others murmured their approval.

'And I am with you, brother. But it is important you understand how those Xhosas hope to defeat us. To kill us. We all know about this sickness.

They are saying we are the only ones who are carrying it, because we do not remove the foreskin. They want us to be like little girls, who run around in the bush in a dress and chalk on their faces.'

The men roared with laughter at the unexpected joke – a reference to the circumcision ritual which Xhosa boys went through to attain manhood. It had long been the butt of humor among Zulus, who said it turned Xhosa boys into girls by cutting off their manhood and dressing them like women, in a blanket, with face powder.

For their part the Zulus preferred a small incision of elastic tissue under the glans, in a procedure called ukugweda, which allowed the foreskin more mobility for improved pleasure. However this procedure had no demonstrated benefit against HIV infection, unlike circumcision which had been shown to reduce risk significantly.

'Now we know why Mbeki did not want these drugs. Because he believed it was only the Zulus who had this sickness, and as a Xhosa he did not want to save Zulus who, in any case, voted against him when he was president. But then he was forced to accept the drugs by the supreme court, and he was chased out of his office by the Zulu elephant!'

Another roar of approval. The sound would have been familiar to any gladiator.

'Now we know why their drug factory is located in East London – because that is the heart of Xhosa territory! If it was here, as it should have been, we would have protected this factory from sabotage, and even now we would be making sure that everybody gets the medicines they need.'

A short pause to tell them the punch-line was imminent.

'But most of all, now we know why they persuaded the United Nations to locate those treatment camps where they did. It is not an accident that there is no treatment camp in any area controlled by Zulus!'

Once again Bhengu's voice drowned out everything else.

'Do not believe anyone who tells you these centers are there to facilitate entry into neighboring countries. Even though KwaZulu has borders with Lesotho, Swaziland and Mozambique, there are no treatment camps in our province! To get treatment, Zulus must pass through territory controlled by the Xhosas and their herd-boys…'

Once again his words had the drivers on their feet.

'Are we afraid of them?'

'NO!'

'Will we sit quietly in KwaZulu until we die?'

'NO!'

'The time has come to show them who are the warriors, and who are the herd-boys! We have plenty of men, we have plenty of weapons, and we have plenty of reasons to go and get those drugs.'

Again the guttural roar of approval, as the group heard what they wanted to hear – an outlet for their anger and frustration! A way to get even!

'What we need, brothers, is enough transport to carry our warriors to their door. And that is why you hold the key to the survival of the Zulu nation!'

As the drivers raised their clenched fists and bellowed their support, Max pictured a convoy of combi-taxis loaded with men and weapons taking the fight to the enemy. They would all be heroes – especially the drivers!

Bhengu spoke once more. 'The founder of our nation, King Shaka Zulu, built an empire by teaching his men to cover great distances at great speed, and still arrive ready to fight. We will move fast – too fast for the herd-boys to see us coming – and we will arrive ready to fight. Ready to snatch their precious prize away from them!'

'Chief, we are ready to leave!' The speaker was one of the older drivers, a veteran of the time when state-owned buses were chased off the highways by taxis. The roar of approval erased any doubt that he spoke for the whole group.

Komatipoort Sunday 22 May

Colonel Rajendra Narain looked around the table at his junior officers. The commanding officer of the Komatipoort Treatment camp had supervised its establishment and fortification, and the only surprise about the news he was about to share with his officers was that it had been so long in coming.

'Gentlemen, we have information that the Zulus are sending a convoy of militia to seize our store of antiretrovirals. They could be here as early as tomorrow, before dawn. Indications are that they are between 500 and 700 in strength, and armed with rifles and handguns.'

There was little reaction from his officers, most of whom were making notes.

'We have no intelligence on their strategy, but we know they are not army regulars – since the South African troops remain confined to their bases – so they are probably a mixture of police, private security personnel, and volunteers. Still, we would be ill-advised to underestimate them.'

The Colonel picked up a billiard cue and moved to a large-scale map of the KTC and its surrounds.

The camp was centered on a 19th century Lutheran mission station on the top of a small hill, so it afforded no vantage point for observers or snipers. The base of the hill was generally too rocky and steep for vehicles to approach. Two dense lines of razor wire had been laid around the perimeter, with an electrified fence between them to make sure that access by foot was equally improbable. The entire perimeter was floodlit at night and continuously watched from armored observation towers, each equipped with a heavy machine gun, backed up by closed-circuit TV cameras feeding into a control centre.

At one point on the hill a spur of land provided a natural ramp for a road, and in another Indian army engineers had built a second road, to provide a 'back door' to the camp. Both roads led to fortified access points. At the main entrance, AIDS patients were admitted for treatment after initial testing at a cluster of prefabricated buildings outside of the perimeter. No drugs were kept or administered in these buildings, and the personnel – along with their testing equipment and reactants – could be evacuated at short notice.

At both access points to the camp itself, heavy concrete blocks forced approaching vehicles to weave, preventing them from moving faster than walking pace. In addition a huge trench had been dug across each road, and steel drawbridges placed across the trenches – an ancient but very effective defense.

The Colonel issued a series of orders while his officers listened carefully. When the time came for questions, none were forthcoming.

***

Max felt his pulse quicken as the convoy cleared the city of Nelspruit. His GPS told him it was just 23 kilometers to the camp. It also warned of a fixed speeding camera just ahead, which normally would have seen him slowing down to avoid a fine. Instead the flash of the camera flickered rhythmically as it photographed each vehicle in the speeding convoy, causing some merriment among the men crammed into the seats behind him.

It was still fully dark outside, and would be for another two hours, but Max could see the long line of vehicles ahead, each illuminated by the headlights of the vehicle behind. At the head of the convoy he could occasionally glimpse the five armored cash-in-transit vans which had been 'recruited' for the expedition, along with their willing crews. Behind he could see a string of headlights when the road curved. It was an impressive sight.

Suddenly the brake-lights of the vehicles ahead began to flick on, as they slowed and turned left onto a gravel road. Next he could see they were turning off their headlights, relying on their running lights to avoid bumping into the taxi in front. A few minutes of slow driving and the convoy entered a parking area, next to a deserted building. As the vehicles parked, men began spilling out, checking their weapons and staring at the hill, 500 meters away. A row of floodlights lit the rocks and razor-wire, and dazzled them, but gave no inkling of what lay behind.

***

Inside the Komatipoort Treatment Camp, nothing much happened. This was because every soldier was already awake and at his post, and had been for several hours. The medical staff and patients would not usually be roused for another hour, and the CO had decided there was no good reason to disturb their routine. They had all, however, been warned that their sleep may be disturbed, and told they would be completely safe if they remained in their quarters.

Suddenly a volley of shots shattered the soft sounds of the night, and several of the floodlights flared out in a shower of shattered glass and sparks. Another volley and the rest of the lights went out, although this time mostly because they were turned off rather than shot out.

Colonel Narain was seated in the control center, watching the CCTV monitors which displayed clear images from their low-light and infra-red cameras. He could see a row of men surrounding the hill – perhaps as many as 700 – mostly armed with assault rifles, shotguns or machine pistols. He waited.

A voice, amplified by a vehicle-mounted loudspeaker, announced that the camp was surrounded, and that a delegation of men wished to speak to whoever was in charge. Still Narain waited.

The demand was repeated several times as the night slowly gave way to a pastel pre-dawn. Finally, as ordered, Narain's second-in-command, Major Bhaskar, used a megaphone to respond.

'Good morning gentlemen. We have been expecting you. We would be happy to receive a delegation of no more than three men, unarmed and on foot, at our main gate, in 30 minutes. Tea will be served. For the rest of you, there is tea and breakfast in the reception centre where you parked your vehicles – please help yourselves.'

The Indian soldiers had orders to stay out of sight and not to laugh, jeer, or make any other sound, no matter what they heard. They had also been instructed not to fire, unless directly ordered to do so. But it was difficult for them to maintain their composure as their surprised 'attackers' broke into clusters to discuss this unexpected reaction, and eventually moved toward the testing centre to find, as promised, tea and a selection of Indian breads and a mild mutton curry waiting for them.

On cue three men appeared at the gate, and were duly frisked and escorted to the CO's office. Their route took them past the vehicle park, where rows of armored personnel carriers were lined up, and past the helipad where a Hind attack helicopter squatted alongside a Dhruv air ambulance and two large MI-8 general utility choppers. Next they were treated to the sight of three companies of blue-helmeted troops with assault rifles and body armor, assembled on the parade ground, being inspected by their NCOs. They could see other troops manning the observation towers and access points, or simply moving about. It looked like the camp was awash with soldiers – all of whom were ignoring their leather-jacketed visitors.

Colonel Narain warmly welcomed the men and made sure they had tea before listening patiently as a somewhat subdued Bhengu explained why they were there. When Bhengu told him that KwaZulu had no treatment camp of its own, leaving Zulus with little choice but to cross 'enemy' territory to get help, the Colonel clucked sympathetically but offered no comment. The Zulu politician concluded by saying that if the Indians handed over their stores of ARVs, nobody would be hurt. The portly policeman and bulky bodyguard accompanying the politician tried their best to look tough and uncompromising.

The Colonel offered Bhengu a fresh cup of tea. 'I'm sure that one has grown cold, Mr Bhengu. We Indians are very fussy about our tea. And we're also very much against unnecessary bloodshed, so I'm delighted to hear that you don't want to hurt anyone. I'm sure you know our mandate is to save lives, not to take them?'

He paused as a white-jacketed steward replaced Bhengu's tea, and refilled the cups of the other two guests.

'However I regret that your long drive has been in vain, because I am not authorized to disburse drugs to anyone – that is the sole preserve of our medical staff. My job is simply to protect them from any interference. And I'm sure you can see that we are well equipped to resist most kinds of interference. In fact I have arranged a little show for you, just to avoid any possibility of a misunderstanding. I think you may enjoy it.'

He stood, and gestured to the door. 'Please, this way gentlemen. Feel free to bring your tea with you.'

The Colonel politely waited until the men had gathered their teacups before ushering them out of his office and onto the verandah of the old stone manse which served as his command post. From here they had a clear view over the plain below, including the reception center where Bhengu's militia was milling about with mugs of tea and plastic plates of bread and stew.

In Hindi he checked with Major Bhaskar that all their 'visitors' had cleared the area around an old bus which been towed the previous afternoon to a small cluster of rocks and trees, about 500 meters from where they stood, and a similar distance from the reception center.

'Gentlemen, if you will observe that bus over there? I'd say it's about the same distance from us as your vehicles and personnel, wouldn't you?' Sure enough, the rows of combi-taxis and cash-in-transit vehicles were neatly parked in the lot alongside the reception center.

The Colonel nodded to the major, who spoke into a two-way radio. Almost immediately there were a succession of four loud popping sounds, about two seconds apart. No sooner had the fourth pop sounded than the wrecked bus disappeared in a flash of white light. An instant later the sound of the explosion reached them – and the men at the reception center.

On the hill, the Indian personnel knew what to expect and had covered their ears, but the Zulus were caught unawares by the monstrous wallop of sound. They barely had time to grasp what was happening before the first blast was followed by a second, then a third, and a fourth. All three men dropped their teacups as they belatedly raised their hands to block their ears. When the smoke cleared, there was a shallow crater where the rocks, trees and bus had stood – and nothing else.

The Colonel took his hands away from his ears, and quietly thanked the major for the demonstration. Then he raised his voice so his deafened visitors could hear him.

'Gentlemen, those were 120mm high explosive shells from our E1 mortars. They are quite impressive, aren't they? Naturally we have other weapons at our disposal, but a handful of those shells would quickly eliminate a cluster of men and vehicles, at that distance.' He pointed to the chaos at the reception center, where men were picking themselves up from the ground and trying to get mutton curry and tea off their clothing.

The colonel chuckled and spoke sotto voce. 'Of course it would have been easy to spike their tea, but that just wouldn't be cricket.'

He glanced at his visitors to see if they had a different perspective on what they'd just seen, but they were transfixed by the scene below. Bhengu became aware that his trousers were soaked with scalding tea, and began to tug the fabric away from his skin. The other two came to the same realization.

Seemingly oblivious to his guests' discomfort, Colonel Narain continued. 'I'd love to demonstrate the firepower of our 50 caliber Browning machine guns. Did you know their armor-piercing rounds can go right through a lightly armored van like those you've brought along, or evaporate those rocks down there? They don't go through the rock, of course, they simply turn it into powder. It's really quite amazing to see. Must be sandstone. Granite would offer better cover, I suppose, but I'd hate to rely on it.'

Narain seemed to become aware that his visitors were preoccupied by their wet clothing. 'But we've disturbed everyone enough for one day, I think. Damn shame about your trousers, gentlemen. You'll want to get out of those as soon as possible.'

He smiled expectantly, as if waiting for thanks or congratulations on the pyrotechnics display, but the Zulus seemed to be torn between shock and embarrassment.

'Well then. I'll have someone escort you to the gate.'

**

Looking back now, it was all so appallingly predictable. After the treatment camps were set up, just three months after the bombings, people and freight started moving across South Africa's borders again, the local currency recovered some of its value, and there was a sense that the worst was over.

The vast majority of AIDS patients were still in good health, and a growing number were inclined to believe the – now explicit – message from their government, that they had all been duped by foreigners into taking unnecessary and toxic drugs. Pro-ARV patients were not particularly worried either, believing Pretoria would take advantage of the European

Union offer to introduce second-line treatment in public hospitals. In good time.

At the same time there were many who read the signs.

The first to leave were those who had a place to go, and little reason to stay. For decades South Africa had been an irresistible magnet for the ambitious and the desperate of Africa. Porous borders and corrupt immigration officials meant the country was now home to uncounted millions of illegal immigrants. But with the balkanization of the country into its tribal constituents, and the shrinking of the economy which drew immigrants here in the first place, the polarity of the magnet was reversed and they began leaving in huge numbers.

At the opposite end of the economic scale, top people in multinational companies, professionals with portable skills, northern expats and South Africans who were thinking of leaving anyway, did so. Soon the airlines were scheduling extra flights, and embassies were working 24/7 to process visa applications.

The government and people of South Africa made it clear they were happy to see them all go. These were the leeches who had been stealing their jobs and committing their crimes. What started as resistance to the hegemony of the pharmaceutical industry was turning into a full-blooded purge of foreign influence. There was a widespread sense that South Africa would be cleaner and stronger, once the hiatus was over. There was even talk that it was high time the Cape went its own way – after all, it had always been different and 'not really Africa'.

For a great many middle-class South Africans this was just what they wanted to hear. They began to quietly wind up their affairs and head for the Cape, where the only passport needed was a negative blood test, or for Namibia, Botswana, Zimbabwe and Mozambique, who saw it as their turn to skim the cream of intellect, skills and capital from a country that had been doing it to them for a century.

South Africa's hemorrhage of human capital happened so quickly that, within a matter of a weeks, many products and services were affected. Corporate executives found their accountant and bank manager were leaving, their key suppliers were closing, and clients no longer needed their services. Professionals discovered their family doctor had gone, along with the man who fixed their Mercedes and the woman who gave their kids extra lessons. Increasingly those who had decided to stick it out changed their minds, and joined the chicken run instead.

One of the most remarkable aspects of this exodus was the relocation of the Indians. The vast majority of South Africa's million-strong Indian community lived in and around the city of Durban, where their forefathers landed 150 years earlier. And even though Durban was ground zero for the AIDS epidemic, Indians had the lowest HIV prevalence of any sector of South African society. Cape Town, a thousand kilometers away, had almost no Indian residents at the start of pharmageddon, but when it was all over they made up a significant part of their population.

At first the Indians' departure was seen as a kind of joke – 'a dash of curry' as one blogger described it – but after a few months the laughter died down, then turned to concern and finally to panic as it became clear that this was not merely the unstopping of a national constipation, but was part of a life-threatening diarrhea. Every day the number of shops, offices and factories which failed to open their doors grew. And when supermarkets and banks closed their doors it was just a matter of hours before the looting began.

Within hours the shelves of stores were emptied, banks and ATMs were bombed, motor dealers were stripped of cars, and businesses and industries of every description were cleaned out. Pharmacies were a popular target although the looters were disappointed to find that most pharmacists had taken their precious stocks of ARVs with them. Gun stores, too, had been quietly emptied before they were abandoned but liquor stores hadn't, which helped many to overcome their disappointment. People who held back eventually joined in as it became obvious this was their best and perhaps only chance to provide for their families' immediate needs.

It took a few more days before the pillage of residences began in earnest, starting with deserted middle-class homes then spreading to those still occupied, along with the mansions of the rich and the hovels of the poor. Once the genie of uninhibited acquisition was let out of the bottle there was no putting it back. But while the plunder of commercial and industrial property was mostly uncontested, the attacks on homes were often fiercely resisted.

For generations white South Africans kept guns in their homes, in anticipation of the day that the black man shook off his shackles. In the twenty years since the peaceful collapse of apartheid, despite a tightening of the gun-control laws, the number of firearms in private hands had spread across all sectors of society, black and white, rich and poor, licensed and otherwise. So when the rattle at the gate or the thud on the door eventually came, it was by no means certain it was made by a black hand, nor that it was resisted by a white one.

The sacking of private property took on the shape of countless sieges. For weeks the rattle of gunfire was everywhere and the streets were hyphenated with corpses. Meanwhile the highways were choked with cars, trucks and buses packed with families and possessions, heading for the nearest border where the Indian army and a treatment camp were waiting for them.

Nobody tried to prevent them from leaving. Instead they focused on moving into newly vacated homes in the suburbs, inhibitions abandoned in the scramble for the best pickings. People persuaded themselves that it was all good as they moved their new possessions into their new homes using their new cars. Some re-started businesses or applied for jobs, and many talked of new beginnings. Unfortunately there was nothing in the stores, no way to replenish them, no banks to provide capital and, most of all, no desire by anyone to pay for anything. Gasoline ran out, power faltered and water supply became uncertain and unsafe.

As the fabric of society unraveled the gang-wars began. Paradoxically it began in the mansions of the powerful, whose strong-rooms were stacked with ARVs, and whose compounds were guarded by men who expected payment in these drugs, both to keep them alive and to use in place of their worthless currency. Their bosses realized their stock of drugs would not last indefinitely, and the only way to acquire more was to send their troops to steal the other guys' stockpile. They calculated their men would bring home more drugs or would die trying – either way was okay by them.

Once again the masses did not understand what was happening. They saw what looked like police or army raids on the ivory towers, and they heard the gunfire, but their own concern was not for drugs but for food. After five months without ARVs, many AIDS patients were now seriously ill, but their condition appeared no different from their uninfected friends who were starving or poisoned by bad food and water. And when they died, as they did in growing numbers, their deaths were blamed on their environment, not the virus in their blood.

As the war of the mansions grew, and the platoons of bodyguards were depleted, men with guns came looking for new recruits – and found them in plentiful supply. All they had to offer was two meals a day in exchange for a man's willingness to bear arms, and a woman's willingness to part her legs. What started as a fight for drugs gradually slid into a tribal war of survival, with politicians reinventing themselves as warlords and recycling centuries of grudges, real and imagined.

As the fighting gathered momentum and the last vestiges of ubuntu – the core African value of humanity – were lost in the bloodletting, untrained and youthful tribal militia took to visiting another venerable form of vengeance on their enemies – the rape of their women and children. In countless conflicts through the ages, rape has been a way of asserting dominance, while leaving a genetic imprint on the enemy. But now the urban legend – that sex with a virgin would cleanse the rapist of HIV – not only added fuel to this deadly fire but dragged the nation's children into the flames, robbing them of their childhood, and leaving most of the survivors with the virus that started it all.

Bloemfontein, Tuesday 7 June

I lay awake all night listening to the sounds of the end. Somehow I knew what the end would sound like – perhaps we all do. It's what we rehearse in our nightmares, so that when it happens, we know.

The sound of the end is mostly silence, which is deeply disturbing in a big city. The background murmur of traffic, and whatever else makes a city live and breath, is simply gone. The void is defined rather than replaced by the isolated sound of cars, some growling past at the lowest register of hearing, some sounding like getaways from a bank heist with screaming engines and wailing tires. But they are alone, there is no chase. One sound I didn't hear the entire night was a siren. It was almost a pleasant change, in a country where nobody with any political clout goes anywhere, at any time, without a phalanx of wailing outriders.

Between the phrases of car engines, the stretched silence was pricked by sudden sounds, every one unexpected, sucker-punching adrenals and yanking at involuntary muscles. The most frequent was the sound of shouting men – confrontational, defensive, triumphant – and women shrieking or laughing, way too loud for humor.

Occasionally – just when you began to wonder whether you'd imagined the last one – there was the single report of a gunshot, or the dreadful rattle of a fire-fight. Unlike other sounds I found I was plotting gunshots on a kind of mental radar screen, each percussion a bright blip on the green screen, showing direction, range and hinting at movement. Was this a running battle or a succession of individual confrontations? My radar was too primitive to tell.

But worst of all were the screams – each as unique as a fingerprint. Some short and final, leaving no room for doubt that this was the last sound to come from that throat. Others, long and appallingly detailed, a repulsive script of appealing for help, begging for mercy and venting terror and pain. Some were far away – screams carry a long way in a silent city – and some were dreadfully close, near enough to hear both cause and effect.

The sound of running feet, the thud of an impact, the voices of attacker and victim doing what voices shouldn't, the ragged breathing of both, or just one, at the end. Some of these sounds came from men, some from women and some, sweet Jesus, from children and animals. It feels like I still remember each one, still carry them all. It's entirely possible some are still alive, but it's inconceivable that any are unchanged, after that night.

I know I'm not.

I didn't want to be here, in the city of Bloemfontein, but I was the guest of the Indian army who had a base on the outskirts of the city. They'd placed me here, in an anonymous city hotel which they used as a kind of staging post for civilians en route to one of their treatment camps. Tomorrow I'd been promised an opportunity to accompany a mission to restore second-line treatment in a regional hospital. More history being made. Joy.

I lay on my bed in the darkened room, listening to everything but looking at nothing, thinking about the end. What did it mean to be here, and how did it feel to think about the end? Why was I here? Was there something I should be doing, other than just… listening? There were no butterflies – I didn't feel scared – but when I put my hand on my chest I was amazed to feel my heart hammering like an impact drill. I wanted to speak to someone in Istanbul, look at someone who wasn't hearing what I was, but I had nothing to say, nothing to ask. I didn't think I'd ever sleep again, but I couldn't keep my eyes open.

Oddly enough I didn't think about survival. I didn't wonder if the army detail downstairs would be overwhelmed, and men would surge up the stairwells and break down the doors. It didn't occur to me that I could die tonight, or be raped, or maimed, or imprisoned. I didn't know how or when I'd get out of here, but it didn't occur to me that I wouldn't. The words: 'things will unfold as they will' kept running around my head, but I was thinking of South Africa and destiny, not myself.

After a while I realized I'd been wondering how a virus could cause the sounds I was hearing outside? Viruses don't have voices. But dropped into the melting pot of human weakness, a virus can change everything. This one had been stewing for a long time. For at least 10 of the past 20 years it looked like HIV would lay waste to most of Africa, and large tracts of the third world, but then the empire struck back.

Sure they made a lot of mistakes – like downplaying our most effective weapon, the humble condom, for god's sake – but through the sheet brute force of ARVs they got the upper hand on HIV. Until those fucking bombs screwed everything up. Even so, the good guys got their shit together and snatched victory from the slathering jaws of a microbe too small to be seen, even under the most powerful microscope. Everywhere except here.

Why not here? Okay, Mandela dropped the ball and Mbeki and his idiot health minister truly cocked things up, but after the sudden change of regime in 2008 it was at last coming together for them. You could almost excuse the panic seizures of ARVs by men with guns, when it seemed like there would be no more ARVs, ever. Power is irresistible to these thugs.

But then there was the UN plan, the promise that if the southern African nations played with open cards they would be looked after. Again, you could forgive the bluster from the politicians and bureaucrats about sovereignty, but they quietly got in line when the opportunities were given to them. Everyone except the biggest fish in this pond, South Africa, and the two minnows attached to its flanks. What on earth was this all about?

Enoch, bless his soul, said he had a handle on it – that it was about slavery, subjugation by the west, even the illusion of a cure. But it didn't hang together. All they had to do was use condoms, and the epidemic would never have got to this level. Okay, Enoch said this was not their strong suite. But first-line ARVs were produced in South Africa – giving them leverage over their surrounding countries, rather than making them vulnerable to the outside world. The only people they depended on was the Indians, for the active ingredients – not an American or Brit in sight.

And what about this belief that AIDS is an illusion? Jesus, I don't know. Millions of South Africans in their twenties and thirties, when they should be at their strongest, falling ill and dying over the past couple of decades. Not a virgin among them. How much proof do you need? And when they started swallowing ARVs, they stopped dying. What were you smoking, Enoch?

But there was something else. They wanted to believe that AIDS was an illusion, not the product of their reckless behavior... no, that doesn't work either. How can an evil plot by the west be no more than an illusion? Okay, so AIDS is real, but it's put there by the developed world to control their population... Hmm, nope. If the idea is to kill them, why give them drugs to keep them alive? Oh, okay, it's not to kill but to subjugate. Keep them dependent on the drugs. Which they make right here in South Africa.

I realized I was in the zone between sleep and wakefulness, my mind churning through the nonsense which had somehow triggered this catastrophe. Outside it was silent... no, there was the distant pop of a gunshot, followed by a shout, and an answer.

Awake, the genesis of disaster seemed reassuringly clear. For as long as the government failed to call its cops to heel, and did nothing to restore ARV treatment in public hospitals, the fuse was burning. But four other countries had snuffed out the same fuse before it reached the dynamite. But why not here? Who stood to gain? What was I missing?

The theory that HIV was concentrated among the biggest tribe, the Zulus, while government was dominated by the numerically smaller Xhosas, really didn't hold water. Surely infection levels weren't THAT different between the two groups? And to use this as means of ethnic cleansing simply beggared belief.

No, there's something wrong with this picture. How could they be doing this to themselves? This... wasn't the virus at all. It was the idea! It was an idea born of a horrible confluence of events. A brave new republic born at exactly the same time that AIDS made its presence felt. A new president who could not believe that, within a remarkable package of hope, there was an unspeakable cancer gnawing away at the nation he was trying to build. A successor who simply wasn't brave enough to say the hard words that needed to be said – the only way to survive is to control our most basic urge, just long enough to put on a condom.

By the time of the third presidency, the world was a different place, and it was impossible to pretend there was no enemy within. Unless... the enemy within was a Trojan horse, planted by the enemy without. And that everything... everything that followed... was simply part of this despicable plot.

But, honestly, this is just paranoia. Sure, paranoia kept many countries in a state of perpetual lock-down. Equatorial Guinea, Myanmar, North Korea... But they weren't democracies. Not even close. South Africa was. But then... so was Hitler's Germany, Milosevic's Serbia, Bush Jnr's America. Mugabe's Zimbabwe, sort of passed for a democracy, until he showed his true spots to even his most mindless supporters.

So... don't lose this thread. What kind of idea could so infect the minds of the Weimar Germans, the Cambodian peasants, the Rwandan Hutus, the

Yugoslav Serbs, the Zimbabwean Shona, that would persuade them to turn on their fellow citizens? I simply don't accept that they all do it because a small group of men tells them to. They have to believe, somehow… But believe what? That getting rid of a part of themselves will solve anything?

No, whichever way I looked at it, what was happening outside was just irrational mass action. Obviously there was an idea, but not one which could survive even the most cursory comparison with history. But still people… thousands, hundreds of thousands… bought into this craziness. And began killing. What a fucked up world, and here I was at the current ground zero of craziness.

I opened my eyes and was surprised to see it was light outside. Then I registered that the silence was undiluted by cars, shouts, screams. It was just silence. I looked at the bedside clock but its glowing numerals were gone. Tried the lamp… no power. Groped for my PDA – 5,30 am. No signal. Well, there's always the satphone.

I lay back again. Maybe I had slept. Maybe those jangled thoughts were actually fevered dreams. Still, it did seem like the only explanation was a cancerous idea, that fed on people's prejudice and fear, that needed no rational justification. Which meant you couldn't attack the idea with facts and logic. Was there such a thing as an antidote to a cancerous idea? Some chemotherapy or radiation that would kill it, but leave the host alive?

This emperor had only an idea wrapped around him, and the people were invested in the magnificence of that idea – but they were ready for another one. A logic bomb, primed and triggered by the innocence of a little boy. From the mouths of babes. What kind of logic bomb could end the pounding feet, the yelling and screaming outside my hotel window at 3 am?

***

'Yes, but why me? I'm a medical journalist, not a war correspondent.'

Captain Singh smiled with his eyes. He was a serious young man, tipped for great things in the Indian military, so I'd been told. Distinguished military service ran in his bloodline, stretching back to the first Sikh resistance to Mughals in the 17th century, or something like that. Certainly he looked comfortable in his uniform and blue UN turban. He was obviously used to the fact that headsets don't fit over a turban because he wore his with the strap around the back of his head, and the microphone pulled down so it hovered above his impressive moustache.

'Surely you've been covering the situation in South Africa from the beginning? And wasn't it you who first called it pharmageddon?'

I was determined to make him smile, to see what happened between the moustache and the beard, so I gave him one of my best. 'Listen, don't tell anyone, but this whole thing was my idea from the beginning…'

It worked. His teeth were perfect – white and even – and contrasted well with his black face carpet. He also had a great laugh – very smooth and deep – which carried clearly over the microphone. He glanced around, and I remembered that everyone on the chopper was listening to our conversation, and I saw that most of them were looking at me. I felt my face warming up. Shit.

He came to my rescue. 'Anyway, we don't need a war correspondent. This is a medical story. A humanitarian mission, as you know.'

'Right. Just make sure there's no shooting. I don't do shooting.'

'That's okay, Dr North. We can take care of any shooting that may be required, so you can focus on the story.'

I wanted to ask him to call me Gipsy, to see if he'd tell me his first name, but there was the small matter of 26 eves-droppers.

'Have you done any shooting so far?' I looked around the soldiers, who made up half of the passengers on the Indian army chopper, to make it clear I meant them all, not only their captain. I saw a few shaking heads before their captain answered.

'Not in South Africa, no. Other than training. Some of the treatment camps have had to let off a few volleys to discourage people who were threatening to use weapons of their own. Fortunately the tribal militia have been too busy fighting each other to worry about us.'

'Or else they're scared of you?'

'We certainly hope so.'

I caught the eye of the lead doctor on the mission, Vijay Bhikar. Although we'd been on first-name terms on the ground, I knew that Indians can be sensitive to familiarity when they're in company.

'So Dr Bhikar, what's the plan when we arrive at Ladysmith Hospital?'

'We're aiming to do three things, Dr North – test, treat and train. Test as many patients as we can, to determine their viral load, initiate second-line treatment, and train their physicians and technicians so they can continue the testing and treatment after we've gone.'

I could see in the eyes of the other passengers that they'd heard this already. So had I.

'Sorry, what I meant was – do we wait in the helicopter while Captain Singh's men secure the area…'

'Oh, yes…' Bhikar looked at Singh, who looked like he was about to explain when the pilot's voice broke in.

'Ladies and gentlemen, we have the hospital in sight. We will approach quite fast and decelerate quickly for the landing, so do not be afraid.'

I thought of clowning around, but suddenly I felt a constriction in my throat and a kind of paralysis in my lower body. Somebody must have farted because there was quite a strong odor, and I could see the soldiers elbowing each other and trying not to laugh.

The engine note of the helicopter changed and to my surprise I saw the top of a tree passing the window. Jesus, I had no idea we were flying so low. Without further warning the front of the chopper reared up and I felt myself been shoved hard into my seat. A second or two later the chopper leveled out and, in the next instant, we landed – hard. The door was yanked open and before I'd even found the buckle for my seatbelt, all the army blokes were out of there.

'Shit, I didn't realize the fart was that bad,' I muttered to myself. I genuinely had forgotten that our headsets were still connected, so I was surprised to find I'd caused a minor riot among the dozen medics who remained on the aircraft with me, and who were now laughing up a storm. Seems like toilet humor does well in India...

Bhikar gave me a broad smile. 'That was just what we needed, Dr North. Thank you!'

'You're welcome, Dr Bhikar.' I wanted to add something like: 'If you're not feeling better, call me in the morning,' but my follow-ups generally fall flat so I didn't. Instead I tried to look out of the chopper, which wasn't easy from where I was sitting. I took off my seatbelt and half stood to peer out of the open door. I felt a hand on my shoulder – it was a soldier standing next to the door, gesturing me to stay in the aircraft. I realized I still had my headset on. When I took it off I realized something else – the engines of the chopper were still going and the rotors were still turning.

Singh was standing a few yards away, flanked by two of his men. They were being confronted by a knot of four or five young African men, dressed in civilian clothes, all carrying rifles of some kind. One of them was shouting and waving his arms.

Singh said something, gave a 'wait here' gesture to the men and walked back to the chopper. His face was neutral but the smile in his eyes was gone, replaced by something which brought the lump back into my throat. I sank back into my seat, as he appeared at the door.

He had to shout to be heard. 'We have a situation here. There is quite a large contingent of militia, and they do not want us to enter the hospital or treat anyone. They want us to hand over the drugs and leave...'

Bhikar looked grave. If he was frightened he did a good job of hiding it. 'Can we not simply take off...'

'They will probably open fire if we try that.'

A woman sitting in front of the door touched Singh's shoulder and he turned to look behind him. A portly man – a doctor, judging by his white coat – was trotting towards us across the sports-field where we'd landed. Singh walked back to meet the winded doctor, and was joined by the militants. I noticed now that Singh's men were standing in a circle around the chopper with their weapons held ready, and I could also see what looked like dozens of men sitting and standing around the sports-field. All of them were armed.

Finally Singh came back, his face still neutral. This time he picked up a headset and held it to one ear. When I got my own headset back on I found he was speaking in Hindi. From the nodding it looked like he was speaking to the pilots and to Bhikar, but then several of the medical team reacted, and one nurse began crying and trembling. I felt a hand on my knee and found Singh was looking at me. His eyes were soft again.

'Stay in the helicopter, Gipsy. Dr Bhikar will explain what's happening.' Then he turned and shouted an order to his men. I heard the sound of the cargo hatch on the chopper being opened, and saw his men offloading crates and carrying them to the edge of the field. Without warning the note of the helicopter's engines changed and we were yanked off the ground with unbelievable force. The aircraft lurched over to the side opposite to the door, and seemed to stand on it's nose. I wasn't sitting properly in my seat and found myself sprawled on the floor, unable to get up because of the G-forces. But in a second we were flying level. I became aware of a heavy thumping on the floor.

'Fuck – what's going on?' I bellowed. A couple of the group looked at me, but nobody spoke into their microphones. Then I heard the pilot's voice say something in Hindi, and several of the medics nearest the door leaned over to drag it shut. Again the chopper lurched, this time to the left, and suddenly I could see the sports-field through the window. It was already some distance away, but I could make out the heavy crates stacked near the edge of the field, in an L-shape.

Then I realized what I was looking at. The Indian soldiers were using the crates as cover. All around them men were running, like agitated ants. I saw one of them fall, and lie still. The chopper swung the other way, and I lost my view – and very nearly my breakfast. One of the nurses wasn't so lucky, and I could smell vomit. I caught Bhikar's eye, and I saw he was pale.

'Vijay – what the hell is happening?'

'Singh said they had no intention of letting any of us leave. So he said he would offload the drugs, but we should remain in our seats. You saw what happened after that…'

'Sweet mother of god. What now?'

Bhikar gave a short shake of his head, but then I heard the voice of the pilot. 'Dr North, we have radio communications with Captain Singh. Or we will have when the situation has stabilized. And then we will attempt an extraction, when it is safe. Right now I am looking for a safe place to leave you all, until the extraction is complete.'

The pilot was a fucking hero, and was still in the middle of a crisis, and he was making time to explain to me what was going on.

'I… thank you, sir.'

'You're most welcome. We have a small mountain dead ahead, where everyone should disembark. You'll be safe there until… you are extracted.'

I didn't like the sound of 'you are extracted'. What's wrong with 'when we come back for you'?

Within ten minutes we were sitting on top of a very chilly mountain, watching our chopper scoot back towards the Ladysmith, about 15 miles away. I thought I could hear gunfire, but it was hard to be sure – it could have been gusts of wind.

We'd taken a couple of emergency boxes off the aircraft, and we wrapped ourselves in silver 'space blankets' to cut the icy wind. I could see there was food in the box, too, but nobody looked hungry. Bhika suggested we descend a few meters below the summit, just to get out of the wind, and we found a sheltered spot.

Then I remembered I had a sling-bag full of the greatest technology man could buy, and in a couple of minutes I was talking to Jim.

'Hey Jim, you may want to press the record button.'

'Go.'

I briefly told him what was going on, and scanned the mini-cam across our shivering group, and zoomed out to the city below. The lens was much more powerful than I expected, and the image was jumping a little as the anti-shake mechanism struggled to steady the image. I leaned against a rock and instantly the picture crystallized. I could see our chopper moving slowly like a bumble-bee. Then it veered sharply left, and it was obvious that it was moving a lot faster than I thought. To my surprise I saw two rockets shoot down from the chopper and explode below, although there was no sound.

'Great pictures Al. Keep rolling.'

Then we heard the blasts, like rolling thunder in the distance. I hadn't realized our chopper had missiles. We watched for what felt like a long time as the chopper weaved and turned above the city. Finally it turned back towards us, and 15 minutes later it was throttling down on the plateau above where we were huddled.

I scrambled up with Bhikar and a couple of others to see what was happening, taking the mini-cam along. The pilot and copilot were sitting in the cockpit, talking into their headsets. Then the copilot took off his helmet, climbed out of the aircraft and came over to us. He began to speak in Hindi, but Bhikar held up his hand.

'English, please.'

The copilot glanced at me. 'Sorry, ma'am. The section has retreated to the hospital building, which they are defending. They have taken some casualties…'

'How many?'

'Two dead, three injured.'

That left six. There was something in the co-pilot's face. I couldn't help myself.

'Who has been killed?'

He looked at me, and I knew before he spoke. 'Captain Singh and Sepoy Mudali. Havildar Chowdary has taken command. Two of the three wounded men are able to fight.'

Bhikar broke the silence. 'What is the plan, lieutenant?'

'Sir, we have two Hinds en route. They should be here in about an hour. They will give us cover while we do the extraction.'

There were so many unanswered questions, but all I could think about was Captain Singh's solemn hazel eyes and his perfect smile. I had no idea whether Sikhs believed in an afterlife, but I was bloody sure his ancestors would be proud of him. His descendants too, if he had any.

'Did you know Captain Singh, lieutenant?'

He looked at me.

'Yes ma'am. We were friends.'

'Did... does he have a family?'

The pilot smiled sadly. 'Yes ma'am. He has a son, already in school. He wants to be a soldier like his father. He also has a daughter, who is very brilliant. Like your good self, ma'am. She wants to be a doctor.'

Oh fuck. That's all I needed. The picture on the mini-cam monitor jumped as I lost concentration, and then I steadied it. And remembered my job.

'And the other soldier? What did you call him?'

'Sepoy Mudali, ma'am. Private Mudali. I didn't know him very well, ma'am. But he was the comedian in the section. Always making the boys laugh. Very popular. And brave, of course, like all of them.'

He seemed to remember something, and said a few words in Hindi to Bhikar. Bhikar gave a hoarse laugh. 'He's just told me the major – the pilot – is wounded, and asked me to send someone to help him.'

It turned out the major had a shallow laceration of his left calf from bullet which had somehow missed the armor-plated bottom of the chopper, or bounced off somewhere else. His leg had bled quite a lot, but he paid it no attention. One of Bhikar's team stitched him up and anaesthetized the area so he could operate the foot-controls of the giant helicopter. I got most of this on camera, with Jim murmuring happily in my ear at the news value.

While they were patching up the major, the lieutenant was sitting in the cockpit with his helmet on, so he could stay in touch with the approaching Hinds. Finally the pilots cranked up their engines again, and were just lifting off when there was the most god-almighty scream as two ugly helicopters shot around opposite sides of our mountain.

I thought they might sort of hover and wait for our guys to join them, but they just kept going towards Ladysmith. I scrambled back to the spot where the rest of the team were waiting, steadied the mini-cam on a rock, and watched while two mosquitoes and a bumble-bee took on an unseen militia.

The Hinds circled around the area of the city where the hospital was, giving off little puffs of smoke as they fired their weapons. This time our bumble-bee didn't swerve and swoop like before, but zoomed straight in, disappearing among some trees and buildings. In an instant it emerged again, flying away from us but then making a big circle and heading back towards us. This time when it landed our medics were ready to scramble into the aircraft the instant it settled on the plateau. The Hinds were back, too, settling a hundred meters away. The noise was indescribable until their engines had faded to silence, then the silence was deafening.

I went over to the big helicopter and trained the mini-cam on the scene inside. The lens, now set on wide angle, instantly adjusted to the relative gloom inside, and I could see doctors and nurses working on several men, on the floor of the aircraft, while others sat on the benches along the side and watched, or waited their turn. I saw one soldier look up, and gesture to me. He probably wanted me to stop taping, but he'd have to drag me away. He rose to his feet and moved towards me. I looked up from my monitor, and realized he simply wanted to talk to me. It was the sergeant. He clambered down from the now quiet aircraft.

'Are you fine, Dr North?'

'What?'

'Captain Singh said I must make sure you are safe.'

'You're joking!'

The man looked confused. 'No ma'am.'

I didn't know what to do with this. At least we could edit it out of the recording. 'I am fine, thank you. How are you, Sergeant Chowdary?'

'I am fine, too, ma'am. I am sorry to inform you that Captain Singh is deceased.'

'We heard. Also private Munali.'

'Mudali, ma'am. And private Sewsunkar.'

'What happened?'

'He died on the helicopter, ma'am.'

'Captain Singh?'

'Oh, no ma'am. The Captain was shot on the sports-field. After we achieved our first objective, we continued to engage the enemy…'

'What was your first objective?'

'To facilitate the departure of the helicopter, ma'am.'

'Sorry, please go on.'

'We had shot many of the enemy, ma'am, and they had ceased firing. They called to us to talk, and Captain Singh approached them to negotiate an exchange of the medicines for a ceasefire, so we could get to an evacuation point.'

He spoke in a sing-song voice, as though he were reciting a poem. 'Unfortunately one of the enemy shot the captain in the head while they were talking. From behind. An execution. We resumed fire, and sepoy Mudali ran to recover the captain's body, but they shot him, too. We had no choice but to leave their bodies and retreat to the buildings. Three of my men were wounded during the retreat, and another one while we were boarding the Mi-8.'

'Do you have any idea how many casualties the militants sustained?'

'It would be many, ma'am. At least 20 deceased, not counting those who were wounded from the helicopters. The Mi-8's missiles hit the building where they were hiding. There would be many more deceased.'

We never learned how many of the Zulu militia were killed, but two of the 10 Indian soldiers, as well as their commander, died in the 'Battle of

Ladysmith'. If it were not for Captain's Singh's bravery our tally could have been 11 soldiers, 12 medics, two pilots and a journalist – whose last words would have been 'I don't do shooting'.

When the wounded soldiers were stabilized, I put Bhikar on camera for an update on their condition.

'Two men are in a serious condition. Unfortunately we don't have all the medical equipment we need so we are leaving immediately. The other wounds are not so serious.'

The record light on my mini-cam was flickering to show the battery was low, but I had to get in one more question.

'Dr Bhikar, what are the implications of today's events?'

He wasn't expecting the question, but he didn't hesitate.

'I will be recommending that we abandon our plan to restore second-line ARVs to major hospitals. Obviously the situation is highly unstable. It is a very sad day for everyone.'

The light on the mini-cam went out.

Lesotho, Saturday 10 September

The giant mountains stood around them – peaks above coated with the last of the winter snow, valleys below filled with rushing icy waters, feeding into the rivers which nurtured vast tracts of land to the east and west. The slopes where they stood were rich and green with grass and low bush, and sprinkled with cattle, sheep and goats. If the mourners gathered to bury Jacob Moloi noticed their surroundings, or the icy wind which cut through the blankets they wore over humble street clothing, they gave no indication. They were used to it.

As a Swede, Miu Andersson was also used to cold weather and was dressed appropriately, but she was aware that she stood out from the small crowd not only for her expensive trench coat but also because she was the only foreigner present. She had been invited by the local headman to attend the funeral of his great-nephew. She came, hoping to get a better idea of the reality of a nation dying from AIDS, so she could lobby even more aggressively for the restoration of universal ARV treatment.

Through a teenage interpreter the headman, Phineas Moloi, told Miu about the young man they were burying. When Jacob was 22 years old his father, a mid-ranking official in the education ministry, died of 'the illness'. Jacob inherited a fifth of his father's livestock – an equal share with his four brothers – and the right to graze them on these slopes which, like most of the country, were owned by the king and administered by the local chiefs.

Soon after his father died, Jacob himself became a father for the third time. His wife, Matumeleng, produced a child while Jacob already had two children with another woman. His inheritance was good news for these children and their mothers, since it meant he could provide for them.

But shortly after his father's death Jacob had fallen ill and, like two of his brothers and three of his sisters, was diagnosed as HIV-positive. He was prescribed antiretrovirals and, within a few weeks, was as strong and vital as he had ever been.

Then the news came – there were no more ARVs. After a few weeks Jacob and two of his siblings took the bus to the clinic at Butha Buthe to plead for their lives, but the nurse confirmed there were no drugs at any price.

A well dressed man outside the clinic told them he could give them a year's supply for about $400 – the price of three cows – each. They had to pay half of this upfront, and the balance when they came back to collect the drugs in two days. When Jacob and his brother and sister returned there was no sign of the man, just a knot of angry people who had also paid over a large part of their meager savings.

The old headman said they never found this man, but they heard he had done the same thing to many people in surrounding villages, and that there were other con-men doing the same across the small country. Some people were so desperate that they paid more than one of these men, but nobody managed to get any ARVs – except of course the politicians, police and army. People with guns and power.

Before she was promoted to a desk-job in UNICEF, Andersson had worked for many years in remote locations like this and was used to witnessing the stoicism of poor people, perennially cast in the role of victim. The headman caught her eye and smiled sadly before continuing his story. His young translator sounded as though she were standing in front of a classroom, reciting a poem, rather than describing the horrors of powerlessness.

Jacob hadn't given up. He went to a local sangoma – a traditional healer – and paid her two goats for a small packet of herbs, which made him vomit and gave him diarrhea but did nothing to improve his condition.

The old man hesitated, and glanced at his young translator, then seemed to reach a decision. After he spoke she continued her recital. 'Just before he died, Jacob told my grandfather that he went to Maseru, where he made friends with a small girl of about eight or nine years. But it turned out that this little girl had many friends already.'

Miu found the headman's eyes were locked onto hers, pleading for understanding. With her own eyes she granted it. He broke eye contact and spoke again, and his grand-daughter relayed his words.

'Jacob's skin became very bad, and his face and body became very thin. He was suffering from diarrhea and had difficulty swallowing food. He began to cough all the time. We brought him some medicine from Butha Buthe, but it didn't help. It is the same for many of our young people now.'

Miu followed the headman's gaze, and found herself looking at a very thin woman with a baby tied to her back.

'Grandfather says that is Jacob's wife, Matumeleng. Most of our young parents have the illness. Soon we will be only old people and orphans.'

Word of a funeral spread rapidly in these mountains because Sotho culture, like that of most African tribes, dictated that everyone who came to the funeral must be fed. In the case of people like Jacob, who was perceived to be wealthy because he owned livestock, attending a funeral meant eating and drinking as much as you could, and taking home as much meat as you could carry. However, as the headman explained, there was little motivation to carry home meat these days, because every day saw another funeral, and another feast.

'Our herds are being slaughtered for funerals, and sold to pay for herbs or for medicines which never come. You may think there are many animals on these mountains,' he gestured at the grassy slopes across the valley, 'but we can already see they are few. The animals will be all gone before I die.'

It took a moment for his meaning to penetrate. Miu turned to the girl. 'But... surely you don't have to slaughter so many animals? Can't you have smaller funerals?' The girl turned to her grandfather but he already understood, and spoke again.

'Grandfather says it is our tradition. If we change our traditions it means we have lost hope in the future – that things will return to normal. Saving our animals will not save us.'

Phineas Moloi gestured towards a cluster of stone and thatch homes, and his grand-daughter said, 'They are calling us to the feast. Please, come with us.'

PART III

New York, February, year three

'But Dr Fujimora, how is this possible?'

'Ma'am... it's our best guess.'

'Help me to understand your guesswork then!' UN Secretary General Maryam Kapur wasn't sure if her horror was the result of the numbers she was looking at, or the fact that she was so intellectually and emotionally unprepared for them.

The senior demographer from the UN Population Division was a genius in his field, but seemed awed to be in her presence.

'Well ma'am, South Africa started with nearly 50 million people, of whom about six million lived in the Cape province...'

Kapur stared at the table of figures in front of her. 'So that's this figure here – a base population of 44 million in the rest of the country?'

'Yes ma'am. The Balkanization process led to a mass exodus of expatriates and people with the means to emigrate. The biggest group by far were Africans, especially from neighboring countries. Nobody is sure of the numbers who left because the borders were simply opened to let them go, but we believe it was more than ten million. In addition, the Cape recorded an ingress of 2.3 million people, through the treatment camps, and about a million are reported to have emigrated or returned to non-African countries – especially Britain, India and Australia.'

'So you've estimated that fewer than 30 million remained? What about mortality?'

'Those figures are also guesses, ma'am. We think around 150,000 people were killed attacking or defending their homes and businesses, but it could be double that number. In the tribal war phase, we believe it is between half a million and a million. Our general mortality expectation includes a million violent deaths... so far.'

'And non-violent?'

'Counting AIDS-related deaths, other disease, starvation – particularly among children – we think at least two million have died from natural causes to date, but some of the team are convinced it is at least double that number.

Kapur stared at the figures she'd been writing down. 'Between three and five million deaths in all?'

'That would be about right, ma'am.'

'So... 25 to 27 million people left?'

'Yes... it could be fewer. Nearly four million are currently located in the treatment centers, so the population in the rest of the country is not much more than 20 million.'

Kapur stared at the table of figures. 'Have you any thoughts... projections... of future trends?'

The demographer held her eye for a moment, saying nothing.

'I need to know, Dr Fujimora.'

He took a breath. 'We… are pessimistic, ma'am. The exodus of so many uninfected people has increased HIV concentration in the country. And we know that social unrest creates an ideal situation for infection – there has been widespread cleansing… raping of women, and children… so we expect adult prevalence will be well into the sixties by now.'

The man looked as though he was expecting a rebuke at any moment, but Kapur was too distracted to notice. 'If prevalence is around two thirds, what does that mean for mortality?'

'As you know ma'am the rate of progression of the disease is related to quality of life –nutrition, stress, exposure to pathogens, quality of medical care. As things are, we believe the median time from infection to death will be between three and four years. Instead of ten.'

Kapur wrote a number in the margin of the table. 'What about further violent deaths?'

'We are hoping that fatalities are falling quite steeply – the tribes are not being re-supplied, so they have to run out of ammunition. But any reduction in violent deaths will be more than offset by AIDS related mortality. But right now our greatest concern is nutritional status…'

'Go on.'

'We believe that stored food reserves – grain, canned goods and so on – were depleted within a year. Agricultural cultivation and processing were interrupted, of course, and the land has been picked clean. Satellite imagery suggests there is almost no new cultivation – maybe five percent of what was done before – and it will be very low yield if it is brought to harvest. The national herd has been wiped out, along with the wildlife. There are not a lot of nutrients left.'

'What is your projection, doctor?'

'Ma'am, unless the people are supplied with food and medical services on a truly massive scale, we think the total number of deaths so far will be doubled this winter. We may see the emergence of… a new kind of violent death.'

Kapur did not feel the need to extract the word 'cannibalism' from the demographer.

'And in the longer-term? Assuming we are able to address the issues of starvation and AIDS?'

'Excluding inward migration, we expect negative population growth for several years. Some of the causes are structural, such as smaller populations of children and men, while others are bio-medical, like the reduction in fertility among HIV positive and malnourished women.'

'So you're saying the only way the population will grow over the next two decades is through immigration?'

'It's unlikely to grow, ma'am. But immigration will help to slow the rate at which the population shrinks. Making a lot of assumptions, we expect a return to positive growth only in ten or fifteen years. By then the population will be around 12 to 15 million. We think.'

'My god! It's just... horrible. Dr Fujimora, I know this isn't your area, but do you or your team have any thoughts on how we could go about addressing the situation there?'

'Well ma'am, we talk about it all the time. Strictly as lay people, of course. None of us believe that air-drops of food and medicine will work – the warlords will simply use those supplies to rebuild their militia. We believe relief can only be delivered through some kind of direct intervention. A military ground exercise...'

'To defeat the militia?'

'Oh, no ma'am. I doubt they will offer any significant resistance at this point. We were thinking of securing hospitals in the major centers to deliver medical care and food-aid...'

'You know the Indians tried that and... it was a disaster?'

'Yes ma'am. But that was, when the tribal militia were at their strongest.'

'And of course we couldn't give the people food rations to take home – they'd simply be targets for the militia. We'd have to feed them in situ. Every day.'

'Only if you are not giving food to the militants as well, ma'am.'

'True, the food will have no black market value if it's freely available. But that implies we would have to cover the entire country...'

The man looked helpless. 'I'm sorry ma'am. The logistics are... we didn't talk about that.'

'No Dr Fujimora, I'm sorry. I didn't mean to imply there was any flaw in your reasoning. I'm simply trying to visualize a solution. I welcome any ideas you have.'

The demographer was encouraged. 'In our coffee break discussions, we assumed that everyone would be fed and given medical attention, almost immediately. We don't think you... we... can talk about restoring order or economic activity until people are eating and receiving medical treatment.'

Kapur was no longer writing, but was staring thoughtfully at the Japanese academic. 'Yes, thank you doctor. What you say makes sense. Now it's just a question of resources.'

***

Kapur had spent her entire career in politics and diplomacy, graduating with a doctorate in political science from Cambridge, then teaching at the University of Karachi for a decade before being drawn into the maelstrom of Pakistani politics.

Her long-standing friendship with Benazir Bhutto meant her own political fortunes tended to wax and wane with those of the heiress to the Bhutto political dynasty, and Kapur served in Benazir's cabinet during her second term as prime minister from 1993 to 1996. When Bhutto was again dismissed by President Musharraf, Kapur accepted an ambassadorial post to Malaysia, the first of several such postings.

The assassination of her friend in 1997, and the election of Benazir's widower, Asif Ali Zadari, as president the following year, gave further impetus to Kapur's career and she was serving as Pakistan's ambassador to the UN when the incumbent secretary general resigned suddenly due to ill health. Maryam found herself the front-runner to replace him – largely, she suspected, because she had somehow avoided making enemies with any of her ambassadorial colleagues, especially those representing the permanent members of the security council.

Kapur had met Yvonne Delgado on several occasions over the years, mainly at international political conferences where the Harvard professor and the Pakistani diplomat were both popular speakers, yet they had never done more than exchange pleasantries, even after Kapur became secretary general and Delgado was appointed secretary of state in the historic 'G-team' of president Norah James – the first in which fully half of the cabinet and cabinet-level administrative positions were held by women.

As she looked at Delgado now, Kapur felt a pang of regret that they hadn't ever found time to get to know each other better. They were about the same age, with similar backgrounds, and both had fought their way to the top without inheriting or marrying into power, while at the same time raising children. Kapur lost her husband to cancer while Delgado was still married – apparently happily – to the senior partner of a prominent DC law firm. The Pakistani resolved to get closer to the American if the opportunity arose.

'I thought it'd be a good idea to do this in private, my dear.' Kapur waited for the steward to pour the tea and leave the room before moving past banalities. 'I'm getting dozens of conflicting opinions on South Africa – both on what's really happening, and about what we should do about it.'

'It's the same in Washington, Maryam. We're getting huge amounts of information, but somehow it doesn't clarify anything.'

The secretary general smiled wistfully and shook her head slowly. 'My heads of agency tell me we did everything we could, and more. After all, our strategy to restore the supply of ARVs succeeded everywhere else. And the treatment camp initiative worked perfectly. And yet the situation in South Africa simply went from bad to worse.'

'Should we have seen it coming?'

'Oh god Yvonne, I don't know! We never got a satisfactory explanation for why the South African government under Mandela did so little about AIDS, or why Mbeki pretended it didn't exist, and then delayed the roll-out of antiretrovirals…'

'What amazed me was that their government acted as though the sabotage of the ARV supply chain somehow vindicated Mbeki's position.'

'And yet when Ambassador Dutta proposed the treatment centers I thought... we all thought... it would allow the South African government a way out.'

Delgado rummaged in her purse and found a pack of sweeteners, dropping two into her tea. 'I agree that the time has come to act, Maryam. Our surveillance is... well, you've been seeing the same data.'

The Pakistani ignored her tea. 'The thought of mass rapes ...'

Delgado put down her own tea abruptly, spilling some in the saucer. 'I'm told the militants set out to rape every adolescent girl in the country. Saying "we're all in this together" or some such thing. But they're also targeting boys and much... younger... children.'

Kapur's eyes glittered, and she absently dabbed at them with the end of her shawl. She didn't speak for a long moment. 'I suppose we'll be told that we should have seen it coming.'

'Maryam, I can't believe that anyone will accuse you, or the UN, of not doing everything humanly possible to avoid this. You've been an example to all of us.'

The secretary general took a deep breath and pulled back her shoulders. 'Right now my particular concern is food security. I'm advised that a combination of starvation and disease is likely to kill several million people during their winter, unless we intervene.'

'Do you have a strategy in mind?'

Kapur handed a folder to her guest and described the contents in broad strokes. Delgado heard her out before returning to one aspect, as Kapur knew she would.

'The strategy makes sense, Maryam. I'm a little concerned about the size of the operation, of course, but more especially the idea of such a massive deployment by India. I can't help wondering where they get all these people from...'

'Dutta says they have Pakistan and China to thank for that! India has the third largest standing army in the world – effectively the same size as your own – but with the growing détente with my government and the Chinese they have little to do. Unfortunately it's not politically expedient for them to demobilize large numbers of men.'

'But what about the doctors and nurses, the engineers, the educationists, economists... this is a truly massive undertaking?'

'Well I understand India now has more graduates than they can accommodate. On medicine alone, they have more than 200 medical colleges, producing tens of thousands of graduates each year. What they're proposing is to offer them a year of practical experience abroad. Their experience with the treatment centers showed a huge latent demand, so I'm told.'

'Even so, I worry about having all our eggs in the Indian basket...'

'My reaction was the same, my dear. Unfortunately it would be impossible for us to put together a multi-national team of that size and complexity in a few months. In fact I really doubt we could do it at all. Yet we must, if we are to avoid millions of deaths.'

'At the same time, Maryam, I feel certain the Chinese will veto any resolution along those lines, on the basis that the South Africans themselves would never approve of it. If they had a functioning government, that is. Of course the truth is that the Chinese would love to extend their hegemony over South Africa. But I'm sure you've thought of a way around that?'

Kapur shrugged. 'I asked my analysts to look into the possibility of a joint Indian-Chinese mission, but the Indians came back immediately to say it was all or nothing. As you may imagine they are playing all their cards – the biggest Indian population outside of India, the Gandhi connection, the similarity of interest and language, the fact they have two years of experience in the treatment centers...'

'I'm not sure I blame them. India and China aren't exactly comfortable bedfellows. The last thing we need is to turn South Africa into a battlefield for two superpowers.'

'That's more or less what Dutta said to me. He maintains they can land the first wave of specialists in South Africa within three months, but he makes no bones about it – they will need material and financial support, and they will need political backing to keep the peace with China.'

'So you're not proposing to take this to the security council?'

'No. That would be to invite a veto from China, and possibly other permanent members. India will simply announce they are sending reinforcements to create a suitable environment to dismantle the treatment centers, which are no longer sustainable.'

Delgado took a sip of her tea and paged through the dossier which Kapur had given her. She knew most of the major players would back the Indian plan – or at least do nothing to oppose it – as long as the Americans agreed first. After all, this really was a remarkably generous offer from the Indians. The key question was whether the benefits of strengthening US relations with India would outweigh the strain on their relations with China. Then again, if the rest of the world stood together, what could the Chinese do about it?

'Of course you understand I can't make a commitment without taking this to the president?'

Kapur nodded.

'But I can foresee two conditions that she's likely to insist on. The first is deniability – we must be able to say we had no idea of the real scale of this project.' As she spoke, Delgado handed back the folder to the UNSG.

'And the second condition?'

'When the time arrives, we will publicly oppose any suggestion of permanence.' Her emphasis on the word 'publicly' drew a tiny smile from Kapur.

'I'm sure the Indians will be very happy with your political and material support for a compact, short-term relief operation.'

Delgado looked at the secretary general with even greater respect. Perhaps she should invite her up to their cabin in the Rockies for a weekend.

'Will you send me a revised proposal? Just the bare bones?'

Without a word Kapur handed over a second folder, and smiled at the American. Delgado could have sworn she heard the Pakistani say that she'd love to meet Vernon and Halley.

Cape of Good Hope, April, year three

For safety reasons commercial flights to Cape Town no longer passed over South Africa, so BA059 from Heathrow was routed over the Atlantic, making landfall somewhere along the Cape's arid west coast just as the sun was rising.

I pushed up the blind from time to time to squint at the empty beaches scrolling past, but the rising sun was too strong to leave the blind open so I concentrated instead on my pink grapefruit salad, eggs Benedict, croissant with cheese and preserves, coffee – and the lifejacket demonstrator.

She was a Brit, late thirties, fine-boned with lively grey-blue eyes, a generous mouth, flawless pale skin and auburn hair caught up in a mass of braids which accentuated her neck. I kept ordering things I didn't want – sparkling mineral water, another espresso, biscotti – so I could swim in those eyes and fantasize about that mouth.

It had been nearly a year since I lost Emily and I was finding it easier to focus on the future. Or at least to stop fixating on the past. But it still felt like I was treading water. Running in place. So when the invitation came to return to South Africa for a tour of the treatment centers, it felt like an opportunity to close the loop, somehow.

I pushed up the blind again and squinted into the dazzling sun. In the distance, rising above the wispy sea-fog which softened the coastline below us, I could see the silhouette of mountains.

'That's the Cederberg.'

Her name-tag said Kimberly Fossett. She was looking into my eyes, not through my window.

'Yeah, I thought it might be. The edge of civilization.'

It was meant to be funny but she frowned. 'Yes. It's a tragedy. But it doesn't seem to have affected the area too much. Having that refugee camp on their border, I mean. They still get a lot of tourists. It's only a couple of hours drive from Cape Town, and there are some lovely lodges and hiking trails. There's even a hot-springs resort, if you like that kind of thing.'

'Do you?'

She rolled her eyes. 'Oh, I'm a sucker for massage, saunas, Jacuzzis, gourmet salads.'

'Toweling robes, oysters, Pol Roger from room service …'

She was laughing now. 'Venison pie and claret in front of a log fire…'

'It's that cold?'

'It can be. It was the last time I visited, which was in September. I got to see the spring flowers…'

Oh well, in for a penny. 'You go there with your mates during a layover?'

'Yes, we try to do something whenever we've got more than one night in Cape Town. Or at least I try – the other girls aren't always interested. Most of them prefer chasing boys in the clubs.'

'How long is your layover this time?'

There! The unmistakable flash of interest. 'Four nights.'

'Well, there you go. Venison pie it is.'

Now she smiled, reading the signals.

'What about you, Dr North? What brings you to Cape Town?'

'Please, call me Gipsy.'

***

'Where are your bodyguards, Mr Minister?'

BT looked like what he was these days, the only surprise being that it had taken him less than three years to change from a rangy radical into a political suit. His black hair had the first streaks of gray and his angular lines had definitely softened, but at least his shirt was open at the throat and his eyes hadn't lost their humor. He chuckled, and for the first time I recognized some of the resonance of his evangelical brother.

'Oh, we don't go in for that kind of thing so much. There's nothing to be gained by killing any of us – we all believe in the same thing. At least, that's what we tell ourselves.' He sidled closer. 'But we take precautions…'

'That's what I love about you, BT. A free spirit with a cautious streak.'

Now he gave one of the wild laughs I remembered so well. 'Hey man, I like that! Can I use it?'

'It's all yours, mate.'

We arrived at a black BMW 750 with darkened windows and he opened the back door for me. I saw there was a driver already behind the wheel, and another man sitting next to him.

'Ah, I see what you mean about precautions.'

BT said something in Afrikaans to the men in the front of the car, and they laughed. 'I just told them we all have new names – I'm Free Spirit, and they are Cautious and Streak.'

As the car eased its way through the morning traffic, over the flank of Table Mountain and into the city center he answered my questions about the transformation of the Cape Province into the independent state of the Cape of Good Hope.

'I don't know anyone here who regrets the secession, but we all feel very conflicted about the fact that we've done very well while the rest of the country has turned into a game reserve.'

'A game reserve?'

He smiled sadly. 'Ja, an area populated by wild animals, with civilization in a few camps surrounded by razor-wire.'

'Do you see any moves to… tame the wild animals?'

'Ag, people have been talking about nothing else for months. From what we hear, the tribes have stopped fighting. Now they are just focusing on survival.'

'What about here in the Cape? Don't you have the same tribes?'

'Ja, of course. Mainly Xhosas, but lots of Zulus too. But we sat down with their leaders, and told them we're all in the same life-boat. If you guys start fighting the boat will turn over, and we'll all drown. All of our ancestors came from somewhere else – we're all immigrants in the Cape – so we might as well forget all that ethnic shit and consider ourselves Kaapenaars. Capetonians. But I must say it's hard to stop thinking of ourselves as South Africans also.'

'What a pity they didn't do that in the rest of the country. But you say they can't wait to lay down their arms…?'

'That's what we hear. Some say they've run out of ammunition, others say they've run out of people to shoot. I think so many of them have been wiped out by AIDS that the others have lost interest in fighting.'

'Any ideas on how to sort things out?'

'Ag, I really don't know. We hear terrible stories. Nobody knows how to fix it.'

'What about the people who left South Africa before the shit hit the fan? Can't they come back and help to stabilize the country? Like the exiles who returned after Mandela was released?'

He shook his head. 'We came back to a country that was politically messed up, but everything was working. Today… well, there are millions of exiles, but the question is whether they want to come back to a country where nothing works. Nothing at all.'

I'd seen this argument on the forums, but it never quite made sense.

'But BT, all the power stations are there, the water-purification plants, the schools and universities, the hospitals and factories, the roads and the cellular towers…'

'Ja, I know what you mean. So why is it such a big deal to get them all working again?'

'Yes, exactly.'

'It's like… if you want to turn on the electricity, you don't just need a few guys to flip switches. You need coal from the mines, which means the mines must be working, then you need the guys who know how to operate the generating plants, and people in every city to sort out the substations and the meters. And you need consumers who can pay for their electricity, which means you need an economy. But you can't have an economy unless you can get the electricity going.'

'Okay, but what about foreign aid?'

'Well, ja, of course, but remember we're talking about rebuilding the biggest economy in Africa, from nothing, when we have huge gaps in skills…' He caught himself and laughed. 'Listen to me, talking about "we" like it's our problem.'

'Isn't it?'

He blew out his cheeks. 'Man, you have a real talent for asking hard questions, Gipsy. Our official position, as the Cape government, is that it isn't – our responsibility is to ensure the security and prosperity of the people who live inside our borders. And we're doing a bloody good job, even if I say so myself. But we all grew up as South Africans first, and Kaapenaars second, so our hearts and minds are on opposite teams.'

***

When BT said my old friends from the secession wanted to see me again, I didn't think we'd gather in the tiny living room of a cottage on the Cape Flats and drink beer like the last time, but he didn't give me many clues on what I should expect – except to 'dress nicely'.

BT's bodyguard was waiting for me in the foyer of the Cape Grace hotel at noon, and it turned out there was nothing wrong with his command of English.

'You can call me Cautious, ma'am,' he said with a big smile. 'Streak is waiting in the car. Minister Abrahams offers his apologies for not being able to collect you himself, but he'll meet you at the premier's house.'

'Thanks, Cautious. Is that your first name or your surname?'

'My surname, ma'am. My first name is Super. The driver's first name is Mean.'

And so it went until we passed through the gates of the premier's official residence, when Super Cautious and Mean Streak fell silent. Super opened my door and assured me they'd be 'ready and sober' when it was time to take me back to the Cape Grace. When I said not to expect the same of me he merely gave a polite smile, obviously conscious of where we were.

As I turned toward the mansion I saw the reason for his caution – the massive bulk of the Reverend Dr William Abrahams, Premier of the Independent State of the Cape of Good Hope, was bearing down on us.

'Gipsy! Welcome to my humble abode.'

I tried to look unimpressed. 'Shit Billy, I really hoped you would make something of yourself since we last met!'

The giant man laughed so loudly that several people appeared at the door to see what was going on. I was somewhat worried myself – fat and jolly is a recipe for an oversized coffin. Billy draped a heavy arm across my shoulders and ushered me into the building, where he introduced me to a couple of dozen people, all holding high office or partnered with power.

In due course we were seated at a series of round tables on the terrace, overlooking an immaculate garden and the eastern side of Table Mountain, now in shadow, and our champagne flutes were kept filled with a lovely bubbly from Graham Beck. After we'd said grace and eaten half an avocado filled with shrimps in a seafood sauce, Billy rose to his feet and rapped on his glass with a spoon.

'Friends, today is doubly special. First, it is exactly three years since a small group of malcontents met in my mother's house in Mannenberg and decided that, somehow, the Cape had to insulate itself from what we all knew was going to happen to the north. I'm not sure any of us truly believed we would succeed but, as you can see, we did.'

He waved his arm at the mansion behind, and the lawns and mountain in front of us. I heard soft calls of 'hoor hoor' and 'hallelujah' from the group, and a few raised their glasses before Billy continued.

'I've often been asked for the secret of our success, and I think the answer is – timing and gearing...'

'Sounds like my old car!' I recognized one of the men from that meeting on the Cape Flats. Like the others he looked older, heavier and better groomed. Billy took the heckling in good spirits.

'Solly, that old Chev of yours couldn't go anywhere that had a hill! But, unlike your car, our timing was good – we found people in power were ready to talk – and our gearing worked, because when we told them who else was supporting us, most of them agreed to join. Even those who were against us at first came around when they saw which way the mood was going.'

'If you talk much longer, the mood will be gone...' BT got his timing just right, and the guests cracked up. I wasn't used to heads of state taking a public ragging, but Billy took it all in his stride.

'Ladies and gentlemen, the Lord gives us our families. Praise the Lord that we can choose our friends!' When he could be heard again, Billy raised his hands for quiet.

'But as always my little boetie, the honorable minister of foreign affairs, is right. So let me tell you the second reason that today is special. When we needed an unbiased observer to witness the birth of our state, there was never any question about who that should be. Gipsy North told us about the bombing of those factories in India, and she gave it the name we all use today – pharmageddon. Gipsy knew who would be affected most by that sabotage, and she flew to Johannesburg the very same day, even before the looting started. She warned us of the dangers of interrupting ARV treatment, and she alerted us to the tribal conspiracy which was the underlying reason for that interruption. Gipsy was here to witness the birth of our small nation, and she's been close to our story, and to our hearts, ever since.'

Billy reached into his jacket and pulled out what looked like a small book. 'Gipsy, last week the Cape Council resolved to recognize your contribution to the Cape by awarding you honorary citizenship to our boutique country. Now you are one of us!'

I stood up to take the passport from Billy, who was on the opposite side of the table, and was horrified to find that everyone else stood up and began to applaud. Then I heard BT yell 'speech' and everyone sat down, leaving me standing with my new passport and my face hanging out. Neat trick.

'Oh... crap! Hey, I bet you do this for everyone who applies for a passport...'

While they laughed, I wondered what would come out of my mouth next. I didn't want to piss on their kindness, which ruled out the 'I was only doing my job' approach, and the 'if I stand out it's only because I'm standing on the shoulders of others' line has been done to death. I wished I hadn't downed two glasses of bubbly on an empty stomach.

'This is just... great, thank you. I always wanted to have a second passport, just in case some mad dictator somewhere confiscates the other one. Hey, did you know that journalism is one of the most dangerous jobs in the world? Second only to politics, I believe. We journalists face constant threats to our lives. Cirrhosis of the liver, diabetes, congestive heart failure, hair-dryers in five-star hotels falling into our bathtubs...' They seemed to be lapping it up.

'But as your newest citizen, I must warn you that journalists can pose a danger to others. Bad grammar, keeping bad company... But the greatest danger, by far, is that we will be asked to speak in public. The World Health Organization has issued a global warning against asking journalists to deliver a speech. Anyone who hears us speak must be disposed of with other toxic waste, in case the contamination spreads.' Time to quit while I'm ahead.

'But before I sit down, in the interests of your health and mine, I do want to say two things. The first is – I'm really touched by this! For the opportunity to see the birth of... what did you call it? Your boutique nation! I love boutiques! And the second thing is – congratulations! You guys turned a crisis into an opportunity, and you've succeeded. Magnificently. But for what it's worth – if you'd failed, I would have written about you anyway.'

It was the right moment to sit down, but I held up my hand. 'Oh yeah, one last thing. Now that you're a country and not a province anymore, don't think for a minute that you can play against Queensland or Western Australia. You may have been able to keep a tribal war out, but there's no way to keep out the Wallabies.'

For a horrible moment I wondered whether I'd blown it – but Capetonians are as crazy about rugby and cricket as any Ozzie, and they didn't seem to mind my jibe at the tribes.

After I sat down Billy raised his glass to me. 'Well said Gipsy. But tell me, now that you're a citizen of the Cape of Good Hope, who will you be cheering for when we defeat the Wallabies?'

'Hey, if you're beating them, I'll cheer for you guys. The golden rule – always be on the winning side.' I raised my glass to him. 'Same goes for your wine. When you learn to make better plonk than we do, I'll be the first to admit it.'

After the thunder of the reverend premier's mirth subsided, he hooked a finger at the wine-waiter and took the bottle from him. I'd seen the label earlier, so I deliberately averted my eyes now. The leader of the fledgling state carefully leaned over and filled my glass with red wine, then cocked an eyebrow at me. By now the entire audience was watching. I took a sip, ran it around my tongue and palate, sucked in a little air, and swallowed.

'Yeah, okay. It's not too shabby. Cab sav. It isn't quite up to the best from Margaret River or McLaren Vale. Also a bit young. My guess is a De Trafford from, oh, 2004.'

'You saw the label!' BT yelled from the next table.

When normality returned Billy turned to me again and asked about my plans while I was in the region. I told him I'd been invited by the Indian army to see for myself what their treatment centers looked like, three years on.

'And what are your plans this weekend?'

'Oh, I heard you made some reasonable wines in the Cederberg, so I thought I might go and see for myself.'

***

The hot-springs resort near the town of Clanwilliam was called 'The Baths' and their facilities were as spare as their name, so we checked into the Clanwilliam Lodge which was a modest step up. Pol Roger wasn't on their wine-list but there was nothing wrong with their local bubblies, nor with their oysters and lobster – or crayfish as we call them in the colonies. They even had toweling robes in their 'presidential suite' and a treatment room for massage.

Not that we really cared. I'd hired a hardy Landcruiser and bought us hiking boots at an outdoor shop, and we spent the two days exploring the mountains, tasting the excellent wines at the highest winery in the country, and talking. And we spent our two nights together eating, drinking, talking and... well, sleeping.

Kimberly was a delightful companion, and a great listener. She probed gently on Emily, and I ended up telling her the whole story. In fact I talked so much that I learned very little about her life, but she didn't seem to mind. And I needed to talk to someone who hadn't met Em, or grown to love her. Which is the same thing.

I told her how we'd met at a medical conference in Dublin, where Em was one of the simultaneous interpreters. I was so taken with her voice as she translated Spanish and Portuguese into my headset that I forgot to listen to what she was saying. At the first opportunity I went looking for the face behind the voice.

The best way to describe her was 'wild'. Her hair, her eyes, her voice, her laugh, even her life and her friends. Wild! I never quite understood what she saw in me but whatever it was, she saw it right away. When the conference ended, we didn't.

It turned out we had a friend in common – Jim Wallace. In fact Em knew him much better than I did. They'd met a decade earlier in Antigua Guatemala, high among the volcanoes and coffee plantations of central America, when they were studying Spanish at one of that quaint city's language schools. Their love was mutual, profound and enduring, but the roll of the genetic dice meant it would never be physical. Jim never married, but he and Em spoke on the phone at least once a week, and made up excuses to visit each other a couple of times a year.

I'd met Jim a few times in the course of my work, and taken a course that he taught in media trends at Columbia. We enjoyed each other's company, but made no particular effort to stay in touch.

When I met Em I was working for BBC World and renting a grungy hole in Fulham. It had cupboards for my clothes, space for a good bed, and a few decent restaurants within walking distance, but it was hardly a place I yearned to be. Em had no trouble finding an outlet for her remarkable linguistic talents in London, and even less trouble renting a bright and warm semi in Chiswick which she made our home for three years. Then came the Economist for me, and a shift to literary rather than verbal translation for Em, and we pooled our savings to buy a cottage in Chipping Norton.

From the beginning I was away more than I was at home, but Em was a social magnet and complained she never had time to herself. And our times together were always memorable. Living near the impossible Jeremy Clarkson was enough reason to buy a sports car, and when we weren't shopping for distressed furniture for the cottage, we spent many wonderful afternoons exploring the pubs of the Cotswolds in our yellow Mazda MX5.

Then, out of the blue, came Em's dizziness, diagnosis and depression. An incurable and unpredictable illness, they said. Not terminal itself, but opening the door to a catalogue of complications, from the niggling to the fatal. For a year we held our breaths but, apart from having to sit down occasionally to avoid falling down, or dropping things, nothing else happened.

Eventually we got tired of waiting for the other shoe to drop and drafted the Concord of Chipping Norton. Whatever is going to happen, will happen. We respectfully decline to live in fear. Instead, we will suck the sap out of whatever we have – time, abilities, opportunities, money – and we'll ignore the things we don't have, or lose along the way. Amen and pass the corkscrew.

Within a week Em found she couldn't call me Gipsy. Her tongue wouldn't make a 'P' sound. So we agreed that Jimsy or Gimme were good, too. But for some reason she took to calling me 'lover' even though she couldn't say 'Ls' either and it sounded unnervingly like 'mother'.

Within three months she surrendered to her first wheelchair. As I lowered her into it she smiled wickedly. 'Hey! Now that I'm a cripple, our parking problems are at an end! Oh, and I can take a dog where other dogs aren't allowed!' A few days later the Mazda made way for an Audi station wagon, which could hold her wheelchair, and a couple of weeks after that Jamie entered our lives, courtesy of the Guide Dog Association.

Em's balance and speech were messed up but her hand-eye coordination was perfect and she continued with her written translations, and her never-ending quest to soak up languages. She also made it clear that, while she was breathing, our home was her responsibility, and she would not tolerate any modification of my career. She made more than enough money to pay a housekeeper and a part-time nurse, and the insurance payout – after she finally litigated it out of her insurers – gave her a sense of financial security.

So we weren't exactly bleeding, and when Shan and Jim's offer came up I was ready to turn them down. It was amusing that anyone should offer me so much money, but it simply didn't compare to my life with Em, and I knew it would mean even longer periods away from her.

But the wild girl of Dublin wouldn't hear of it, happily throwing the Concord of Chipping Norton in my face. 'We suck the sap out of whatever we have, lover. Including opportunities. If you turn Jim down, Jamie and I are outa here. Oh, no, that won't work – I'm the cripple. Okay, if you turn him down, you're outa here.'

An even bigger surprise was her insistence on moving to Istanbul, even though we could easily have stayed in Chippy. 'I've only ever lived on one or other side of the Irish Sea. And I've already started learning Turkish…' She didn't need to say that it would also be the first time she'd be living near to Jim.

Em loved everything about our villa in Fenerbahçe. The view, her staff, my colleagues from TWO, and especially the fact that Jim visited most evenings for a drink or supper. When Jamie finally made it through the Turkey shoot, as Em called their quarantine regulations, it seemed her life was complete. We were sucking the sap as hard as we could.

When the second shoe fell I was at home. I heard Kenan's yell from the terrace, where I was hammering at my laptop. He told me later that Jamie fetched him in the kitchen, the dog's body language powerful enough to make him drop his coffee mug and sprint to the bathroom, where Emily was lying between her buggy and the bog, her eyes alive but her lungs not taking in air.

He lifted her onto the bed and began resuscitation before bellowing for help. Despite my medical degree I knew my limitations, so I left the first-aid to Kenan while I held onto Em's hand with both of mine – one hand for reassurance, the other taking her pulse – and talked to her eyes. I could hear

Arda speaking urgently into the phone, so I couldn't think of anything more to do.

Even though her body had stopped working, her mind had not. I saw her eyes flick over to the side of the bed where Jamie always lay, now out of her line of sight. I said his name and in an instant he was on the bed, snuggled against her side. Em's eyes were on me again, saying what her face and her lungs couldn't.

'You're welcome, my love.'

As Kenan kept working, I found myself dredging up crap from our lives together, just to fill the silence. Or to cover the sound of the BVM resuscitator which Kenan was squeezing rhythmically.

'Hey, you remember that time when Nikki stayed with us in Chiswick? Before we bought the sleeper-couch? Didn't she say there was some guy in her life? I think she met him in Geneva, but she never said how. Or what happened. She never tells me anything important – just about global epidemics and shit like that. Did she tell you what happened to that boy? You're much better at wheedling that kind of information out of people. Remember to ask her about it when we next see her, won'tcha?'

After a few minutes I offered to take over on the resuscitator, but Kenan said he was okay so I rattled on mindlessly, trying to persuade myself that Em's pulse wasn't fading. Arda appeared at the door to say the ambulance would arrive in a couple of minutes, but I knew they couldn't do much more than we were doing. Em's eyes told me she also knew this wasn't going to end well. They also said she wasn't ready. Not yet.

'Whatever is going to happen, will happen girl.'

There was movement at the bedroom door but it wasn't the ambulance guys, it was Jim, his face white with shock.

'Arda called...' he said, crawling over the pillows to find a spot near Em's head, from where he could stroke her hair. It was getting really crowded on the bed. I smiled at him and then looked back at Em, to find her eyes had changed. Now she was ready.

I must have said something, or maybe not. In any event Jim began crooning: 'It's okay my love. We won't let go. Ever.' And something else in Spanish that sounded like a poem.

Em's pulse fluttered and then disappeared, like a moth discovering the open part of the window. Now her eyes were... just eyes. I put a hand on Kenan's arm and he stopped aspirating, then he dropped his head to his knees and cried like a baby. There was a commotion as the EMS guys finally arrived, and we all had to leave the bed while they confirmed what we knew.

After they'd gone Jim, Jamie and I all lay next to Em, saying nothing, for a long time.

A few days later Nikki flew in from her office in Geneva to join Jim and me as we scattered Em's ashes from a rented boat halfway between the Fenerbahçe marina and the Princess Islands. Then we held a noisy wake at the villa, attended by pretty much everyone from the office, just as Em would have wanted.

Jim was the last to leave the party, and I walked him out to his car. As he opened the door Jamie brushed past him, scrambling onto the passenger seat then sitting motionless, his amber eyes fixed on me.

Jim was surprised. 'Hey boy, where d'you think you're going?'

But I understood. 'If you'll have him Jim, he wants to be with you.' Somehow I resisted the temptation to add: 'at last'.

***

The invitation that brought me back to the Cape had been signed by a Major General Ao at army headquarters in New Delhi. It simply said I was invited to tour the 'UN installations in South Africa'.

I was asked to allow a week, which seemed like a long time to visit a few camps. The plot thickened when a Colonel on Ao's staff told me I was the only person on this tour.

'Why me? And why now?'

'We understand you have a unique record as a witness to the... situation in South Africa, doctor. We would be sorry to see your batting average drop, at this late stage of the game.'

I hate sporting analogies, but I let it go. 'And the timing?'

'Well, I'm told the heat of summer is over, so it is a pleasant time to visit. It is also three years since the treatment centers were established, so it is time for a review, we believe. You will have an opportunity to meet General Ao, who has been appointed GOC – general officer commanding of our peacekeeping forces in that region.'

I sensed that I was supposed to be intrigued by these platitudes. I was, a bit.

The bases for the reserve Indian army forces inside South Africa, including the one I'd visited in Bloemfontein, had been evacuated shortly after my last visit. New brigades were deployed instead to Lüderitz in Namibia, Francistown Botswana, Maputo Mozambique and Saldanha Bay, an hour's drive north from Cape Town, where I was expected.

I may have been the only person on the 'tour' but I wasn't the only passenger on their Mi-8 for the three-hour flight to the Three Sisters Treatment Center. This time I was given ear protectors rather than an audio headset, so there was no question of talking to the other 19 passengers. They all appeared to be Indians – a collection of medics, soldiers and bureaucrats from the looks of them.

Now, as we circled the camp, I got a buzzard's eye view of how this little patch of desert had been transformed since I ate barbecued corn and potatoes on this spot, more than three years earlier. The center was set against the small hill, exactly where we'd assembled that night. I could see the highway now had some kind of concrete barrier, and the little hill had acquired a hard-looking nipple which I guessed was a gun emplacement.

A makeshift road ran from one side of the barrier across the highway, around the hill, arriving at an open parking area just outside the camp's perimeter. A couple of prefabricated buildings stood alongside the parking area – presumably where the testing took place. A control point with a boom guarded another gravel road, linking back to the highway south of the barrier. The gun emplacement on the hill made sure nobody broke the rules.

The only thing wrong with the picture was that the roads and car-park were utterly deserted, even though it was 10,30 on a Monday morning.

Inside the perimeter fence, the camp itself was a sprawling mass of brown and olive tents, clinging to a spider's web of roads. At the center of the web was an improbable circle of green – a park of some kind, with grass and trees.

Between the road that ran around the park and the next circular road, I could see three clusters of buildings and four dust-colored open areas – a vehicle park, a helicopter landing area, and a parade ground or sports field. A vivid red cross inside a bright white circle painted on one of the larger buildings left no doubt as to its function while the others appeared to be a school and the military headquarters.

Moving still further from the green dot in the middle, hundreds or even thousands of tents filled my field of vision. As we moved slowly toward the landing area I could see clusters of outside toilets and water points, with people lining up to make use of one or fill plastic drums at the other. Finally my vision was obscured by a cloud of diarrhea-colored dust, and we settled on the ground. I fumbled for my carry-on as the engine note changed and finally disappeared, along with the dust. The door was yanked open, and the dry desert air and silence blew in.

Outside not much was happening – just a few soldiers in sand-colored desert fatigues and pale blue UN helmets watching us and looking bored. Nobody told us what to do, but the other passengers straggled towards a prefab which served as an arrival and departure area.

Inside the building a man wearing the uniform of the Indian Voluntary Service was holding a little placard with my name on it, seemingly oblivious of the fact that I was the only peppermint in a box of chocolates. He solemnly introduced himself as Sunny, took my bag and led me outside and a few paces along the circular road to a building bristling with satellite dishes, antennae and airconditioning units, which turned out to house both the military commander of the base and the civilian camp administrator, Mahmud Khan.

After a couple of minutes Khan emerged from his office, a small man in his mid-forties wearing a white dhoti kurta, like a long shirt over a skirt. He said he was delighted I'd accepted the invitation from the GOC to review 'his' camp – a sentiment not entirely shared by his eyes – and ushered me into his small office. After a few pleasantries and a cup of spiced tea with milk and sugar already added, Khan asked what I wanted to know.

I'd been sent a bunch of figures by Ao's people, so I asked for a history lesson.

'When we set up the camps we were expecting a lot of patients to arrive very quickly – to be swamped you could say – because nobody was getting treatment in their own hospitals. But we were surprised to find that a lot of people who tested positive did not want treatment, but went back to where they came from. In the first week we admitted less than three thousand patients across all ten camps.' I noticed that Khan didn't refer to any notes.

'We finally learned the reason for this from your own good website, Dr North. It was the myth that our treatment centers were actually death camps, and that nobody who was admitted would leave. Well, not alive anyway.' He seemed amused at the thought.

'But at the time all we could do was wait. The observers sent by the South African authorities seemed to be happy that people were not making use of our facilities. Unfortunately, most of the patients who did ask for treatment were at a very advanced stage, so our mortality rate was high. And it seems the government may have used this fact to reinforce the rumors.'

'When did the number of patients pick up?'

'Not until three months after we opened. By that time patients could no longer purchase ARVs on the black market, or they were becoming resistant to those drugs, and they were no longer so accepting of rumors.'

'That would be around the time of the Ladysmith expedition...'

'Yes indeed. A terrible tragedy. We have named the fountain in our memorial garden after Captain Singh, at the request of our patients.'

'Oh?'

'Yes. They regard him as a hero, as we do of course. He gave his life trying to save the lives of others. Not just those of you on the helicopter, but the people who needed medical treatment to save their lives. A lot of patients heard of the Ladysmith massacre, and realized they had been misled about our intentions.'

'I'm glad his death served some purpose. At the time it just seemed like a huge... waste.'

Khan nodded, and seemed to be waiting for me to say something else.

'I gather your inmates are all women and children. Why is that?'

'Ah yes. Well you see at first we were admitting patients only long enough to stabilize their condition, and then we discharged them. The government observers insisted we send them home, but of course the patients found they couldn't get treatment there, so they came back with their families and camped outside our fence.'

'What – here in the desert?'

'Yes, it was horrible. They had no shelter, no water, no sanitation... but what could we do? We took them food and water, and we re-admitted those who were sick, but our mandate prevented us from admitting uninfected family members, and the observers were such... sticklers for detail. Then, after some time, the observers withdrew and we decided – Delhi decided – to expand our perimeter to accommodate the outsiders, as we called them. Unfortunately, by that time those gangs were preying on them, stealing their food and medications, holding their children hostage and so on...'

'Couldn't your peacekeepers chase away the gangs?'

'Oh, it wasn't so simple. There was no way to decide who was a family member or a gangster. I mean, they didn't threaten anyone openly. So when our reinforcements arrived to expand the camp, they decided as a temporary measure to admit only women and children inside the perimeter. Until we could sort the civilians from the militants, so to speak.'

'How did you do that?'

'Unfortunately we failed. Our plan was to interview all the men, and verify their stories with the women inside. But it became ugly – some of the men threatened our volunteers – and then one night they all disappeared.'

'Disappeared?'

'Yes, we woke up to find they were all gone. All except for a few old men. We heard they were forced to join the tribal militia. We also heard there was a rumor that we were going to poison the food we took out to them, but I don't know about that.'

I tried to blank out the horror of men being forced to abandon their wives and children.

'So... Mr Khan, what proportion of your patients are HIV positive?'

'In this center, more than 80 percent of the adults, and a third of the children. That's why they came here in the first place. It varies between centers – on the coast they have a higher proportion of uninfected people.'

'Have you had uninfected people coming here for food?'

'No. Well yes, but just a few. They had many in some of the other camps, which are closer to populated areas, and they tried feeding them, but of course they couldn't admit them all to the center, and the local gangs kept harassing the outsiders, and eventually they left.'

Khan's matter-of-fact tone and slight smile formed a bizarre counterpoint to the human tsunami which had washed up against the razor wire perimeters of the camps. He went on to describe the logistics of trucking in food and supplies donated by wealthy nations, and busing Indian soldiers, medics and support personnel.

He seemed surprised when I asked about transport for patients wishing to return to their homes in South Africa. 'But... nobody wants to leave. If they didn't die from AIDS, or starve, they could be killed by the militia.'

Time to take another tack.

'I'm curious about your own background, Mr Khan.'

'Thank you for asking, doctor. I am a member of the IAS – the Indian Administrative Service. It is like a professional association for senior civil servants. Before I was posted here I held the post of joint secretary in the national Ministry of Health and Family Welfare.'

'Where does a joint secretary fit into the organogram?'

He smiled. 'We have our own way of doing things in India. After we are trained by the IAS we start as magistrates and work our way up. A joint secretary is the fourth highest rank in our national government service. The next step is additional secretary, then secretary, then cabinet secretary, which is the top position.'

'In a country of over a billion people that sounds like a pretty big deal.'

'Thank you. It is a great honor to serve my country.'

'So… why are you running a desert camp in South Africa?'

The man looked genuinely surprised. 'Well we… our government attaches a very high priority to these centers, Dr North. I was one of many applicants for this job, and I was very honored to be chosen.'

This was getting dull, so I decided to push a little. 'What kind of powers do you have here, Mr Khan?'

'We run each center by committee – the military commander, the chief medical officer, and the chief administrative officer. The committee is chaired by the brigadier who is responsible for the three centers bordering the Cape.'

'And your daily responsibilities?'

'I am the administrative manager, chief accountant, and also a magistrate. So I hear disputes among patients or staff. I even have the authority to conduct marriages!'

'And who is your boss – who do you answer to?'

He sat very still, but answered immediately. 'The secretary for external affairs in Delhi, who gets his instructions from the foreign minister. The minister chairs a special cabinet committee established by the prime minister to oversee our… engagement in South Africa. It includes the ministers for defense, health and family welfare and population.'

'Thank you – I hope you don't mind me asking?'

'Not at all Dr North. We have nothing to hide.'

Buggered if I wasn't getting exactly the opposite feeling, although I had no idea why. Khan asked whether I'd like to meet the brigadier. Silly question. He ushered me across the hall and into another waiting room, much like his own. Several soldiers leapt to their feet when we entered, but there was no saluting. A secretary – who hadn't stood up – picked up her phone and spoke briefly in Hindi before showing us through to the brigadier's office.

Brigadier Bhardwaj was every inch the military officer, tall and thin with a fine handlebar moustache and graying hair, and his eyes were friendly and inquisitive.

'Ah, Dr Gipsy North. I was hoping we'd get a chance to meet.' He grasped my hand firmly and held on. 'I've been following the development of TWO since it's inception, d'you know. A wonderful tool. Long overdue. Real antidote to war.'

'I'm glad you feel that way, brigadier. I certainly share Dr Gupta's view that the truth can set us free.'

'And you have done a truly admirable job of covering the unfolding drama that brings us all to this dusty spot. It seems to me you've done so much more than simply present the news…' There was a twinkle in his eye.

'Well, I could tell you everything, but then I'd have to kill you. And Mr Khan.'

Bhardwaj threw his head back and roared with laughter. I caught a fleeting look of distaste on Khan's face, quickly concealed. I wondered if it was my crook humor or Bhardwaj' lack of inhibition that Khan objected to.

'And now you have joined us to witness the beginning of the end of this affair?'

I caught Khan's reaction from the corner of my eye, and saw Bhardwaj' eyes move to him. 'Ah, I think I have said too much too soon.'

Khan shrugged. 'I was leaving it for you to tell Dr North, brigadier.'

'Well then, let's make ourselves comfortable.'

Bhardwaj offered tea and cold drinks. I sipped a club soda with ice and a sprig of mint while we covered the standard pleasantries and background. I was scheduled to be here for a week, so I saw no need to push Bhardwaj to explain right away what he meant by 'the beginning of the end'. There was often more to be gained by approaching a big story from the side.

As Khan had already told me, the brigadier headed the 'southern cluster' of three camps adjoining the Cape. Other brigadiers ran the western cluster, alongside Namibia and Botswana, and the eastern cluster next to Zimbabwe and Mozambique. Bhardwaj and his colleagues reported to Major General Ao in Delhi.

'Tell me about your assignment here, brigadier.'

'We're mainly policemen – policemen and border guards. We don't expect any external threat. Just a case of keeping the peace. A classic UN mission.'

'But I heard that it can get a bit… hectic sometimes. Like that attempt by the Zulu militia to take ARVs from the camp on the border of Mozambique?'

A deep chuckle this time. 'Heavens, I would have loved to see the look on those gangsters faces when Narain planted those 102 millimeter mortars. I gather they wet themselves.'

'I heard they spilled tea on their trousers.'

'Ah, but who could tell the difference? They got themselves into hot water of some kind!'

'Have you had anything like that here?'

'No, m'dear. We had reinforcements here when we expanded the camps, so the hostiles kept their distance. We've had a few of them taking pot shots at our patrols, but we go out in Casspirs, so no harm done. We never retaliated, in fact we've not fired a shot in anger.'

'Casspirs?'

'Yes – armored personnel carriers. Strangely enough India purchased them from South Africa. Very good they are, too. Ironic, really, shipping them back here for this mission.'

'What about inside the camp? Any agro in here?'

'Well, when you put a bunch of men together there's always excitement. But we're used to that in the army. Our Indian boys are pretty well behaved overall. The UN loves to use us for peacekeeping.'

'Do you have any problems with... what do you call it in the military... fraternization, between your men and the civilians?'

'No no no. Well, not with the patients. Our fellows are very well behaved. Mind you, I told them I'd cut off their balls if they used them anywhere except the cricket field!'

Now we both guffawed. I could see Khan was uncomfortable with the tone of the discussion, but Bhardwaj paid him no attention. 'Mind you Dr North...'

'Please, call me Gipsy.'

'Thank you, m'dear. I was going to say that my unattached boys take a keen interest in the Indian nurses and teachers, but our girls are very... straight laced, I suppose you'd call it, by western standards. And of course our married soldiers are allowed to bring out their wives and children after a year.'

Out of the corner of my eye I caught a reaction from Khan, so I turned to him. 'So that's why you mentioned that you are able to conduct marriages, Mr Khan. Have there been many?'

The administrator glanced at Bhardwaj before replying. 'A growing number, yes. A lot of our staff – military and civilian – have opted to extend their tours here. It means they have additional privileges, like having their family stay with them, or getting married.'

From the little I knew of Indian custom, it seemed odd that their young men and women would choose to get married so far from their homes and families.

'Do you think many of these couples are hoping to stay after the camps are closed?' Ah, a definite reaction from them both, but Khan responded smoothly.

'It's something which they are certainly talking about. At this stage there's no policy from Delhi, but I think some of our staff would like to help restore public health services in South Africa. Time will tell.'

'Is that what you meant by the beginning of the end, brigadier?'

'Yes m'dear. In fact the GOC has asked me to brief you on Operation Truro. Unfortunately I can only give you the broad details, because if I told you the specifics...'

'Then you'd have to kill me! And Mr Khan?'

Again Bhardwaj bellowed at the ceiling. 'Oh heavens! No, I think I would spare Mr Khan. I wouldn't want his job. And don't you know the IAS is a protected species in India?'

'Okay, tell me about your operation. What does Truro mean?'

'It's the name of the ship which carried the first indentured laborers from Madras to Durban in 1860. I believe they named the operation after that ship because India is now sending more people to help restore the society that our people helped to build.'

'Restore society?'

'Indeed. Obviously we cannot continue with these treatment centers indefinitely, but at the same time we cannot abandon nearly four million people who are depending on us. So the only way to break this impasse is to restore order in South Africa, including their public health system.'

I was making a show of taking notes, but I looked up when he stopped. 'And how will you do that?'

'Well, our approach is straightforward. In the first phase we will secure points of entry for a team of civilian assessors. During the second phase they will decide what's needed to restore services and infrastructure. And in the third phase we will operationalise their recommendations.'

'Okay. Sounds simple enough.'

Bhardwaj smiled at my tone, but waited for a question.

'What are they expecting to find? Your assessors.'

'Our intelligence chaps believe a lot of city dwellers must have barricaded themselves in buildings and compounds, and lived on canned food and so on, but they would have run out by now or been overrun by militants. Aerial and satellite surveillance suggests the cities are now mostly depopulated, and the survivors are scavenging off the land or on the sea-shore.'

I told them what BT had said about the Catch-22 of restoring the South African economy, and the two men listened attentively, and Khan responded.

'Yes, we've had the pleasure of meeting minister Abrahams. He is an astute man.'

'So when will this operation begin?'

Bhardwaj smiled. 'Ah, I could tell you that, but...'

Before we could milk the joke for the third time, Khan cut in.

'It's important that the world understands that South Africa is going to need a lot of... hand-holding... for the foreseeable future. I've heard Dr Jha likening this project to caring for a premature baby...'

'Dr Jha?'

Khan rose to his feet. 'Yes, our CMO. Chief Medical Officer. Let's see if he's at home.'

'At home?'

'Receiving guests.'

Bhardwaj must have read my surprise at the abrupt termination of our interview but his wry smile told me resistance was futile, so I gave him a small wave and followed Khan out of the office, and the building. We walked into the central park and up to a modest fountain inscribed with Captain Singh's name and regiment, and an inscription in Hindi and English: 'He kept his head, while all around were losing theirs.'

Khan looked to me for a reaction. 'We Indians do like a bit of Kipling.'

I didn't have the heart to tell him that Captain Singh had lost his head so that the rest of us could keep ours.

'It's quite moving. Doest the Hindi say the same thing?'

'It's not Hindi – it's Gurmukhi, the script used for Punjabi language, and in the Sikh scriptures. I don't read it, but I believe the inscription says "He follows humbly in the footsteps of Guru Tegh Bahadur". Tegh Bahadur was one of the ten gurus who formed their religion. He was a great warrior, fighting against the Mughals who were trying to impose Islam on the people of India. In fact his name means "mighty of the sword".'

'What happened to this guru?'

'He was beheaded by the Mughals in the main marketplace in Delhi.'

I wanted to ask whether the guru kept his head while all around were losing theirs, but recognized the devil sitting on my shoulder. 'Where do you get the water for the grass and trees – and the fountain?'

'It's piped to us from a storage dam outside Beaufort West. I hope you do not feel this small patch of green is inappropriate? It's part of the Indian tradition to have parks.'

'Does everyone in the camp have access to this park?'

He looked uncomfortable. 'Yes, but not all the time. The patients conduct their Christian worship here on Sundays, and some of our Hindu festivals and wedding ceremonies take place here. But if we allowed unrestricted access the park would rapidly be reduced to a dust-bowl. The garden is more symbolic than practical.'

As we crossed the inner circular road and entered the hospital building, Khan explained the camp received power from the Cape's two nuclear power stations – the second completed a few weeks after secession.

Dr Dinesh Jha was remarkably young – early thirties, I guessed – and had the darker skin and features of the southern Indians, unlike Khan who had the caramel skin and Roman nose of the people in the north. Bhardwaj had been harder to place, with darker skin and aquiline features.

For the third time that morning I was offered refreshments and allowed to enquire as to the background of my host. Like Khan, Jha held a fairly senior job in the Indian public service – in the Ministry of Health – but was very pleased to be chosen for this post. Once more I was given a bunch of statistics and background, but as soon as I could I steered the conversation to the forthcoming push into South Africa. Jha was animated, but seemed to be choosing his words carefully, glancing at Khan from time to time.

'From a medical and social point of view, it promises to be one of the most interesting projects of our times.'

'How so?'

'Well, how often does one have an opportunity to rebuild all the components of a functioning public health system from scratch? It's like assembling a giant puzzle, with some of the pieces missing, or soon will be...'

'Soon will be?'

'Yes, when you consider the extreme levels of HIV, the life expectancy of many health workers will be limited. Transferring skills will also be difficult...'

'Because those who could be trained do not have the basic education, or may also have a limited life-span?'

'Exactly!'

'So... if you want to restore medical services, doesn't that mean you need to restore schools and universities, and also infrastructure like water and sanitation? And won't that take many years? Or a vast army of people?'

Jha glanced at Khan. Aha, it's about the people! Who they are, or how many. And, connecting the dots, it's about their intention to remain here. Once again Khan cut in.

'As the Brigadier mentioned earlier, military reinforcements are already on their way. Once they have secured the airports, civilian experts will be flown in to assess what's needed. Dr Jha and I are not in a position to guess what they will find.'

A definite stonewall! Yeah, baby!

'How many people are being sent from India?'

I saw the shadow of a smile on Jha's young face as he watched the administrator shift in his seat. 'I really don't know...'

'What about an estimate, Mr Khan? I'm sure it's been discussed? I was told I could ask any questions, and you said you have nothing to hide.'

Khan was getting rattled. 'Dr North, we are not hiding anything from you. You will have an opportunity to see for yourself how many people are involved.'

'What do you mean?'

'The GOC has invited you to witness the launch of the operation.'

'Oh... great! What does that mean?'

'It means, first of all, signing an agreement of confidentiality.'

Khan produced a document which said that I agreed to withhold publication of any and all information which I learned for a period of seven days. I checked that it did not limit what I could write, or photograph, only the timing of publication. For the duration I would have to surrender all communications devices.

'And I thought Brigadier Bhardwaj was joking when he said that if you told me everything, he'd have to kill me!'

Jha registered shock, but Khan said something in Hindi and the doctor chuckled.

'Okay, guys. Here's what I suggest. I have my regular Monday afternoon editorial conference this afternoon. Let me bounce this off my colleagues, and then I'll let you know whether I'm in or out.'

Khan looked surprised that I would think twice, and he seemed to hesitate over what to say next, but finally surrendered with a simple 'very well'.

***

I didn't need Jim's blessing, but I wanted to tell the others what I knew so far, without worrying about breaking any agreement. Of course Linus was the most experienced in matters military, and he said restrictions on information were quite normal – keeping critical information from the enemy – and in fact the terms I'd been offered were pretty relaxed.

'Sometimes they list all kinds of stuff that you can't report – ever. Other times they want to check your copy and recordings before you post them. A simple time-embargo is... well, it's actually amazing. But then again this is just a mercy mission. Hey listen Gipsy, why don't you pass it over to me?'

Before I could blow a raspberry at him, Russ cut in. 'Gipsy, you said you were asked to allow a week for this tour? Surely that means the Indians are going to land their reinforcements in the next couple of days...'

'But... they don't have a mandate from the UN.' Georghe had a light-bulb flashing over his head. 'Guys, they aren't afraid of Gipsy tipping off the tribal militia – they're worried about someone trying to stop them before they get there!'

Jim raised a hand towards the camera lens. 'Hold up a second. I don't believe India would risk international confrontation. Surely Georghe, if they don't have a UN mandate they will have cleared it informally with the big guys?'

'Well, I'll check with my contacts of course Jim, but I can't imagine any way that China would agree to an expeditionary force in South Africa, unless it's their own. They've been trying to muscle into Africa for years.'

Russ nodded. 'It's true. The Chinese declared 2006 the Year of Africa, they've written off a lot of government debt, lent a lot more, paid for infrastructure, propped up failing states like Zimbabwe in return for access to their natural resources...'

'Are there any circumstances in which India wouldn't need a mandate from the Security Council to send more troops to South Africa?'

'Jim, I may have the answer.'

'Yeah, Gip?'

'The Brigadier says this is the only way they can dismantle these camps. They have to restore public health services so the people in the camps can go home. But to do that, they have to restore public order first.'

Linus blew out his cheeks. 'Well, I don't know if that's enough to by-pass a UN mandate, but it may be enough to persuade some of the superpowers to sit on their hands. If the Indians tried for a Security Council resolution, you can be bloody sure China would veto it.'

I could see Jim wanted to move on. 'Okay okay! Georghe, you're going to check on the legality of the Indian position, and whether they're getting tacit support from the superpowers. Linus, can you follow up on the military angles, and together with Georghe watch for the Chinese reaction when it comes? Russ, how about a refresher course on the international push for economic hegemony in Africa? But listen, all of you, we need to play this very close to our chests. No posting until we agree it's safe to go. Gip, how much of this can go on record right now?'

'Jim, I think they cocked up today. I'm pretty sure the guy in the night-dress was supposed to get me to sign his piece of paper before they told me anything about their Operation Truro. If I post anything now, I think they may withdraw their invitation to see all the fun.'

'So what else have you got?'

'Oh, quite a lot of touchy-feely stuff on the camps themselves. I'll do a walk around this evening, chat to the patients...'

'Okay, go with that for now. The rest of us will get our ammunition ready for when the fighting starts.'

'Shit, nobody said anything about fighting!'

Jim didn't laugh like the rest. 'Gip, I'm sure you realize this has Pulitzer written all over it. If you need anything, anything at all...'

'Thanks Jim. Just hold your thumbs while I'm on the dark side of the moon.' We used the term for when we were out of contact – which didn't happen often.

***

I was back on the mountain overlooking Ladysmith, watching as the Mi-8 and the Hind gunships returned with the survivors of the Battle of Ladysmith. Once again the noise was overwhelming until their engines wound down. I ran over the coarse grass to the big transporter, my mini-cam rolling. Inside the wounded lay, but against the far wall of the chopper I saw the blue turban and calm eyes of Captain Singh. He held my eyes and gave a half-smile before turning back to the groaning soldier at his feet. I saw he was holding a drip, while a medic worked on the man.

Sergeant Chowdary touched my arm. 'It is time, Dr North. They are asking for you.' His touch became more insistent, and I turned to him but I couldn't see him. My eyes were closed. It wasn't Chowdary, and I wasn't on the mountain, I was on a camp bed in the 'guest tent' at the Karoo Treatment Center, and a female soldier was patting my arm.

'I'm... sorry. What?'

'The General has arrived, ma'am. Breakfast will be served in 20 minutes, then you will be leaving.'

'Twenty minutes? Oh crap! Okay, I'm up.'

Twenty five minutes later I was in the officer's mess, where we'd eaten the night before. I walked over to the table loaded with brass, and the men all rose to their feet. Major General Ao looked more like a martial arts instructor than a soldier. He was about my height but lean and hard, with slightly oriental features and hands designed to break things. He offered one of his deadly weapons and I shook it. It was as yielding as the handle of a tennis racket, but his grip was gentle. His accent was typically north-Indian but his eyes were gray-blue and his very short hair was brown, graying around the temples.

'Dr North. Pleased to meet you.'

He rattled off the names of three officers at the table that I hadn't met, and two that I had – the Brigadier and the Colonel in charge of the camp. He also pointed to six officers in overalls eating at the next table and introduced them collectively as the helicopter pilots. They waved back.

As soon as we were seated I was given a plate of spicy Indian food, without being asked what I wanted. They all had empty plates and full coffee-cups in front of them. While Bhardwaj pretended not to mind, Ao checked that I'd signed and understood the confidentiality agreement, and surrendered all means of communication.

'Good. You come very highly recommended, Dr North. Both for your journalistic skills and your experience in this… affair. I am also told you are a person of great integrity.'

'I can't imagine who would have told you that, General.'

He was taken aback by my response, but Bhardwaj smiled. 'Dr North has a rather… Australian… sense of humor, sir.'

'Oh, I see.' He giggled. 'A spin bowler.' The other officers echoed his giggle. Arse-wipes.

'Dr North, you are about to witness history being made. We ask only that you record it faithfully.' He looked me directly in the eyes, engraving his words in stone. 'Will you forgive me if I continue to speak to my men in Hindi? We have much to get through. Please, continue with your breakfast.'

Twenty minutes later the General, his two minions and I were on board a Sea King helicopter as the engine spooled up. The Hind gunships were already airborne, circling and ready to kill anything that threatened the General. The Sea King was smaller than the Mi-8 but more comfortable. General's transport. I learned later it was the same lump of machinery as the American president's ride, Marine One. With the door closed it was quiet enough to hold a conversation without headphones, just. However most of the discussion was in Hindi, and I wondered whether my inability to speak it was one of the reasons I was there.

One of the officers turned out to be the guy I'd spoken to when I was clarifying the invitation on this 'tour', Colonel Sewraj, and it appeared that one of his tasks was to look after me. He told me we were on our way to join the reinforcements, and that it would be a long flight. When I asked where we were meeting them, he smiled and said he didn't want to spoil the surprise.

Ao spent the first hour of the flight talking into a headset, but he must have run out of things to say, or maybe lost his radio link to whoever he was talking to, because he took his headset off and began to make conversation with me.

It turned out he was born in the north east Indian state of Nagaland, on the Burmese border. He followed his father and grandfather into the army. His grandfather was killed during the siege of Kohima in 1944. I'd never heard of it, but later looked it up to find it was a major ding dong – the turning point of the Japanese push into south Asia. What google didn't tell me, but Ao did, was that Indians served and died in terrifying numbers on both sides.

'My grandfather enlisted for the Assam Rifles, and his unit happened to be stationed in Kohima when they heard the Japanese were coming. The commander of the 14th army General Slim ordered the 161st Indian Brigade into the area – they were the crack troops of their day, and the fighting started on the fifth of April.'

Ao got a faraway look as he was telling me the story, and I could tell he'd relived it many times in his imagination.

'They were surrounded on the ridge, fighting 14,000 Japanese troops. The main battlefield was the deputy commissioner's bungalow and tennis court. It sounds almost funny now, but thousands of men died right there, on the sidelines. They were issued a pint of water a day, which was parachuted to them along with food and ammunition by the RAF. The officers didn't write much about their enlisted men, but we know grandfather was still fighting when the siege was lifted on 19 April. We think he was killed during the counter-offensive, sometime in early May. His grave is right there on the tennis court.'

Ao's father joined the army to honor the memory of his grandfather, and rose through the ranks to retire as a major, despite never seeing a shot being fired in anger. Apparently he now spent his days reminiscing with the other old timers and boasting about his son, whom he'd insisted should be burdened with the Christian names of Randle Harman – the surnames of two soldiers awarded the Victoria Cross after the Battle of Kohima, which cost more than 9,000 lives.

As for the man sitting opposite me, he joined the army because there 'wasn't much else to do in Nagaland'. He gave the credit for his meteoric rise to a series of lucky breaks, but I guessed he'd made his own luck. He'd fought against the Pakistanis in the Battle of Tiger Hill in Kashmir in 1999, and served with UN peacekeeping missions in Sierra Leone and Burundi. He was now based at Army HQ in New Delhi where his job involved 'doing anything that needs doing outside our borders.'

I was interested to see the glow of hero-worship in the other men's eyes. Their guy was clearly the sharpest edge of India's military machine.

Like every Indian, Ao followed cricket and knew every name on the Australian squad – which was more than I did – but he professed to be passionate about polo, to enjoy reading biographies, and to be married to a professor of constitutional law and to dote on their nine-year-old daughter.

'You look like you spend some time in the dojo, general.'

He smiled, but didn't respond. The other guys were closely following our conversation and I guessed they didn't often have the opportunity to grill their commanding officer, or know what a 'dojo' was. He wasn't about to tell them.

Having told me his first names, and how he got them, General Ao asked about mine and it seemed churlish not to tell him about my father, Bertie North, who nurtured a life-long belief that he was a great painter despite all evidence to the contrary. It certainly wasn't his artistic skills which attracted Briana, my mother – she told me he was funny, charming and built like a brick outhouse, but couldn't paint to save his life. In other words it was a fling.

Inspired by the exploits of Frances Chichester, who was knighted for his amazing feats of seamanship in the cantankerous ketch Gipsy Moth IV, Bertie's dream was to build a yacht and sail around the world, living off the proceeds of his pastels of waves crashing on rocks and craggy seamen mending nets. Unfortunately for him one of his own semen found a safe harbor in my mother's egg and his dream floundered, while Mum abandoned any dreams of her own to support three dependents – me, my father and then my brother – on a legal secretary's salary.

After sending me down the slipway, Mum was anxious to get back to work and entrusted Bertie with the registration of my birth. Fortified with one too many ambers he decided there were already too many Mary Janes in the world, and wrote 'Gipsy Moth North' on the dotted line. My mother only found out when she had to produce my birth certificate to register me for school, at which time I was old enough and opinionated enough to decide I'd much rather be Gipsy Moth than Mary Jane.

Mum died from a stroke shortly after I graduated from medical school, proud but exhausted, and Bertie promptly drank himself to death rather than confront his inability to cook, clean or support Mag and me.

'Mag?'

'Yeah, it's short for Magnetic. Actually his birth certificate says John William – mum took care of the registration herself – but Mag decided that if I could choose my name, so could he, so he called himself Magnetic Due North. Mum thought it was a fad, and he'd drop it after a while, but he didn't.'

The other two guys in the chopper decided Mag's name was the funniest thing they'd ever heard, and I watched them trying to swallow their hysteria in a paroxysm of coughing and holding of breath. Ao was of sterner stuff.

'Where is... Magnetic... now?'

'Good question, General. I think he inherited Bertie's genes, and he's using the legal degree that my mother paid for to find the best surfing wave in the world. I get an occasional email asking for money.'

'And whose genes did you collect?'

'Well, definitely my father's aversion to taking responsibility. Being a doctor seemed too... dangerous to me. One slip and someone dies. In my final year of medicine I dated a newspaper editor, and he said he would give me a job until I decided what I wanted to do with my life. From there is was just... a series of lucky breaks, I suppose. Just like you.'

He smiled at me. We understood each other. 'And your mother's genes?'

'Well, I look like her. A bit. And she also loved the finer things in life, even if she could never afford them. Sometimes I feel as if I'm having fun for both of us.'

'But she was also a warrior, wasn't she?'

I gave him a taste of his own inscrutability.

***

After that we lapsed into silence, rapping on our laptops or staring into our heads. There was a call from the pilot and Ao put his headset back on and started talking to someone in a calm tone. Then, without warning, the helicopter banked to one side. I looked out of my window and saw nothing but blue sky, while the opposite porthole showed only a small square of ocean. Then the chopper banked the other way and... my brain refused to accept what my eyes were telling it. The great span of brilliant blue ocean below was peppered with ships!

I grabbed for my mini-cam and pointed it out the window. I counted 24 vessels laid out in a huge rectangle, smaller ships around the sides, bigger ones in the center. The smaller ones looked like warships – pale gray with stubby guns, lots of antennae and boxy appendages which I assumed were missile housings. In the centre of the rectangle the boats got bigger, with a couple of bigger warships, some freighters and small tankers. Right in the middle were five enormous passenger ships and an aircraft carrier.

Colonel Sewraj leaned over so he wouldn't disturb Ao's discussion. 'She's the Viraat. It means "giant". She was designed at the end of World War 2 and commissioned in the 1950s as HMS Hermes. We bought her from the British in 1985 after the Falklands War and refurbished her. Twice. She's already past retirement age and we have another carrier which we bought from Russia, the Vikramaditya, and a third we built for ourselves, the Vikrant. But the Viraat is perfect as a floating air-base for this particular operation.'

I had been trying to regain my breath. 'Holy mother... that's quite a sight! But I thought aircraft carriers were... bigger.'

I heard Ao giggle and saw that he'd removed his headset. 'Oh, she's big enough Dr North. Well over 200 meters in length, and carrying a dozen Sea Harriers and the same number of helicopters. But next to those ocean liners... well, they're enormous – more than double her tonnage. We chartered them to carry two divisions – that's 30,000 men under arms – and a lot of support staff. The freighters are carrying equipment and supplies of course. And the destroyers and frigates are here to protect us all.

'So... I suppose this is a fairly typical... reinforcement?'

This time Ao caught my 'Australian humor' and smiled.

'I suppose it would be more accurate to call it a liberation. Liberating the division of Indian troop who are confined to the treatment centers. And of course the patients they are protecting.'

We'd been flying in a giant arc around the fleet and now I could just make out the coast – a thin line on the horizon. I pressed the zoom button and watched the line grow fatter and acquire a white frilly skirt from ocean breakers. Although the picture was hazy I could make out green coastal bush broken by a speckle of small buildings. As I panned to the right and left I saw modest clusters of larger buildings.

'Where are we?'

There was a pause as Sewraj waited to see if the general wanted to respond, before he spoke himself. 'We're about 30 kilometers north-east of Durban. Directly opposite the city's international airport.'

'Ah! When are you going to take control of it?'

I swung the mini-cam around towards the men in the chopper, and caught the two officers exchanging a look, before Ao answered. 'We already have.'

'Oooh-kay! Any resistance?'

'No. The airport was deserted, as we expected. There is a small chance that militants may attempt to eject us from the airport, so we're in the process of... making sure they can't.'

I was going to ask what would happen next when the movement of the chopper changed again. I swung the mini-cam back to the window to find we were now low over the aircraft carrier, with a man in a yellow shirt and helmet signaling with ping-pong bats, just like in Top Gun. I could see rows of Harriers and a few evil looking choppers, similar to the Hinds I saw in action at the battle of Ladysmith. A moment more and we hit the deck with a heavy thump. The army obviously doesn't reward pilots for passenger comfort, just survival.

Sewraj asked me to stay put while the General disembarked, so I squatted at the open door with my mini-cam as Ao was welcomed aboard by a line of sailors and a clutch of naval officers. Indians look sensational in white – not a paunch to be seen anywhere. When Ao and the penguins had disappeared the other officer on our flight – who hadn't uttered a word – along with the colonel and I were escorted into the part of the aircraft carrier that sticks up above the flight deck, which Sewraj told me is called an 'island'.

Inside I dug into my war-movie lexicon and told a female sailor who appeared to be hanging around for my convenience that I desperately needed the 'head'. She turned to Sewraj in confusion. He presumably told her to take me to the crapper because that's what she did. Just in time. Then I was escorted down some stairs to the officers' mess for lunch with the guys – more curry and Hindi. Again I was introduced to a lot of brass, who solemnly shook my hand if they were near, or waved at me if they weren't. This time Sewraj and I weren't at the top table, which contained two captains and a rear admiral along with Ao and another man in civvies. And a lot of serious discussion.

Sewraj told me there'd be a briefing for the journalists after lunch.

'Journalists? Plural?'

'Yes. You're the only international reporter, but we have two from the military and two from the Indian press.' I wondered how many TWO stringers there were, scattered around the fleet. Although I doubted they'd have cellular reception or access to satellite telephones.

Ao conducted the briefing, flanked by the Rear Admiral and the civilian, who was introduced as 'a representative of the parliamentary defense committee.' My 'colleagues' from the Indian press were a subservient lot – the civilians kowtowing just as much as the military hacks – and it was left to me to ask most of the questions.

Ao told us what I already knew about the background to his operation and immediate goal – to secure points of entry for the assessment group which would follow.

'General, how many airports will you secure?'

'Six, Dr North. Three civilian and three military. And three harbors.'

'Harbors?'

'Yes – Durban, Richards Bay and Port Elizabeth, so we can land troops, equipment and supplies.' He explained they would secure a part of the harbor entrances and quays so they could safely dock the liners and freighters. Then they would secure the surrounding cities, and push inland to do the same for some of the bigger cities. In the process the army would re-open a dozen major hospitals in those cities, set up a hundred or so distribution points for food aid, and escort the assessors while they developed a recovery plan.

I was beginning to understand why they'd brought 30,000 troops along with them. In fact I was beginning to wonder... 'General, I imagine by the time you've spread yourselves across the country, the army won't be able to run the hospitals and food distribution. Are you bringing in more medics and volunteers – I mean in addition to those already working in the treatment centers?'

'Very astute, Dr North. Army personnel will simply kick-start the process. We have already recruited civilian teams to take over from them as soon as it is safe to do so. It will be a kind of rolling operation...'

'So give us an idea of how many people will be arriving over time.'

He gave me a small smile and nodded at a soldier standing at the side of the room. The man handed out folders while the General turned the sheet on a flip-chart, revealing a table of numbers just like the first page in the folder.

'Here are our deployments. In round numbers we already have one division – 15,000 troops – and 15,000 medical staff in the treatment centers right now. And we have a second division in reserve, divided between the bases in Namibia, Botswana, Mozambique and the Cape. Taking into account army support personnel, administrators and volunteers we have roughly 50,000 Indian nationals in South Africa.'

I wanted to ask how many family members there were, but not in front of my 'colleagues'

'In this expeditionary force we have two more divisions – that's another 30,000 professional soldiers and about half that number of support personnel, not counting the navy sailors and airmen. Within five days we will have a lakh – 100,000 personnel – on the ground, including several mechanized and armored battalions.'

He paused and looked at me, but I didn't think he was waiting for questions. I got it – I was here to make sure the world heard these numbers. But not yet. He continued.

'As soon as we have secured our points of entry we will begin flying in 15,000 medical personnel, about 12,000 multi-skilled volunteers, and about 5,000 assessors and their staff. This phase will be completed in ten weeks...'

He was cut off by the roar of jet engines, and waited until he could speak without raising his voice.

'That's one of our Harriers. It's on a reconnaissance mission – to over-fly and photograph one of the points-of-entry. Of course our aircraft are equipped to deal with any eventuality, not just reconnaissance missions.' It sounded more like he was planning to fight a modern army, rather than the emaciated survivors of a tribal war.

'And phase three, general? What about the time-line' I could see some numbers on the table in front of me, but no dates.

'In our planning we are assuming phase three will start in between one and three years from today.' He read the question on the other hacks' faces. 'Phase three is when we implement the recommendations of the assessment group. The recovery plan. But the numbers you're seeing are the rotation of staff, when their tours of duty end. They are all on a one-year rotation.'

'So until phase three your numbers will remain at 130,000 Indian nationals?'

'Yes, roughly that number on active service.'

'What happens at the end of their rotation? Do they go home?'

He seemed surprised by the question. 'Well... yes, I imagine most will want to return to their families. It's up to them.'

'So they can stay if they want?'

'They are free to volunteer for a second tour, Dr North.'
It wasn't what I asked, but I knew the answer anyway.

New York, April, year three

Weng was too experienced to show emotion, but he left no doubt about his government's feelings.

'Madam secretary general, the Indian action is in direct violation of their mandate. It must be stopped.'

'Excellency, how do you respond to Ambassador Dutta's argument that there is no other way to close the treatment centers without risking the lives of their patients?'

'With respect, madam, it is a disingenuous argument. Naturally we concur with the need to restore social order in South Africa, but the correct procedure would be to develop a multi-party response, supported by a Security Council mandate.'

'And the Indians' concerns that this would take too long?'

'The People's Republic of China would be happy to relieve the Indian forces, so they can repatriate their people while the international process continues…'

'I'm sorry, excellency, but I think their concern is for their patients, not their own people. The best estimates are that if we do not provide blanket food aid and medical support immediately, we are looking at two million deaths among the civilian population.'

'Madam, is that not the function of the World Food Program, and the World Health Organization?'

'Indeed. But they are not equipped to launch an operation on that scale, that soon, or without military protection. Apparently the Indians are.'

'Then why the need for the secrecy? Why not ask for an extension of their mandate from the Security Council?'

'Excellency, is Dutta wrong when he says your veto was a foregone conclusion? And that in the event of a veto their hands would be tied?'

Weng was too experienced to fall into this trap.

'Madam Secretary General, we propose to table a resolution in the Council condemning the Indian intervention, and calling on them to submit their forces to independent command.'

'To what end, excellency?'

'With a view to phasing out their assets, and replacing them with teams from other countries.'

'Again, may I ask why?'

'Because it is inappropriate for a single nation to impose themselves on another nation, even if the subject is in… disarray, and even if their motives are ostensibly humanitarian.'

'You have the right to table such a motion, of course, but you understand that in so doing you will be giving India a platform to defend their actions on the global stage? A debate between the world's two largest nations, on the world's biggest stage?'

'Of course.'

'It's just that… they are widely perceived as heroes in this matter, excellency. Their work has already saved hundreds of thousands of lives, and it promises to save many more. They have asked for nothing in return, merely the opportunity to restore a country which is home to more than a million Indian descendants, and to honor the memory of the father of their own nation, who found political enlightenment in South Africa.'

Weng permitted himself a small smile. 'Not to mention the refuge they have provided to the Dalai Llama, ever since the Chinese army stole his country?'

'Excellency, it is not for me to put words into Ambassador Dutta's mouth. However, for better or worse, we live in an age when public opinion weighs at least as much as military might in shaping the future. It does seem the Indians have managed to combine the two with… some skill.'

'Madam secretary general, do not expect the People's Republic of China to concede defeat like a second-rate chess-player.'

'But excellency, I do not. I was rather hoping you would attempt instead to seize the moral high-ground in this matter.'

'In what way?'

'Why, by playing to your strength, of course. You have the world's biggest economy. Instead of focusing on a withdrawal of Indian military, why not offer to support the rebuilding of South Africa's economy? We all know the balance sheet is a much better indicator of control than a head-count.'

Weng remained dead-pan, and said nothing.

'It is hardly my place to suggest your strategy in the Security Council, excellency, but I would imagine a resolution by the People's Republic of China to establish and lead a global reconstruction fund for South Africa would not only attract considerable support from the Council members, but would do for China's public image what India's military initiative has done for theirs. Not to mention the number of heart attacks it would cause in Delhi when you put your queen into play…'

Weng's poker face melted into a broad smile.

Bangkok, June, year five

When there's no moon, and no cloud to reflect the light of the city, the only lighting at the Breeze restaurant comes from the lamps on the tables and the bluish glow from beneath the translucent floors. It may not be the best light to read a menu, but it certainly picks out the silver and glassware – and it made the sequined edging on Nikki's jacket sparkle as she turned slowly, scanning the restaurant for me. Her dark hair and black outfit were invisible against the night sky, leaving her pale face floating like a three-quarter moon over a dark ocean. When finally she saw me waving she smiled, her teeth shone, and I forgot all that crap about moons and oceans.

Somehow the blur of life had conspired to keep us apart since Emily's funeral, two years earlier, although we chatted in one medium or another at least a couple of times a week. Now we stood for a moment, just looking at each other. I hoped the strange light was as flattering to me as it was to her – she didn't look any older than when she descended like an angel of mercy to help me through those first couple of weeks alone in Fenerbahçe. In fact she looked younger. Radiating a kind of peace, instead of the anxious concern of our last intersection.

After Nikki left me I had pretended for a few weeks that I could adjust to living in the villa without Em, but it was a lost cause so I moved into a hotel on the European side of the city, near the office, while I considered my options.

Along with most of the senior editors at TWO I'd renewed my contract at the end of the first three years. The notable exception was Enoch, who said he was ready, in every way, to retire. He'd slipped away from his beloved South Africa with his wife and two grandchildren, and was now living quietly in Lusaka, Zambia, where he'd been stationed with the ANC-in-exile during the latter days of the struggle against apartheid.

In the months after Em's death I considered basing myself somewhere else, or even resigning from TWO, to start over. Everything about Istanbul, my job, and what was happening in the world, reminded me of her. I'd like to tell you that I reached a decision but the truth is that I became distracted by other stories, other travels and – after Kimberly's quiet ear in the Cederberg – other people.

As things evolved at TWO, Jim encouraged us to step outside our respective beats, and to focus on one region of the world. He used the analogy of a British cabinet minister who is responsible for a specialized national portfolio, but also for the varied needs of the constituents who elected him to parliament. With Enoch out of the picture – or at least missing from his little square on my computer monitor during the weekly news conference – Africa was a natural choice of constituency. And Africa has a lot to say for herself.

About a year after Em's funeral, Nikki and I started looking for opportunities to get together again, but somehow every plan was scuttled at the last moment – until this one. The UN's regional office for south east Asia was hosting a media briefing in Bangkok to prepare journalists for the forthcoming World AIDS Conference, to be held in Kuala Lumpur a month later. Nikki was there as one of the presenters, and I managed to get there as well..

Now, as she latched on for a second hug, I felt something turning over inside me and realized it was a sob. I pretended it was a gasp. 'Jesus, Nik, have you been working out?'

She held onto my hand, and my eyes, as we sat down, her own face code-sharing between a smile and concern. 'How are you, Gip? I mean, really?'

This was ridiculous. I had no reason to be choked up, but I found I couldn't speak. At that moment a waitress arrived with menus and a wine-list. Nikki turned to the girl. 'We're waiting for one more person, but let's order a bottle of wine.'

This was the first I'd heard of a third person. 'Oh, good...' Nikki knew my tone meant exactly the opposite, and she gave me another dazzling smile.

'Yeah, I asked him to arrive a little late so I could get you drunk first.'

'Him? How drunk do I need to be?'

She pretended to look me over like a traffic cop checking for signs of inebriation. 'Oh, I think you're drunk enough...'

'Ossifer, I'm not as thunk as dreeple pink I am.'

She'd heard it before but smiled anyway. She directed her attention to the winelist, ordered a bottle of Krug, and turned back to me with her best naughty child expression, then broke the news. 'I'm engaged!'

I must admit that my eyes began to water. At the time I tried to pass it off as tears of happiness for Nikki, but I was really thinking that this was supposed to be our evening – our time to get maudlin and reconnect. A third person – a stranger – wasn't in the script! But whatever she thought of my girly tears, she held onto my hands with both of hers and waited for me to grow up.

'I'm so... sorry, Nik. I'm such a dork. That's wonderful news.' I took a deep breath and tried hard to change gears. 'Where did you find the suck... the fellow?'

She smiled to reward me for pulling myself together. 'In Shimla.'

For one bizarre moment I pictured her walking down the aisle with Shan, who happened to be married to a Bollywood starlet with whom he'd produced a couple of picture-perfect kids. 'Shimla?'

'Yeah. Remember when I went there to advise on Shan's plan to convert his research lab to produce API? There was a guy there... an American. An army intelligence colonel, from the Office of the Director of National Intelligence. We clicked, and one thing led...'

'You dirty dog! That was ages ago.' I punched her shoulder – a little harder than I intended. Consciously, at least. 'Why am I only hearing about it now?'

'Ow! That hurt!' She sat rubbing her shoulder and looking at me like a kicked dog.

'So?'

'Well, I thought... we thought it was a fling, at first. Keeping warm in the Himalayas. But after Shimla... well, we stayed in touch. I mean, we've seen each other here and there. His job is to keep tabs on the whole pharmageddon thing, so there have been... plenty of opportunities.' She gave me a wicked leer.

'And… what? You want to do the whole house-in-the-burbs, kids-in-school routine?'

She laughed at that. 'Oh god no. He's got two already, from a previous marriage. Both in high school, in Chicago. Anyway, I'm not the mommy type. But… it feels right. Right time, right guy. I want… we both want someone to go home to…'

I saw her face freeze, and I realized she was thinking of me going home to Emily. I wanted to tease her, tell her not to walk on egg-shells around her oldest friend. But then it hit me. I remembered exactly what it was like to have someone as a reference point for every action, every observation, every thought. Someone to go home to. But it was so much more than a memory – I lived it again, for the first time in years. And, maybe for the first time, I truly understood what I'd lost. What I'd been hiding from. Without Emily, I was homeless. Lost. And it felt like someone had turned on an irrigation system built into my face.

'Oh fuck, Nik. I didn't… I don't want to lose you, too.' For a while it wasn't pretty. Certainly not what is supposed to happen at the highest open air seafood restaurant in Asia. I filled a couple of the Breeze's beautiful linen napkins with tears and snot while Nikki held me, stroking my back and telling me not to worry, it would all be okay.

'You said she'd be happy for you.' A deep American voice. I looked up to see a tall black man in a tweed jacket and white shirt, open at the neck. He had a look of gentle concern, wrapped up in humor. I liked him immediately.

'Sorry Art. She doesn't hold her liquor very well…' Nikki recoiled as though expecting another punch, and I found myself laughing. I stood to make space and to shake his hand but instead found myself caught up in a hug, with Nikki's moon face swimming nearby in my tears and the Breeze's funny lighting.

'Listen,' he said, sotto voce, his mouth only an inch from my ear. 'Whoever did this to you, I can have them killed. I know people.'

'It was her.' I pointed a deliberately shaking hand at Nikki.

'Oh. Well, I'm afraid I offered her the same deal first, so I'm going to have to throw you off this balcony. D'you want to go before or after dinner?'

I stayed inside the hug, but now I was only pretending to sob. 'After, please. The lobster here is worth dying for. And the abalone salad. And the…'

I could see what Nik saw in Arthur Baldwin. He radiated a kind of… strength. Just sitting at the same table made me feel that everything would be alright. For her, I mean. As the meal unfolded I learned more about him, and about his assignment to monitor the still unresolved investigations into the sabotage of the ARV supply chain.

Nikki gave a hilarious rendition of the instant attraction between them, and their clandestine schnogging in and around Shan's compound. It turned out that it was only here in Bangkok, while strolling around the Grand Palace just three days ago, that they'd decided to make it official. Apart from Nikki's mum, I was the first to know.

It felt good to see that my closest friend was so happy. Still, as soon as it was decently possible I shifted the subject to the other thing that Arthur Baldwin and I had in common. 'Okay, so spill the beans, soldier. Who dunnit?'

He looked uncertainly between Nikki and me, the whites of his eyes flashing in the blue light. 'Done what?'

'The bombings, of course. The sabotage.'

His teeth flashed brightly. 'Oh, that. Tell you what, why don't I tell you about the things I've succeeded at?'

I looked sternly at Nikki. 'Nicola Kershaw, you want my blessing on your union with a self-confessed failure?'

Art barked so loudly I wondered briefly if they could hear it on the street, fifty floors down. 'Well, hang on a minute, Gipsy North. It's true that we don't know who did it, but we also know who did not.'

'Like who?'

'The FBI are very sure it wasn't big pharma. They got the word from the White House not to leave any stone unturned, and they didn't. Their investigations put a lot of strain on party funding, so I hear. The CIA and military intelligence are pretty sure it wasn't Al Qaeda, for all kinds of reasons....'

'What about simple blackmail?'

'We heard of a few cases of attempted extortion, in several countries, but they all turned out to be opportunists – people who thought they'd make a quick buck by saying they planted the bombs, then threatening some corporate that they'd do the same to them. One or two had us going for a while...'

'White supremacists, Chinese pharma?

He smiled. 'No and no. And we had a good look, believe me.'

'And the black hole?'

His smile broadened. 'You mean, did the US government blow up those factories to save taxpayers' money?'

I smiled back, partly because I realized that I was enjoying myself. I knew what he was getting at – the US government had ended up spending far more as a result of pharmageddon than they would if it had never happened.

'Okay, fair enough. But what about the South African government? I mean, they practically admitted they did it.'

'Not really. We reviewed everything they ever said or did. We even tracked down Minister Makeba in Dar Es Salaam...'

'I'd like to track him down myself. Tear him apart with my bare hands for what he did to Bettina and her family...'

'Actually, we don't think he ordered that. It could have been a rogue cop, but I think it was probably a genuine accident.'

'But he threatened me…'

'No, Gipsy. I listened to the recording of your conversation. I can see how you felt threatened, but Makeba denied it. And his story checks out.'

'What story?'

Art hesitated. 'Well, it turns out a lot of your speculation was right on the money. Makeba did have a controlling interest in that pharmaceutical plant, and they did build up a secret stockpile of ARVs…'

'Well, there you go.'

'Yeah… except when we added up the facts, we came to a different conclusion.'

'Oh?'

'Sure. Turns out the stockpile was ordered and paid for by his government, and they were given regular reports on it. It was active ingredient, by the way, not finished drugs…'

'Well, Shan did tell me a lot of countries had undisclosed reserves of API…'

'Yeah, in case there were problems with global supply. For perfectly legitimate reasons, like shortages of raw materials, shipping snafus or currency fluctuations…'

'I still don't see why it was a big secret.'

'Makeba said that if the world knew they had plenty of API, they wouldn't be given a share of the global stockpile – in fact they'd be forced to share what they had. But he was adamant that neither he nor his government wanted ARV treatment to be interrupted. In fact, he blames you for it.'

It took me a second to process his words. 'WHAT? Are you out of your mind? How… why would I do that?'

Somehow I wasn't surprised that Art wasn't offended. He simply laughed and held up his hands in surrender. 'Hey, I'm just the messenger. Like you.'

'Sorry mate. But shit, that's some fucking accusation. From Makeba. The truth is that I did my best to prevent the treatment interruption. Ask Nikki – she was in on it too.'

Nikki shook her head sadly. 'And Bettina…'

Art's eyes moved between us. 'You mean your plan to trick the cops into returning the drugs?'

Somehow I wasn't surprised that he knew about our scam. 'Yeah. What did the fat toad have to say about that?'

'As a matter of fact, he was surprised to hear that you guys cooked it up. He thought the police had told Bettina that they were going to return the ARVs, and she was just doing what she was supposed to, by releasing that media statement.'

'What?'

'Yeah. Makeba admitted the government had... limited control... over the police. They kinda stayed out of each others ways, because...'

'People in glass houses?'

'Exactly. So there was no question of ordering the cops to return the drugs. Instead, the government's plan was to tell the cops that they had this strategic reserve of ARVs, and they were ready to re-supply the hospitals. Which meant the looted drugs would be worthless on the streets.'

'So? Did they tell the cops...?'

'Yeah. Just an hour or two before Dr Shabangu's statement appeared on your site. So naturally...'

'Oh crap! Makeba thought that the cops told Bettina they were going to return the drugs, and the cops thought that Makeba told her the same thing. And all the while, we thought...' I looked at Nikki, and I could see she was also reliving that night.

'I know, Gip. Talk about coincidence.'

I turned back to Art. 'But... what about the contamination of that batch of ARVs from Nguni Pharmaceuticals?'

'Makeba thought some rogue cops may have arranged that. Because they were angry that they were losing their windfall, and wanted to make sure there was no fresh supply of ARVs.'

I sat there, staring at them both. 'So that's that?'

'No, actually it isn't. When we looked more closely, we found the timing doesn't work. The contamination had to take place a week or so earlier. It would take that long for spiked drugs to be manufactured, packaged and dispatched.'

'Shit, that's... weird. So who was responsible?'

'It must have been the same people as the attacks in India, Sweden and Iceland. Same timing, just a different method. This one was designed to have a delayed reaction.'

I was beginning to feel like I was suffering from vertigo after all. 'But... the API itself wasn't contaminated, was it? So why didn't the South Africans just make more drugs?'

'According to Makeba it took them the better part of two weeks to find out exactly what was contaminated – or rather, to find out what wasn't contaminated, because they never did pin down the actual contaminant. Then they had to "apply their minds" to what to do next.' He drew the quotation marks in the air.

'Meaning?'

'Meaning that, by the time they realized they could safely make more medications, it was too late. The drugs would have reached the hospitals more than six weeks from the start of the treatment interruption...'

'So there'd be a lot of drug resistance...'

Nikki cut in. 'Not only physiological resistance. We were convinced that patients wouldn't want to take the same medications that made people sick before. It got a lot of publicity.'

'So… what? The government gave up?'

Art shook his head. 'No, they came up with another plan. They tried to buy the old ARVs back from the police, to tide them over. Apparently they offered the cops a fortune.'

'Oh, right. So what happened?'

'The rumor happened. That Xhosa-nostra thing. And the cops turned down the government's offer – decided they'd be better off with the drugs than the money.'

Sweet Jesus, what a mess. 'But if the government had been straight with the UN – with you, Nik – surely they would still have been okay?'

Nikki pulled a wry face. 'Yes, but they didn't think they were in trouble… even after the cops refused to sell the ARVs back to the government.'

She glanced at Art before continuing. 'After Shan announced that he was planning to make API for second line ARVs, Makeba and his cronies decided they'd be okay after all. They thought they could overcome drug resistance by putting everyone on second-line medications. They even started re-tooling Nguni to make the PI-based drugs. And president Shezi announced that better drugs were on the way – to keep everyone cool.'

'Holy crap, Nik. Then there was the rumor that the new drugs were reserved for Xhosas. And after Shezi announced they'd go to the Zulus first, we were told the drugs would be toxic…'

She nodded. 'No matter what they tried, they couldn't get it right…'

Art picked it up. 'Makeba blames you for the rumors, Gipsy, but we think they were planted by the cops, so people would buy their looted ARVs rather than wait for the new ones.'

'But then Shan realized he couldn't make second-line API in his research lab after all…'

Nikki and Art exchanged another look. She spread her hands on the table. 'Well, about that…'

Art cut in. 'Just when the South Africans began to see how much trouble they were in, along came the UN's offer of treatment camps.'

'But… hang on a mo, Art. The camps only came a couple of months later. After the South Africans turned down the UN offer to send peacekeepers to restore treatment in their hospitals…'

'Yeah, about that. We discovered that the African ambassadors didn't see that coming – they were actually stalling for time when the Chinese threw out their veto. Makeba's comment was that it all happened so quickly, and they only truly understood the seriousness of their position after their neighboring countries restored treatment and the Cape seceded.'

'Fuck, what a mess. What about the Indians' attempt to restore second-line treatment in Ladysmith hospital?'

Art shook his head. 'That happened only in June, by which time the Balkanization of the country was complete. By then the government wasn't running the country – the cops were morphing into warlords, and…'

'Oh yeah, of course. If the Indians had succeeded in restoring universal treatment, the drugs which gave the warlords their power would have become worthless...'

He nodded. 'The advantage of the treatment centers, from the government's point of view, was that they didn't step on police toes. So they leapt at the opportunity.'

I left them for a minute, staring over the bright lights of Bangkok, with the little ferries scuttling up and down the Chao Phraya River far below. So Makeba was a gentleman crook after all, someone who was willing to milk the system for money, but hadn't set out to hurt anyone ...

I turned back to them, and found them staring at me with worried expressions. I gave them a bright smile, and their faces softened.

'Rumors and bad luck.'

'Huh?'

'That's what killed South Africa. So are we going to order some desert or what?'

Pretoria, July, year five

Through the tinted windows of the white Mahindra SUV the city of Pretoria looked much the same as it did five years earlier. The gardens surrounding the ornate seat of government, the Union Buildings, looked as neat as they were on the day Mandela was sworn in as the first president of a democratic South Africa – the only difference being the twin flagpoles bearing the colors of India alongside those of South Africa.

It was getting dark and the streetlights were coming on as we drove slowly through the city, stopping at traffic lights – or robots as they call them in South Africa. Many stores had not yet been reopened, but a couple of restaurants looked like they were getting ready to open for the evening and most of the downtown hotels were showing signs of life. The only thing wrong with this picture was that other cars were so rare that, when we saw one, we craned to see who they carried – who else was allowed access to the tightly controlled reserves of fuel?

I didn't feel like talking to the guys in front – the driver and the suit who met me at the airport – and they seemed content to leave me alone with my thoughts. After a while we left the downtown area and drove into the leafy suburbs, now mostly restored and occupied, until finally we were waved past the gate-house of Mahlamba Ndlopfu, the official residence of the head of state.

The suit let me out of the car and I turned away from the mansion to take in the spectacular view over the grounds and across the charcoal landscape to a distant range of hills, reaching into a salmon sushi sky. As the last light drained away so did the warmth of the day, and it felt like someone had opened the door to a refrigerator. Suddenly something soft brushed against the back of my neck and I ducked instinctively and tried to brush it away, before I realized what it was.

'Not another bloody pashmina…'

Shan's familiar laugh sounded in my ear.

'Ah, but this one has the insignia of the Indian administration in South Africa. It's a collector's item.'

I turned to look at him and the mansion behind, the lights inside competing with the reflection of the sunset on its windows.

'This is quite a place, Shan.'

'Isn't it? It was built in 1940 for the prime minister of the day and renamed 'The New Dawn' in 1995. I can't get my tongue around the Shangaan name. Are you ready to come inside?'

The car which brought me was gone and only a white-jacketed steward was waiting for us at the brightly lit entrance. Although the door was wide enough for a marching band, Shan stood back so I could go first into the impressive foyer, with its grand staircase and reception rooms leading off to each side. I walked into the middle and swung around, taking it all in.

'I'll take it! How much did you say it was, again?'

'Oh, it comes free with the country.'

'And how much is that going for?'

'Hmm, it's only available on short-term rental. But the rent is enough to make the richest nations on earth complain.'

As we talked Shan ushered me through to a beautifully decorated study, where he waved me to an easy chair and brought me a glass of red wine. He poured himself a glass of water from a jug.

'Oh yeah, this is grand. How much work was needed to restore the place?'

'Not much. For some reason the warlords left it alone after the president went into exile. We think they were saving it for whoever emerged as the top dog, but nobody ever did.'

'And the other government buildings?'

He shrugged. 'A lot of movables were looted – furniture and so on – probably by politicians going into exile. Some offices were used by the militia as barracks, but the damage to government buildings was nothing compared to the shopping malls. They were totally gutted, as I'm sure you know…'

He tailed off and sat smiling at me, then he raised his glass. 'To living in interesting times. It's really good to see you again, Gipsy.'

'To interesting times. Past and future.'

We sipped. The wine was excellent, but before I could ask what it was Shan spoke again.

'We have a rather… military… evening ahead of us. I've invited Dr Kershaw from UNAIDS, and her husband Colonel Baldwin, who is some kind of high level… spook… for the Americans.'

I smiled at the word I'd taught him. 'Yes, I've met them both.'

He hesitated a microsecond, as if waiting to see if I was going to say more, before going on. 'And then I've invited General Ao who, as you know, commands the peacekeeping forces here. He's bringing his wife.'

'Uh-oh. Husbands and wives. What about Mrs Gupta?'

'Vasanthi is still at home, in Shimla. She says... we both feel... our children are still too young for boarding school, and education here isn't up to scratch as yet. We have some very good private schools in Shimla. But maybe things will change in time...'

'How long do you think you'll be here?'

'We're working to a five-year timetable, from the day our reinforcements arrived. Two down, three to go. It's ambitious, but Delhi says it's not negotiable. The reconstitution process here is costing us a fortune.'

'What? Hiring you as governor?'

He gave me a sideways look. 'No, I'm probably the cheapest person they have here. It seemed... inappropriate to ask for a salary. But I'd just as soon you don't share that particular piece of information with the world... if you can see your way clear.'

I gave him an as-if-I-would look. He smiled back and carried on.

'No, the cost is related to the sheer scale of this operation. It's... big. I thought an industrial conglomerate ate money until I discovered what it costs to run an army. And you can't open hospitals with just nurses and doctors – turns out they are barely half of the essential personnel. Re-opening schools is... a financial and logistical nightmare. To say nothing of restoring power, water, sanitation, food distribution, law enforcement, communications networks...'

'Are the Chinese giving you the money they promised?'

'Oh yes, they've been very generous. And we're getting a huge amount of technical and material support from many other governments. But it's all for South Africa, Lesotho and Swaziland, not for our contingent. I mean, just the cost of transporting our people here...'

'I'm told the cheapest long-haul flight in the world is from Johannesburg to Mumbai...'

Shan laughed and finished my sentence. 'Yes, because all the return flights are empty! But speaking of flights...' he looked at his watch, 'I imagine you'd like to unpack and get ready for dinner? The other guests will be arriving in an hour and a half. It would be nice if you...' he looked a touch embarrassed, 'could welcome them with me. Sort of play the role of hostess?'

I punched the air. 'Yeah, baby! I always wanted to be a governess!'

Shan roared. 'No, I'm sorry, I can't help you with that, Mary Poppins. But you can pretend to be a governor's wife if you like, at least until the guests go home.'

***

The steward showed me to a guest suite, where my suitcase stood unopened. He offered to send someone to help with unpacking and getting ready. It sounded like fun but I felt like being alone.

As I showered and dressed I thought about Shan's invitation to visit South Africa, two years after the Indian liberation forces landed. His invitation promised a week of interviews with people at the coal-face of the reconstitution process – an irresistible lure for someone trying to guess where things were heading in the most newsworthy nation in Africa.

But instead of thinking about the issues I'd need to cover while I was here, I found myself dwelling on that little pause after I told Shan that I'd already met Nikki and Art. He definitely thought I was going to say more – I could see it in his face. I wondered whether he knew how close Nikki and I were. He was a man who did his homework, after all, and our friendship wasn't exactly a state secret. But I'd never mentioned it to Shan, and Nikki confirmed just a couple of days earlier than she hadn't either.

It all started because she didn't want to be identified as my deep throat inside the UN, but since then it had became a kind of game we played, with Shan as the unwitting subject. Like Nikki, Art continued to have regular dealings with Shan, but he'd been sworn to secrecy so we could have our fun.

This evening Shan acted as if he didn't know about our friendship, but still… there was that little pause. It occurred to me that maybe he wasn't an unwitting subject in our game after all, but an active player. Interesting thought.

After a while there was a tap at the door, and a smiling middle-aged woman introduced herself as the housekeeper, asked if I needed anything, and tactfully mentioned that our guests were expected in ten minutes. I took the hint.

***

General and Mrs Ao arrived first, the CO of the Indian forces looking impressive in his dress uniform. He introduced his wife Gitanjali, a slim and striking woman dressed in a black silk tunic and a finely embroidered Jamavar shawl in muted autumn colors. She had the Aryan features of north India, rather than the oriental features of her husband, and she shook my hand firmly and said she'd heard all about me. I vaguely remembered her husband said something about his family, so I said the same to her and she accepted the lie gracefully.

Nikki and Art arrived hard on their heels. Art was also wearing his uniform while Nik looked terrific in a deep emerald green evening gown. I had decided to abandon our game so I threw my arms around them in turn, whispering in Nik's ear that we should talk asap. Shan made no comment at our familiarity but when our eyes met I thought I caught a hidden smile, like someone caught bluffing in a friendly card game.

263

As soon as we could, Nikki and I escaped to my room where I told her that I was sure that Shan knew about our friendship, and I thought we should play it straight. Back downstairs, the conversation had already zeroed in on the one thing we all had in common – South Africa.

Art was a member of a five-person American mission to South Africa to monitor and report back on the Indian reconstitution process. His team had already been in the country for three weeks and, in line with his brief to look at issues relating to national security, he'd met General Ao several times. It was obvious from their body language that they'd struck up a rapport, although they still called each other by their rank.

When Nikki and I rejoined the group the men stopped talking and Gitanjali Ao gave us a grateful smile. 'Welcome to the old-boys club.'

The men laughed, general Ao's high-pitched giggle rising above Shan's hearty guffaw and Art's booming bark.

'Don't take my wife too seriously, Dr North. Gitanjali is just as involved in developments here as any of us. Do you remember I told you that she was a professor of constitutional law?'

It came back to me then, along with his comment that they had a nine-year-old daughter. 'Of course. And I believe you said you had a daughter? I suppose she'd be eleven by now?'

I saw from Gitanjali's smile that I'd scored a brownie point. 'Yes – Sophie. She's visiting her grandmother and my extended family in Guwahati.'

General Ao looked proudly at his wife. 'Gitanjali is one of the founding professors at the new National Law University in Delhi, and she's presently advising the Indian government on constitutional development here in South Africa…'

'Is that connected to Art's… Colonel Baldwin's mission…?'

Gitanjali spoke for herself. 'Oh yes – I've been working with one of Colonel Baldwin's colleagues, who has a similar task to my own. And there are other experts from China, the European Union and the African Union. We're meeting with local delegates to finalize a format for the restoration of democracy.'

Nikki cut in. 'How far have you got with that? My husband never tells me anything!'

Gitanjali laughed. 'You too? Actually, we've made a lot of progress. We're looking at a general election in just under three years…'

I saw the gap. 'Will Indian expatriates be able to vote?'

She turned to me. 'That's the thinking, yes. The issue of citizenship is rather… up in the air… after this hiatus, so the thinking is to allow everyone to stand for election, and to vote. Unless they are employed by a foreign government, such as our own…'

'That'll make the numbers interesting.'

'What do you mean, Gipsy?' Shan's half-smile said he knew the answer, but wanted me to tell the others anyway.

'Well, math was never my strong suit, but I did a little cigarette-box doodling...'

He laughed delightedly. 'Oh my. I haven't heard that expression for some time! So what did the tobacco leaves foretell?'

General Ao was looking a touch unsettled but the others were smiling expectantly so I plunged on.

'Okay, two years ago, when you landed your reinforcements here, General Ao, you said there'd be about 130,000 Indian nationals in the country. If I remember correctly they were all doing a one-year tour of duty, but they could elect to stay for a second year – in which case they'd be allowed to bring out their relatives to join them. Or they could retire from the service and stay on in South Africa.'

Ao shrugged. 'Yes, I think that's about right.'

'Well, for the sake of my doodling, I assumed nobody went home, and they brought out an average of three relatives. That's 390,000 civilians, bringing us to 520,000 Indians. Now your soldiers and nurses have all reached the end of their second tour of duty, so I'm assuming they all elect to stay here as civilians, with their relatives, and that you'll bring out fresh troops and medics to replace them. That's another 130,000 people, bringing us to 650,000 Indians.'

I could see Shan and Ao wanted to speak, but I kept going. 'Let's say that, in a year's time, the new guys all opt to stay another year, and they bring out another 390,000 relatives. And two years from now – your election year, Gitanjali – you'll bring in a third batch of 130,000, when the new lot finish their second tour. The third batch won't be eligible to vote, but by then you'll have a million Indians who can. In theory, at least...'

General Ao was looking concerned but Shan was beaming, and when he caught my eye he mimed applause.

'Bravo, Gipsy! Of course the reality is a little different, but your final numbers aren't too far out. In fact most of the relief troops, medics and support staff are already here. But according to the latest population estimates, we're still outnumbered by at least twenty to one – and we're expecting our numbers to reduce from next year, as our people gain the experience they were looking for and go home to India.'

Nikki cut in. 'Shan, what about those population estimates? Our own research shows that mortality here is still very high, even with ARVs and food aid. And the birth-rate is way down, so the indigenous population is shrinking as fast as expatriate numbers are going up...'

Which made me think of something else: 'And we mustn't forget the 600,000 South Africans of Indian extraction who are expected to return in the next couple of years...'

Not to be left out of the old-girls club, Gitanjali spoke up. 'Actually, one of the South African delegates in our forum accused us of trying to turn her country into the 37th state of India. But really, I think that's a bit far fetched. I can't see how expatriate voters will come anywhere near to the number of indigenous voters.'

I wanted to ask Shan whether anyone had modeled the population trends to see where they'd be in ten or 15 years, but he spoke first. 'For what it's worth, I can tell you there's no grand plan to absorb South Africa into India. Never has been. The way I see it, we have a very different opportunity here.'

Aha! 'Like what?'

He stared at me reflectively for a moment, then smiled. 'This is my own cigarette-box doodling, Gipsy. Except it's not about numbers – it's about opportunity.'

He scanned the group, just as he did the day we met in Istanbul. 'Do you know what the biggest barrier to innovation is? It's experience. Tradition. Culture. People not changing the way they do things, because that's the way they've always done them. Having social conventions makes us feel secure, but it robs us of our power to change. It's why we still have the caste system in India, even though it's been officially abolished. We're scared to let go.'

Arthur Baldwin leaned forward. 'But, governor, as a soldier I believe that being trained to do things a certain way, to the point that it's almost instinctive, gives us a solid base for improvisation. And in the scientific field, didn't most of the great innovators – Da Vinci, Newton, Edison and so on – live in extremely conservative times?'

'Good points, colonel. But I'm not talking about physical skills or decision-making processes. I'm talking about people's world view. Most of the great geniuses in all fields are misfits, mavericks, odd-balls. They don't buy into the conceptual paradigms which define the lives of ordinary people. They see the status-quo as something which doesn't need to be preserved, but rather to be built upon.'

Nikki was looking confused. 'I agree, governor, but I don't see what this has to do with…'

'With reconstituting South Africa? Dr Kershaw, the most successful nations today are those who have re-invented themselves. Transformed themselves from feudal, culture-bound societies to the greatest innovators on the planet. Germany did it during the Nazi era, the Pacific Tigers did it after their wars, and China and India are in the process of doing it right now – without a war, thank god. All of us have managed to shake ourselves loose from our past, re-set our cultural clocks, and we've overtaken the new world – all in a single generation.'

I could see that Art Baldwin didn't like this, but he said nothing. Nikki asked: 'And South Africa?'

'In 1994 when apartheid ended, South Africans had an opportunity to re-set their clock. And in many respects they did. But they didn't focus on educational standards like we did in Asia, they lost control of crime and corruption, and instead of creating equal opportunities they replaced one oligarchy with another.'

'Okay... so?'

'So they failed to achieve the three key predictors of economic success – a large pool of highly educated and skilled people, a direct relationship between hard work and reward, and a stable and honest social environment. In other words they blew their first opportunity.'

'So you're giving them another one?'

'Well, let's just say that fate has given them another opportunity, and we're doing everything we can to help them to use it well.'

I needed to know: 'But, Shan, what's in it for you... for India?'

'I think a lot of us see it as repaying a debt. A debt to those Indians who were forced by poverty and discrimination to accept what amounted to slavery in South Africa...'

'And a debt to Gandhi?'

'Absolutely. The Mahatma's ideas were directly formed by the racial discrimination he found in South Africa. We feel the spirit of modern India was born right here.'

'And that gives you some kind of hold over the country?'

'Not a hold, no – it gives us an obligation. Gandhiji carried the flame from here to India in 1915, and used it to create the world's biggest democracy. Now we're carrying the flame back again.'

Suddenly he smiled self-consciously, looking at each of us in turn. 'I'm sorry, I know it sounds like I'm delivering a speech, but it's what I really believe...'

I looked at General and Mrs Ao, who looked like they wanted to applaud, and at Colonel and Mrs Baldwin, who looked more skeptical. Nikki asked: 'So how do you picture the future? What would you like to see happening here?'

'Oh, you'd laugh.'

'Try me.'

'Alright. I picture a country without a past. Well, let's say without baggage. A nation which attracts the best talents and ideas from anywhere and everywhere, without insisting that those ideas fit the preconceptions of those who are already here. While other countries build enterprise parks and enterprise cities, this could be the first enterprise nation. Not on the basis of infrastructure or tax benefits, but psychological freedom. No limits.'

Nikki looked surprised. 'But won't immigrants bring their own limits with them? And South Africans have legitimate values and expectations...'

'Perhaps, but I believe there's been enough of a shake up that people will be able to re-invent themselves, if they're motivated to do so. Locals and newcomers. This could be the place where anyone can be whatever they want to be. Only their ideas and their skills will matter, not their past.'

I found Shan's eyes were on me, as if he was looking for approval. Validation. I gave him an indulgent smile. 'It sounds like the wild west. Ye-haaa!'

He guffawed. 'You have a talent for bringing me down to earth, Dr North! But you know, I've always dreamed of a country where the past doesn't get in the way of the future. I suppose at some point South Africa began to fit that dream. Or vice versa.'

Suddenly a light went on in my head. A lot of people were querying India's motives and intentions in South Africa. There was a very active thread on TWO-cents entitled 'The 37th state of India?' – no doubt where Gitanjali's delegate got the idea. And my so-called cigarette box math was hardly original.

But, like everyone else, I'd been thinking in terms of old-world strategies – military control and packed electorates. But now I saw that such blunt instruments weren't needed, it was enough to create an open playing field, where gifted and ambitious people could strut their stuff, and to make sure the cream of India's crop got there first. Just like Shan said, talent and hard work would do the rest.

And it occurred to me that this was nothing new for South Africa. For centuries this had been a land of opportunity, from the early African and European settlers, through successive gold and diamond rushes, followed by a century of immigration as people flocked to find their fortunes in their mines, industries, farms and homes.

'Gipsy?'

'Sorry… I was off in my own head-space.'

I saw the others were getting to their feet, and Shan was holding his hand out to me. 'Care to do something about your stomach space? Dinner is served.'

***

'Good morning Gipsy! Did you sleep well?' Shan was looking relaxed in a brightly colored cotton kurta, washed out jeans and leather sandals. I wasn't sure how formal breakfasts at the governor's residence were, so I'd dressed more conservatively.

'Hi Shan. Naah, not really. My mind was going round in circles all night. I think I drank too much of this…' I held up my coffee cup.

He looked concerned. 'I'm sorry. Are you okay now?'

'Oh sure, thanks. Nothing that more caffeine can't fix. I enjoyed the evening, by the way.'

'Me too. I had no idea that General Ao was such a raconteur...'

'I had a taste of it on the day I flew with him to the aircraft carrier. He told me all about his family's tradition of military service.'

'Did he, indeed? I read about his background in his file, but it also says he's slow to open up to strangers, and to talk about personal matters.'

268

'Ah. That would explain why the other uniforms on the chopper were soaking it up.'

'And it would explain why you make such a good journalist.'

'Thank you, boss. Flattery will get you everywhere.'

He smiled as he helped himself to fruit salad. 'Actually I was surprised that we didn't talk more about... the events that brought us all here, last night.'

'Yeah. Ignoring the elephant in the room. Maybe it's not surprising, since we don't know where the elephant came from.'

He laughed. 'There's a profound thought. When we don't know the provenance of something, we pretend it's not there. The invisible elephant.'

'Yeah. It's just bizarre that someone so... evil... never claimed responsibility for their actions.'

'I remember your op-ed about evil. Rather well, in fact. It was premised on the belief that the saboteurs intended to kill millions. Or at least were willing to use them as pawns. Do you still believe that was their motive?'

'Oh come on, Shan! They did such a good job of disrupting the supply of ARVs, how could they not have wanted anyone to die?'

'But what do you make of the timing of the bombs? And the fact that the only countries with any significant mortality were South Africa, Swaziland and Lesotho?'

'Well, maybe it was easier to plant the bombs over the New Year's weekend...'

'Uh huh.'

'And, maybe they didn't foresee how effective the international response would be – getting ARV production going again.'

'Is that a realistic assumption? Remember, in the beginning nobody seriously suggested there would be large-scale mortality. If we couldn't restore first-line treatment, we would have geared up the production of second-line drugs in plenty of time. It would have been difficult to re-start treatment programs at hospitals, but not impossible.'

'Okay, but what about the contamination at NguniPharm? That made sure that South Africa, at least, landed in the shit.'

'Did it? Nguni supplied all the southern African countries, not only South Africa. They all had looting of ARVs from their hospitals, but only South Africa, Swaziland and Lesotho failed to respond appropriately. Or to turn to UN for help.'

'Yeah, I know. That's why the South African government was such a strong suspect for me, although Art... Colonel Baldwin seemed to think it was just a combination of stubbornness and bad timing that brought South Africa crashing down.'

Shan stared at the distant hills as he spoke. 'So, if the South Africans weren't behind the bombings, who was?'

'I can only think it was extortion, and that we never heard who was targeted. But they paid up and we never heard from the blackmailers again.'

'What if it was a mistake?'

I gave a real school-yard laugh. 'A mistake? Riiight! Shit, we didn't mean to plant those bombs! Soh-reee!'

He didn't respond to my sarcasm, but kept staring into the distance. 'No, I mean the outcome. What if the perpetrator didn't foresee that anyone would die?'

I wondered briefly if he was teasing me, but his tone was serious so I decided to play along. 'Oh-kaaay. Well... uh... they obviously meant to threaten the supply of ARVs...'

'Yes.'

'Which would have been enough for blackmailers. They just wanted to flex their muscles.'

'And if it wasn't?'

'Well, if they didn't mean to kill anyone, it rules out Al Qaeda, white supremacists, the Indian government...'

Shan sat back in surprise. 'The Indian government?'

'Sure. To create the population and power vacuum, which you've so ably filled.'

Now he laughed. 'Brilliant! Unless you're an Indian, of course. The idea of extermination is just so... alien... to our culture. Ever since Ashoka embraced Buddhism around 260BC. It was the golden age, the Maurya dynasty, after which I named my company. It's still central to Indian thinking.'

'Well, okay. And I very much doubt the US administration would resort to genocide to climb out of their funding black hole. Unless it was a rogue agency within their government who thought they'd take the initiative, and the administration tried to cover it up...'

'I agree. There were no signs of a witch-hunt in any of the agencies, or of departmental heads falling on their swords. I'm quite sure one of your stringers would have told us. And I'm equally sure the Director of National Intelligence would have withdrawn your friend Colonel Baldwin, if he knew who did it.'

That made sense. 'And nobody in pharma seems to have benefited significantly. No single company, anyway.'

'Who benefited from the attack on Vikmed?'

'Anyone who really wanted AIDS patients to die, I suppose. Didn't you say their injectable could be fast-tracked into production, and used to save the day if there was a treatment interruption?'

'Yes. But what if the bomb at Vikmed was different... was planted for a different reason to the others?'

'Like to distract us from the real reason for the other bombings?'

'Or vice versa.'

'Vice versa? You mean, Vikmed may have been the real target, and the others were just a... smokescreen?' I tried to compute this, but it didn't make sense. Shan wasn't any help, as he turned to his fruit salad.

I hate it when I'm put on the spot like this, but I wanted to see where Shan was leading me so I tried to work it through. 'Well, okay, let's say the bomber wanted us to THINK his goal was to disrupt first-line ARVs, even though he knew they'd be restored before any serious harm was done. And we know somehow that his goal isn't extortion?'

Shan had a mouthful of food, but he nodded.

'Art told me recently that if the bomb at Vikmed had gone off, it wouldn't have interfered much with their research. The real damage was done because someone wiped their data off their computers.'

Shan nodded again. I caught the flash in his eyes.

'So the bomb at Vikmed could also have been a... smokescreen? Deleting their research data could have been the main objective.'

Shan swallowed, and wiped his mouth with a napkin. 'Only deleted?'

I stared at him. 'You mean, it was copied? The real agenda was to steal their data?'

Shan smiled and began to help himself to more fruit salad.

'But... didn't you try to persuade Kurt Hohner to let you in on his research? At the UN meeting, I mean? Maybe you planted the bombs!'

Shan's hand paused in mid-air, leaving a serving spoon loaded with colorful chunks of mango, kiwi-fruit, strawberries, gooseberries and roasted pine nuts hovering above the pristine white tablecloth. But in a moment the spoon continued towards his bowl, leaving the linen still unmarked.

'Well, that would certainly fit the facts.'

My heart stopped. While watching his spoon I'd been trying to decide whether to beg forgiveness for the biggest faux pax of my life, or to pass it off as a joke. And now... this! Maybe he was teasing me, to give me a taste of my own medicine. It had to be.

'So how do you think the others would have reacted last night, if you told them that you are the API bomber?' I pronounced it like a French woman saying 'happy bomber'. I have no idea where it came from. 'Or does General Ao know already? Or Art Baldwin?'

'No, you're the only one who knows.'

Oh Jesus! 'Ah... this is interesting!'

'Isn't it?'

'Can I finish my breakfast before you have me dragged away and shot. I really can't face it on an empty stomach.'

He laughed, his usual guffaw, without any reserve. 'I have no intention of doing anything to you, Gipsy. I think the question is, what will you do with me?'

I swallowed the last of my espresso, to buy time. My hand wasn't nearly as steady as Shan's. 'So we're not joking, here?'

Now he looked a little more serious. 'I don't think the deaths of millions of people is a joke. And I know you don't.'

'No... but you said it was a mistake.'

'Yes it was. But that's not really a defense. I should have foreseen the possibility.'

'Why didn't you?'

He frowned. It struck me that I'd never seen him looking unsettled, until this moment. 'It... seemed too far fetched. I just couldn't imagine... couldn't foresee what actually happened, here in South Africa.'

The enormity of my situation began to sink in. I could barely breathe. I didn't have any of my electronic wizardry on me – I didn't even have a pen and paper – so it was my word against his. But I was desperate not to break the spell, so I pushed on.

'So... what? It was just business?'

He gave me a strange smile. 'It seemed like a good idea at the time.'

I struggled to get past that. 'How so?'

'Well, we... I... had two priorities. The first was to get hold of the research data from Vikmed, on their bio-engineering methods. We'd reached a dead-end in our own research, and I had to know how they resolved certain issues. A lot depended on it. Like the future of our bio-engineering division. Maybe the whole company.'

'You mean, the technology of making the injectable ARV?'

'Only indirectly. That drug was the product of a lot of new thinking and new science. I wasn't interested in the drug itself so much as the technology and methods they used to develop it.'

'And you couldn't just hack into their system?'

He shook his head. 'No. I tried, believe me. It was well protected. I had to get someone inside their plant... physically. But even then I realized we couldn't extract the data without anyone suspecting, and I knew that if we were found out it would lead straight back to me. I had to create another script for the story. A... diversion.'

'Some diversion!'

'Well, yes. It started out as a more modest exercise, but I got... sort of caught up in it. I'm afraid I have a tendency to do that. I persuaded myself that a challenge to the ARV supply chain would show everyone just how vulnerable developing nations are to this kind of thing. Not only drugs, of course. Materials, technology, information. And I... well, I became obsessed with finding out if it was possible to get away with something on... such a grand scale. To beat the global security establishment.'

I saw Shan's eyes move over my shoulder, and my heart lurched again. I turned to see the steward approaching. He asked what we'd like from the kitchen and, to my amazement, I realized I was hungry, so I asked for an idli sambar with scrambled eggs and another espresso. It felt like a lifetime since Dolly brought the same breakfast to me on Shan's Gulfstream. It also felt appropriate, somehow, to order the same dish. When I turned back to my host he was smiling, waiting patiently for my next question.

'So blowing up your own factory made you look like the victim, rather than the perpetrator?'

272